THE BLUEGRASS FILES: DOWN THE RABBIT HOLE

THE FIRST IN A SERIES OF MYSTERIES SOLVED BY THE AGENTS OF BLUEGRASS CONFIDENTIAL INVESTIGATIONS

F J MESSINA

Blair Brooke Publishing

ISBN: 978-0-9998533-0-6 (Soft Cover)

ISBN: 978-0-9998533-1-3 (MobiPocket)

ISBN: 978-0-9998533-2-0 (Epub)

PCN: pbi1503

❀ Created with Vellum

ACKNOWLEDGMENTS

Most writers learn to write ... then they write their first novel.

I wrote my first novel ... then I started to learn how to write.

I give all the credit to my dear friend, Edie Maddox Torok. After reading a "completed" draft of my first novel, she patiently walked me through not only the novel itself but the process of writing. She was much more than an editor, she was a teacher, a friend. Without Edie's help, this book would not work nearly as well as I hope it does. I thank her husband Dale for sharing her with me for so many hours during the spring of 2016.

There also needs to be a special place here for my sister, Judy Thompson. She is one of the few people who read this and my other novels while they were in process and who made suggestions along the way, suggestions that significantly impacted the path the books and characters took.

Then there is my daughter Kristin Morford and her husband Logan. Kristin's help as line editor (and resident millennial) was invaluable. Together, they did a great job in developing a photographing a great cover concept. In addition, if it were not for their incredible work leading the social media effort that supports this book, many of you may never have had the opportunity to read it.

I'd like to thank *some* of my beta readers, my dear friends George McCormick, Linda Vangellow, Debbie Lutz, Tom Hailey, Marcos Valdés (who's help with the Spanish in this book was invaluable), Pat McClure (who poured over the MS so carefully and made important suggestions), and my daughter Jennifer Alrikabi. Without their support and comments Sonia Vitale might have turned out to be a somewhat different person.

And finally, of course, my most special thanks go to my wonderful wife Denise. When your husband turns to you and says, out of nowhere, "I'm going to write a novel," it's not easy to say, through your words and your actions, "Go for it." Through all the literally hundreds of hours I have spent crafting this novel and the two that follow it, through all the other hours spent learning how to bring these books to fruition through our own publishing company, Blair/Brooke Publishing, through it all, her love and support never faltered. I am grateful.

So, as you can see, although writing can be a solitary experience, bringing the books of The Bluegrass Files to life has been a family affair—family and friends that is. I hope that as you read these books *you* will find yourself experiencing a sense of family—mine, and Sonia Vitale's as well.

PART I

Come along for the ride as Sonia Vitale takes her first steps on a dangerous, action-packed journey that will eventually lead her from novice PI to consummate yet compassionate professional.

1

He remembered. He'd known it from the time he was a kid. It was always there—deep, deep, in the recesses of his mind—but always there. He'd been sure that someday, someway, it would come.

It had started with the glasses, needing them by age four. Not just corrective lenses. No, they had to be the damn coke-bottle kind, the kind that distorted what his eyes looked like to the rest of the world, big and kind of glassy.

Not that he'd cared at that young age. Then, it was about being careful, always being careful. His mother's voice. "No rough-housing! You don't want to break your glasses. Your father paid a fortune for those things." Over and over again, gnawing at him like the buzzing of a mosquito in his ear. Always. "Be careful. Don't break the glasses. Can't you play quietly?" It was as if she still lived somewhere deep in his middle ear.

And small. Always so small. The other guys, Pete and Eddie and Joe, even as young boys they'd liked throwing themselves against each other, testing the weight and strength of their growing bodies against those of their friends. Sometimes it had turned into a real scuffle. But all had been forgotten in moments.

They were friends to the end, learning what it meant to be boys, then men. But not him. He had always stood by and watched, knowing full well he was out of his league even with the normal-sized kids, no less the bigger ones.

Not that he'd been a peace-maker. For him, it was simply avoiding physical confrontation at all cost. The few times he'd been drawn into a situation he simply couldn't steer clear of, he'd reacted with the ferocity of a trapped animal, biting and scratching, fighting for survival. His friends had stepped back, shaking their heads, giving him strange looks. "What's with him? We're just messin' around." They'd had no idea of the fear that lurked in his soul.

It got worse when his mom died and the state took him away from his alcoholic dad. Placed in a home with "lovely Christian folks," his foster parents turned out to be bible-thumping fanatics. Too much of a "sissy" for his temporary father, attempts to turn him into a God-fearing man came with the song of a switch or a belt whistling in the air toward his soft body.

And then there was high school. Every kid had seen all the movies, the dorky kid being stuffed into his locker by the Neanderthal jocks. Great laughs for everyone. But what if you *could* fit in your locker. What if your buddies thought it would be funny to do that to you, you know, "just for laughs." What if they didn't know that you were so claustrophobic that you would actually die in there, your lungs cramping with fear, refusing to work, your heart bursting? What if even as an adult you couldn't make love to your wife or play with your kids in certain positions because having a body over your head in some fashion would drive you into a mini-panic.

Time passed. He'd "grown up." Childhood fears had receded . . . some of them. But others had made their indelible mark on his soul. And this fear, the fear that had darkened his inner life, had never gone away. Not really. It was as if he always knew that no matter what changed in his life, how he left childhood behind and became an adult, even a successful adult, it was inevitable. It was going to catch up to him. It was going to cost him. Something terrible had been following him for years, coming after him. Slowly . . . slowly . . . always. It wouldn't be his fault. It wouldn't matter. Someday it would catch up to him and he would pay the price.

His eyes screamed as he watched the rough hands stretch the noose, ready to slip the rope over his head, laughter all around him. He felt it tighten against his throat, tearing his skin, burning. He couldn't breathe. He couldn't swallow. He heard the barking of commands as they pushed the bales of hay out from under his feet. His body flailed in the air. As darkness began to fill his vision, it hit him. He shook his head. Tiny movements. He almost smiled. It had found him.

SONIA TURNED AWAY from the window overlooking East Main and sat at her wooden desk, more yard sale than antique shop. She pushed the few papers there into neat piles, those items needing the most immediate attention at the top. Then, since her partner, Jet, was not yet in, she set about making a few notes in the Dylan file:

3/17 – Two hours spent on case

- Quite certain that Mr. Dylan is involved with another woman. Have photographs of both the woman and him entering the building on Clay Avenue at separate times. Includes images of a wooden box that could possibly be used for sex toys of some sort.
- Have been unable to get photographic evidence of the actual sexual relationship thus far. Hope to accomplish that and close file by next Thursday, the 24th.

SONIA KNEW that it was best that she wrote the firm's reports. When Jet wrote them, words and phrases like, "slimeball," "bitch," and "whore," often found their way into the reports. Having grown up in a strict Italian family and, of course, gone to Catholic schools, rarely did Sonia let anything more than the occasional "damn" roll off her tongue. Her reports maintained a more professional tone. Accordingly, the report failed to mention, as Jet's would have, that Mr. Dylan's associate appeared to be, "built like a brick whatever." Sonia shook her head. I guess that's how he likes them.

She closed the Dylan folder and placed it on the top shelf of her small, black, metal file holder. As she did, Sonia couldn't help but shake her head in muted disbelief. Who was she to be writing reports on someone else's behavior, reports based on clandestine observations. There was no question that there were reasons Jet had asked her to be her partner—her skillset, her background with computers, but definitely not her personality. She was certainly bright and quietly self-confident. But she wasn't the type of person you would expect to step covertly into some dangerous situation or cavalierly come face to face with impending harm. Still, there were times when she felt her new job might just take her into situations she never could have imagined.

Getting back to work, Sonia turned her attention to some of the new equipment she and Jet had just purchased. She began with the photographic weaponry. She knew that in most TV shows and movies, PI's are armed with cameras that have gigantic lenses. And it was true that Sonia had at her disposal a great digital SLR camera, to which she could attach a giant telephoto zoom lens. But she also knew that, in reality, a PI with that kind of camera in her hand would be as unobtrusive as a Clydesdale at a pony ride. She would be more likely to use her trusty gold iPhone. She could turn her back to her subject and appear to be taking a selfie, and no one would ever think a thing about it. Sonia and Jet had also obtained a killer audio device for monitoring and recording conversations, a notion that still felt a little creepy to her.

Sonia leaned over her desk and took the laptop computer they had purchased out of its box. She turned it on for the first time. As she waited for it to boot up, her phone cooed like a pigeon. She looked. A text message from Jet.

C U SOON.

Sonia had just put her phone down when it sang out its silly *Star-Spangled Banner*. Remembering that Jet had gotten her hands on Sonia's phone and changed its ringtone, Sonia sighed. I've got to change that stupid thing. She picked up the phone, assuming it was Jet on the line. Still, she answered, "Bluegrass Confidential Investigations. This is Sonia Vitale."

"*Is this the ladies who hunt down putos boy friends who can't keep their pinches pitos in their pants?*"

Sonia leaned forward and pushed the laptop off to the side. "Yes, it is." She picked up a pen and scooted a notepad in front of her. "I mean, this is Bluegrass Confidential Investigations, if that's who you're looking for."

"*Si. Oh, yes. I'll tell you who I'm looking for. I'm looking for someone who is gonna help me catch that pendejo boyfriend of mine with his pants down so I can—*"

"Yes, yes," Sonia cut in. "We're probably the right folks to help you find out if your boyfriend is involved with someone . . . something untoward."

"*I'll tell you what that bastard is going toward. He's going toward getting his pito cut off if I find he's been cogiendo around with some other puta.*"

"Ma'am," Sonia said. "Before we go any further, I have to warn you that if you make any physical threats against your boyfriend, and then something actually happens to him, I might be required to report that to the police." Sonia checked the clock. Ten fifty-three. She noted the time on her pad. "Let's just say that you would like to find out more about your boyfriend's activities when he's not around you. What did you say your name is?"

"Teresa Torres. My name is Teresa Torres, and his name is Marcos Torres, but we're not married. We just both come from the same small village in Mexico. Lots of people there have the same last name."

Sonia jotted down the name. She spun her swivel chair around and looked out the window that overlooked East Main. "Well, Ms. Torres, my name is Sonia Vitale. I'm one of the partners here. And before we go any further, I should tell you I can probably help you, but our fee for that kind of work is $75 per hour."

"A carbón! Seventy-five dollars an hour?"

"Yes, plus any expenses."

There was a pause. When Teresa spoke again, Sonia could tell that she was less agitated, getting down to business. *"And how long will it take for you to catch that bastard screwing around?"*

"Well, I can't tell you for sure." Sonia swiveled her chair around. "It normally takes me six or seven hours work to wrap up a case. I could try to do it as quickly as possible to save you some money, and if it were all in-town work there would probably be no other expenses. Still, I think you're looking at five to six, maybe seven or eight hundred dollars. Does that work for you?"

"And what if you never catch him? Do I still pay?"

"Ma'am, I can assure you that when you get my report you'll have a very good idea of what your boyfriend's been doing. It's not my job to make it look like he's doing something wrong if he's not. I'll just let you know what I find out about what he *is* doing. I'll stop looking whenever you tell me to, and whatever you do with the information I give you is up to you. I have nothing to do with that."

"Five or six hundred dollars?" Teresa said quietly.

Sonia wondered if five or six hundred dollars or more was too much money for Teresa. Her eyes ran across all the expensive equipment they had purchased for just this kind of work.

"Okay, you do it. I'm pretty damn sure you'll catch him pretty quick. He's pretty dumb."

Sonia wrapped up the conversation and made arrangements for Ms. Torres to drop off a $200 deposit at the office that afternoon. She went on to collect a little more information about Marcos Torres, no relation to Teresa Torres, and ended the phone call. Almost immediately, Sonia started to plan her strategy. She shook her head. *"Ay caramba."* Snorting gently, she laughed at her own terrible Mexican accent.

2

S onia looked at her watch. Eleven thirty, time for a break. She slipped her slightly tired blue pea coat over a white sweater and jeans that hugged her shapely bottom, something that had gently sparked her pretty smile as she'd checked herself in the mirror that morning. She knew that at thirty-two years old, her dark brown hair, long and wavy, and her olive complexion made no secret of her Italian heritage.

She also pulled on the beige cloche hat that she, a big Downton Abbey fan, had just purchased at a cute little shop on West Main Street, Feather Your Nest. It's a place where you could spend hours poking through all the antique and period clothing and items they had. The hat just seemed to call out to Sonia, and she really didn't care that Jet kept teasing her, saying the hat looked like a bell sitting on top of her head.

Sonia walked down the long, white, wooden staircase running along the side of the brick building that housed her office. At the bottom of the steps, she stepped around the corner of the building and pushed open the door of one of her favorite places in the world, Magee's. It was a bakery that had been an icon in town since the 1950s. Brick interior walls, open ceiling, hardwood floor, the environment was warm and welcoming. As she entered, she was greeted by the most wonderful smells.

Hildy, the same thin-faced, grey-haired woman who was always there in the morning, looked up at Sonia from behind the counter. "Morning." A sweet woman, she'd had some problems with Sonia's name, Lexington not having much of an Italian community from which she could learn proper pronunciations. It had helped when Sonia had said, gently, "*Sewn*-ia Vital*ay*, with an accent on the "tah" and a long "a" sound at the end." Hildy asked the same question she asked almost every day. "Coffee and an almond croissant?"

"As usual," Sonia replied, glad for the sense of familiarity that came from seeing the same folks in the same place every morning. Sonia grabbed her croissant, wrapped tightly in a white paper bag with the Magee's logo on it. Then she headed toward the coffee bar next to the large picture windows at the front of the building. As she stirred in a packet of raw sugar, she looked out across the street, staring at the brown-brick building that housed the central offices of the school district that served Lexington, Kentucky.

Her coffee sweetened appropriately, Sonia swallowed a bit of frustration, tightened up her coat, and walked back out into the brisk morning. She knew that having the BCI offices over a bakery was pretty cool. She also knew that having to access those offices via an outdoor stairway was another thing entirely. This was especially true since this set of stairs went straight up to the second story without a turn-around landing. Fortunately, the steps at her carriage house apartment above a garage on Central Avenue were a bit shorter. Sonia looked up to the top of the steps. Steps at work. Steps at home. She sighed, laughing at herself. Sonia, the little girl with calves like The Hulk.

Sonia climbed the stairway, turned the ancient knob, pushed the heavy door open and stepped in. Given the outdoor staircase and limited heat—Jet was constantly complaining that it was colder than a witch's whatever in there—Sonia wondered for the millionth time why they had ever rented the place. Of course, cheap rent and being right there on East Main Street were key, especially since Magee's was a big deal in Lexington. Also, it didn't hurt that being over Magee's—Sonia took a deep breath—her office always smelled like Christmas cookies.

Sonia walked through the BCI space ruminating on the cases before her, an attempt by a sixty-four-year-old man to locate an old girlfriend, the Dylan case, a new client that Jet would be meeting with this afternoon, and now the Teresa Torres case. Had she been wearing heels, as some of her clients did—not that she was going to go up and down those darn steps ten times a day in heels—their sound would have reverberated off the wooden floor and bare brick walls as she walked. The raw wood ceiling only made the sounds more intense.

Trying to organize some sort of work plan in her mind, Sonia stepped to the window and took in the familiar view across East Main. The school district's central office, a building from which she had recently been exiled, loomed slightly to the left; the only other commercial buildings she could see from that window were a small restaurant and an old white house. The restaurant, it seemed, kept changing hands, and therefore names, at least once a year. First, it was Cajun food, *The Crazy Cajun*; then French food, *L'Escargot*; then All-American food, *Beef & 'Taters*; and then Cajun food again. Sonia chuckled. Coming soon: *Entrails On Main*.

The old white house had been turned into office space for three or four professional businesses. It seemed to Sonia that at least one of the units was always empty, but that the lawyer and the accountant who had established residency had been there quite a while. Finally, and this was the kicker for Sonia, the fourth space was occupied by Semper Fi Investigations. It made Sonia crazy that the only other PI firm in town was right across the street, and seemingly quite a bit busier than BCI. She shrugged. That's just part of starting a new business.

Pulling herself back to her work, Sonia turned and sat down at her desk. It would take her an hour or so to transfer files to her new laptop. After that, she would spend the rest of the day searching the internet for any details that would flesh out her report on the sixty-four-year-old's long-lost love. She'd located the woman living in Phoenix. However, before she got the old guy's hopes up, she wanted to know, for sure, if the woman was married or single. She thought it might also be a good idea to check the woman's legal history. No use sending him out to Phoenix only to find that her home was a cell in the county or state prison system. Medical records, of course, were off limits. Nonetheless, Sonia was determined that by the end of the day, the end of the week, she was going to be able to put a report and some photographs taken off the woman's social network postings into a nice crisp envelope and send them to the old guy. She would also include an invoice. BCI needed the cash flow.

3

Monday morning, after getting her coffee and pastry at Magee's, Sonia climbed the stairs and discovered the door unlocked. She stopped, took a breath, then entered. She found Jet sitting in her office, speaking with a male client. Sonia guessed it was Clay McCormick.

Jet looked up at Sonia in brief recognition and smiled, her long blonde hair setting off her pretty, blue-eyed face. Sonia was just a bit jealous of Jet's Scandinavian looks and that perpetual ponytail which Jet had learned to whip around for effect at times. At five-foot-six and athletic, Jet was the same age as Sonia, but about two inches taller. Whereas Jet was lean, Sonia was more shapely. As she moved to her own space, Sonia could hear Jet speaking to Clay McCormick and was pretty sure Jet was really turning on the charm.

In the past, Sonia had been told that she, like most folks in the mid-west, had little or no recognizable accent. She was also well aware that Jet, like most central-Kentucky millennials, had worked hard to eliminate any southern accent from their everyday speech. Nonetheless, Jet had told Sonia that slipping into the southern dialects that had teased her ears in her youth came to her naturally. As naturally as "slidin' out of its skin comes to those damn cottonmouths that were all over my granddaddy's farm."

The girls had divided the former attic into three rooms, using wood and glass walls. Clients entered at the back and stepped into a large waiting room. It was a nice area, and they were planning on decorating it in an equine motif. The size of the room, however, made that a pretty expensive undertaking. So far, other than a leather couch, there was little evidence of what was to come.

The front area had been divided into two offices, Sonia's to the left, Jet's to the right, each with a window onto East Main. The wooden floors and open ceiling continued in each of their spaces. The large glass sections of the wall offered privacy for any discussions, yet, because they could still see each other, Sonia and Jet felt less vulnerable when they were in their office with men they didn't know. On the wall of each office hung a picture of Sonia and Jet at a shooting range and copies of their licenses to carry concealed weapons. Those were meant to convey a certain, *"Listen, fella. I'm carrying a gun and I know how to use it,"* message.

Sonia slipped off her pea coat and sat at her desk. Friday afternoon, Sonia had asked Jet to tell her about McCormick, their newest client. Jet had said that he owned a large restaurant in town and good-sized pieces of top quality meats and fish were disappearing from the restaurant's refrigerator. This would be good work for BCI since the rate they could charge would be much higher than the "Snap & Burn" work—snap the photo, burn their asses—they did for jilted spouses and lovers. On the other hand, this would entail setting up video surveillance and hours of reviewing images before the culprit was caught.

Sonia tapped her Cross pen, a thin, silver, "fine writing instrument," on her desk. It was pretty old school, but her parents had given it to her as a graduation gift from college, and it sometimes gave her heart a warm tickle when she used it.

Since coming to Lexington, Sonia had found that the Mexican-American community had become a vibrant and positive element in the fabric of the city's daily life, many of the first to arrive finding work on the horse farms that surrounded the city and gave it its unique character. Ms. Torres had told Sonia that was where she would find the cheating "*puto*," Mr. Torres, no relation. Marcos was a farm hand on Dahlia Farm, a small horse farm out on Pisgah Pike.

Sonia had done a little digging with her new computer and found that Dahlia Farm was managed by Steve Hollings and owned by John Abbott Hensley, a very successful attorney in Cincinnati. Given that his business was located across the river in Ohio, she guessed Hensley was also very much an absentee owner. Sonia assumed that, as so often happens, the successful business that allowed him to own the farm rarely afforded him the opportunity to enjoy it. She guessed he only came to the farm a few times each year.

Having grown up in Cincinnati proper herself, Sonia loved the idea that in order to observe Marcos she would have to go out into the beautiful horse farm country that was only minutes from downtown. Yet, this also created some serious problems. First, farm hands don't exactly clock in at ten in the morning, as Sonia had gotten used to doing. These farm hands were probably showing up at five. Second, it wasn't like she could just park her car outside Marcos' place of employment and sit there unnoticed. Surveillance of his arrival and departure from work was going to be one pain in the butt.

Ms. Torres had said Marcos, "came home from work smelling like he'd been with another woman a few times a week." As best as she could guess, Sonia figured that Marcos was either slipping out at lunch to meet with this "*puta*," or stopping on the way home. After all, work schedules for farm hands were less than regular. He could easily leave at three in the afternoon, stop in for a little personal liaison, and tell Teresa he had gotten off a little before four. Which, Sonia knew, could be true, in a manner of speaking.

As she ruminated on how she would observe Marcos, Sonia turned and looked out the window onto East Main. It was another sunny day, quite a bit warmer than the days before had been. It was a perfect day to take a ride out to Dahlia farm and check things out. As she stood to slip on her coat, however, she couldn't help but look at the white house across the street and the sign that read Semper Fi Investigations. She wondered how Brad Dunham, "Mr. Semper Fi Investigations," would handle the Marcos Torres surveillance problem.

Sonia walked out of her office and down the steps. She got into her car, turned left on East Main, and within minutes was on the road that took her past iconic Calumet Farm, perhaps the world's most famous horse farm. It had produced eight Kentucky Derby winners—two Triple Crown winners. She passed Blue Grass Airport and historic Keeneland Racetrack, known by jockeys, breeders, trainers, and racing fans alike, as one of the most beautiful horse racing venues in the country. Finally, she drove a few more miles and reached another local landmark, an odd replica of a European castle that was now being used for special events. The castle was such an unusual sight that Sonia, like many other first-time visitors to the Bluegrass, had Googled, "Lexington Castle," soon after she had first seen the stone walls and high turrets.

At that corner, Sonia turned right onto Pisgah Pike and was almost immediately surrounded by horse farms. She struggled to keep her eyes on the narrow road, rather than let them drift to the beautiful, white, wooden fences and lush green fields.

Sonia slowed as she passed Dahlia Farm on her left. A long gravel driveway left the road and created a straight path onto the property, a good-sized barn on its right, an old but well-kept house on its left. There was no visible activity that she could see, but she assumed that was not so unusual for a horse farm.

According to what she knew about horse farms—and that wasn't much—there were busy times in the mornings and late afternoons. Some days there were important things to do in between. Other days there were some lulls in the activity. Sonia hoped she wasn't missing something important, but she was pretty sure that driving past a horse farm and not seeing any human activity was sort of par for the course.

About a quarter-mile past the farm, Sonia stopped and made a difficult U-turn on the narrow road. She drove past the farm a second time, going even more slowly and taking in as much information as she could. Before taking the turn at the castle and heading back into town, Sonia pulled to the side of the road and spoke a few notes into her phone:

Teresa Torres case, Monday, March 21, first impressions:

ONE: Farm is as small as I had expected. Little activity.

Two: Farm must be doing well, or at least be well funded. House, barns, and fences all in excellent repair.

Three: Electronic gear on top of house indicates that the farm is well connected to twenty-first-century communications.

SONIA TAPPED out of the MEMO section of the phone and started to put it back into her purse. Something else struck her. She made one more note.

Four: Surprised to see five pickup trucks parked in the farm's small lot. One must belong to the farm manager. Seems like each of the farm hands also has his own truck.

THAT SEEMED a little unusual to Sonia. She would have assumed that many farm hands would be more likely to share a ride to work. Then she added another item.

Five: Each of those trucks is pretty darn new and in good condition. The farm must be paying its employees well.

As SHE DROVE BACK to her office, still not sure how she was going to keep an eye on Marcos Torres, Sonia mindlessly tapped her fingers on the steering wheel. Is that little farm really doing that well? I'll bet there are some financial filings I might be able to get my hands on.

4

Sonia arrived back at Magee's and walked into the bakery. She had seen Jet's car in the parking lot, so she sent Jet a voice text: I'M DOWNSTAIRS GETTING LUNCH. WANT SOMETHING?

Within a few moments, she got a reply: NO TKS. COVERED

Sonia decided on her 'personal' sandwich, one she had invented, and let her mind and eyes wander as she waited in line to order. She couldn't help but notice the guy at the counter. He was six-foot-three or four and must have weighed at least two-twenty-five, and it was clearly all muscle. He was wearing some sort of military boots, a pair of pretty tight jeans, and a puke-green tee shirt. Surprisingly, he wasn't wearing a coat. Sonia didn't recognize him, but whoever he was, he seemed to be quiet, the kind of guy who kept to himself. A small smile crept across Sonia's face. Hmmm. Now there's a delicious-looking lunchtime treat. Sonia was well-aware that the elementary school nuns had curbed her tongue, but not her appetite. She was, after all, Italian.

Hildy handed him his order and he turned around. What

Sonia noticed first were bright blue eyes, set in a rugged face. His hair was cropped very short and his hairline was beginning to recede just a tiny bit. The next thing she noticed was the anchor and globe insignia of the United States Marines on his tee shirt, book-ended by some serious biceps. Not that Sonia cared, but this guy was pretty hot. As he walked toward the door, carrying a white Magee's bag, Julie, one of the owners, popped out from behind the counter.

"Goodbye, Brad" she called in a bit of a singsong voice. It was completely obvious she also thought this Brad guy was pretty sexy.

Sonia smiled and chuckled to herself. Then it hit her. Holy moly. That's Brad Dunham, Mr. Semper Fi himself. Whoa, no wonder most of the women who want a PI go to see him instead of us. But Sonia knew that looks weren't all Mr. Semper Fi had going for him. No one runs a business in a small city without developing some sort of reputation and Brad Dunham's reputation was that of a hard-ass. Maybe it was because he was on a military pension and didn't really need the money, but Sonia had heard that he often turned down work because he didn't like, or didn't believe, the client. He'd also been known to get a little physical with some of the people he'd been hired to investigate—and come to think of it, with some of the people who had hired him. Brad Dunham might be eye candy, but Sonia was quite certain that he was clearly not her type. Too much muscle. Probably not nearly enough brain. She would just leave him to Julie. After all, Julie was a friend.

A few minutes later, Sonia had climbed those stairs again and walked into their offices, lunch in hand. Instead of going to her own workspace, she went directly to Jet's and plopped herself down in the padded red chair across from Jet's desk. She took her sandwich out of its white paper bag. "I've got a problem."

Jet looked up from her work. "And that is?"

Sonia didn't like asking for help, but she dove in nonetheless. "I've got to figure out a way to watch the comings and goings of one Marcos Torres who just happens to work on a horse farm." She shook her head. "I can't exactly park on the road across the street from the farm and go unnoticed. I might as well put out a black and yellow sign that says, 'Private Investigation Under Way. For More Information, call Bluegrass Confidential Investigations.' "

Jet smiled and her pretty blue eyes sparkled. Sonia returned the smile—they were on the same wavelength. Sonia unwrapped her avocado and peanut butter sandwich, a combination which had brought a grimace to Hildy's face the first time Sonia had placed that special order. But now, like today, Sonia could count on a little extra avocado and a wink whenever she ordered it.

Pushing away the yogurt and apple that were on her desk, her "healthy lunch," Jet's smile broadened. "I may just have exactly what you need." She reached down and pulled a box on the floor close to her. Then, with both hands, she lifted it onto the desk and placed the package right in front of Sonia. Slowly, with a bit of a dramatic flair, Jet pulled out a small black object with a tiny antenna, obviously some sort of transmitter. Then, as she intoned the magic words, "Abracadabra," she produced a small video recorder. "These, my friend, will solve all your problems."

Sonia's sandwich was half-way to her mouth. She was speechless.

Jet continued. "Remember how I have to record the deliveries at Clay McCormick's restaurant?"

Sonia nodded.

"Well, we needed to get the right kind of video recorder to do that. And given that it's not such an easy place to set up the camera, I went ahead and got this transmitter gizmo to go with it. It'll send the signal at least a half-mile, maybe up to a mile. You can set the camera up across the street from the farm and watch it on that bad boy lap-top of yours from almost a mile away."

Sonia smiled. "Awesome! That's brilliant. But—oh crap." A chunk of avocado had fallen on her jeans. She picked it up gingerly and popped it into her mouth. "Five-second rule." Then she did her best to wipe the mess off her pants. "But don't you need that equipment for the restaurant gig?"

Jet tapped her hand on the recorder. "Listen, I told McCormick I'd have to order the equipment, then I found it right here in town. He's expecting that it'll take a few days for me to get the surveillance up and running. By then you may have all you need on Marcos Torres."

Sonia stood. "Cool. Let me take this sandwich over to my little corner of the world and, after I've eaten lunch, we can figure out how to set all this stuff up."

Sonia left Jet's desk and headed for her own. Earlier, she had wondered how Brad Dunham would have solved the problem of keeping tabs on Marcos Torres. Now, she smiled. How 'bout them apples Mr. Semper Fi?

After lunch, Sonia stepped into Jet's office carrying her laptop. Jet scooted over and she and Sonia got started figuring out how the new equipment worked. Sonia was in her element and happy as they spent the next hour working together and getting the video camera to transmit a wireless signal to Sonia's laptop. Around three o'clock, Sonia took the camera and walked down the long staircase and onto East Main, all the while transmitting back to Jet in her office.

The camera was small and inconspicuous, therefore, Sonia could keep recording as she walked the two-block area around Magee's. They had also set up voice communications from Jet to the earpiece Sonia was wearing. Just for practice, Sonia would listen as Jet gave her instructions and called for certain images. *"Give me a close-up of the optometrist's office . . . . Now give me a long shot of the school district office across the street.... Can you zoom in on the Superintendent's office?"*

Things were working out pretty well. Sonia walked across the street and turned around to get a long shot of Magee's. Then she slowly walked toward the white house.

"What are you going for?" Jet asked. Sonia zoomed in on the sign that said Semper Fi Investigations. Holding the camera in one hand, Sonia spun it, turning the image on the laptop upside down.

"Feeling a little mischievous, are we?"

Sonia answered in the only way she could, by moving the camera up and down, creating an image on the laptop that resembled shaking her head, "Yes." Then she grinned, turned the camera off, and headed back to the office.

AT AROUND FIVE-THIRTY THAT EVENING, Jet and Sonia piled into Sonia's red, seven-year-old Subaru Forester and headed out to Dahlia Farm, transmitter, receiver and two-way communications system lying in Jet's lap. It was getting quite a bit colder, but the cover of dusk would afford them a greater chance of going undetected. Directly across from the entrance to the farm, Sonia slowed to a stop. Jet, wearing boots, jeans, and a dark green jacket, hopped out of the car as quickly as she could. Sonia took off immediately, hoping to get around the bend in the road before anyone noticed her.

Sonia had given Jet instructions to move quickly into some low bushes that were on the side of the road, across from the farm. She hoped Jet would be able to set up the camera in such a way that it would have a reasonable view of the farm and, at the same time, be pretty inconspicuous. Sonia felt guilty sitting in her warm car while Jet was out in the cold.

"Are you getting anything?"

Sonia fiddled with her earbud. "I'm definitely getting something, but it's pretty dim. Let me try to enhance the image."

With her laptop leaned against her steering wheel, Sonia worked with brightness, contrast, and some other image parameters. The picture on the screen brightened a bit. "I'm pretty sure we're doing okay. I've got the entrance to the barn and the entrance to the house," she said into the microphone. "But there's just not enough light anymore. Without some sort of night vision imaging, this just isn't going to get it in the dark. Let's hope that Mr. Torres does all his cavorting during daylight hours."

Sonia closed the laptop. "I guess that's the best we can do for now."

"Great. Now get me out of here before I freeze my ass off."

Sonia put the laptop on the back seat. She stepped on the gas and within moments brought the Subaru around the bend. Jet had already run across the street, so when Sonia stopped, it only took a few seconds for Jet to hop into the car before they drove away.

Jet gave Sonia a look. "Well, that was lots of fun."

"Like it's going to be a barrel of laughs sitting in the car all day tomorrow, watching the grass grow green?" There was a snarky smile on Sonia's face.

Jet hugged her body with her arms. "Well, the adventure begins. Now, what have you got in that thermos?"

Sonia's eyes were on the road. "Coffee, just the way you like it. Hot from Magee's and with a serious dose of Jim Beam bourbon."

"Jim Beam Black or four-year-old?"

"What? Now you're a bourbon snob?" Sonia gave her a quick look. "Listen, if you're looking for their best stuff, it certainly won't be cut with coffee."

"Okay, okay." Jet returned the glance. "But when we get back to the office I'm pouring us some of their new Double Oaked, neat. Man, that stuff is earthy. I love it."

Sonia smiled. Before she'd moved to Lexington she'd never

had a single taste of bourbon. Now she was all but arguing the attributes of different bourbons and their uses. Strange. They got to the castle and turned left, back toward town.

5

Nine-thirty on Tuesday morning, early for her, Sonia walked into Magee's and up to the front counter. "Large coffee and an almond croissant?" Hildy asked with a smile.

"Not today." Sonia shook her head. "I need a large coffee *and* a thermos of coffee. I'll also need a club sandwich to go."

"Another thermos of coffee?" Hildy raised her eyebrows. "Got a lunch with a special somebody?"

"Nothing like that. Just going to watch how horses spend their afternoons."

"Alright then," Hildy shrugged, "large coffee, more coffee, and a club sandwich to go. That's order number forty-seven."

Sonia smiled at her then walked back to the coffee bar to pour that first cup and fill her thermos. As usual, she glanced at the school district offices across the street. Her gaze drifted over to the white house.

Sonia squinted and her face wore a tight-lipped little smile. Well, Mr. Semper Fi Investigations, I'm on my way out to do some fieldwork. I wonder what you're up to today. Probably just working out at the gym, polishing up those "guns" of yours. She knew she was being a bit catty, but darn it, it had kind of bugged her the way he moved through the place yesterday like he owned it. Just because he was good-looking and buff and a former Marine didn't mean he was special. For all she knew, he could be a pretty terrible PI. Maybe the only reason he got all those clients was that he was some sort of stud.

Sonia wagged her head sharply, almost a shudder. Wow, get a hold of yourself. A little jealous, are we? I'd better start thinking more about Marcos Torres and less about Brad Dunham.

A few minutes later, Sonia pulled out of Magee's parking lot and headed for Dahlia farm. The camera was already in place, so as Sonia passed the entrance to the farm, she slowed for just a moment and turned the camera on remotely. The prior evening, with more time than she'd had that afternoon, Sonia had found a turn-around spot just around the bend. It would have been a grassy spot, had it not been for all the vehicles that had used it to change directions on the narrow road. Paint marks and a few broken boards on the classic horse farm fence made it clear that drivers had sometimes misjudged the available turning space the area allowed.

Less than a mile away from the camera, Sonia tucked the Subaru into the turn-around, wondering how long she could stay without arousing any suspicion. There was no question that she might have to move every once in a while. There was also no question that she would have to have some believable story about why she was sitting there if someone stopped to help her. "These Kentucky folks are awful darn friendly," she said softly.

By one o'clock, Sonia had filed her nails, cleaned out her purse, and caught up on her Facebook and Instagram pages. She was bored. Several hours may not seem like a long time when you're at work, or out to dinner, or watching a movie, but it's a darn long time to sit in a car watching a computer screen upon which not much is happening. Yes, she had her coffee and her lunch. And yes, she had Spotify to listen to. But this stakeout thing was much tougher in real life than it was on a one-hour TV show. The way she figured it, a TV stakeout probably lasted only about six seconds before the partners had a brief conversation, and no more than a minute and a half before someone said, "Check it out. Here they come!" She'd already been sitting there almost three hours.

Sonia was pretty darn pleased when her camera/computer told her that Mr. Torres, no relation to Ms. Torres, appeared. A smallish man, dark-haired, wearing blue jeans and a dark green jacket, he was getting in the truck Teresa Torres had described. He was thick, almost pudgy, and significantly shorter than his girlfriend. Sonia snorted quietly, remembering the picture of him dressed as Zorro that he had posted on Facebook. Given his size and the shape of his body, it was an epic fail. Starting her car, ready to roll, she opened the voice recorder on her phone and noted that it was 1:17 PM.

Sonia watched as Marcos Torres fired up the vehicle and left the property. Watching the monitor carefully, she saw him turn right as he entered the road. She pulled out immediately and was close behind him as he turned left at the castle. Within a few minutes, he was passing Blue Grass Airport and going up the ramp to the road that circled the city, New Circle Road. She had backed off and was following approximately a half-mile behind.

A mischievous little smile crossed Sonia's face. Well, Mr. Torres, it appears that you're an afternoon delight kind of guy. Shame on you. Ms. Torres is at work, planning on making you a nice dinner this evening, and you're out here on your way to hook up with your little *puta*. As she drove on, careful to not get too close, Sonia wondered what *puta* actually meant in Spanish.

Sonia was relatively certain this would be a pretty short trip. After all, Marcos probably only got an hour for lunch. Maybe he could stretch it a bit, but his little *puta* would have to live pretty close if he were going to get there, "get down to business," and return, all on a lunch hour—even a long lunch hour.

At the top of the circle, Marcos and his dark blue Ford 150 got off the circle and headed north on another major road. Sonia was certain Marcos would be pulling in somewhere pretty soon. To her surprise, that didn't happen. About a mile-and-a-half up the new road, Marcos turned right, driving up a steep, curving ramp onto I-75 north. Soon, Marcos was out in the left lane. It seemed clear that he was heading out of town on a trip of some length.

Thinking about Teresa Torres' financial situation, and the fact that there was every chance that Marcos was not, at this moment, headed for a liaison, she headed for the next exit. Turning left at the end of the ramp, and left again after she had crossed over the interstate, Sonia was back on I-75. She was on her way home with nothing to show for the day.

6

D ay two of the stakeout, Wednesday, was even less eventful for Sonia. She knew that arriving around ten o'clock she was missing most of the morning activities, but that didn't seem to matter to her case. She wasn't shooting a documentary on the life of a working horse farm. She was, as her partner had so delicately put it, "trying to catch a cheating, slimeball boyfriend boffing some slut while his poor girlfriend was at work." She shook her head. Ah, two years as a college English major has given Jet such a rich, descriptive vocabulary.

Sonia curled up on the couch in her tiny living room that evening. The CNN anchor and his roundtable guests were talking about yet another political impasse on her television, but she and her glass of merlot were pretty much ignoring them. She listened to the notes she had made on her phone that day:

Teresa Torres case, Wednesday, March 23:

11:07— FEDEX TRUCK ARRIVES. *Makes a quick delivery. Leaves immediately.*

12:36—Young man arrives. Probably driving his own car. Jimmy Johns sub sandwich company sign on the roof. Quick delivery. By the smile on his face, there must have been a good tip.

1:57—Red tarp-covered truck drives onto farm. Magnetic sign attached to door.

Mid hyphen West Feed and Hay Company. Truck backs partially into barn. Can't tell how much feed and hay is delivered. Whatever.

4:36—Black Lincoln Continental drives onto farm. Might be owner or client?

Man comes out of house to greet driver. Dressed better than farm hands. May be the farm manager.

4:39—Car leaves. Looks like farm manager was just giving the driver directions to town or something. Was able to get license plate MDB-619. Thank you, Ohio, for demanding cars have two license plates.

As Sonia sat on the couch, the folks on CNN still grinding on and on about a political possibility that didn't have the slightest chance of ever happening, Sonia was frustrated. After two solid days of work, Sonia had not a bit of evidence that Marcos Torres was doing anything at all untoward.

The third day of the stakeout, Thursday, was significantly different. At ten o'clock Sonia was in her appointed position. The routines of the day had, at first, seemed about the same. There was another FedEx delivery and, right around lunchtime, the

Jimmy Johns boy showed up with more sandwiches. Later, however, something very odd occurred.

At 2:07 PM, a white, late model, Mercedes pulled onto the property. It was driven by a man in a bright orange and red jacket. Sonia assumed, from his dark skin and black hair, that he was Hispanic. Accompanying him in the car were four women, all of whom were dressed in some combination of skirts and tops that clung tightly to everything below the waist, and gave important things above plenty of room to breathe. Sonia noted that it was not likely these women were there to consider purchasing horses, though the word "studs," did cross her mind.

Sonia sat up and adjusted the angle of her laptop screen. What the . . . . He's not going to his *puta*; his *puta* is coming to him. Only in Kentucky, the land of beautiful horses and fast women.

Sonia watched the farm manager, Steve Hollings, come out to greet the ladies, escort them to the barn, then turn and walk away. Sonia noticed he had a habit of running his fingers through his hair. A few minutes later, she saw all four farm hands, including Marcos Torres, enter the barn, laughing and joking. Sonia made the assumption that somewhere in that barn there were places more fit for humans than for horses, and those places were about to be used in the service of the world's oldest profession.

It made Sonia uncomfortable to sit in her car watching the motionless computer screen. Although she could see nothing significant on the screen, her head was filled with images that belonged in some porno flick—not in the mind her Italian mother had tried so diligently to protect.

Sonia's foot tapped as she waited for the four prostitutes to service the farm hands. She had already successfully caught several men and women in compromising positions, but this was entirely different. When a spouse gets involved with another person, thinking they've fallen madly in love, that's one thing.

Four prostitutes servicing four farm hands in the same barn at the same time, that's another. Yuck.

On the other hand, she knew she should be pleased. She was here to catch Mr. Torres with his pants down, and it was pretty obvious that was precisely his state of undress at the moment. Unfortunately, Sonia wasn't peering through some window getting a photograph of his behavior. She was around the bend in the road and couldn't even see inside the barn. All she could see on her computer screen was a beautiful white Mercedes in the foreground of a lovely pastoral scene. Heck, it looked like a slick car commercial. She could show Teresa Torres this image and tell her the Queen of England was in that barn drinking tea with Elton John, and the image on the computer would neither confirm nor deny the story.

No, what Sonia needed now was some photographic evidence that would bring this case to a conclusion. She had expected to follow Marcos Torres to his rendezvous. Now, with the woman, or women, coming to him, she had been caught off guard. She hadn't been in place to get shots of the prostitutes and Marcos walking into the barn. Neither was she in position to get shots of them doing the deed. She could try to get some shots of them leaving, but to attempt that in broad daylight, without a plan, seemed a bit reckless. Sonia was going to have to wait for another opportunity, one she was pretty sure would present itself in a week or less. "And trust me," she whispered to the motionless computer screen, "next time I'll be ready."

Sonia waited until the four ladies left the barn and piled into the Mercedes, seemingly none the worse for wear. She did note that none of the farm hands had bothered to be gentlemanly enough to walk them to their car. So much for chivalry. The time was 3:14 PM, just a tad over one hour since the women had arrived.

Sonia was stiff and sore from sitting in the car all day. She decided it was time to call it a day, so she headed home. She turned off the camera; she wished she could turn off her frustration the same way.

Sonia's day was over, but not her night. It was Thursday, and she knew that every Thursday evening Mr. Dylan met up with his muse and danced the dance of young love, or was it young lust? Either way, she had plans to meet Jet after dinner and wrap that case up. This time they would snap the incriminating photos they needed and burn the guy by handing them over to his loving wife.

7

A t eight o'clock that evening, Sonia met Jet in their office. It was a short walk to the house on Clay Avenue. A simple one story with a large front porch, it appeared to have been built in the '40s or early '50s and probably hadn't seen a fresh coat of paint since the '80s. This should have been a pretty easy affair—it wasn't turning out that way. First, they were walking, one in front of the other, carrying a six-foot ladder they had awkwardly attached to the top of Sonia's Subaru and then transported to within a few houses of the "bimbo's" residence. Second, it was pouring rain. The whole scenario made Sonia feel more like Barney Fife than a real private investigator.

Jet and Sonia had already gotten all the shots they needed of Mr. Dylan and his mystery woman entering and leaving the house on Clay Avenue. They were also pretty sure the window at the back of the building would give them a view of the man and his paramour. Given the fact that the ground around the back of the building sloped downward, the problem was getting high enough to see through it. They were confident the ladder they were carrying would give them the height they needed to get the shots that would clinch the deal.

The early spring storm was making it pretty miserable, with cold rain and a whipping wind—and, of course, prickly bushes outside the house. Things turned worse for them when lightning lit up the sky, followed by a significant boom of thunder.

Sonia whispered. "Are you sure we need to do this tonight?"

The look on Jet's face told Sonia the answer, but she got Jet's retort nonetheless. "Hush now chil'," her voice was all fried green tomatoes and collard greens, "because of a little wind and rain?"

"And lightning and thunder." Sonia ran her fingers through her wet hair and wiped the moisture off her face with the back of her hand. "C'mon Jet. Just because Mrs. Dylan thinks her husband Robert is cheating on her—"

"Bob," corrected Jet. "*Bob* Dylan."

"Okay, Bob Dylan," said Sonia, acknowledging the running joke they'd developed about the twenty-four-year-old man whose parents had unfortunately named him Robert Dylan.

Jet placed the ladder against the building, her eyes on its upper end. "You bet your ass we're doing this tonight. I'm not gonna let a little weather keep me from catching this son-of-a-bitch. We're getting him tonight and ending this little love affair first thing in the morning."

"Ooookay," said Sonia, knowing full well that once Jet was on the trail of some "slimeball cheat," there was no dissuading her. She also knew that if they missed this opportunity, they would have to wait another week to catch ol' Bob and turn his latest version of "Lay, Lady, Lay", into his final refrain.

Cold rain splashed in Sonia's face as she heard Jet say softly, "And here we go." She watched Jet go up the few rungs necessary for her to see through the window. Then, mixed with the wind and rain, Sonia heard Jet's singsong commentary. "And there she is, naked as a jaybird, walking around the room, not a care in the world."

"Get the shot and let's get the heck out of here. I'm freezing." Sonia's arms were wrapped around her body.

"Give me juuust one more minute. I haven't got ol' Bobby in the picture yet. He'll be there in a second, I'm sure." There was no question Jet was enjoying this.

CRACK! The sky lit up and the thunder shook the girls almost simultaneously. There was no need for them to count the seconds to try to figure out how far away the lightning had struck. It had struck right there. Not three hundred feet away, a transformer on a pole blew, sparks flying everywhere. Within seconds the whole block went black.

Sonia froze.

"Damn, damn, damn. I can't get the shot. I can't get the damn shot."

Sonia knew better than to say a word. She just held the ladder still as Jet climbed down and muttered, "Well doesn't that just take the cake? That's one lucky boy in there, one lucky boy."

"Look, Jet, let's just get out of here, okay? Everybody will be looking out their windows. It's bad enough we've got to walk to the car carrying a ladder. Come on, let's just go. We'll be lucky if another bolt of lightning doesn't light up the ladder and us with it."

"Yeah, yeah, yeah." Jet pulled the ladder down and they marched off, back toward Sonia's car. Ol' Bob Dylan had slipped out of their grasp yet again. Another night wasted. Sonia knew that Jet would now be more determined than ever to get that slimeball in the end, and soon the times would be a-changin' for ol' Bob. She was starting to feel the same way.

Jet led them on the short walk down the street, bent into the wind. "Come on baby girl, tote that end of the ladder. I ain't no pack horse up here you know."

Sonia felt cold water splash on her ankle. She bent her head as well, sighed, and plodded on.

~

THURSDAY NIGHT HAD BEEN a wet and soggy disaster, and Friday morning found Sonia in a foul mood. Nonetheless, Sonia had gotten herself out of bed and out the door. By ten in the morning, she had already stopped by to see Hildy, picked up her coffee and sandwich, and was pulling into the little turnaround just around the bend from the Dahlia Farm entrance.

Sonia slouched in the driver's seat with little hope of anything special happening that day. Her job was to catch Marcos Torres in the act with another woman, and Sonia was now pretty certain that his other woman was a prostitute. So, here she was, once again, with Spotify and her laptop computer, watching the day go by.

The only ray of sunshine in her professional life was the message she had received from Jet. Apparently, the sixty-four-year-old client who had hired BCI to find his ex-girlfriend had called the office. He had gone on and on about how much he appreciated the fact that Sonia had put in the extra effort to not only find the woman but to establish her current situation. "I'm so glad she stopped me from going all the way out to Phoenix only to find her married to the head honcho of some scruffy and aging motorcycle gang or whatever they are. You thank that Ms. Vitale for me, Okay? She really went the extra mile and I'll be eternally grateful." The compliment and appreciation had gone a long way toward brightening Sonia's mood.

Just past one in the afternoon, the truck from The Mid-West Feed and Hay Co. had shown up on the farm and backed partially into the barn. Sonia sighed in boredom. Horse farm, feed and hay truck. No big deal. But then again, something in the back of Sonia's mind said, "This *is* a big deal." The few horses on the farm were going through an awful lot of feed and hay. She was no farm girl of any sort and certainly knew less about horse farms than most folks in this town, but she would have imagined this truck showing up every week or two, not just two days after its last visit.

Sonia wished she could watch the farm hands unload the delivery, but with her limited view, and the truck being backed into the barn, that was impossible. Sonia squirmed in her seat. It would be great if I could just stroll up there and ask a simple question about directions or something, just so I could get a peek at that delivery.

In fact, she was beginning to come up with just such a plan. She would simply drive onto the farm and go looking for someone to give her directions to somewhere, maybe the apple orchard that was nearby. She sat up taller in her seat. Unfortunately, before she could get her plan clear in her mind and pluck up the courage to put it in place, the driver hopped back in the truck and took off.

It wasn't too long, however, before Sonia saw some new activity and her frustration dissipated a bit. She sat up again. One by one each of the farm hands was backing his truck up to the barn's entrance and then going inside. The one in the oldest-looking truck backed in first and left the farm almost immediately. Then the driver of the dark red Toyota Tundra followed the same procedure.

Marcos Torres was third. He backed his truck into the barn, spent a few minutes in there and then left the farm headed toward the castle. Sonia was tempted to follow him as she'd done the other day. She thought better of it. She knew where he was getting his extra-curricular action, and she was willing to bet that was going to happen again soon. She paused with her hand on the key. She didn't turn it. I should really just sit here and see if that last pickup truck follows suit.

The last farm hand backed his truck into the barn and, a few minutes later, took off. Sonia had to fight hard to resist the temptation to follow that last pickup. She scratched her head. Something very strange was happening out there and she was dying to know what it was.

8

T en o'clock Monday morning found Sonia sitting in her car, just around the bend from the farm, monitoring her laptop. The prostitutes had been there last Thursday, and Teresa Torres had said, "a couple of times a week." So, it was possible that Monday could be another "Hooker of Your Choice Day." Sonia would be ready this time.

Once the girls arrived, she would wait a bit and then drive right onto the property. With her professional Cannon camera completely on display, although with a small, reasonable lens attached, she would walk right into the barn. If anyone stopped her, she would just say that she was a tourist from another part of the state and hoped nobody would mind that she was taking pictures of one of Kentucky's beautiful little horse farms. Of course, they would chase her tail right off the property. Still, if she could sell the story, it was more than likely that no one would make a big deal of her having walked in.

Sonia was surprised when, at 10:47 AM, the large red truck from The Mid-West Feed and Hay Co. arrived again, maneuvering on the driveway and backing into the barn. A few minutes later, Marcos and his colleagues—laughing, shoving, fooling around—arrived and went into the barn as well. Sonia tried to quit thinking about the fact that this was yet another frequent delivery. She folded her arms and leaned back in the seat, reminding herself that her job was catching Marcos cheating, not figuring out what the men on that farm were up to.

Sonia sat up straighter just after eleven and spoke into her phone. "A white Jaguar convertible has just pulled onto the farm." Sonia wasn't familiar with the model numbers of high-end cars, and she had no idea what kind of Jaguar it was, but she knew one thing: this baby had to go sixty or seventy thousand bucks at least. The car drove right up to the house and Sonia watched a blond man in white pants and a madras shirt step out of the car. He was smallish, maybe five-foot-five or less, and slight, a hundred and twenty pounds or so. He seemed at ease in his fine clothing, well-coiffed hair and thickish tortoise-shell glasses. He walked up the steps, onto the porch, and right through the front door.

A few minutes later, the man stepped out the front door and back onto the porch. He stopped for a moment and surveyed the scene, looking left to right and into the distance. Sonia squinted at the computer screen, wishing she could see his face more clearly. However, his body language indicated a certain sense of well-being. He walked casually down the steps and toward the barn. Steve Hollings followed. It appeared to Sonia that Hollings was speaking and pointing in another direction as if he wanted the man to go with him out into one of the fields. The blond shook his head slowly, although apparently not disturbed, and continued toward the barn. As he neared the barn, Hollings hustled up to him again. Sonia sensed Hollings still urging the man to follow him in that other direction.

Sonia shifted herself in her seat. Without sound, the images on the screen were simply not giving her enough information to figure out what was going on. She banged her fist on the steering wheel. "Dang."

The blond man seemed determined to walk into the barn, and that was exactly what he did. Hollings shrugged and followed the dapper little man in his hip clothing. For quite a while, Sonia could make out nothing new on her screen. Her intuition, however, told her now was not the time for her to go poking around the farm posing as a tourist.

Forty-five minutes or so went by and, at 11:59 AM, Sonia jerked herself upright quickly, popped her earbud out, and spoke into her phone. "A local police cruiser has just come onto the property. What's that all about?" The cruiser pulled up the farm's driveway and stopped directly outside the barn. As the officer exited the car, Sonia saw that he was not in uniform. She stared at her laptop. Must be off duty, or maybe a detective. With his image so small on the screen, however, there was not much more she could tell about him as he went quickly into the barn. Sonia brushed a wisp of hair out of her face and let out a sigh.

Only seven minutes later, at 12:06 PM, the policeman emerged from the barn. Having seen plenty of cop shows on TV, Sonia could almost see him already, standing outside his car, one foot on the door ledge, holding the microphone from his radio and calling in a report or a request for help. Instead, the cop got directly into his cruiser and made a pretty dramatic U-turn in the driveway. Kicking up a lot of dust, he left the property. The feed and hay truck followed right behind him.

Sonia picked up her phone and noted the cruiser's arrival and departure. She wished she could add more. Had the police been called simply to calm down a situation? Was it just a coincidence that the officer had arrived when he did? Sonia shook her head. What the heck is going on? It didn't feel right. It might not have anything to do with the Marcos Torres case, but it didn't feel right, and she damn well knew she wasn't leaving until she had figured out what was going on.

By three in the afternoon, nothing else had happened. She was tired of watching horses meander around a field, munching slowly on grass. And unfortunately, Sonia had been sitting in her car drinking Magee's coffee since ten in the morning. The phrase, "having to pee like a racehorse," seemed appropriate to her in so many ways. She should give in to her biological needs and head to the BP station just a mile or so away. Sonia put her hand on the ignition key. Before she could turn it, however, a black Lincoln Continental appeared on her computer screen—a third surprise visitor. The weather had been very dry over the last few days and when the car sped up the driveway it kicked up so much dust that it transformed the image on the screen into swirls of gray.

Sonia squirmed in her seat and picked up her phone: "3:07. Black Lincoln comes onto the property. Similar to the vehicle seen last week, but not the same one. Couldn't see the license plate"

The screen cleared. Today's driver was accompanied by a passenger, another blond man, but his look was entirely different. He was tall and very thin, his haired slicked back, a closely trimmed blond goatee adorning his chin. Dressed in black pants and a black shirt, he appeared to carry himself with a definite sense of authority, almost of menace. While the driver stayed outside, the tall man went directly into the barn.

Once again, the duration of the visit was very short. Sonia noted the Lincoln was gone by 3:18 PM—only eleven minutes. The tall man had simply walked out of the barn, flicked his hand, indicating to the driver that it was time to go, and gotten into the back seat. When the car blew out of the farm's entrance, turning right onto the road without stopping, Sonia missed her only other chance to get a look at the car's license plate.

By three-thirty, Sonia couldn't put off her need to pee any longer. And she was pissed. "If I was that damn Brad Dunham, I'd just go behind a bush and relieve myself. But no, I've got to leave the stakeout and go find a freakin' bathroom."

Sonia made the world's quickest trip to the BP station and back to her surveillance post, hoping she hadn't missed anything that had happened on the farm. Marcos' truck was gone, but that was no longer her main concern. It was what was happening in that barn that she was focused on. As long as the Jaguar was still there—and it was—Sonia was not going anywhere.

By four o'clock, Sonia was so bored she decided to go over her notes. Damn, I never recorded when that stupid truck left the barn, or Marcos either. She knew the truck had left at the same time as the police cruiser. Having been gone only about ten minutes on her pee run, she guesstimated when Marcos had left. But the Jaguar was still there. That just didn't seem right.

By six o'clock Sonia had listened through her entire iTunes library, mostly *Smashing Pumpkins*, *Radio Head*, and *Over the Rhine*, a local Cincinnati group that she had followed since she was a kid. The Jaguar was still there. Where was the guy in the madras shirt?

By eight o'clock, Sonia checked for local headlines on her phone. Nothing about Dahlia Farm. Her stomach was reminding her that she hadn't eaten since lunch. Her butt was reminding her that she'd been sitting in the car all day—again. At 8:36 PM, the computer screen filled with the red and blue lights of a police cruiser. It was followed by another and then another. Sonia tracked the movement of each vehicle, including the ambulance that followed. Less than twenty minutes later, a small SUV from the local NBC affiliate arrived.

Sonia was certain the time had come to get more aggressive. She twisted her lips, mustering her strength, pushing herself forward. Dang, I knew something was going on. Surely, with all that commotion, I could walk right onto that farm see what the heck is happening. She started her car and drove to the edge of the property. With her iPhone concealed in her hand and recording video, she started to walk up the driveway, right toward the barn.

A uniformed police officer stepped in front of her when she

was only twenty-five yards onto the property. He lifted his hand. "What's your business here?"

Sonia gave him a big smile. "Oh, I just saw all the commotion and I wondered what it was all about." She batted her eyes and looked around him. "The lights. The cars—A TV van? Did a famous horse die?"

"This is now a restricted area. I'm afraid you'll have to leave ma'am." There was no smile on his broad face as he looked down at her.

Sonia played her best innocent bystander. She stood on her tiptoes, looking around his big body. "Can't I just stay right here and watch?"

"No, ma'am. Restricted area." His long arms were already not-so-subtly pushing her in the direction of the road. "Don't want anyone to get hurt or to interfere with the emergency vehicles. And this is private property. I'm afraid I'm going to have to insist that you leave— immediately."

Sonia's opportunity had slipped away. Not wanting to press her luck, she walked back to her car, at a total loss for what to do next. Deflated, she got into her car and started toward home. *Something's going on there, and I'll bet they would have let that son-of-a-bitch, Brad Dunham, in to see it. Damn him.* In her mind, Sonia could see Mr. Semper Fi standing at the counter in Magee's and then walking through the place like he owned it—the puke green shirt bulging with his muscles. Her Italian blood boiled. *That son-of-a-bitch.* Then it hit her. She didn't really know a thing about Brad Dunham, and now he was a son-of-a-bitch. Sonia blew that same wisp of hair out of her face. *Man, I am tired.*

When Sonia walked up the steps to her apartment she was worn out and stiff. She took a half-empty bottle of white wine out of the refrigerator and poured herself a glass. She plopped into her favorite chair and started munching on a large handful of pretzels. *So, this is dinner?*

Sonia turned to the *Ten O'clock News* on the local Fox affiliate, the earliest news show in town. The attractive young female anchor opened the program. "Thank you for joining us. This evening our 'Big Story' concerns one of our local horse farms. Police report that the owner of Dahlia Farm, Mr. John Abbot Hensley, has committed suicide."

PART II

9

S onia couldn't sleep that night. By five in the morning, she had given up and gotten up. She had turned on the local Fox affiliate again, hoping to learn more about the suicide of John Abbott Hensley. All she saw was the same story and the same video that had aired last night at ten. By seven o'clock it was time for the *Today Show* on NBC, which she knew would have local cut-ins. She poured herself a third cup of coffee and turned it on, figuring that they would now be reporting with a little more depth. She was right, but just barely. The reports now gave a little more background on Hensley. He was a lawyer who lived in Cincinnati. He owned the farm. He seemed to be in town for a routine visit to the farm. Blah, blah, blah. She had already discovered that information on her own. And, in fact, she knew more than they did. She had seen his demeanor when he walked around the farm. She knew exactly when he entered the barn—pretty much. She knew, pretty closely, when they had found the body. The reports kept referring to it as a suicide, but all the while that she watched the reports Sonia kept saying softly but intensely, "*Stronzate. Stronzate.*" Italian for bullshit.

She kept running it over and over again in her mind. Hensley had arrived in his fancy car, with his white pants, his madras shirt, his stylish glasses. He was confident, all smiles. Then he'd headed for the barn, but Hollings kept trying to show him something out in one of the fields. She hadn't thought about it then, but now it seemed to her that there had been a bit of tension between Hollings and Hensley. Sonia paced around and around in her tiny apartment. They go into the barn, the cop comes, but then he leaves. The guy in the black Lincoln comes, then he leaves. Then Hensley commits suicide? It just doesn't add up. Damn it, it just doesn't add up.

By nine in the morning, she was frustrated and antsy. She had no real business report to file, but she went to the office anyway, forgetting to stop by and get her coffee and croissant. She hardly noticed climbing the stairs. She entered the office, hoping to find Jet there. But it was no surprise to her that, at nine-fifteen in the morning, Jet had not yet come in. Sonia paced around her office, in fact, around the entire BCI space. She would stop occasionally and stare aimlessly out the front window. Her eyes, of course, settled first on the school district building, then on the white house. I wonder how Brad Dunham is doing this morning.

Finally, after forty-five minutes, the door squeaked open and Jet pushed her way in. "Have you heard?" Sonia asked, standing in the doorway to her own space.

Jet slipped off her jacket on the way to her desk. "Heard what?"

"Heard about last night's *suicide*?" said Sonia, making quotation marks in the air with her fingers. "John Abbott Hensley?"

Jet stopped. "I heard something on the radio, but I didn't pay much attention. Hensley? Isn't he connected to Dahlia Farm?"

Sonia's eyebrows arched. "Connected? Yeah, he owns it."

"Whoa." Then, after a long moment, "Soooo?"

"So, I was right there when it happened. Right there."

Jet's eyes opened wide. "You saw him do it?"

"No." The words flew out of Sonia's mouth in a quick stream.

"But I was staking out Marcos Torres all day, and I saw Hensley show up, though I didn't know it was Hensley at the time. Then later, much later, the cops were all over the place. I tried to get close but they wouldn't let me. They say he committed suicide right there in the barn. That's bull. I don't know what happened, but I know one thing. That was no freakin' suicide."

Jet stared wide-eyed. "What?! What do you mean, not a suicide?"

"I'm telling you." Sonia was rising out of her seat. "I was there. That was no suicide." Her voice shook.

"Hold on there, baby girl," just a hint of Paula Dean in her voice. "Get a hold of yourself and calm down. It's okay. Where's your coffee?" She looked around Sonia's desk.

"I don't have one." Sonia shrugged. "I guess I didn't go downstairs this morning."

"Well, let's go get you that coffee and your croissant. I'm buying."

They walked down the stairs arm in arm. The weather was nicer, but with no jacket on, Sonia still felt a little bite in the air. She didn't mind. The cold seemed to wake her up. It was refreshing. As they reached the bottom of the steps, Jet opened the door for Sonia and ushered her inside. Sonia could still feel the tingle of the brisk air on her face as she entered a place whose warmth and wonderful smells usually offered a sense of comfort and safety. Usually. Today, however, Sonia wasn't feeling it.

Sonia and Jet sat down at a small table by one of the front windows. Sonia had her coffee and croissant, and Jet had given into temptation and ordered a cherry-cheese Danish. They talked quietly.

Jet leaned in just a bit. "Okay, so, tell me again. Let's start from the beginning."

Sonia looked across the table. She leaned in as well. "Listen, I was there all day. I saw what happened. I'm telling you, Hensley didn't kill himself."

"Now, you didn't really see it go down, right?"

"No, you're right." Sonia stirred her coffee so hard it almost came over the top of the cup. "I didn't really see anything. It's just that something's not right. I mean, I saw him arrive—Hensley that is. I saw him arrive and he was all smiles. He went in to see Hollings, that's the farm manager, and then he came out and walked over to the barn. He didn't seem upset or anything. It just all looked normal."

"You didn't see anything out of the ordinary?"

"Well, that's not entirely true." Sonia stirred her coffee again. Her speech slowed. "It did seem that Hollings wanted to show Hensley something, but Hensley didn't seem interested. In fact, Hollings tried several times to get Hensley to follow him into one of the fields. I just don't know what he wanted Hensley to see."

Jet took a sip. "So, they just went into the barn then?"

"Well, yeah, they just walked into the barn."

"What happened then?"

"Nothing. Nothing happened for a long time. Well, not until some cop showed up."

A middle-aged man and his wife walked past the table. The man looked down at the girls and smiled.

Jet smiled back, then leaned in and whispered furtively. "A cop showed up?"

"Yeah, a detective or something. I never got a look at his face. He was only there for a couple of minutes, but now that I say it, I kind of had a sense of relief when he showed up. Honestly, I realized this morning that I might have been sensing some tension between Hollings and Hensley."

"They were getting into it?"

"No, it was much more subtle than that. It was like Hollings really, really wanted Hensley to follow him into that field, and he was frustrated when Hensley wouldn't go."

"Then what happened?"

"Then that other guy showed up."

Jet squinted. "What other guy?"

"Well, this other guy shows up in a big black Lincoln Continental. He was real tall and thin, and he looked kind of mean. He goes into the barn for a few minutes, comes out, and leaves."

"What was he doing there?"

Sonia's fists fell to the table. Her voice rose. "How the hell do I know?"

Jet took a beat before she spoke again. "And nothing else happens?"

"Nope." Sonia's answer was much more controlled.

"And you don't know who he is?"

"Nope."

"Had you ever seen him before?"

"Well, no. But there was just something weird about him, something ominous."

"And you think something was going on there?"

"Yes, I think!" said Sonia. Her voice rose again, so much so that she feared she was attracting attention. She brought her voice down, almost to a whisper. "That's why I'm so rattled. There was something going on there and I don't have any idea of what it was. And now John Abbott Hensley is dead. I mean, what the . . . ."

"What the hell is right." Jet wagged a piece of her Danish at Sonia. Her voice lowered. Conspiratorial. "So, what are you going to do?"

"What do you mean, what am I going to do? What can I do?"

Jet gave her a snarky look. "Well, you could put on your big-girl panties and go to the police, couldn't you?"

"And tell them what?"

Whispering even more quietly, Jet leaned in across the small table. "Tell them you were there and something smells fishy."

Mirroring Jet's movement, Sonia brought herself within inches of Jet's face. "I'm not going to the police. I don't have any proof. Hell, I don't even know what *I* think happened. It just seems . . ." Sonia paused, slumped back in her wooden chair, and sighed. "It just seems all screwed up."

There was a long pause as they both sipped coffee that was getting cold and ignored their pastries. Finally, Jet said slowly, "You've got to do something."

Sonia noted the gentle concern on Jet's face. "I know. I know I do. I can't just let this go. But I don't know what in the world I should do."

"Well, we're private investigators, aren't we?" Jet tipped her head. "Don't you think we should go investigate?"

Taking a deep breath, Sonia nodded. "Yeah, but how?"

"Questions." Jet shrugged. "We go ask questions."

"Questions," Sonia said, her voice subtly reflecting a growing sense of energy, "we're going to go ask some questions." She sat up taller. "And we're going to start with the police. C'mon. Finish your coffee and let's walk down to police headquarters. It's right down the street."

"Sure 'nuff," said Jet, sitting up tall in her seat as well. "But listen. Better one person than two. You're the one who was there, and you're the one who knows the players best. Don't make a big fuss. Just slip in there and ask some polite questions. See what they're willing to share. And if they ask, tell them you have every right to know." She smiled. "You are, after all, a licensed private investigator. And you were, if it makes any difference, watching the property because you were on a legitimate case." Jet stood. "We have the paperwork to prove it."

Sonia decided that both her coffee and her pastry had passed their moment of expiration. She stood as well, threw her trash in the can, and headed for the door. Jet joined her. As they stepped out into the sunny but still somewhat chilly air, Sonia shivered. "I'd better head upstairs and get my coat before walking four or five blocks." Sonia stopped and looked up to the top of the stairs. She turned to Jet. "In fact, screw it. I'm going to drive. It's too damn cold to walk, but I'm going. I'm going there, and I'm going to find out something about what happened last night."

S onia walked through the front door of police headquarters and right up to the front desk. She asked to speak to one of the detectives who was investigating last night's suicide.

The officer behind the desk looked so young and squeaky clean to Sonia that she couldn't help but wonder if he was old enough to drive. "That would be Detective Sergeant Adams, ma'am," he said. "But he's not in right now, can I help you with something?"

The officer was being polite, but Sonia's Italian blood had gotten a bit stirred up. "Well, I need to talk to somebody who knows what's going on. When will he be back?"

"I really don't know, ma'am. He's out working the case, I guess. Can I have him give you a call?"

Sonia's insides churned. *I want some damn answers right now.* Still, there was no use making a scene. "Yes, please have him give me a call." There was an edge to her voice.

"Absolutely, ma'am. Just write your name and number on this sheet and I'll have him call you as soon as he gets back."

Sonia jotted down her information, left, and drove the few short blocks back to her office. She huffed. *Well, that didn't get* me very far, did it? Still, she had at least gotten started. As she pulled into the parking lot, it struck her that what she needed to do was listen to her recorded notes and get that information down on paper. That way she would tell a coherent story when Detective Sergeant . . . "Oh crap, what was his name. Oh well, whenever Detective Sergeant 'What's-His-Name' calls, I'll be ready." Back in her office, she went to work cleaning up her notes and did some research on John Abbott Hensley. As she did, she couldn't help but wonder what kind of man this absentee owner was, with his madras shirt and his really thick glasses. She had seen the smiles on the faces of the Steve Hollings, the farm manager, and the others, but they had seemed less than authentic. Was Hensley oblivious? Did he not sense the shallowness of their smiles? Or was he just used to that kind of reception? Did that all fit the general tenor of his life? She wondered.

~

IT HAD BEEN LESS than two hours since she had left police headquarters, but Sonia was wondering when the heck this detective, "What's-his-Name" was going to call her. Finally, right around 1:15, her cell phone rang.

"Bluegrass Confidential Investigations, this is Sonia Vitale speaking."

"Ms. Vitale, this is Detective Sergeant Adams calling. You left your name and phone number with the officer at our front desk?"

Sonia grabbed a pen and jotted down the detective's name. "Yes, I'd like to talk to you about last night's suicide," Sonia said, hoping her disbelief didn't show in her voice.

"You mean Mr. Hensley?"

"Yes."

"Do you have any information you'd like to share with us?"

"Well, I might. But I have a few questions I'd like to ask as well. Can we meet somewhere?"

"I'd be glad to come to you. Are you somewhere here in town?"

"Yes, right here on East Main. It's Bluegrass Confidential Investigations. We're up above Magee's."

"Great. I could be there in about ten minutes or so. Does that work for you?"

"Absolutely. I'll see you then."

"Yes, ma'am. See you in ten minutes."

Sonia hung up and looked around her office. It was in pretty good shape, but she set about straightening it up a bit anyway. Somehow, she had liked the sound of Detective Sergeant Adams on the phone. Sonia watched her hands organizing a small pile of mail. Weird. You haven't even met this guy and yet you're acting like you want to show him what a good homemaker you are. Get real Sonia girl, this is business.

THIRTY-SEVEN MINUTES LATER, Detective Sergeant Adams walked up the stairs and into the BCI offices. Sonia wondered why anybody ever bothered to say they'd be there in ten minutes.

Adams was a tall, attractive man. His looks reflected the strong influence of the Scots/Irish/English immigrants who had made their way west to Kentucky, from Virginia and North Carolina, through the Cumberland Gap. Tall, sturdy, somewhat rambunctious folks, they had created a life for themselves in the hollers and on the sides of the mountains in Eastern Kentucky, Tennessee, and West Virginia. His demeanor was quiet and polite as he took a seat in Sonia's office.

Adams asked the required questions about what Sonia had seen and why she had been there. He took copious notes in his pad, glancing up briefly at Sonia when she mentioned the visit from the police officer and also when she mentioned the arrival of the blond man in the black Lincoln.

Sonia let out a sigh. She'd finished telling her story.

Adams stood up suddenly. "I want to thank you for sharing this information, Ms. Vitale. I'm sure it will be helpful in our investigation."

Sonia was sitting at her desk. She had become more and more relaxed as she shared her story with this attractive, almost gentle man. But when he stood and began to leave, she popped up like an English muffin coming out of a toaster. She had been playing her part as the concerned citizen, but now it was her turn. "Aren't you going to answer any of my questions? Like how he died? Of if there was anyone else there?"

"I'm sorry, ma'am, but any information we gather is strictly confidential. I'm sure the County Attorney will be releasing a statement to the media sometime today or tomorrow. You're welcome to attend that press conference, or just listen to the news."

She walked around the desk after him. "Now wait a minute. I just gave you lots of information you would never have gotten without me. I'd like to know exactly what happened to Hensley. Did he shoot himself? Did he hang himself? How'd he do it? Who found him? Was he already dead?"

The questions came flying out of her mouth. She had lots of questions and she wanted answers. She wanted them now. The problem was that she was already talking to the back of Detective Sergeant Adams. He had walked out of her office and was already halfway through the waiting room, headed for the door.

"Thank you for your co-operation, Ms. Vitale," he shouted over his shoulder. Then he was out the door and gone.

"Damn him!" Sonia said, literally stomping her foot. "*Figlio di puttana!*" Sonia knew just a few choice words in the language of her forefathers, and loosely translated, those choice words meant, "Son-of-a-bitch!"

Way back in Cincinnati, John Eckel, the man who had asked Sonia to marry him, had learned not to mess with her when she started speaking Italian. Even Jet had seen a hint of Sonia's Italian temperament when she was angry—and Sonia was angry now.

Sonia walked around her office talking to herself, while Jet sat at her own desk, unusually attentive to her paperwork. "That son of a bitch. I told him everything I knew and nothing. That bastard told me nothing. Damn it. Well just because you won't tell me what the hell is going on, doesn't mean I'm not going to find out. Screw you, Detective Sergeant Shithead. I'm going to find out."

Sonia heard the door to the outside stairs click closed. Apparently, Jet had suddenly decided it was a good time to go to lunch.

AT FOUR-FIFTEEN ON FRIDAY AFTERNOON, Sonia found herself standing in the lobby of one of the two beautiful new court-houses that had been built downtown. The high ceilings, stone walls, and tile floors gave the space a chilly feeling. She was part of a small crowd, mostly news media folk, waiting to hear a statement from County Attorney, Estella Cabrera. She had been stymied over the past two days, with nothing of importance happening on the farm. She was determined that today, at least, she would find out what had happened to Hensley.

As she waited for Ms. Cabrera to begin, Sonia felt a light touch on her elbow. She turned to find Detective Sergeant Adams standing there.

"Good afternoon Ms. Vitale."

"Good afternoon Detective." Sonia's eyes quickly took him in from head to toe. She looked away. Doesn't he look nice in that dark gray suit? She liked how quietly he carried himself.

Adams stood at her side and looked around somewhat surreptitiously. "Listen," he spoke to her while his eyes stared straight ahead, "I hope you realize that any information you shared with me is now part of the official investigation. I wouldn't ask any questions here, or say anything that would compromise any of that information."

Sonia was completely taken aback, literally speechless.

"Good," Adams said. "Have a nice day."

Sonia watched him turn and slip away into the crowd. There seemed to be an empty space where he had just been standing. The reporter to her left moved a few inches forward and Sonia turned to see Estella Cabrera stepping in front of a bank of six microphones, several of which were capped with the logos of local TV and radio stations. The young woman's light-gray suit and white blouse set off her long, almost lustrous black eyes and hair. Well-known in the city for her intelligence, her appearance made her seem almost more TV star than prosecutor.

The County Attorney began. "Good afternoon ladies and gentlemen." Sonia turned to listen. "I'm here today to share with you our conclusions as to the death of Mr. John Abbott Hensley, which occurred in our jurisdiction this past Monday evening, March 28th. Our conclusions are as follows:

WE BELIEVE THAT, sometime between 7:00 PM and 9:00 PM, Mr. Hensley took his own life by hanging himself inside one of the barns on Dahlia Farm, a horse farm he owned and operated as an absentee owner. The body was found by the farm manager, Mr. Steven Hollings. Police and medical professionals were called as soon as possible, but Mr. Hensley was declared dead by the County Coroner at 9:51 PM.

Medical Examiner Dr. Xin Li, has determined that the cause of death was strangulation by rope, the same rope found around Mr. Hensley's neck at the time of the discovery of his body. There were no signs of foul play.

SONIA'S INSIDES ROILED. No foul play? Who is she kidding? Mr.

Sunshine didn't just walk in that barn and off himself. And of course Hollings is the one who found him. He's the one who went into the barn with Hensley and he never came out! No frickin' way. Ms. Cabrera continued.

IN A PRELIMINARY INVESTIGATION of the finances of Dahlia Farm, we found that the farm was under financial duress. We believe this may well have been the motive for Mr. Hensley's having taken his own life. We have, therefore, determined and declared the death of Mr. John Abbott Hensley a suicide, and no further investigations will be undertaken. I will now take questions from the media.

SONIA HEARD the rustle of hands being raised and voices calling out, as different reporters tried to be the first to get their questions answered. There were several questions, but they were mostly routine. The level of energy in the room was more subdued than Sonia would have imagined. Dahlia Farm was small. Mr. Hensley was not part of the Lexington scene and was rarely visible in town. Bottom line, somebody who owned a farm in Lexington, but didn't live in Lexington and wasn't famous, had taken his own life. Blah, blah, blah. Film at eleven.

Sonia walked out of the press conference and toward her car, her head spinning. What the hell were they thinking? There's no way he killed himself. Something was going on in that barn and they missed it. "*Idioti.*" The word came out of her mouth with utter disdain. And what was that crap from Adams? What was he implying? My information was part of the official investigation? But Estela Cabrera said the investigation was closed. Was he trying to intimidate me? Why would he do that? What the heck is going on?

As she walked to her car, Sonia pulled her spring jacket up

close to her chin and neck and wrapped her arms around her body. It had turned colder again, but her actions were probably more a response to her emotional state than her physical condition. Something wasn't right, and that knowledge sent a shiver through her body. Her mind told her to just let it go. But her gut was telling her something entirely different.

11

A t eight o'clock that evening, Sonia walked back into the offices of BCI. She was still rattled from her encounter with Adams and the press conference in general. Yet, it was another Thursday evening and, therefore, there would be another attempt to close the case of Robert "Bob" Dylan. This week the weather was a little chilly, but not problematic. Jet was ready to go with the six-foot ladder they had once again strapped to the top of Sonia's car. The batteries were charged in the camera and there didn't seem to be anything that wasn't locked and loaded. Bob's girl-friend might be singing, "I'll Be Your Baby Tonight," but Sonia and Jet would be watching. By evening's end, ol' Bob Dylan would be knock, knock, knockin' on heaven's door, trying to get away from his troubles. Sonia laughed at herself. *I guess all those hours listening to Dad's old cassettes must have really warped my mind.*

At eight-fifteen, Sonia stood in the bushes, holding the ladder as Jet climbed up the rungs. She watched her partner's head get high enough to peek through the window. Jet seemed to be enjoying herself. "Well, I'll be." Her voice was, suddenly, all hush-puppies and black-eyed peas. "There she is naked as a jaybird

once again, and she's just sitting there waiting for him. Come on
Bobby. Come to Momma. Step right up there and hop on your
lady friend. Let's get this rodeo started."

Sonia looked upward. "Nice, Joyce Ellen."

Jet flashed her a look.

Sonia was fully aware that little Joyce Ellen Thomas had
hated it when her parents insisted on calling her by her full
name, Joyce Ellen. When she'd become a bit of a girl's track star
in high school, she'd reveled in the fact that other kids had
started calling her The Jet. Soon it had become simply Jet and
she'd adopted that as her official, if not legal name. All of that
made it more fun for Sonia to call her Joyce Ellen whenever she
needed to make a point.

Jet got back to business, and a minute or two later she huffed
and shook her head in frustration.

Sonia could tell there was still no sign of Bob. His lover must
have been sitting there waiting and waiting. Every once in a
while, Jet would whisper down that Bob's lover was saying something, but she could never tell Sonia what it was. "Geez, how long
can this go on?" Jet asked.

Suddenly, Jet gasped and looked down at Sonia with her eyes
open wide. Then she whispered loudly, "I've got it. I know what's
going on."

Jet stepped down from the ladder and put her hand up to
Sonia's ear. "That son of a bitch in there is doing some nasty,
messed-up shit. He's doing some weirdo thing and making that
poor woman watch." Jet was twisting and turning, wrapping her
arms around her body. "Son-of-a-bitch. He's in there doing who
knows what. Yuck, I feel dirty just being near it. It's disgusting.
He's disgusting."

There was a part of Sonia that wanted to climb up the ladder
and take a peek. But she knew better. If she ever saw what this
pervert was doing she might never be able to forget the image. A

chill ran up her spine. Her shoulders twitched. Damn, utterly repulsive.

Sonia had no idea what to do next, and Jet seemed to have had enough as well. "Let's get the hell out of here. We don't get paid enough to sit here in the dark while "Mr. Play-with-Himself" does some perverted show in front of that poor woman. Screw it, we'll be back next week with an entirely different plan."

Sonia let the ladder slide quietly down and grabbed one end. "I'm all for that."

"What I need right now is a good shower," said Jet. "Yuk, I can't stand knowing what I've just seen, and what I feel like." She moved to the other end of the ladder and took hold.

"Well, perhaps I know what will rinse that feeling off," Sonia said as she led the way past the side of the house.

"And what would that be?"

Sonia smiled. "Oh, I don't know, maybe some hot coffee laced with some Bailey's Irish Cream?"

Jet cocked her head. "You know, I believe that's just what the doctor ordered."

By a little past nine, Sonia and Jet were sitting in a bar in a part of town known as Chevy Chase, a name that existed long before the actor/comedian's birth. The bar, Charlie Brown's, was in the middle of a block of connected buildings. It had a wooden edifice and was dark and cozy inside with lots of plush seating near an open fireplace. The coffees in front of them were strong and hot and laced with a noticeable dose of Bailey's.

Sonia and Jet had chosen a well-worn couch, bookended by two even more well-worn tables. Settling into the couch, Jet spoke first. "I don't know how the hell we're going to nail ol' Bob, but we'd better come up with something soon. Mrs. Dylan is getting impatient." Jet took a tentative sip of her coffee. "In fact, so is

McCormick. Do you think you can be done with the camera soon? I've got to get on that restaurant thing ASAP."

Sonia blew on her coffee. "You know what? I know where Mr. Torres is dippin' his wick, and I'm pretty sure those ladies will show up again in the same car." She took a tiny sip, carefully blowing on the hot drink first. "I'll just park somewhere between the castle and the farm and keep my eyes open. I'll know when they resume their conjugal visits."

"Based on how you described Marcos Torres," Jet snorted, "they sound more like pity visits." They sat in silence for a minute, enjoying the warmth of the cups in their hands. "Any idea how we're finally going to snag Mr. Dylan?" Jet asked.

"I don't know." Sonia put her mug down on the marred table next to her. "Honestly, all I can think of is the Hensley case."

"Oh, it's a case now, is it?" Jet tipped her chin down and looked over the glasses she wasn't wearing. "And exactly who's paying us?"

"Well, you know what I mean. It's just chewing on me. I did some research on the guy. Mom died when he was young. Dad was an alcoholic. The state took him and put him into foster care. From what I could tell, those folks were some kind of religious fanatics. Must have been tough on him. Still, he goes on to become a really successful lawyer, marries a beautiful woman, buys himself a horse farm." She shook a finger at Jet. "Listen, I know damn well that Mr. John Abbott Hensley most certainly did not kill himself. Yet the police call it a suicide. Even the medical examiner called it a suicide."

"Have you seen the Medical Examiner's Report?"

"No, but I'm going to. It's public record, isn't it?"

"Honestly, I don't think so." Jet shook her head. "It's not like on all those TV shows, where everyone knows everything. Damn, with all those HIPAA rules, the receptionist at your dentist's office could get in trouble just for telling one of your friends that you dropped in to get your teeth cleaned. I'm pretty sure you'd have a hell of a time getting your hands on that report."

Sonia sat in silence, her eyes roaming past several rows of books on a dusty shelf—books that hadn't been touched in years, but were at least real books. Finally, she sat up taller. "Well, then, I'm just going to have to get it from the horse's mouth."

"What do you mean?"

"Well, you know how Magee's has its regulars, right?

"Yeah, Magee's has its regulars," Jet shrugged. "As a matter of fact, don't we qualify?"

Sonia bobbed her head. "I guess we do."

"So? . . . What?"

"Well, one of those regulars is the medical examiner herself, Dr. Xin Li. Every Friday afternoon she stops in around one o'clock. She has a cup of coffee and just sits there. No book, no phone. She just sort of meditates. Then she stands up and walks over to the counter, and Hildy usually has a box waiting for her. I think she brings her family a cake or something every weekend."

"And?"

"Aaand, I've had a few passing conversations with her on occasion." She took a long sip of her coffee and felt the warmth of the Bailey's slip down her throat. "Aaand, tomorrow being Friday, I plan to be in Magee's right around one o'clock." She set the mug back on the table. "Aaand, I'm planning to have one of those conversations with our esteemed medical examiner." She gave Jet a knowing smile.

Jet laughed. "And she's going tell you everything you want to know, HIPAA be damned?"

"Oh, I have my vays," Sonia said with a terrible German accent. "I have my vays."

Jet rolled her eyes.

12

Spring can come relatively early in Kentucky, and this year it had. Friday's warmth felt good to Sonia as she walked down the stairs from her office to Magee's. It was her goal to be seated at the corner table when Dr. Xin Li arrived for her weekly visit.

Sonia got a cup of coffee and chose a seat along the brick wall, a place from which she would have a clear view of everyone who came into Magee's. Shortly after she settled in, Sonia's ears were accosted by the sound of a woman's rather raspy voice coming from behind her. At first, she tried to ignore it. Within a few moments, however, Sonia's ears perked up as she heard three words that had become very, very, important to her—John Abbot Hensley.

Sonia leaned forward, her elbows on the table, her coffee cup held in both hands, close to her lips. Making a distinct effort to not turn around and look, Sonia strained to hear every word the woman was saying. ". . . not sure anyone really liked him. I mean, with those coke-bottle glasses, and the way he dressed." The woman chuckled derisively. "Do you believe it? The man wore some of the most ghastly clothing." She paused, Sonia assumed to take a sip of her beverage. "You would think for a little man, he would have been more concerned with his choices in that area."

There was a pause. Sonia strained to hear if there was another voice at the table. There was, but it was much more discreet and Sonia couldn't really understand the other woman's words. Finally, the raspy voice began again. "Oh, no. He was very successful, but that didn't mean he fit in here." The voice lowered. Sonia strained. "He would show up at one of the affairs in town with that *wife* of his." She almost snarled the word. "I mean, *really*."

Sonia was entirely focused on the women's conversation when her attention was suddenly drawn to the smell of fine perfume. An attractive blonde-haired woman in her late forties walked by, dressed in obviously expensive clothing. From behind, Sonia could hear the raspy voice turn syrupy sweet. "Martha, Martha. How lovely to see you. Come. Sit with us."

Sonia put down her cup, trying to control her disdain. What she couldn't control was her curiosity. Reaching into her purse, she retrieved her compact. Ostensibly checking her own makeup, Sonia turned the mirror so that she was able to see a large, red-headed woman with expensive clothing, bright red lipstick and entirely too much hair—a bouffant that appeared so heavily covered in hairspray that any accidental contact with it might actually tip the woman over. Sonia was quite certain that the red-head was the source of the irritating voice and disparaging conversation. She went back to her coffee, disappointed that she had not learned anything new and important about John Abbot Hensley.

Just past one o'clock, Sonia watched the county medical examiner walk in the door. Dressed in a simple white blouse, black pencil skirt, and black pumps, she carried a black cardigan sweater over her arm along with her functional handbag. Her black hair was cut in severe bangs, matching the look on her face. She wore rimless glasses.

As usual, Dr. Li made her way to the counter and spoke a few words to Hildy. After she had paid, she turned and walked back to the coffee bar, poured herself a cup, and found a seat at an empty table near the window. She sat, sipping her coffee, lost in her thoughts for over thirty minutes.

All the while, Sonia was seated near the door, surreptitiously observing Dr. Li. She knew she couldn't muster any good reason to interrupt the Medical Examiner's quiet time, so she would have to catch her on the fly, as she was leaving.

Sonia had sat at her table for a little over twenty minutes as she waited for Dr. Li to arrive. That twenty minutes had certainly been interesting. On the other hand, the thirty minutes or more that she waited as Dr. Li simply sat there staring into space seemed interminable to her. Sonia had gotten up and poured herself another cup of coffee then sat there doodling impatiently on the pad in front of her. This kind of static waiting was anathema for Sonia. Sonia looked down at her pad and was surprised. She had been mindlessly writing out a drill she had been forced to do seemingly hundreds of times during her school years.

Having grown up Italian in Cincinnati, it was no surprise that Sonia's family had sent her to Catholic schools. The nuns she had studied under in those intermediate years had been all about classical training: memorizing long passages, finishing sentences with brief phrases in their original Latin, learning to use Roman numerals. Now, waiting for the motionless Dr. Li, she was well along in writing out the numbers from one to one hundred in those same Roman numerals.

Finally, Sonia saw Dr. Li stand. She dropped her pen, popped up, and headed for the counter. She got to the counter just before Dr. Li and, loudly enough for the medical examiner to hear, asked Hildy what type of cake she recommended Sonia bring home for the weekend.

Hildy seemed dumbfounded. Sonia had never asked a question like that before. In fact, Hildy knew Sonia didn't even have a family to bring a cake home to. But before Hildy could say much of anything, Sonia turned, trying to be nonchalant, and said to Dr. Li, "Oh, hello. How are you?"

Dr. Li looked at her with a bit of surprise, then seemed to recognize her. "Oh, yes, hello."

Sonia turned back toward the counter for a moment, and then back to the doctor. "It's so hard to know what everyone will like. They all have different tastes, don't they?"

Dr. Li replied a bit timidly, "Yes, that's always a problem. It's hard to make them all happy."

"I just don't know. Do you have any suggestions?"

"Well, I bring home the yellow cake with the milk chocolate icing and the almonds around the side every week. That way they all know what's coming and no one bothers to complain. It's simple that way. Plus, they all seem to like it."

"Hmmm." Sonia put her finger to her mouth. "You're probably right. Just keep it simple. By the way, you're the county medical examiner, aren't you?"

Dr. Li's eyes squinted in reaction to the sudden shift in gears, but she managed to get out a quiet, "Yes, I am."

"I saw you on TV yesterday. You were there at the news conference. Wasn't that awful about that man, Mr. Hastings?"

"Mr. Hensley. John Hensley."

"Right. They say he committed suicide, don't they? Oh, I'm sorry. I guess it was you who said that he committed suicide. Is it hard to tell sometimes?"

Dr. Li shrank back a bit, becoming somehow smaller. "Sometimes it's obvious. Sometimes not so."

"Well, what about Mr. Hensley? Was it obvious with him?"

Dr. Li stiffened. "As our report indicated, it was our conclusion that he did, in fact, take his own life. If you'll excuse me, I really do have to get home to my family."

Sonia pressed. "But there was nothing out of the ordinary, was there? It was clear that he had done it to himself?"

"There was no indication otherwise." Li stood on her toes and said over Sonia's shoulder, "I'll take my cake now, Hildy." Then she glanced back at Sonia as briefly as possible. "Have a nice day, I mean evening." She shook her head. "I mean weekend. Goodbye."

With that, the Dr. Li walked around to the side of the counter and, with her back to Sonia, waited for Hildy to bring her the cake. Her weekly order in hand, she all but scurried out of Magee's, seemingly glad to be getting away from the nosey lady at the counter.

Hildy looked at Sonia waiting for some sort of decision. Sonia simply waved her hand, turned, and walked out of Magee's. She trudged up the stairs, into the office, and plopped herself down in the red chair opposite Jet's desk.

Jet looked up. "Did you get anything out of her?"

"Yeah, bring home the yellow cake with the milk chocolate icing and the almonds around the side. The whole damn family will love it."

"Huh?"

"No! Nothing. I got nothing." Sonia stood up again. She walked past Jet's desk and to the front window. She looked outside, her eyes scanning the same scene she saw almost every day. Then she spoke, her words reflecting off the window and back to her own ears. "There's no freakin' way Hensley killed himself, but the cops and the medical examiner all say it's an open and shut case. Now that I think about it, I'll bet if they sent me the Medical Examiner's Report and I read the whole damn thing I wouldn't know a bit more than I do now. And that bullshit about the farm being in financial straits? I don't buy it."

Sonia paused and thought for a moment. "No, if I'm going to find out what actually happened on that farm, I have to come up with another plan. Try a whole different approach. Problem is, I don't have one."

Jet didn't respond.

As usual, Sonia's eyes drifted first to the school district building and then to the white house. This time, however, she not only saw the house and the sign that said Semper Fi Investigations, she saw a big rugged man walking out the door and down the steps. Although it would have been impossible, it seemed to her that she could see his bright blue eyes from all the way across the street. "Brad Dunham," she whispered.

Jet swiveled her chair around to face Sonia's back. "What?" she asked softly.

Sonia watched the man disappear around the building. "Nothing. Nothing."

"Oh no, you said something."

Sonia turned around and looked directly at Jet. "We need to talk to Brad Dunham."

Jet stuck out her hands, palms up. "What the hell for?"

"Listen," Sonia said, as she walked back around Jet's desk and took a seat.

Jet swiveled in her chair to follow her.

"This PI thing, it's cool. Really, it's a trip, and we're doing some good work. What is it, twenty-one people we've helped in the last year or so? We've done everything from cheating spouses and lovers to that man who hadn't seen his daughter in over four years. But this is different." Sonia looked directly into Jet's eyes. "Come on Jet, are we really the kind of PIs who can deal with a murder case by ourselves? Are we?"

Jet leaned back and crossed her arms. "We don't know it's a murder case."

Sonia could feel the energy rising in her chest. She straightened her back and leaned toward Jet's desk, placing her hands on her own thighs. "Well, we damn well know it's not a suicide. And even the medical examiner isn't saying Mr. John Abbott Hensley died of natural causes. This is big-time stuff, Jet, and we can do this, but we can't do it unless we get the help we need."

Sonia thought she saw hurt in Jet's eyes, and she immediately felt bad. "Look," she said quietly, as her body relaxed, and she leaned back into her chair. "Two years ago, I was a technology specialist at the school district. You were a work-from-home wife with one little sideline after the next. What was it, vitamins, then makeup, then air purifiers?" She shook her head. "Then you caught him cheating with that slut and all hell broke loose." She leaned in. "You realized you've got a passion, a passion for catching folks doing bad things. And I've got to admit you're pretty damn good at it. That's why you started BCI.

"Then I came along. Two years past being left at the altar in Cincinnati, I move to Lexington to work in the school district, helping teachers help kids. Then budget cuts come and I'm out of work. I was emotionally and financially drained. You knew I was good with technology, so you offered me a job. I was grateful, and I still am. We did good work together. And," she said softly, looking directly into Jet's eyes, "we've become friends, close friends."

Sonia sat further back in her chair. "But what does that all add up to if someone did something very terrible to Hensley. Don't we owe him the best that we can do, even if it means swallowing our pride and asking Mr. Hotshot across the street for help?"

Now it was Jet's turn to stand up and look out the window. It seemed clear to Sonia that Jet was struggling, turning things over in her mind. Sonia gave her time, watched her stroke her ponytail.

"Look, if you want to go over there and talk to Mr. Hotshot you go right ahead," her voice was defensive, "but this is not an official case for us." Jet turned, her voice even more pointed. "If you want to go, you go, but I'm staying out of it. You're on your own with this one."

Sonia heard more hurt in Jet's voice than anger. And the last thing she ever wanted to do was hurt Jet's feeling. She stood up and walked toward the door. "Okay," she said softly, "I'll see you tomorrow." Then she left BCI and headed for . . . actually, she had no idea where she was headed; she just felt the need to put some space between her and her dear friend. She hoped that as Jet had time to think about it, she might come around to seeing Sonia's point of view. One way or the other, though, Sonia was more and more convinced that she needed to try to enlist help from Brad Dunham, former Marine. She owed it to John Abbott Hensley.

SONIA HAD TAKEN the weekend off again. She felt that she absolutely had to clear her mind.

Saturday had been warm and sunny, with a light spring breeze. So, after her morning run, Sonia had decided to get in her car and just drive through the beautiful rolling hills of central Kentucky. She had eventually found herself in a picturesque little town called Midway, one commercial street in town, a railroad track running right down the middle of it.

For all her efforts, however, Sonia had not been able to shake her obsession with the death of John Abbot Hensley. As she had stepped out into the street in Midway, a fancy sports car with a Jaguar hood ornament drove by. Sonia had immediately caught a mental glimpse of Dahlia Farm. Questions had danced around in her mind. Why didn't I figure out what was going on? I was right there. Why didn't I do something to save that poor guy's life? Shouldn't I have been able to do something?

Driving back to her apartment on Saturday, Sonia had made a very difficult decision. The last thing she wanted to do was to go to Mr. Hotshot, Brad Dunham, and ask for help. But, this was about a man's life. I can't let this go just because I'm not experienced enough to figure out what to do. I just can't. I'm going to have to walk across the street and ask Mr. Hotshot for help. I don't want to, but I have to. I just have to.

After she'd made that decision, Sonia really couldn't wait for the day, and the weekend, to be over. She knew what she had to do and she couldn't wait to get started.

∼

Monday, at nine fifty, Sonia stepped out of the BCI offices and walked down the steps toward East Main—toward the white house. She fought back a sense of trepidation.

She had made her decision and was about to embark on the first case in which she didn't have Jet's unconditional support. In fact, the conversation she was about to have might begin the unraveling of her partnership with Jet, the relationship, other than the one with her family, that was now the most significant in her life. An ugly feeling roiled through her stomach. She was pretty sure it wasn't from the three cups of coffee she'd already had that morning.

At nine o'clock, she had called Brad Dunham and, without telling him where she worked or what she did, made an appointment to see him. Actually, she had been surprised that he had been in his office so early. But then again, he was a former Marine.

Sonia walked up the steps to the white house, running her hand over the smooth, freshly painted hand-rail. She remembered that the building itself had not been in very good shape when she'd started working at the school district. Now, however, the building was in much better shape. Mr. Dunham's presence in the building seemed to be having a very positive effect.

Sonia walked through the big doorway and into a dark hall. She found Brad Dunham's office on the first floor, to her left. She knocked on the door and heard a deep voice politely say, "Come in."

PART III

13

S onia put her hand on the doorknob. The door itself was old,
just like the door to the BCI offices; but, whereas the doorknob at the top of that long set of stairs was tarnished and difficult to turn, the doorknob that led into the offices of Brad
Dunham and Semper Fi Investigations was new and shiny. It
worked smoothly. A small quiver ran through Sonia's body as she
turned the knob. Dang, this is how you enter the office of a
successful organization.

As she stepped into the room, nothing she found gave her any
reason to change her impression. The room was an unusual, yet
very effective, blend of old and new. Hardwood floors and high
ceilings of an older era contrasted with the latest in sound and
photographic equipment. There was a highly-polished, antique
wooden desk, upon which sat what appeared to be the Dell
computer one of the local retail outlets had been pushing so hard
recently. Two eight-by-ten framed flags hung on the wall: one, a
framed miniature United States Marine Corps flag; the other, a
flag Sonia didn't recognize. On the desk were photographs of
three people and a desk nameplate. Sonia's eyes quickly scanned
the three photographs: the first, a standard official portrait of a

Kentucky State Trooper; the second, a high school football coach with his arm around one of his players; the third, a woman Sonia guessed to be in her early forties, probably a family member. The nameplate, on closer inspection, was a placard which simply read, "Do the Right Thing."

For Sonia, however, the focal point of the room was not a piece of furniture or a decoration. It was the large, quiet man who stood behind the desk and captured her with his incredibly bright, blue eyes. He was staring right at her, but he waited before he spoke—as if to give her a moment to take in the room. Finally, he addressed her. "Ms. Vitale?"

Sonia snapped out of the trance into which she had fallen. "Yes, uh, Vitale. I'm Sonia Vitale. And you are Mr. Dunham?"

"That's me." Brad Dunham nodded his head toward one of the two wheat-colored cloth seats that faced his desk. "Would you like to sit down?"

Sonia sat down in the chair on the right. She sank into it. *Dang, these chairs are low. Oh, I get it. This guy's playing power games. You find yourself looking up at him, and that puts him in the stronger position. I'll bet most clients don't even notice that. Dang, he's good.* She kept her hands on the arms of the chair, trying to elevate herself a tiny bit.

Brad Dunham sat as well—in his executive desk chair, simple, black, functional. A few moments passed. Brad Dunham said nothing. He just waited, his elbows on the arms of his chair, his hands tented in front of him. *More power play.* Then Sonia started. "Mr. Dunham—"

"Brad. Brad will do."

Sonia chuckled inwardly. *Oh, power and "Mr. Nice Guy." This guy does have his stuff together.* "Yes, Brad, I'm here because I need your help . . . or at least I think I do." Sonia felt her body collapse just a tiny bit. *Nice going. Now he's all power and strength, and you're such a crumbling cracker that you don't even know if you need help or not. Crap.*

Brad's only response was a small, ever so small, nod of his head.

"Listen, here's the deal," said Sonia, trying to rev up and get the conversation back on track. "I'm a private investigator—"

His hands relaxed and he stirred just slightly in his chair. "Bluegrass Confidential Investigations. Offices right across the street, over Magee's. Nice location, but I'll bet it's pretty cold up there in the winter. And I wouldn't want to have to climb those stairs all day long." There was a small smile on his lips.

It was Sonia's turn to sit in silence. Are you kidding me? This guy already knows who I am, knows all about us. Sonia's foot began to tap. Something she often did unconsciously.

"We passed the other day inside Magee's. You were wearing your dark blue pea coat with the plaid scarf and had that bell hat on."

Sonia squinted. "You mean a cloche hat?"

He cocked his head. "Yeah, I guess, if that's what you call it. Anyway, I think you had on a white sweater underneath the coat." He shrugged his shoulders. "I don't know, though, it was hard for me to tell."

Sonia blinked involuntarily. Are you kidding me? Do you want to tell me what color panties I was wearing too? She struggled to sit up taller. "How observant of you, Mr.—I mean Brad. Do you always keep such close track of those around you?"

Brad was silent for a moment, his hands tented again. Then he said softly, "In certain environments." There was something about the way he said it that made the hairs on Sonia's neck stand up.

Brad remained silent for another moment. When he spoke, his voice was more upbeat. "How can I help you, Ms. Vitale?"

Sonia felt like this was turning into quite a chess game. She remained tall in her seat—as tall as she could—and pressed on. "As you obviously know, I'm a PI, and I was staking out Dahlia Farm the other day. That was the day, and evening, that John

Abbott Hensley died. I use the term 'died,' because I don't believe for an instant that he committed suicide." She leaned forward.

"And you were staking out Dahlia Farm because?"

Sonia was stunned. No real response to a possible murder? Her mind scrambled for a moment. "Well, why I was there is really none of your concern. Client privilege and all, you know."

Brad, again, sat in silence. His elbows still on the arms of his chair, he interlaced his fingers and began unconsciously moving them in and out. Finally, Sonia continued. "As I said, I was staking out Dahlia Farm and I saw several things that made me come to the conclusion that there was no way that John Hensley took his own life."

His hands became still. "And you're not willing to tell me what those things were?"

"No. I mean yes. Well, of course, I am. I'll tell you all about that. I just don't see what my reason for being out there has to do with anything."

"Ms. Vitale—"

"Sonia," she interrupted, leaning in and trying very hard to get on the same psychological footing as her ... her what? Was he her adversary?

"Sonia," he restarted. So did his hands. Sonia noticed the movement. Stronger. Intimidating. "My point, is that to truly understand anything, we have to bring to bear every bit of information we might possibly gather. And in that context, the reason for your staking out Dahlia Farm might have everything to do with what we're discussing." His blue eyes locked in on her. "Wouldn't you agree?"

Sonia took a deep breath. "Well ...."

"Okay, then." Brad leaned back in his chair. "So, tell me why you were staking out Dahlia Farm. Then, of course, I'd like to hear what convinced you Mr. Hensley didn't commit suicide."

Sonia braced herself and jumped in. She started by sketching out the details about Ms. Torres and Mr. Torres, no relation. Once she got into the events surrounding Hensley's death her tempo quickened, as did her level of determination.

As she spoke, Brad sat in silence, obviously listening very intently, his elbows on his desk, and his fingers tented in front of his mouth. His eyes never left Sonia's face. In fact, Sonia was starting to have trouble discerning whether Brad was listening intently or just staring at her. And with those bright blue eyes, it was all a bit unnerving.

When Sonia finished her account, they sat in silence until Brad sat back in his chair. "So now you're determined to find out what actually happened to Mr. Hensley?"

Spent both from verbally sparring with Brad Dunham and from reliving the lengthy story, Sonia just nodded.

"And you would like to know the why and the who as well?"

"Yes."

"And you've come to me for help because you really don't know how to proceed on your own?"

Sonia sat up in her chair. This is starting to feel a little demeaning. What the hell? "Well, more like I would appreciate the professional courtesy of your input," she said with noticeably more energy, "and perhaps your assistance."

Brad remained relaxed in his chair. "And you would like me to do this pro bono?"

Sonia's nostrils flared. Holy crap. This jerk expects me to pay him for his help? I can't believe it. She glared at him silently.

After a few moments, Brad finally spoke. "Listen, Sonia, I know you don't have the money to pay me, and I wouldn't take your money anyway. I respect what you're doing. Honestly, I'm crazy busy, but I'll find the time to help you. Really, I will."

Sonia pursed her lips. She locked eyes with him. The clock on the wall ticked. This bastard is going to help, but only after he demeans me and makes me feel like I couldn't possibly accomplish this on my own. To add insult to injury, he makes me feel like I should pay him. Then he rubs it in by saying I couldn't afford it, and he wouldn't take my money anyway. The gall of this guy.

Sonia had to say something. She wanted to stick it to him, but she did need his help. She tried to hide her frustration. "And why are you going to do that?"

His gaze drifted to the placard on his desk, then he looked intently at her with those blue eyes. "Because that's what I was taught."

14

For the second time since she had entered the room, Sonia looked at the placard on Brad's desk. " 'Do the right thing'? Like it says on your desk?"

"Like it says on the desk."

He had said it so softly Sonia knew there was more. She waited for him to elaborate, but he said nothing. The clock ticked again.

Brad stood up and started to walk around the room. He spoke. His voice was still soft, his words slower than before. "Listen, I was born up the road in Paris, Kentucky."

Sonia turned and watched as he moved to the window, looking out on East Main—black polo shirt, well-fitting khakis, black belt, black leather shoes—his broad shoulders, his trim body in silhouette.

"My dad, that's his picture there, was a Kentucky State Trooper." He'd said it without turning around. "When I was thirteen, my dad was killed in the line of duty—doing the right thing—shot during a liquor store robbery. Those were *his* words, 'Do the right thing.' "

Sonia sat silently. She saw his fingers run absently over a

window frame. She waited, trying to understand. Is his game shifting?

"Until I was seventeen, I lived alone with my mom. She was a nurse, and she worked at one of the hospitals here in Lexington. After he died, Mom started saying, 'Bradley, do the right thing, honey, do the right thing.' " He turned and looked directly at her. He smiled. A real smile. "I think it was her way of honoring my dad, keeping him a part of our lives."

His eyes were so bright, so intense. She smiled back at him, then felt uncomfortable for having done so.

"One night, it was in February, the roads were icy and there had been a bunch of accidents. She was at home, but the hospital called and said she needed to come in. She just went and put on her coat and boots. And as she walked out the door, she said, almost more to herself than to me, 'Do the right thing. Just do the right thing.' "

There was a pause, and Sonia cringed inwardly.

"You know, some people call the road between Paris and Lexington the prettiest road in Kentucky."

Sonia knew it was a beautiful ride between Lexington and Paris. She and Jet had made the trip several times, up to a shooting range they occasionally practiced on. Horse farms. And beside the road, miles, and miles of stone fences, some of which were actually built by slaves before the Civil War. But Sonia knew this wasn't a story about horse farms and beautiful scenery. She already knew the end of the story. She didn't want to hear it.

"But that night it wasn't the prettiest road in Kentucky, it was the deadliest. She slid off the road, right into one of those stone walls."

Sonia looked down at her hands. Why is he telling me all of this? So personal.

Brad turned, moved back to his desk, and stood in front of it. He leaned against it, putting himself between Sonia and the desk. He picked up the picture of the football coach.

Sonia could hear him speaking. Words came into her consciousness . . . "Aunt and uncle . . . coach . . . took a special interest in me . . .," but they slipped by. She was trying to take the measure of the man, his strength, his sharp mind, but also his vulnerability. Her mind strained to grasp the whole of him. Who is this guy? What makes this guy tick?

". . . but he knew how important the phrase, 'Do the right thing,' was for me." Brad had finished speaking. He was smiling at her.

Sonia felt she should say something, but nothing came to her.

There was another long pause. He looked down at the picture and tapped it with his thumb. Then he turned back to Sonia. "You know, that could have become something I hated, 'Do the right thing.' I could have rebelled against it, but I didn't. Instead, I took it on as my own."

Sonia adjusted herself in her chair, and that seemed to break Brad's train of thought. Brad put the picture back on the desk. He seemed ill at ease, as if he suddenly realized he was sharing too much. He straightened the picture several times. His eyes rose to hers momentarily. "Sorry." The words were soft, almost mumbled.

Sonia noticed the gentleness with which Brad had placed the photograph back on the desk. Gentle man? Tough guy? Which one? Both? Sonia's eyes drifted to the miniature Marine Corps flag on the wall. Trying to break the intensity of the moment, she asked, "So, you were in the Marines?"

He looked at the flag himself. "Yeah." His tone of voice was much lighter. "When the first Gulf War started, I wanted to go fight, but I was too young. So, I finished high school and went to the University of Kentucky." Brad turned his blue eyes back to her. "But I knew that as soon as I graduated, I would enlist in the Marines.

"It's funny." He shrugged. "Because I had a college degree, I could have gone into the Marines as an officer, but that's not what

I wanted. I wanted to be more of a, well, a first responder. I wanted to be on the front lines. I wanted to actually be *doing* the right thing. So, I went in as an enlisted man and served in combat in the second Gulf War. It was years before I became an officer. Twenty years later, here I am back in horse country.

Brad moved behind his desk and sat down. He was back in his simple, black, functional, executive chair. In charge. He looked at Sonia, "And now, Sonia Vitale, you're sitting in front of me, telling me you want to find out what happened to John Abbott Hensley; you want to do the right thing. *That's* why I'm going to help."

Sonia took in a deep breath and wondered about the man in front of her. Is he the Boy Scout all these stories would imply, or is he just conning me? Unclear of where she stood, she said the only thing she could think of. "So, how do we move forward?"

15

At eleven fifteen, Sonia walked back toward her office, shell-shocked. When she passed the entrance to Magee's she stopped, thought for a moment, then turned inside. I need a cup of coffee and a chance to just sit and chill. She walked to the counter and, with just a word or two to Hildy, she went to the coffee bar and got her coffee. Then she took a seat in the front corner of the bakery, a seat which offered her the solitude she needed.

She sat there, lost in her thoughts. Her mind kept flashing back and forth in fragments. His mom and dad . . .Those blue eyes . . . That son-of-a-bitch . . . Of course, I'm competent! . . . But I don't even know where to begin . . . Damn, he's hot . . . He wants me to pay? Son-of-a-bitch . . . But he *is* going to help . . . . She took a careful sip of her very hot coffee. Get a hold of yourself girl. You're supposed to meet him at three forty-five, out here in the parking lot, and you'd better get your act together. Be ready. Be a pro. Do this thing.

Sitting in the corner, facing the door, Sonia's eyes had been seeing but not perceiving. Suddenly that changed. The door opened and Detective Sergeant Adams walked into Magee's. She woke from her trance. *What the hell is he doing here?*

Adams cruised right past her without appearing to notice. He went to the counter, and it seemed to Sonia that he had paid only for coffee since he walked toward the coffee bar with nothing in his hand. Sonia sat quite still. After her experience with him at the news conference, she didn't want the detective to notice her.

After he filled a large cup with dark roast coffee, Detective Adams turned and looked around the room, apparently searching for a place to sit. When his eyes connected with Sonia's, he walked directly over to her.

"Ms. Vitale. How nice to see you."

"Nice to see you as well, Sergeant Adams." Sonia picked up her phone and slipped it into her purse on the floor, hoping to send the message that she might soon be leaving.

"Please, call me Johnny." He looked around the room. "Nice place."

"I don't think I've ever seen you in here before," said Sonia. *Damn, I should have let that go by.*

"No. I haven't been here for a very long time. But coming by on my way to visit with you the other day, it struck me that I should stop in sometime. Would you mind if I joined you?"

The words that came out of Sonia's mouth were, "Certainly. Have a seat." But the words that were running through her brain were two-fold. Part of her brain, her temporal lobe, where sexual attraction occurs, said, *"He's wearing that dark gray suit again. My, it does look good on him. Nice smile, too."* Another part of her brain, her cerebrum, where thinking takes place, said, *"What is he doing here? Is he after something? Can I trust him?"*

All of a sudden, Sonia realized Detective Sergeant Johnny Adams was talking and she had not the slightest idea of what he had said. The voices in her brain had drowned him out. Quickly, however, she caught his gist.

"—was the right time of day for it. I'm so pleased that I happened to run into you."

"Yes," she said, hoping the answer made sense.

Johnny Adams smiled and leaned in. "Listen, I'm so glad you took my advice and didn't ask or say anything at the press conference. I was worried that you might, somehow, get yourself into a difficult situation. It's good that the department got that whole issue wrapped up, and so quickly."

Sonia felt her guard go up. "Yes, it was."

"You don't have any more questions or issues? You're comfortable now that the medical examiner has filed her report?"

Sonia decided to play things close to the vest. "Yeah. I guess you guys got it all figured out. Must've been my imagination running a bit wild. You know how we PIs can get."

Detective Sergeant Johnny Adams sat back in his chair. "Good. I'm glad to hear it." He turned around in his chair and took in the mural and the stained-glass sign in the room. "Gosh, this *is* a nice place, isn't it? Is this around the time you usually come in? Lunchtime?"

"No, I'm usually here and gone way before this." Damn, he didn't need to know that. "It's just that I had . . . I just came from a meeting with a client and thought a second cup of coffee would be nice. You should try the Southern Pecan. It's delicious."

With that, Sonia stood up. "I've got to get up to my office. I've got to work on some things with my partner. It was nice to see you."

Johnny Adams stood up as well, the perfect gentleman. "Well, again, it was nice to run into you. I hope that happens again."

Sonia scooped up her purse, and with a quick "Bye now, Sergeant Adams," moved around him and headed for the door.

"Johnny. You can call me Johnny," he called after her. And as Sonia hustled through the door, he added, "Bye!"

Sonia climbed those damn stairs, even more annoying now that Brad Dunham had mentioned them. *Aren't I a hot mess?*

Now her brain was not only conflicted by dual thoughts of Brad Dunham, but by dual thoughts of Detective Sergeant Johnny Adams as well. Sonia was a very attractive woman who had been pursued by more than her share of men. She stopped at the top of the steps, with her hand on the door. Is he trying to get something out of me? She thought for a moment and opened the door. Either that, or he just wants me. She smiled.

16

At precisely three forty-five, Sonia walked down the stairs, put her brown leather purse on the ground, and leaned against her car, waiting to drive Brad Dunham out to Dahlia Farm. He had said that he needed to get a feel for what was going on out there. As she stood by her red Subaru, which was in pretty good shape for its age, a very new-looking Corvette pulled into the parking lot and stopped. It was a real muscle car—a deep rich blue. The sound of its engine was a deep-throated rumble. She smiled a sad smile. Yet another gray-haired old man driving the car of his teen-aged dreams. The car door opened and Brad Dunham half-stepped out. He yelled at her over the door. "Are you coming or not?"

She picked up her purse. Jerk. Of course he thinks he's driving. She walked to the Corvette. Yes, Your Highness. Your humble servant is on her way. How may I serve you?

As she slid into the supple leather seats, she smelled that unmistakable fragrance. "New?"

"Just this week. Thought it was time I got rid of the Porsche and bought American again. Got myself a 'Vette. Nice, huh?"

Sonia's eyes roamed around the cockpit of the car. Corvette

logos. LED displays. Stick shift. High tech navigation system. High tech everything. She let out a deep breath. Oh, brother. She managed a "Very nice."

Brad turned the car around effortlessly and took a left onto East Main. Sonia watched the streets go by. "Do you know where you're headed?"

"GPS." Brad kept his eyes on the road.

Sonia turned her head and looked out the passenger window. And so it begins. Butthead.

They were both silent as they worked their way out of the city and past the airport. Brad turned at the castle. As they approached the farm, Sonia said, "It's right here on the left."

Brad slowed way down, stopped for a moment, then drove on. They approached the place in which she had parked her car those several days that she was staking out the farm. "We can turn around right here."

Brad smoothly palmed the 'Vette's steering wheel, turning the car around and pulling into the spot. He reached toward the dashboard and slid down a plastic cover between the dash and the console. Sonia's eyes opened wide. "What's that?"

"That's one of the images I just took as we passed the farm." He was nonchalant. "The car is equipped with four cameras, one facing each direction. They all feed into this mini- computer. I can take stills or video of anything, no matter what side of the car it's on. Of course, for our purposes now, it was better to take stills."

Sonia swallowed hard. Whoa, we're not in Kansas anymore, Toto. She didn't say a word.

"Okay, let's see what we've got here." Brad scrolled through several images. He stopped. "Is that the barn where it happened?"

"Yes, and the entrance they walked through is right here." She pointed at the center of the screen.

"And that's the same entrance the truck backs into?"

"Uh huh."

Now it was Brad pointing. "Do you see this electronic gear on the roof?"

Sonia squinted at the image. "Yeah."

"That's pretty damn high-tech for satellite TV. I'm guessing they have a very sophisticated communications system in that house." He looked at her. "Are there any outlying buildings on the property?"

"I don't know." Sonia was a little embarrassed that she hadn't asked herself that question. Then she realized she hadn't needed to. She was only there to watch Marcos Torres.

"That's all right. We'll check Google Maps." Brad checked his rearview mirror.

She looked at him. "Okay, but that's not always totally up to date, is it?"

Brad checked his side mirror. "The version I check is." He put the car in gear. "Okay, let's go. I got what I needed."

Sonia looked away. You mean what *we* needed. She remained silent.

They took off down Pisgah Pike. Sonia couldn't resist. "So, you have your own personal version of Google Maps?" She was caught between being in awe and just plain pissed.

"Not really, just access to a version that most of the public doesn't have."

Sonia waited for more, but nothing came. Her foot started tapping. Finally, she asked, "And that's possible how?"

He shrugged. "Some old acquaintances." He turned left at the castle.

Sonia tipped her head and turned toward Brad. Okay Mr. Hotshot, you want to play this game again? "And who would those old acquaintances be?"

"Just some guys I used to work with."

"I thought you said you just got out of the Marines."

"That's true." His eyes remained on the road.

"So, you had, what, a part-time job on the side?" Her foot tapped faster.

"No, ma'am."

"So exactly when did you work with these guys?"

He checked his mirrors. "While I was in the Marines."

"So, they were in the Marines too?"

"No, ma'am, they weren't."

She took a deep breath. "So, you were in the Marines, but you worked with guys who were not in the Marines?"

"Yes, ma'am."

This "ma'am" crap was driving her crazy. Both feet were going now. "So, who the hell were these guys?"

"NCIS ma'am."

"NCIS? Like in the TV show?" Her feet were playing conga on the floorboard.

"No, ma'am. NCIS. Like for real."

"So, you were in the Marines, and they were in NCIS, and they just gave you access to things that they use? Why would they do that?" She heard the snarky tone of her voice and didn't care. She was looking right at him.

"Because I was NCIS as well."

"What?" Her feet stopped. "I thought you were in the Marines?"

"I was ma'am."

Sonia stomped her foot on the floor. "Explain yourself, Marine!"

There were several moments of silence before Brad relented. His voice was calm and a bit demeaning. "Listen, the Marines are technically part of the Navy. NCIS stands for Naval Criminal Investigative Service. Most of the folks with NCIS are not in the military, but there were two hundred or so of us who were in the Navy or Marines and assigned to NCIS.

"I told you I was in combat in Iraq. After we'd completed our mission, I was very disturbed by what happened next. We were the best fighting force the world had ever seen, but with all the constraints on us, and given the impossible mission of trying to turn modern-day tribal warfare into a democracy, we had no chance of succeeding. Eventually, I asked for a transfer. I had a background in electrical engineering, that's what I studied at UK. Somehow that all came together and I was transferred to NCIS."

"Your background in electrical engineering got you into NCIS?" Her voice sounded somehow accusatory.

Brad looked at her for a moment, then turned back to his driving. "Listen, when someone says, 'Gain access to that facility,' and so on, that usually means someone has to override a security system. Nowadays that can usually be done by hacking into it with a computer. When I first joined NCIS, we were still doing that by getting in there and messing with it manually. Knowing how electrical systems worked came in very handy. It still can."

By then they were back on East Main and approaching Magee's parking lot. Sonia's brain was swimming. He was a Marine. He was NCIS. He was hot and apparently pretty damn well off. And sometimes—he was a total jerk. Sonia crossed her arms. Damn, I need a cup of coffee . . . or maybe something stronger.

Brad turned the car into Magee's parking lot, interrupting her thoughts. "I'll pick you at zero three hundred hours. Be dressed for walking through a field or two."

"When? Why?"

Brad turned those bright blue eyes on her. "Three AM, dear. We're going to place some additional surveillance devices on the farm, and it usually works best to do it while no one is watching." He let out a snarky sigh of frustration.

Sonia climbed out of the car. She wanted to kick his damn tires. Jerk. Still, that was real progress. She had to keep herself focused on the goal, finding out what happened to John Abbott Hensley.

"Three," she said, before closing the door—still reluctant to accept being told what to do. "Where shall we meet?"

"I'll pick you up at your place."

"But I haven't told you where I live."

Brad just looked at her with those eyes.

"Got it. Three AM." She closed the door.

17

By four thirty-eight in the afternoon, Sonia had made it up the steps to the BCI offices. It had already been a hell of a day. As she pushed the door open and walked in, she saw Jet sitting at her desk.

Jet looked up and waved Sonia into her office. "Well, if it isn't Amelia Earhart, back from the dead. Where have you been all day?"

Sonia blew a wisp of hair out of her face. She studied Jet, looking for signs that she might have accepted Sonia's choice to engage Brad Dunham in her search for the truth—Sonia certainly hoped she had. After a close inspection of Jet's expression, she didn't see the hurt that she'd seen on her partner's face the other day. Hmm. I think she's over it. Sonia sat down in Jet's red chair and relived the day for Jet, starting with the pretty amazing meeting with Brad Dunham. She felt herself getting a little emotional as she shared the stories of Brad's dad and mom losing their lives and how it shaped his moral compass—"doing the right thing."

Sonia then told Jet about going into Magee's for coffee and the surprise visit from Detective Sergeant Johnny Adams. Finally, she recounted the trip to Dahlia farm, the Corvette, the cameras, and the revelation that Brad had spent all those years with NCIS.

Jet tipped her head. "NCIS? Like the TV show?"

"NCIS. Like for real," Sonia answered, mimicking Brad's answer to the same question. She glanced at the concealed carry license hanging on Jet's wall, next to the picture of both them at the range. She tried to sound matter-of-fact. "He's going to pick me up at zero three hundred hours to go put surveillance devices on the farm . . . and I've got to be dressed for field work."

Jet had listened intently the whole time. Now, however, a smile broke out on her face. "GI Joe is gonna take you on a late-night recon mission, at, what was it, zero alpha delta bogie hour?" She laughed.

Sonia ignored Jet's comment. "Yeah, yeah, I know. I guess the military time thing is just an old habit for him. Still, you really do get the feeling this guy knows what he's doing. And the car? With the cameras? Dang, he's into the latest stuff. You should see the equipment he has in his office."

Jet's chin dipped downward and she looked over her imaginary glasses. "Yeah, but what does he have in his brain?"

"Oh, he's smart. He's really smart. And his heart? Did you hear what I told you about his 'doing the right thing?' "

Jet pushed her chair back from her desk, letting it roll freely a few inches. "Heart, schmart. You're leaving something out. I can tell. I want the deets, spill it."

Sonia's mind drifted back to her first meeting with Brad. He'd been hard and sharp, like a rock; yet he could be soft and sensitive—the proverbial iron fist in the velvet glove. And those eyes . . . . "Well, he does have the most intense blue eyes you've ever seen. And the rest?" She made a big circle with her finger. "Yeah, it's pretty intense too. I've got to tell you that when he was sharing that story about his dad, and then his mom, I just wanted to hold him . . . and I'm not sure it was entirely for altruistic reasons."

"Oh, do tell." Jet sat up straighter and scooted her chair back to her desk. "He's pretty delicious, is that what you're saying?"

"Oh, trust me, I'd take him over one of Magee's almond croissants any day."

They both broke out into full-throated laughter. Shortly, Sonia shook her head. "But he can be a real jerk too. The way he ran me through the wringer in his office . . . his assumption that only he could drive us out to the farm—although he is the one with the cameras mounted in his car. And then, as I was trying to understand how he got his hands on all that stuff, all I could get was, 'Yes, ma'am,' 'No, ma'am,' 'Yes, ma'am.' He was driving me crazy."

"Well, honey," Jet's voice was all maple syrupy, "you've got to take the good with the bad. And it sounds to me like there's plenty-o-good to go around there."

"True, true." Sonia began absently straightening a pile of papers on Jet's desk.

Jet reached out and put her hand on Sonia's. "Now what's the deal with this Detective Sergeant Johnny Adams? Are you getting any vibes from him?"

"Oh, yes, but not so much about the case." Sonia slipped her hand out from under Jet's. "The biggest vibe I get from him is that he wants to jump my bones."

Jet's eyebrows went up. "No shit. Go on."

Sonia ran her hand through her hair. "Well, like I said before, he came into Magee's to," she wiggled her fingers in the air, " 'sit and enjoy a cup of coffee.' Then within a millisecond, he's walking toward me like I've got a 'Sailors Welcome' sign hanging around my neck.

"And?"

"And what?"

"Don't hold back on me, girl. You wishin' you had a 'Sailors Welcome' sign handy?"

Sonia's smile was coy. "Well, I do have to say, he's no sack-apotatoes. He's tall, thin, has a nice smile. He's attractive but not rugged, more clean-cut than anything. And quiet. Quiet and unassuming. Yeah, he's nice. But I'm not sure I trust him either. That stuff, when he came to the office and wouldn't answer my questions? And then he shows up at the press conference and 'warns' me," Sonia made quotation marks in the air with her fingers, " 'so I won't get in trouble.' I don't know; it's all just a bit confusing."

"Well, well, well. Looks like my partner's drought is over, one man after another pouring life-giving rain down upon her wilting blossoms, trying to get next to her. And meanwhile," Jet's voice became airy and sad, "I'm left here alone." She paused, then leaned back in her chair, elbows on the armrests. Her voice strengthened. "You know, we've got three other clients and I'm dealing with them all by myself. And that doesn't even count Marcos Torres and Bob Dylan." She turned her palms upward as if pleading for an answer. "Are you ever going to be able to get enough time away from your admirers to help me? Any chance we could make this business something like a profitable endeavor? Are we ever going to wrap up the Torres and Dylan cases?"

Sonia felt a pang of guilt though she knew Jet was half-kidding. She had gotten so involved with the John Hensley case, not that it was really a case, that she had stopped working on everything else. "I'm so sorry. I promise. After tonight I'll get back to work that pays. It's not fair, you having to do all the work that actually brings in money."

"Don't worry about it, really." Jet smiled at her and flipped her hand across her face. "Look, it wasn't your fault that you were sitting out there when Hensley bought it. We said the other day that you can't just let this go. Maybe you should give yourself a break and follow Mr. Hotshot's mantra: just *do the right thing*. Ol' Jet will keep the home fires burning. Yes, she will."

Sonia stood up. She needed some rest before her 3:00 AM

mission. "I've got to get home and get a little sleep. I need to straighten up the place, too." She stopped. She could clearly hear her Italian mother asking her if the place was ready for company. Really? Am I that woman? She walked out the door and down the steps. This has turned into one crazy mess.

18

Sonia lived in a one-bedroom carriage-house apartment over a garage on Central Avenue, just blocks away from Magee's. At 2:55 AM she was standing outside at the curb. It was cold, but she had come dressed in warm clothing, all black, a black quilted vest, and comfortable shoes, ready for "field work." She had a travel cup of hot coffee in her hand. At precisely 3:00 AM, Brad Dunham, Mr. Semper Fi, former Marine, former NCIS, Mr. Hotshot, pulled up in his new Corvette. It was such a deep, dark blue that it looked black in the half-moon night.

"Hop in, agent." He took off while the door was still closing.

Sonia didn't know if he were just teasing her, or if he had slipped into his professional personae. *Does he really think of me as an agent on his team?* "I assume you have everything we need?" She regretted the comment immediately. *Of course he has everything he needs. She'd just had the need to say something and that's what came out. Just keep your damn mouth shut.*

Brad never said a word as they drove, and his silence was certainly increasing her apprehension about this evening's plan. Sonia furrowed her brows. *Maybe that's exactly why professionals operate this way. It's a form of psyching yourself up for a* difficult challenge.By then they were at the castle and Brad was turning onto the road that would lead them directly to Dahlia Farm. "ETA one minute," he said quietly and without emotion. Sonia felt a chill run down her spine.

Brad drove past the farm and turned into the pull-off that Sonia had been using for her stakeouts. He reached into the tiny space behind Sonia's seat and pulled out a leather bag. Taking out a tin marked "Camouflage Face Paint," he handed it to Sonia. "Put this on your hands and face."

Sonia recoiled. "You're kidding, aren't you? We don't really need to put this stuff on, do we?"

Brad's look was serious, his voice terse. "Do you have any idea how the human face reflects light, even on a night like this? If they have any kind of sophisticated cameras at all, they'll see you from three hundred yards out. You've got to cover up. Just get that stuff on and let's get moving."

Sonia's heart rate rocketed into high gear. Ho-ly shit. This is no place for . . . I don't want to do this. Crap!

"Get a move on!" Brad whispered with sudden authority. "But be careful with that stuff. If you get it on the leather, I'll never get it out."

Without thinking further, Sonia opened the tin and started applying the camouflage paint to her face. It felt slick and smelled like old bacon grease. Soon she was done. "Now what?"

"Your hands. Do the tops of your hands as well."

She didn't even ask. She rubbed the greasy stuff all over the tops of her hand, but was totally lost as to where to wipe them. She struggled, just barely managing to put the lid back on the tin. "I think I'm ready."

Brad reached over and took the tin. He started, in his most serious whisper, "Listen, I need you to get out of the car here. It's only about a half click to the back of the barn—"

"Click?"

"Kilometer." He let out a small sigh. "About a half mile." He pointed into the darkness. "It's straight through that field. I can't afford for them to confront you if you approach the barn straight on with me. When you've made your way to the barn, if you haven't encountered any alarms or lights, I want you to work your way to the front. Come around on the side away from the house."

Sonia was almost panicked. She wanted to write these instructions down somehow. What if I forget? What if I don't know if there's an alarm or not?

"When you get there, I'll be waiting by the front door to the barn. Now, if I'm not there, you wait three minutes. If I still don't show, then something's gone wrong. Just get the hell out of there. Head for the road first, then turn left and come to the car. I'll leave the fob in the car, so all you have to do is put your foot on the brake and push the start button. Then drive like hell. Go directly to police headquarters and tell them what's happened. You got that?"

Sonia nodded her head. She couldn't speak.

"Really, do you have those instructions? I've got to know you're clear on everything."

"Yes," she whispered. "I've got it." She didn't believe herself.

"Okay then, out you go." His voice was soft but husky. "I'll meet you at the barn just after zero-three-thirty. Now go!"

Brad reached across her and unlatched the door. Sonia opened it with her elbow and carefully climbed out, closing the door gently with her hip. Swallowing her fear, urging herself forward, she crawled through one of the horse farm fences, out into the field. Fortunately, the wind was relatively calm. Still, at three-fifteen in the morning, in early spring, it was pretty damn cold. There was no snow on the ground, but the grass crunched beneath her feet. At the same time, her feet sank into the not quite frozen ground. All in all, it made for difficult walking, even in comfortable shoes.

As Sonia slogged on, her mind raced. Go to the barn. Look for alarms. No alarms, walk around to the front. Come on the side opposite the house. Not there, wait three minutes. Still not there, get the hell out. Go to the car. Drive to the police. Sonia was glad that she did, at least know how to drive a stick-shift car. Still, her mind was swimming.

She took another few steps, and in the darkness the shape of the barn appeared to her; but as she quickened her pace to reach the barn, she tripped over a large rock, falling to her hands and knees in the mud. What the hell am I doing here?

Sonia stood and wiped her greasy, muddy hands on the black jeans she had just bought last weekend. A few minutes later, she was close enough to reach out her hand and actually touch the barn. So far, no alarms had gone off, from what she could tell. No spotlights had come on, not even the kind of motion-detection light that many people have on their homes. Brad must have made it safely.

Slowly, she walked behind the barn to the corner and turned right to walk along its side. Then, peeking around the corner, she saw Brad Dunham leaning against the barn, a smile on his face. He was right there at the corner waiting for her, only a foot or so away from her face. It startled her. A huge breath escaped her and she realized that she had barely been breathing for the last few minutes.

Brad glanced back at the barn door. "It's done, let's get out of here."

Every cell in her body screamed silently. Yes! Yes! Let's get out of here!

Without another word, Brad walked straight down the driveway toward the road. Following, Sonia kept to the side of the driveway as much as possible. Brad didn't seem to care. As soon as they got to the end of the driveway, Brad turned to Sonia. "Stay here. I've got one more thing to do. Just crouch down and stay here. Don't move."

Sonia did exactly what she was told. She was cold, and it was damn uncomfortable to be crouching down in the gravel, but at that point, she was committed to doing exactly what she was told when she was told. Brad hurried across the street and into the bushes.

Sonia shivered. This is what it's like to be a soldier. Somebody gives an order, you do it. You don't think, you don't ask, you do it. Wow.

Less than four minutes later, Brad reappeared. "We're all set. Now let's get to that car and get going." Without waiting for a reply, he took off toward the car.

Sonia stood up, her legs aching from crouching, and followed. Her heart rate was starting to fall. She was just beginning to breathe normally again. We did it. We got in, did it, and got out. The sense of having done something so dangerous so well was making her giddy.

It was no short walk back to the car, but their energy moved them quickly. It seemed like only moments and Sonia was wiping her hands on her pants and crawling back into the Corvette. Sonia didn't even try to hide the big grin on her face. And when she looked across at Brad she could see a definite twinkle in his eyes. Those beautiful, blue, twinkling eyes, surrounded by that rugged, manly face. Sonia had a powerful urge to just reach over and kiss him. She wanted to kiss Brad Dunham. She wanted to share this moment with him passionately. Those eyes, that face . . . . She pulled back. "Your face?"

"What?"

"Your face?" Her voice rose. She was beyond the fear of getting caught. "There's no camouflage paint on your face. Why is there no camouflage paint on your face?"

Brad smiled broadly and said nothing.

19

"Tell me! Tell me!" Sonia insisted. "Why don't you have camouflage paint on *your* face?"

Instead of answering, Brad started the car and took off. Then he said, "Well, about that." His voice trailed off. He kept his eyes on the road.

Sonia's voice sizzled. "What about that? What the hell is going on?"

"Now don't get your panties in a wad." His voice got just a little edgy. "It's just that, well, this could have been a pretty dangerous operation, and I couldn't just let you walk into it unprepared."

Sonia's chocolate brown eyes were burning—throwing flames right at him. "So you made me dress up like a clown? What the hell good did . . . wait a minute. I didn't need to march through that field, either, did I? You sent me on a damn wild goose chase, didn't you?"

Brad turned left at the castle. "Listen, I was just concerned for your safety." But as he spoke, Sonia saw the smile on his face get bigger. Eventually, she could swear she actually heard him chuckle.

Sonia reached over and slapped Brad's muscular arm. "You son-of-a-bitch! You damn son-of-a-bitch! *Figlo di puttana!*" She slapped him again, the words flying out of her mouth. "You're so full of your ex-Marine, ex-NCIS self, it's unbelievable. How could you do that to me? How could you?" Sonia reached up, pulled down the sun visor, and flipped open the vanity mirror. She felt Brad's eyes snap to what she was doing. She turned back to him, but his eyes were locked on the visor, locked on the handprint she'd left on the tan leather.

Suddenly his hand was on hers. "Be careful with that sweet—"

Sonia wrestled her hand away, elbowing him in the chest.

"That's right babe. You wipe that mess on me, not on my car." He grinned. "Come on. You've got to admit it's pretty funny. You look hilarious in that stuff. And I kept you from getting hurt, didn't I?"

Sonia's mouth dropped open. Her silence lasted only a moment. "Well, obviously, *you* weren't too worried about getting hurt, now were you?" Sonia pawed Brad's arm with her greasy, muddy hands. "No damn paint for you, was there?" He lifted his arm in self-defense. His elbow in her way, she changed targets, wiping her hands on his leg. "Was there?" Sonia was madder than she had been in a long, long time.

Suddenly Brad got serious. "Now look. For all I knew this could have been a dangerous operation. I sent you off to stay safe. When I used my electronic gear, I found out the place had a pretty sophisticated security system. Damn sophisticated. What if you had set it off? I'm starting to get the feeling these boys play for real. I'm glad I sent you out of harm's way."

"And tell me again, why no paint for you?" The pace of the conversation had become furious, razor-sharp. Her foot was tapping like crazy.

"Because I took care of the security system before I went in. I took care of it."

"And how exactly did you do that, 'Mr. NCIS?' " She spit the words at him.

He paused. "That's exactly how I did it."

"What the hell are you talking about? How did you take care of the security system?" Underneath the camouflage paint, her face was bright red.

"With some help from NCIS, that's how."

She could sense he felt back in control.

"Oh, I get it. You just put in a phone call to your old buddies, and they sent you something to take care of it? Is that how it works?"

Brad checked his mirrors. They were the only ones on the road. "Well, I do have to pay for it."

"Pay for what? What the hell are you talking about? You just bought some help? You placed an order and the operator said, 'That'll be twenty dollars, please. Please deposit your money in the slot?' Or did you do it by credit card?" She put on her TV-ad-man's voice. "That's right, order today by phone. Credit cards accepted. Just call 888-888-9Iscrew you, that's 888-888-9Iscrew you. Call today!"

Brad let out a heavy sigh. "Are you done?"

"Not hardly." She crossed her arms, the sound of her tapping foot almost audible.

"Listen, remember when I said I sometimes used my electrical engineering skills to get past security systems, but now you can usually do that with a computer?" He turned his blue eyes to her.

Sonia blew the wisp hair out of her face, that same piece of hair that seemed to stray only when she was frustrated with something. She waited for his explanation.

"Well, I have this piece of equipment that can scan an area and tell if any security systems are operating, and what kind they are. When I found out these guys had a sophisticated system with

24-hour video surveillance from several cameras, I was able to use the same device to disable the system."

"How?" The tapping was slowing down. She was curious. She was, after all, a techie.

"Well, it sends a signal that forces their video feed to become a freeze frame. We can pretty much assume that the images those cameras are seeing stay pretty static. My device made them freeze altogether. Unless someone was carefully monitoring the time stamp live, no one would notice that the file ran a few minutes short over the course of the whole evening. Even if they fast forwarded the video in the morning, just to check to see if anyone had been on the property, everything would still look copasetic."

"And you can do this because you have all the 'latest and greatest' electronic gear?" Sonia asked with a clear note of disdain.

They were on Broadway and headed for Vine and then East Main. "Actually, what I have is the *almost* 'latest and greatest' gear. You see, when new gear comes out, and the department decides the agents need it, they go out and buy it. And what do you think happens to the old gear?"

Sonia looked out the passenger window. "I don't know." She didn't want to give him an answer.

"They sell it, of course. And who do you think are the first people to hear about the sale of that kind of gear?" He looked at her. "Former agents, of course. So, with a little help from my friends, I was able to purchase some of that *almost* gear, and I used it tonight. We now have three cameras inside the barn and two different angles from outside, thanks to the good ol' NCIS Procurement and Disposal Program."

Sonia unfolded her arms and looked directly into those blue eyes. "Inside? Three cameras?"

"Yup. We'll be able to see what the boys are unloading from that truck and what they do with it. We'll also have a view of both of the stalls that have been made into accommodations for any special female guests that join the workers." He gave her a little smile.

Sonia furrowed her brows. "Only two stalls? But there were four of them. Four prostitutes."

"Well, share and share alike they always say."

Sonia thought for a moment, then turned and looked away again. "Oh, that's disgusting."

Brad waited, then asked, "Are you okay?"

Sonia wanted to snap back a nasty retort, but when she looked at him she saw that twinkle in Brad's eyes. Yes, he'd played her for a fool and sent her marching through a half-mile of cold, muddy, frozen, grass. But she had to remember how scared she was. Things really could have gone very, very wrong. Sonia turned and looked out the passenger window again. These guys do seem to play for real, and he really did keep me out of harm's way. Besides, when his eyes smiled that way, he really was damn cute, almost irresistible.

Sonia stared out the window for the remainder of the ride back to her place. She'd had one hell of a night and would have one hell of a story to relate to Jet the next morning. She also had one hell of a conundrum going. First, she was totally frustrated that Brad had not really let her participate in the night's operation. But second, she was grateful that they now had eyes on most of the operation on Dahlia Farm. Third, she really wanted to slap Brad silly for making her dress up in that greasy stuff and stumble across a field at three in the morning. And fourth, she was pretty sure that when they had gotten back in the car she had wanted to pull him close to her and kiss him passionately . . . . Now, she was pretty sure she still did.

20

Around eleven-thirty Tuesday morning, Sonia pulled into Magee's parking lot. A quick glance up those damn stairs sent a wave of fatigue through her body. She blew that wisp of hair out of her face and changed her mind. She walked from her car, past the steps, to the bakery's front door. She was beat, and she needed a cup of coffee desperately. As she stood at the counter waiting for Hildy to come out of the back, she looked up at the beautiful mural on the wall behind the counter. It was a scene that portrayed Julie and her brother, the owners, working in the kitchen along with some long-time help. The image continued and the walls of the bakery dissolved. A lovely, peaceful rural scene drifted out to the horizon. Sonia wanted to be out there in those fields, no pressure, no fatigue, just peaceful sunshine.

"Miss your appointment today?" Hildy asked, startling Sonia.

"What?"

"Your appointment. Weren't you supposed to meet someone here this morning?"

Sonia wrinkled her tired face. "I don't think so. Was someone here?"

"That man you had coffee with the other day, the tall, thin man in the suit. You know," Hildy half-whispered as she leaned over the counter a bit, "the good-looking one."

"Detective Adams? What about him?"

"Well," said Hildy, still sounding conspiratorial, "he came in about eight o'clock, got coffee and an almond croissant and just sat there. Checked his phone every once in a while, but he sat there near on an hour. I was pretty sure he was waiting for you."

Sonia looked at Hildy blankly. "I didn't have an appointment with him this morning." Sonia fumbled in her purse for her slightly over-used credit card. Just as her fingers reached it, she stopped. Ohhh. I told him I usually come in early, and he was hoping to just 'run into me'. Sonia smiled. Well, well, well, Detective Sergeant Adams, apparently, you didn't realize that for me, 'early' means ten o'clock. Her smile turned just a bit smug. And I'm ever so sorry I had a late night last night and didn't get here 'til now. Sonia paid and walked to the coffee bar in the front of the room to get her morning pick-me-up. Still, I am flattered that you would wait a whole hour just to catch me unexpectedly, Detective. How sweet.

Sonia filled her cup, put a lid on it, and walked out of the bakery. She turned left and left again, then headed up the stairs. Pushing open the old door, she entered and walked straight toward Jet, who was sitting at her desk.

"What the hell happened to you?" said Jet, looking up from her desk. "That must have been quite a night you had." Jet shot her a sly look. "Did your trip to the farm end with a roll in the hay?"

"What?" Sonia's head bobbed backward. "No way, Jose. It was pure business all the way. Pure business."

"So, how did it go? Tell me." Jet grinned. "Did GI Joe lead the charge? Did you guys take the hill?"

"GI Joe was one damn jackass, thank you very much." Sonia sat down opposite Jet's desk and related the whole story of being told to put camouflage paint all over her face and hands, and having to walk through the mud and frozen grass. When she admitted to Jet that it was all a trick, that Brad had not used any paint, Jet lost it.

"That's the funniest thing I've ever heard. He did that to you?"

Sonia was certain that the look on her face made it very clear that she didn't think it was one-bit funny, but that didn't stop Jet from laughing.

"Sorry, lady. But you've got to admit, it's a least a little bit funny."

"If you like sick jokes." There was a moment of uncomfortable silence.

"Well, look at it this way," said Jet, "at least he kept you safe. Right?"

"Yeah, he did. And based on the kinds of security systems these guys have, it does look like they're up to something out there."

"Listen, I'm glad he kept you safe. What if you'd gotten into something really bad out there? I'm glad he protected you." Jet leaned back in her chair and took a sip of the coffee she had on her desk. Shaking her head, she chuckled silently. Sonia could tell Jet had images of her covered in camouflage paint running through her mind. Finally, Jet said, "Did you guys get anything accomplished?"

"Well, that's the good news. It turns out that Brad has a bunch of used NCIS surveillance equipment. We now have two angles on the outside of the barn, and three cameras inside. There's one pointing at the door. The other two are covering the stalls the farm hands use when they hook up with the prostitutes. It shouldn't be long before we lock down Mr. Marcos Torres once and for all."

"Cool. Very cool. But why only two cameras on the stalls? Aren't there four prostitutes?"

"Don't ask." Sonia finally lifted the lid off her coffee and took her first sip. Ah, southern pecan. "The great thing is that we don't have to sit out there monitoring the cameras anymore. Brad used a system that connects via 4G and sends those feeds anywhere. We can watch from right there in his office."

"Nice."

"And, we're recording everything. We'll be able to go through and check on anything that happens when we can't be monitoring. It's great what his stuff can do."

"Thank you NCIS," said Jet.

"Absolutely."

Jet's face turned softer. "So, are you going to be able to get some rest today? You look pretty beat."

"I'm supposed to meet with Brad this afternoon, but then I'm headed home. I'm going to turn in early tonight unless something pops out there."

At that moment, Sonia's iPhone chirped out its funny *Star-Spangled Banner.* Remembering, again, that Jet was the one who had changed her ringtone, Sonia gave her a frustrated look as she answered the phone. "This is Bluegrass Confidential Investigations, Sonia Vitale speaking . . . Ah, yes, Detective Adams. How are you?"

Jet grinned slyly.

Sonia waved her off. "Well, I don't know, I had a difficult evening last night and I'm pretty tired."

Jet mouthed some words, but Sonia ignored her and tried to focus on the phone call. "I guess an early dinner wouldn't be too much to handle. Where should I meet you?"

Jet mouthed more clearly, *"Niiice."*

"Actually, I've never been to Joe Bologna's. It's on Maxwell, isn't it?"

Jet began licking her lips and rubbing her stomach.

"I'm sure I can find it. There really is no need for you to pick me up."

Jet made kissing motions with her lips.

"Well, if you insist. What time should I be ready?"

Jet's motions became more exaggerated, and Sonia recognized the gestures. Jet was holding someone in her arms and kissing them passionately.

"Okay. My address is—"

In the ensuing silence, Jet stopped and tilted her head, a curious look on her face.

"I should have known a detective wouldn't have any trouble finding me. I'll see you at six then." Sonia ended the call. She smiled at Jet and said in one of Jet's voices. "He wants me." She batted her eyelashes. "He wants me real, real bad."

Jet's smile matched Sonia's. "Oh yeah? And how would you know that?"

"Because he sat downstairs in Magee's for a whole hour this morning hoping," she made air quotes, "to 'run into me.' And since that didn't work out, he's taking me to Joe Bolonga's for dinner. That's how."

"Well bless his little heart."

Sonia chuckled. That was one of the few down-home country expressions Jet hadn't been able to eliminate from her vocabulary. Sonia looked down at her phone. "It's almost twelve-thirty. This coffee's not going to be enough. I'm going downstairs to get something to eat, and then I'm going across the street to meet with Brad. Want to come?"

"To lunch?"

"To lunch and to the meeting. Do you want in on the Hensley case?"

Jet looked directly at Sonia, and Sonia could feel the warmth in her eyes. "Listen, thanks for the offer, but there are two reasons I can't get involved, at least right now."

"And those are?"

"Well, somebody's got to earn some damn money around here, and traipsing through the mud in the middle of the night with you is not going to get that done."

"And?"

"Aaand, it sounds to me like you and Mr. Hotstuff might just be on your way to a meeting of something . . . more than your minds. I don't want to interfere with that . . . although it does seem that Detective Sergeant Adams is definitely intent on doing precisely that." Jet's voice was Southern Belle now. "My, my, how a girl has to struggle when the men line up to get just a moment's time with her. Oh, I believe this is all givin' me the vapors." She feigned passing out and dropped her head to her desk.

Sonia stood. "And with that, I'm outta here. I'll let you know what happens with Captain Dunham."

Jet's head popped up, her southern accent thicker than ever. "Oh, it's *Captain* Dunham. I wonder how that makes *Sergeant* Adams feel. Will you let me know how things go with *Sergeant* Adams as well?"

Sonia headed for the door. "Get a life, Jet." And then over her shoulder, "Listen, I can only be with one of them at a time. I'll send the other one your way."

"I'll be waiting." Jet called out, and Sonia recognized it as the voice of a woman whose friend was finally catching a break.

21

Precisely at two o'clock, after a light lunch and an unexpected conversation with an old acquaintance from her days at the school district, Sonia crossed the street, walked up the few steps, and entered the hall of the white house. Turning left, she knocked on the door, turned the smooth new handle, and waited for that deep voice. Nothing came, so she knocked again, this time louder. Finally, she heard, "Come in," and a smile flickered across her face.

She opened the door. "Good afternoon Captain Dunham."

Brad stood to greet her. "Hi."

"It is *Captain* Dunham, isn't it? Isn't that what's engraved on the plate that's with your Marine Corps flag."

"*Was* captain. I enjoyed my years with NCIS, but once you were assigned there, you sort of stepped out of the normal flow of routine promotions. Honestly, being a captain was okay by me. Get much beyond that and you're stuck doing administrative work the rest of your life. I liked being out in the field. The captain thing suited me just fine."

"Well, it's better than sergeant," Sonia said quietly to herself.

"What?"

"Oh, I just said I was glad it suited you."

Brad looked at her, his face clearly showing that he wasn't buying her last statement. "Look, I've got some stuff for us. Come over here and let me show you what our electronic surveillance picked up earlier today."

Together, they walked over to the table on which the surveillance computer perched. Sonia stood right next to Brad. She watched a video segment he had selected out of the morning's recordings. She missed the first moments of it, however, since her mind was distracted by his smell. Manly. Earthy. She wondered. Is it a cologne, or maybe just soap and deodorant? Or is it just him? His essence?

"Well?" Brad said.

"Well?"

"Well, what do you think?"

Sonia had been caught, lost in thinking about Brad. She tried to recover with, "I'm not sure, let me see it again."

Brad gave her another funny look, but he played the video again. This time Sonia gave it her full attention.

"That's it. That's the truck. That's the Mid-West Feed and Hay truck, and it sure as hell doesn't look like they're unloading feed or hay." She smiled broadly at Brad.

"Well, you're right and you're wrong."

"What do you mean?" Sonia's face turned warm and she looked again at the screen, afraid she'd missed something important.

"You're absolutely right, they sure as hell aren't unloading feed or hay."

"But?"

"But, that's not the Mid-West Feed and Hay truck."

She looked back to the screen again. "Sure it is. It looks exactly like the truck I've seen before, even down to the magnetic signs."

"Well, a few things come to mind." He tipped his head and

smiled at her. "First, how often does a successful company use magnetic signs on their trucks? They almost always have their logo or information painted on the truck. Second, note the unusual spelling of Mid-West. Most Americans would correctly spell it m-i-d-w-e-s-t, with no hyphen. Finally, and I do believe this is the clincher . . ." Brad paused.

"What? What?"

He smiled at her. "There is no Mid-West Feed and Hay Company. The whole thing is bogus."

"How do you know that?" Her eyebrows furrowed.

"Former NCIS agents still have friends who have access to computer information that would blow you away. According to my source, which must remain nameless for obvious reasons, there is no Mid-West Feed and Hay Company anywhere in the continental United States or any of its territories. For that matter, nowhere in North America, South America, or Europe." Brad put his hand to his chin and raised one eyebrow. "I guess they could be based out of Antarctica."

"Good work, Sherlock. We're definitely on to something, aren't we?" She shuddered inwardly. Was that "Sherlock" comment too much?

Brad didn't react. Looking down at her, he smiled and said, "We're definitely on to something," He'd said it in a way that felt inclusive to Sonia.

After a pause to think things through, Sonia asked, "What now? How do we proceed from here?"

Brad walked over to his desk and sat down. He motioned for her to do the same. Remembering the feeling of sinking into the chairs across from his desk—a subordinate position—she remained standing.

Brad didn't seem to notice. "Well, it seems clear to me that those packages wrapped in white plastic are drugs, probably cocaine. So now our surveillance strategy changes. We can no longer just wait to check the video after things happen. We're going to have to start monitoring the feed in real time. The next time the truck pulls in we should have about a half-hour to position ourselves to follow Marcos, or one of his compatriots, to see where those drugs are going."

Making a note on his calendar, Brad continued. "Now it seems that the deliveries are being made during the day. That's probably because if you're supposedly delivering farm supplies, it's actually less noticeable to work during the day than at night. So, we won't have to monitor the feed 24-7. But starting tomorrow we're going to have to figure out a way to watch those feeds for most of the day."

Sonia leaned forward, putting her hands on the edge of Brad's desk. "That's not going to be easy." She was enjoying the fact that she felt that he and she were working shoulder to shoulder at the moment.

"You're absolutely correct, my dear, this is not going to be easy with just the two of us. Clearly, we're going to need some help. Any ideas?"

"Jet. Jet can do it." As soon as she said it, however, Sonia regretted speaking so quickly. What if Jet is still not on board? What if I have to come back and say she won't do it? Sonia desperately didn't want to seem like some sort of a loose cannon to Brad, and Jet had made it pretty clear she wasn't yet willing to work on the Hensley "case."

"Are you sure?" Brad asked as if he sensed the second-guessing going on in Sonia's mind.

Sonia stepped back and stood a bit taller. "She'll help. We're friends, we're partners. She'll help if I ask her . . . nicely." The last of those words came out much softer than the rest. Still, Sonia did believe she could count on Jet. If she couldn't, maybe their relationship wasn't what she thought it was.

22

"Good," said Brad, "with Jet's help we should be able to keep track of what's going on at the farm. And we don't all have to watch the surveillance feeds from my computers here. We can send that signal anywhere."

"I can make that happen. Remember, technology is my thing." Then, Sonia remembered it was Brad who had set up the whole surveillance system. She had been out tramping through the mud. Of course he could do that. Still, she wanted him to know, and acknowledge, that she was bringing something to the table as well.

Brad stood and walked back to the surveillance computer. "Oh, I know, sweetheart. I haven't forgotten. I've got big plans for you and your techiness."

Sonia's heart flipped. Sweetheart? Was that a little term of endearment? Or was that sheer sexism?

Brad continued without a pause. "Remember all that high-tech equipment on top of the farmhouse?"

Sonia walked up behind him, hoping she hadn't missed something else. She peered at the screen.

"Well, I believe that if we can hack into that system, we may be able to find out a whole lot about the operations of the Mid-West Feed and Hay Company. And that may well lead us to a much better understanding of what happened to John Abbott Hensley last week." Brad turned and looked directly at her, waiting for a response. Getting none, he asked, "Do you know how to hack a sophisticated system?"

Sonia took an unconscious step backward. Crap. I was in the top ten percent of my class in a top-notch computer science program, but they never got around to teaching us illegal techniques like hacking into a truly sophisticated system. And I just played the "remember-technology-is-my-thing" card. "Look, I . . . I certainly understand the basic concepts of hacking. But if it's really a sophisticated system it might take me quite a while to work my way in."

She looked into Brad's eyes and knew immediately that he wasn't buying it, that he knew she probably could never hack into that system. She took another unconscious step backward. Is he going to hammer me now? Embarrass me? Drop the case and leave me on my own right now, just when we're really getting started?

Brad's piercing blue eyes seemed to cut right into her, right into where she was feeling so vulnerable. "You're probably right," he said, turning his attention back to the computer. "And we don't have time to wait a day or two for you to get in. Is it alright if I get you some help?"

Sonia was almost speechless. Both he and she knew that this task was beyond her experience, but he had let her off the hook, gently. A sudden warmth rushed through her body, to her face, to her chest, to other places. "Yes. That'll be fine." She turned and walked away from him, toward his desk, her face flushed.

"Okay then. I'll try to set up a telephone meet between you and one of my former colleagues. We'll do it tonight at seven."

She spun around to face him. "Seven?"

He turned to face her as well. "Yes, seven. Is something wrong with that?

"Well, I've got . . . I've got to . . . I've got another commitment at that time tonight."

"Commitment?" he asked, sounding very much like *Captain Brad Dunham, U.S. Marines.*

"Yes, a, uh, commitment."

"What kind of commitment? We've got to get going on this."

Sonia's eyes fell to the floor. She didn't want to lie, but she knew how bad this would sound even before she said it. "I've got a date." She wanted to say it was with one of the police offers involved with the case, but the words never came out.

He was finally starting to work with her as a colleague, at least a little bit. He had just let her off the hook on the hacking thing. And now she was telling him she couldn't get the training she needed to accomplish the mission because she had a date. She waited for the explosion.

It never came. Sonia looked up and into Brad's face. It was still without expression. He never said a thing about the date. Finally, he asked in his most professional and detached tone of voice, "Is there sometime tomorrow morning that would work for you?"

"Anytime. Anytime at all."

"Okay," he said, turning away from her. "I'll check with my colleague and let you know what time the session will start. Bring your laptop and be ready to go."

"Okay." *Yes, sir.*

Brad stared silently at the computer. In her mind, she could all but hear him say it. *Dismissed.* She turned and started walking toward the door.

"One other thing," s*oldier.* "I've got some more good news for you."

Sonia turned, hoping that this was not leading to some other dressing down.

"We've got Marcos Torres on video. It appears they've been laying low with the whole operation for a little while, probably because of Hensley's death. But now that the deliveries have begun again, it seems like whoever is in charge thought it would be a good idea to get Marcos and the boys fully charged up. Earlier today the joy wagon showed up with four hookers. Trust me, a good time was had by all. We've got it all recorded."

A smile lit up Sonia's face. "That's great." Finally, some good news to bring to Jet. "Jet'll be pleased. We'll clear the case with Teresa Torres and get paid. That'll certainly help when I'm asking Jet for assistance with the video feeds."

"Hold on just a moment." Brad motioned her back to a chair. "Let me ask you a question." He sat down behind his desk. "Exactly what are you planning on telling Ms. Torres? 'We've got your cheating boyfriend on video? You can see him boffing some whore? Oh, and by the way, we got the images because we're getting video feeds from the farm while we investigate a drug operation and a possible murder? Please don't mention to Marcos how it is that we have those images. And if you do, please ask him to not mention it to his employers." His questions hung in the air.

Sonia was silent and stunned. She sat down in one of his chairs, leaning forward on its edge.

"I'm afraid you're not going to be able to let Ms. Torres see those tapes."

Sonia collapsed back into her chair. "Yeah, sure. I know you're right. But she's been calling for days, asking when we were going to . . . well, close the case, though those weren't her exact words. I guess we'll just have to put her off a bit longer."

"Wrong. I'm afraid you're going to have to call Ms. Torres. You'll tell her that, after exhaustive surveillance, you've come to believe that Marcos is not having liaisons with other women."

"What?" Sonia sat up and squirmed. "Why?"

"Because if you don't, Ms. Torres is going to start poking around on her own. Right now, we can't afford for the boys out at

Dahlia Farm to have even the slightest notion that anyone is watching what they're doing, not even Teresa Torres. You've got to shut down that whole operation. Agreed?"

She knew he was right. She knew she would have to call Teresa and tell her that Marcos was a real boy scout. Still, this was a killer for her. Now she was going to have to ask Jet for help right after she tells her that they're bailing on the Torres case. Sonia leaned back, unconsciously folding her arms. This sucks.

"Listen," Brad said. "There's one thing that might help sell this to Ms. Torres. You remember that I grew up here and spent a lot of time around horses? Well, I just happen to know that there's a nice-smelling shampoo that stable hands use. It's called Mane and Tail. Its fragrance is so strong that the horses smell almost as if they're wearing women's perfume. Some women even wash their own hair with it. You can at least try to sell Ms. Torres on the notion that that's why Marcos comes home smelling like a French whore every once in a while."

Sonia sighed, dropping her hands to her lap. It's not much. At least that might give me a tiny bit of credence with Teresa. After all, she should be happy that a PI is telling her that her boyfriend is not running around on her. Of course, that's not going to help a bit with Jet.

Letting out another big sigh, Sonia stood and walked toward the door. "Okay. Thank you," she said softly. Suddenly, she remembered, however, they now knew what was coming out of the truck. They now knew that there was no Mid-West Feed and Hay Company. They now had Marcos on video having his way with one or more prostitutes. And someday, when this was all over, Sonia was going to go back to Teresa Torres and burn Marcos' ass so bad he would wish he'd never left Mexico. Sonia put her hand on the doorknob and pulled. But for now, for now, I'm just going to go home and get ready for dinner. I simply don't have the strength to face Jet right now.

23

S onia heard footsteps on the stairs to her apartment and a knock on the door, Detective Sergeant Johnny Adams, picking her up for dinner. Right at six o'clock. Precisely as promised. Sonia checked herself in the mirror over the entry table near the door. Given her shapely body, dark brown hair, eyes the color of dark chocolate, and beautiful smile, Sonia could be quite stunning. Normally, she wore minimal makeup and did her hair in a casual, relaxed manner. When she wanted to, however—and tonight she wanted to—a little extra makeup and a little extra effort on her hair took her beyond attractive.

Unfortunately, just below the surface, Sonia was feeling like one very tired puppy. For all intents and purposes, Sonia had been up since two-thirty in the morning. After her meeting with Brad, she had tried to get a little sleep, but thoughts of John Hensley, The Mid-West Feed and Hay Company, hacking a sophisticated communications system, and Brad Dunham, had kept her from sleeping more than a few minutes. In addition, she was a bit apprehensive about going to dinner with Johnny Adams. Yes, he was attractive, polite, attentive. But she was still a little put-off by the way he had handled his first meeting with her, and the warnings he had given her at the recent press conference. All in all, she had no idea what to expect from tonight's date.

She opened the door and looked up into the eyes of the much taller Johnny Adams. Sonia could tell that her primping for the evening was having the desired effect. Johnny's eyes looked her over from head to toe, apparently drinking in how beautiful she was. No one could have missed the fact that Detective Sergeant Johnny Adams seemed quite taken by Sonia.

"You look . . . lovely."

Sonia smiled. "I'm ready."

"Well then, let's get going."

Sonia slipped on her pea coat and her beige cloche hat. They walked down the steps to his car, a one-year-old Honda Accord. It was a nice car, a dark red, modern, well kept, and not ostentatious, as was another car in which Sonia had ridden recently. "You know," Sonia said as Johnny opened the door for her, "I've been in town for over two years now and I've heard about Joe Bologna's a bunch of times, but I've never been there. I'm really looking forward to this."

"Oh, I promise, Joe's will not disappoint." Johnny slid into the car. "Just wait until you've had one of his breadsticks, it's like a whole loaf of bread: hot and delicious and drowning in a sea of garlic butter."

"Sounds great." As they drove, Sonia looked out the window. Downtown Lexington—always so clean, so nice, so comfortable. She was more comfortable with *it* than she was with the near-stranger sitting next to her.

After a few moments of silence, Johnny asked, "How was your day?"

"Fine. Just fine." It was the most normal question a person might ask in a situation such as this, and it really bothered Sonia that she couldn't help but attach to it some sinister motive. Is he trying to get something out of me, keeping tabs on me? Goodness girl, just drop it. He's just a guy taking a girl out to dinner, making small talk. Still, it was hard for her to shake the feeling that there was something behind his questioning. "And yours? How was your day?"

"Same old, same old. That's pretty much what it is for a cop. Sounds like an exciting career, but mostly it's the same thing every day."

Sonia noted the new floral hangings the city had put up along Main Street. "Uh huh."

They crossed over to Maxwell Street, then stopped in the parking lot of a building that had, at one time, served as a Jewish synagogue, an unusual history for an Italian restaurant. It was full, as she'd heard it always was at dinnertime.

A hostess seated them and then their server arrived. "Hi, I'm Nathan, and I'll be your server tonight. Can I get you something to drink?"

"Water with lemon," said Sonia.

"Oh, come on. We're out to dinner. Let's have some wine." Johnny turned to Nathan. "What kind of wine do you have?"

"We have a nice red table wine, a pinot grigio, and a delicious rosé."

"Two glasses of the red," Johnny said, without asking Sonia. Then he turned to her as if looking for approval.

"Yes, that'll be fine." She wasn't really sure she should be drinking wine when she was so tired.

They spent the next few moments in silence, each looking over the menu. When she had made her decision, Sonia looked around, taking in the ambiance. The highly-polished, yet well-worn, wooden floors created a striking contrast with the intricate stained-glass windows—a remnant of the religious history of the building. "This really is a nice place. It's comfortable. It feels right."

"Joe's got to have been running this place for thirty years or more now. It's a real Lexington icon."

"Well, thanks for bringing me here. I like it."

Just then Nathan returned. "What can I get you folks tonight?" He turned, of course, to Sonia first.

"I'll have the cannelloni and manicotti combination."

Nathan seemed a bit taken aback by her proper pronunciation of the Italian dish—*mahn-uh-gaw-tah.* "Oh, I guess you're Italian?"

"Uh huh."

"Excellent. Would you like me to have them put a little extra spinach on the cannelloni for you?"

"Sounds great."

Johnny ordered the lasagna and Nathan scooted off to put in the order.

The next few minutes were spent exchanging pleasantries until Nathan showed up with the salads and breadsticks.

"Oh, my goodness," Sonia's eyes widened. "The breadsticks. They're huge." She touched hers carefully with her fingertip. "And obviously right out of the oven."

Together, they oohed and ahhed over the breadsticks and salad. By the time Nathan appeared with the main dishes, Sonia was certain that she'd never be able to eat the cannelloni *and* the manicotti. Sonia eyed the cannelloni, deciding she would start there. *I'll just bring the manicotti into the office tomorrow. I'll bet Jet would love it for lunch.*

Before she could pick up her fork, however, Johnny said to Nathan, "Bring us two more red wines, okay?"

"Oh, no," said Sonia. "I really shouldn't."

"No, no, no. It'll be fine. Let's really enjoy tonight."

Sonia shook her head tentatively. "Okay," she said, promising herself she absolutely wouldn't finish her second glass. Forty minutes later, however, having finished her salad, her breadstick, and her cannelloni, Sonia also found herself putting down her empty wine glass. Much to her surprise, the table came up to meet the glass faster than she expected.

"Listen, Johnny, this has been great, but I think it's time you take me home. I've got a big day in front of me tomorrow." She chose not to mention the fact that she was feeling pretty lightheaded.

"Sure, sure." Motioning to Nathan, Johnny got the check, left a hefty tip, and walked Sonia out to his car. As they walked, Sonia's ankles seemed to keep buckling inward. These damn heels.

Minutes later, when they had climbed the stairs to her apartment and were standing on the tiny porch outside her front door, Sonia could feel Johnny looking deeply into her eyes. He had a broad smile on his face, and she had a feeling that her own smile was warmer than it had been when he had picked her up. Her mind was racing. She desperately wanted him to pull her close and kiss her lips, but somehow it didn't feel right. Still, she couldn't deny that she wanted to feel her body pressed against his.

Right in the middle of their small-talk goodbye, something seemed to change for Johnny. It was as if he couldn't resist. He reached out and put his arms around Sonia, almost lifting her off the ground as he pulled her close to him. No talking, no excuses, no explanations, he just kissed her. And she kissed him back, her Italian blood beginning to stir.

Sonia felt like a teenaged girl, standing outside her front door, passionately kissing this attractive man. He was turning her on more deeply than she had been for, well, literally, for almost three years. But this was like making out on the front porch with the captain of the basketball team after the championship game. Somewhere in the back of her mind, she got the feeling that her father, like so many Italian fathers, was going to flash the front porch lights—indicating to her and her horny boyfriend that it was time to call it a night.

Instead, Johnny asked, "May I come in?"

Sonia froze. She had not been holding anything back as she was kissing him. She could feel her body pressing against his, tighter and tighter. Her thighs were telling her that there was no question whatsoever that Johnny Adams was all man and ready to go as well. Still, in her now slightly drunken haze, there were alarms going off.

Fighting every sexual urge that was coursing through her body, Sonia pulled herself away. "No, Johnny. Not tonight. Please. Please understand. Not tonight."

Sonia watched as Johnny's manners kicked in. "Sure. Sure. I understand. I'm sorry. It's just that ..."

Sonia reached up and touched her fingers to his lips. "Shh-hhh. It's alright. Just not tonight. Okay?" She heard the slight slurring of her own words.

Johnny stood there for a long few moments, staring into her eyes. "Absolutely. Listen, I've got to go. Thank you so much for a great evening. I've got to go. I'll call you, okay?"

Sonia nodded. And with that, Johnny turned, went quickly down the steps, and left. Sonia simply leaned against her front door, pulling herself together, catching her breath. Finally, she turned, unlocked the door, walked into the apartment, and went straight into her bedroom. Without even taking off her clothes, she fell onto the bed and was asleep in moments. It wasn't a restful sleep.

24

Just before eleven on Wednesday morning, Sonia walked into BCI and headed straight into Jet's office.

Jet looked up. "Look what the cat drug in."

Sonia plopped down in the red chair across from Jet's desk.

Jet sat up a little taller and looked down at Sonia's hands. "I see you've gotten your coffee from downstairs. No croissant?"

Sonia gave her a look that clearly indicated the thought of eating a croissant right now would make her puke.

"That must have been some date last night. Are you okay, sweetie?"

Sonia's eyes dropped to her lap. "Yeah, I guess I am."

"Well . . . c'mon girl, spill."

Sonia took a deep breath and let it out slowly. "Okay, so he picks me up promptly at six. Nicely dressed, we get in his nice middle-class car, he takes me to Joe Bologna's, where I've never been before. We have a lovely dinner, some wine . . . ."

"Aaand?"

"And then he takes me home and we make out like two horny teenagers, right outside the door to my apartment."

"Are you kidding me? Right outside? You didn't go in?"

"No. He asks, but I say, 'No.' "

"Why? Was he groping you? Was he all hands and tongue?" Jet seemed excited.

"No, he was great. He was hot and sexy, but he was still a perfect gentleman. I know he wanted to go inside and, you know. But as soon as I said, 'No,' he dropped it right away. He just said, 'Goodnight' and left."

Jet rocked back in her chair, tapping her chin with her thumb. "Was he pissed?"

"No, that's the thing." Sonia put her coffee on Jet's desk. "He was all revved up, but as soon as I asked him to stop he did. He was a real gentleman about it."

Jet squinted at Sonia. "Are you going to see him again?"

"He said he'd call and I'm sure he will."

"Yeah, but will you see him? You look wrecked."

Sonia rubbed her forehead with her thumb and forefinger. "Well, part of it is that I'm so damn hung over. I never should've been drinking wine when I was that tired. It just wiped me out."

"And the other part of it?" A snarky little smile crept across Jet's face.

"I don't know. He's nice. He's pleasant, he's polite, he's very good looking, and he's just . . . nice."

Jet raised her eyebrows and leaned forward, resting her arms on her desk. "And the problem is?"

"Somehow it just doesn't feel right."

"And when was the last time it did feel right?"

Sonia's eyes lowered. "A long time ago." She took a sip of her coffee and looked into the cup she held with both hands. "With John Eckel, back in Cincinnati, I guess."

"The guy who broke your heart? The son-of-a-bitch who left you standing at the altar?"

"Yeah, that's the guy."

Jet's face and voice softened. "Honey, you can't judge every man by what that jerk did. Maybe you just don't remember how it's supposed to feel anymore. Couldn't it be that you're just gun shy?"

Sonia looked up. "Do you blame me? Standing there in the narthex, dressed in my wedding gown, and my uncle comes up to me and tells me John's a no-show. I'm absolutely clueless as to what happened. And now you expect me to know what it's supposed to feel like?"

Sonia rolled the cup in her hands. This was a memory she had been keeping locked away as much as possible for a long time. Just saying the words *narthex* and *wedding gown*, she wanted to groan. Aspirin would eventually take care of the pain in her head, but no amount of pain reliever would touch the ache in her heart.

"Well," said Jet after a few moments. "You know what they say in Kentucky. First thing you do after you fall off a horse . . ."

"Yeah, I know, get back on. It's just not that easy." Sonia put her coffee down on Jet's desk.

Jet smiled, turned her chair around, and stared out the window. "And what about the other one?"

"What other one?

Jet spun back around and nodded her head toward the white house. "Mr. Hotshot, former Marine, former NCIS."

Sonia sat straighter. "What about him?"

"Now don't tell me that you weren't all hot and bothered for him when you got back from your mission the other night."

"Oh, geez." Sonia thought back to how she felt when she first crawled back into Brad's Corvette after sneaking onto Dahlia Farm. "Yeah, he's hot, but he can be such a jerk, too."

"Well, you seemed ready to let that slide the other day. C'mon, don't you really have it for him too?"

"No, no. Sure he's hot but . . ."

Jet stood up and reached for her purse. "Look, let's go downstairs and get you some soup. I'll bet you haven't eaten a morsel this morning, and that's the last thing your body needs. C'mon."

Sonia lifted her hand. "Wait, I'll go, but first I have to tell you something."

"There's more?" Jet paused and looked closely at her friend. "Wow, that must have been some date."

"No, it has nothing to do with last night. It's about work."

Jet sat back down in her chair. "What about work?"

"Well, first, we now have Marcos Torres on video, doing his thing with the prostitutes."

"Do tell." A big smile spread across Jet's face.

"Yeah, we picked it up and recorded it from the feeds out at the farm."

"Ka-ching!" Jet bent her arm and pulled it downward. "At least now we can get paid for that one."

"Not so fast."

Jet's head bobbed backward. "Not so fast? Why?"

Sonia paused and looked right into Jet's eyes. "Well . . . it turns out that if we tell Teresa Torres that we have Marcos on tape with a prostitute, she'll be happy, but we'll have blown our investigation of the Hensley thing. I mean, she's certainly not going to keep that to herself." Sonia got a momentary vision of Teresa beating the living daylights out of a very cowardly Marcos. "And what's worse, we have to make certain that she doesn't go poking around there herself."

Jet scrunched her brow. "Which means?"

Sonia shook her head slowly. "Which means we actually have to tell Teresa that we're sure Marco *isn't* fooling around. That he's being a damn boy scout."

Jet moved to the front of her seat. "Really?"

"Really."

It was Jet's turn to shake her head slowly. "I'll be damned. That sucks."

Sonia lightened the tone of her voice and picked up the pace. "I know. But trust me, as soon as we get this whole thing wrapped up we're going to go back and burn ol' Marcos Torres so badly he'll wish that Teresa had cut his balls off a long time ago."

Jet cocked her head, surprised at Sonia's language. Then Sonia saw her brighten up and stand. "Okay, let's go get you that soup."

"Wait, there's more."

"What the . . . ." Jet plopped back down. "Come on, spit it out. Just know you're killin' me here, Vitale. You're killin' me."

Sonia's eyes dropped to her lap. That wisp of hair fell in front of her face. "We need help." She reached up and ran her fingers through her hair.

"Who needs help? You and I?"

"No, Brad and I. We need help."

"Oh, so it's Brad and I now, is it?" She gave Sonia another snarky smile. "With what?"

Sonia looked back up. "Well, not only do we have Marcos on tape, we also have the Mid-West Feed and Hay Company truck on tape. They're back at it."

Jet rocked back in her chair and drummed her fingers on its arms. "Back at what?"

"You know how I've been watching that Mid-West Feed and Hay company truck come and go on the farm."

Jet nodded.

"Well, it turns out that there's no such thing as the Mid-West Feed and Hay Company."

Jet looked out over glasses that weren't on her nose.

"It's just a cover for some guys who've developed an elaborate system for delivering drugs. And now that we know that, we have to switch from checking tape to live monitoring. Bottom line, we have to have someone monitoring that feed from eight in the morning 'til at least five or six in the evening. And we've got to be ready to roll. As soon as we see the truck pull in, we've got to get out to the castle and be ready to follow one of those pickup trucks as it goes on a delivery."

"And what kind of help do you need?"

Sonia moved forward in her seat, her eyes pleading just slightly. "Help monitoring the feed. We can do it from here, as well as from Brad's office, but we need at least three people to trade off watching the computer."

"Just watching the computer?"

"Yeah, just watching the computer . . . I guess."

Jet's cocked her head again. "You guess?"

"I don't know," Sonia shrugged her shoulders, "it's just that this thing seems to get bigger and bigger by the minute. But right now, all we need is help monitoring the feed."

Jet's face broke into a sly smile. "Three people, huh? And do you have any idea who that third person might be?"

Sonia picked up on Jet's new mood and matched it with her voice. "Well, I do happen to know a professional private eye who is already sitting around watching hours of boring tape from a restaurant that's been having meat and fish pilfered from its refrigerators."

"Oh, you do, do you? And who might that be?"

"The fastest female runner in Woodford County High School history." Sonia's chocolate eyes twinkled. "That's who."

"Okay, okay." Jet broke out in a full-throated laugh. "No need to reach back into ancient history."

"Aaand?

"Aaand, for you, baby girl, anything." Jet stood up again. "For better or worse, wherever it leads, if you're in, I'm in. Now let's go get you that soup."

PART IV

25

J ust before one in the afternoon, Sonia knocked on the door of Semper Fi Investigations. While she had been eating lunch with Jet downstairs at Magee's, she had received a call from Brad. In his clipped, military voice, Brad had informed her that she would be having a telephone meeting with one of his unnamed colleagues from the past. He had made it clear that the phone would ring at precisely 1:00 PM; she needed to be at her computer and ready to move forward immediately. Given Brad's apparent need to know exactly what was going on, Sonia was quite certain he'd meant that she should bring her laptop to *his* office.

At 12:59:30, sitting at Brad's computer table, Sonia readjusted her laptop for the fifth time. She leaned back in the chair, uncomfortable with how it almost swallowed her, uncomfortable that it was *his* chair. But this was not the time for being uncomfortable; this was the time to be ready for the challenge. As proud as she was of her own computer skills, messing with an NCIS computer hacking expert was another ball of wax altogether. She pursed her lips. Am I going to be able to keep up with this guy? Is he going to make me feel like an idiot? Do they even use a computer language I'm familiar with? Will his voice be dark and electronically disguised?

As the second hand on her watch indicated 1:00:07, the phone rang. She made the obvious mental note. *My watch must be seven seconds early.*

"Ms. Vitale?" the voice came. But it was not dark and electronically disguised. In fact, it wasn't even a man.

"Yes, this is Sonia Vitale." Sonia cringed. Her words had come out a little too loudly.

The voice was warm and friendly. *"Listen, as you can imagine, I can't tell you who I am, but if Dunny vouches for you, I know I can trust that you're okay. Are you ready for this?"*

Dunny? Dunny? Sonia's head jerked backward a bit. Her mind rocketed to a new place. *His friends call him Dunny?*

"Are you there?"

Sonia cleared her throat. "Yes, yes, I'm here. And I'm ready. I just hope I can do what you ask of me."

"Look, Dunny says you're a techie. As long as you know some HTML and Javascript, we'll be just fine. Is your computer open?"

Sonia sat up tall. She placed her fingers on the keyboard. "Yes, it's open."

"Okay, I know it seems crazy obvious, but most people don't have the slightest clue about technology security. I'll bet we can find a backdoor into that whole communications system right through their public website."

"They wouldn't do that, would they?"

"You'd be surprised. They buy the heavy-duty equipment, they spend the time setting up their internal communications system, then someone walks in and says, 'Hey, we need a public website. Can you set that up too?' Rather than starting fresh, the guy says, 'Sure,' then takes the easy way out by just making it an add-on to their whole system. Let's give it a try, okay?"

Sonia braced herself but was still afraid this might not work. "Okay. What's first?"

"What's the name of the farm you're interested in?"

"Dahlia Farm. It's a horse farm."

"Yeah, okay. Do a search for Dahlia Farm, and let's see what we get. Now I've got to tell you; I can't follow along with you from here. If I go to that website and then something goes south, I'll be caught with an empty cookie jar and crumbs all over my electronic fingertips. I can't even take over control of your computer, I'd leave one gigantic electronic footprint."

"Sure, sure. I can do this." Her hands flew across the keys and a string of results flickered on the screen. Finding a home page was easy, but that was only step one. She wasn't at all sure she could do steps two through whatever. "Okay, found it. I'm on their home page."

"Good. Let's go find us a backdoor." There was a smile in her voice.

For the next thirty minutes or so, Sonia and her faceless, nameless, co-conspirator worked together. First, they found a backdoor into the website; then, they followed the electronic path all the way back to the main communications link for the whole system.

Finally, Sonia whispered, "Ho-ly moly! I'm looking at every communication ever sent on their internal network." Her voice crescendoed. "The whole thing! Every message!"

"That's my girl. Are you sure you're in? Can you move around to different messages?"

"Yes! Yes! I'm in!" Sonia grabbed the edges of the laptop's screen with both hands. She was thrilled that she had actually found her way into the sophisticated system "The last message was . . . let's see here . . . just about an hour and a half ago." Sonia smiled. "We're in. We did it. You did it. Thank you, thank you."

"No, you did it. You got there on your own. I just gave you a few hints along the way. Seriously, you really do know your way around this world. Trust me, there's no way I could have led Dunny through this maze."

There it was again—Dunny. She cocked her head. Hmm. His friends call him Dunny. It sounds so casual, so fun-loving. Is there another part of this guy that I've never seen?

"*Okay?*" The voice interrupted her thoughts.

"I'm sorry?" Sonia apologized for being lost in her thoughts.

"*I said I'm going to let you go now. Is that okay?*"

"Yes, yes. This is incredible." Sonia sat back in her seat, but her eyes never left the computer screen. "We should be able to figure out everything from here."

"*Well, don't get too cocky. Just because they failed with their electronic security, doesn't mean they're going to be careless in their communications. Here, check this. Do you see any names, actual names?*"

Sonia scrolled through the file list. "Uh, no. I see information being passed, but no names. Like here, it implies that some guy, person, named "Forty" will be looking for a new shipment from "Toro" on the twenty-first, but that's an old message."

"*Look, it's not like on the TV shows. The bad guys may make mistakes, but that doesn't mean they're not trying their hardest to keep things on the QT. Good luck trying to figure out the codes and who's who. If I could plug you into our mainframe, the computer could look for matches in a million different places. But that's something I just can't help you with. I'm afraid you're on your own with that.*"

Sonia's shoulders sagged and she let out a heavy breath. Her eyes continued to drift across the messages on her computer screen. "Yeah, I guess I am."

"*Hey, don't get down.*" Her voice was still bright. "*You've got Dunny, and I've never seen a better investigator than him, ever. I've never seen a better . . . well, let's just say, he's good at a lot of things.*"

Sonia waited for more, but the conversation was over.

"*Listen, I've got to go. Good luck with your investigation. Good luck with . . . everything.*"

Sonia heard a click as the line went dead. Good luck with everything? What did she mean by that?

Then, appearing out of nowhere, Brad was suddenly behind her, his voice, only inches from her ear. He was leaning over her shoulder. "Are we in?"

Sonia turned and took in his presence—his strong hand on the desk, the warmth of his breath on her shoulder, the smell of his starched shirt. Nothing could be more exciting than what she'd just discovered . . . nothing except . . . . She whispered. "We're in." Then louder, "We're in." *We're in Dunny. We are in.*

26

S onia stayed seated but stretched a long deep stretch, her
hands reaching over her head. She had been hunched over
her computer, working intently, for over a half hour, but the sense
of pride and new-found confidence that filled her heart more
than compensated for the stiffness in her shoulders. As she
stretched, she could feel Brad's eyes on her, as if he were drinking
in every part of her while she moved in front of him. When she
glanced at him, however, he quickly diverted his eyes. She looked
away. Hmm.

Sonia directed Brad's attention to the screen. "Okay, before us
lies the entire communications record of the organization. Now,
all we have to do is figure out is who is who, and what the heck
they're doing."

Brad pulled up a chair and they worked shoulder to shoulder
for the next two hours.

Brad eyes were on the computer. "Okay, it appears we know
this much. The Mid-West Feed and Hay truck is being
dispatched by someone called Toro. I assume he's pretty close to
the origin of the internal distribution system here in the states.
We're not certain, but it may be that the drugs involved in this

operation enter the U.S. and are delivered to Toro." He pointed to a particular message on the screen. "He then dispatches the Mid-West Feed and Hay truck, and I'm guessing several others, to move smaller shipments around the country." Brad turned and looked at Sonia. "I'm also guessing that Lexington is not the first, nor the last, stop for that truck. I believe the drugs that have been dropped off at Dahlia Farm, and places like it, are then expedited to other, smaller locations for final distribution to dealers and users." He put his hand on her shoulder. "It's your boy Marcos and his buddies in those pickups that are doing that."

Warmth flushed through Sonia's face. She liked his touch, but she couldn't quite tell what that hand on her shoulder implied. She turned her eyes to the screen.

"Well, assuming you're correct Captain Dunham, what's next? Isn't it time to call in the cavalry?" Sonia could see by the furrow in Brad's brow that he wasn't sure if the use of the term, "Captain," was a compliment or a barb. She continued. "Really, it's time for us to call the FBI, isn't it?"

Brad pushed his chair back from the computer. Picking up a pencil, he began tapping on the edge of the desk as he spoke. His eyes were still on the screen. "No, not now. First, it wouldn't be the FBI, it would be the DEA, the Drug Enforcement Agency. Second, we're not ready yet. We need to know more about the operation."

"Why? It's not our job to stop the drug ring."

Brad turned, his bright blue eyes locking Sonia's. "It's not a drug ring, it's just an operation. The ring would be much larger than what we're looking at. And, *of course* it's our job to stop the operation."

Sonia looked away, breaking the contact. After a very long pause, she asked softly and slowly, "Why, again, is that our job? We're not the authorities." She assumed she knew what he was thinking. In his mind, after all those years, he still feels like he *is* the authorities, *we are* the authorities. She didn't say another word.

Brad reached out and touched her arm gently. "Okay. You're right. We're not officially charged with this, but I'm not calling DEA until I can tell them a hell of a lot more than what I know now."

Sonia waited a few moments. Then she looked into his eyes and quietly asked, "Why?"

"Because. Just because."

Brad stood up and paced around the room. She waited for him to continue, feeling how thick the silence had become.

Brad came to a stop, standing by his desk, looking down at her. "Listen, the guy I would most likely call at DEA is Roberto Alvarez. We call him Robbie. He and I go back quite a ways. We served together in Iraq. While I stayed in the Corps and got assigned to NCIS, he eventually left and hooked up with DEA. Unfortunately, the last time I called him with what I thought was a solid lead on a big drug operation, the whole thing went south. I don't know if my informant was wrong, or if he was setting me up. Maybe someone in DEA leaked something. But Robbie trusted me and made a big move on a bunch of Cubans in Miami. The raid produced nothing but a bunch of hand-woven baskets, and Robbie was left with his you-know-what hanging out—not to mention an official reprimand in his jacket. All in all, a very bad deal all the way around."

"So, you're afraid to let him in on this?"

"Well, maybe not afraid, but I certainly want more to go on before I bring him in. I owe that to him."

Brad started pacing around the room again. Sonia turned and stared at his back. She was far from convinced that it wasn't a better idea to just call the real authorities and turn this over to them. Still, they had begun to figure out how this whole drug thing worked, and that would help her get to the bottom of what she really wanted to know—who had done in John Abbott Hensley. She'd never believed he had committed suicide—and he sure as hell didn't accidentally hang himself. Now, at least, she was pretty certain what the motive was.

Brad stopped in front of the window that looked out onto East Main, the window from which he could see Magee's—and, of course, the offices of BCI. Sonia's heart jumped a tiny bit as she wondered if he had stood there as many times looking at her offices as she had stood at her window looking at his.

"Here's what we need to do." Brad turned to her. "It'll be a two-pronged operation. The first time the truck comes in, and according to what we think those messages are saying, that's Friday, we follow one of those pickups on its delivery route. We won't interfere with anyone. We'll just be trying to gather enough information to make a real case that Lexington is, in fact, a hub in a larger distribution system."

Brad moved briskly to his desk and sat down. He made a notation on his calendar. "Then the next time the truck from Mid-West Feed and Hay comes in we'll follow it. There's no question that eventually that truck is heading back to its base of operations." He looked up at Sonia. "God only knows how long that surveillance will be or where it will take us, but . . ." He stopped and cocked his head a bit. "Have you ever ridden a trail horse? You know, the kind you rent by the hour, and the poor animal walks the same path over and over again, several times a day, day after day?"

Sonia stood and walked toward Brad's desk. "Actually, I've never been on a horse." She took a seat across from him.

His piercing blue eyes popped open and stared at her. Then a big grin slowly passed over his face. "Well, we're just going to have to take care of that someday. Yes, we will. And it won't be on one of those trail horses, either. I'll take you to one of the farms I used to work on up in Paris . . . Kentucky, that is," he said smiling. "Then we'll do some real cross-country riding, through fields and streams. It'll be great."

Sonia smiled, not sure what to make of the invitation.

"Anyway," he continued, waving a finger, "if you were to fall off one of those trail horses, hell, the horse would hardly notice. He'd just walk right on back to the barn and stand there waiting for someone to unsaddle him. I'm guessing that's exactly what this truck does. Same route every few days. And we're going to follow that nag right back to the barn."

Sonia understood what Brad was saying, but the invitation to go riding had her mind spinning just a bit. She wasn't at all certain she wanted to be crossing streams and galloping through meadows on horseback. But . . . .

Brad looked down at his desk calendar pad, "Alright, you'd better clear your schedule. This surveillance might take several days."

Sonia looked at him in surprise, taking in a breath.

He plowed on. "Now, if our reading of the messages is correct, that part of the surveillance won't start until Tuesday. But you never know. I think they're still trying to make up for deliveries they missed when John Hensley bought it. The truck has been pretty irregular. We just need to keep our eyes on those messages and our computer feeds."

Sonia looked at the short-cropped hair on the top of his head while Brad was still making notes on his calendar—blocking out four days of the next week in red. They were going to be out on the road together, probably for several days. Several days? How does that work? Where do we sleep? In motels, I guess. Her brain was running at top speed. And what about the bad guys? Do we all agree to stop at the end of the day and eat dinner together, then retire to our rooms? 'See you guys in the morning. Let us know when you're leaving and we'll be surreptitiously following behind you all day. But listen, we'll let you know if one of us has to pee, so you can—'

Wait. Retire to our *rooms*? What about the rooms? One room, two rooms? Does he expect me to share a room with him? A bed—

"Right?" Brad said, breaking into her thoughts.

"What?" Sonia's mouth was open.

Brad shot her the "Are-you-with-me?" look. Then he outlined his expectations very slowly and clearly. "You will be able to clear your calendar next week? Right? I mean you don't have a date or anything, do you?"

Sonia could feel the heat in the question. She could also feel the heat in her own face. Was that pure annoyance, based on the fact that she had put off last night's session because of her date with Johnny? Or was there just a tinge of jealousy in the comment. She hoped it was the latter. She took a quick breath. "No. I can be ready to go. But are you sure this is the right way to proceed? You said, yourself, that these boys play for real."

"Trust me. We'll do this by the book, and at this point in my career, I could have written the book." He had lowered his chin and was marking on his calendar. No room for discussion here.

Sonia averted her eyes. Well, we are pretty self-assured, aren't we?

Then Brad paused as if he were re-thinking his last statement. He put down his marker and looked directly up at Sonia. "I'm sorry. I know this is not as routine for you as it is for me. This is what I did for all those years. Trust me, I do know how it's done properly, and we'll be extra cautious. Is that okay?"

Sonia's heart leapt a tiny bit again. She could hear the concern in his voice. This was Dunny speaking. And she was quite certain that it wasn't often that Dunny would have made an appearance in this type of planning session. She was becoming convinced that somewhere under the façade of Captain Brad Dunham, former Marine, former NCIS, Dunny might be starting to have feelings for her.

Sonia looked up at him. "Yes, I'll be ready." *Yes, sir. I'll be ready, sir.*

Brad's attention turned back to some other paperwork on his desk. Sonia cleared her throat. "Listen, I've got to get back to my office. I've got to clear some things from Friday and," she shuddered, "all of next week." She stood.

Brad put his hands on the arms of his chair as if to rise.

"No need." Sonia gestured for him to remain seated. "I can find my way out. I'll talk to you later."

"Yes, later." Brad nodded and returned to the work on his desk.

As Sonia reached the door, her iPhone emitted its silly *Star-Spangled Banner*. Frustrated at not having had time to change the ringtone, she shook her head. "Hello?" she said as she closed the door behind her.

27

"Sonia? *This is Johnny Adams. Am I calling at a bad time?*"

"No, not at all." Sonia struggled to shift gears. She walked out of the white house and down the steps onto the sidewalk. "I just finished a meeting with . . . I'm just walking out of a meeting. What can I do for you?"

"*Well, I wanted to talk to you about last night. Are you okay?*"

A flash of the sensations from the evening before coursed through her body. "Sure, sure. I'm okay. Maybe a little under the weather from too much wine, but I'm fine." She was at the corner now and waiting for the light to change.

"*Good, I'm glad. I know things got a little intense last night. It's just that, well, I hope I didn't —*"

"Hey, don't worry about it. We're cool. Everything is okay. Things did get, like you said, a little intense though. I just needed to back away for a bit. But don't worry, we're okay." It suddenly struck Sonia that this sounded like a conversation between a couple in a long-standing relationship; when, in fact, they had only gone out for the first time the night before.

"*I'm so glad to hear it. I didn't mean to, well, you know, come on so strong.*"

"No, don't worry about it. Like I said. It was my fault for drinking so much wine. I should've known better. Not to worry."

Sonia crossed the street and headed for her office. *Oh, my gosh. Now I'm apologizing to him. He really didn't do anything wrong last night . . . but neither did I. Why the heck am I apologizing?*

"*. . . so glad we're okay, because I really did have a great time with you. I was wondering if maybe we could catch a light dinner somewhere tonight. You know, after you get off work?*"

Alarm bells went off in Sonia's brain. He had wanted to kiss her. She had wanted to kiss him. They'd kissed, passionately. Both their bodies had responded. Hers with a passion she felt all over her body, all through her body, his in the way any man would when being passionately kissed by a beautiful woman. Still, Sonia knew she wasn't ready to face that temptation again.

"Thanks so much, but I've got a whole bunch of things to do before tomorrow. And, in fact, I'm still beat from not getting any sleep last night. Some other time, okay?"

Johnny's polite upbringing came through. "*Okay. How about tomorrow morning?*" There was a chuckle in his voice. "*That's some other time. What do you say I just meet you at Magee's for coffee and one of your favorite pastries?*"

"I don't know, Johnny." *Geez, can't he just let this go?*

"*Come on, Sonia. I just want to spend some time with you. Over coffee. It's no big deal.*"

Sonia hesitated. "Okay, but just for coffee. I've got a lot of things on my plate, and I've got so much I've got to accomplish tomorrow."

"*Yeah, sure. Just for coffee. What time is good for you?*"

"Uhm, let's say ten o'clock. Ten o'clock at Magee's."

"*Yeah. That'll be great. I'll see you at Magee's at ten. Okay, then, until tomorrow. Bye.*"

Sonia hung up her phone. *What the heck is it with this guy? Is he really that eager to spend time with me? Is he up to some-*

thing? Or is he just a really nice guy who's a bit lame when it comes to dealing with women?

Sonia had reached the bottom of the steps that led up to her office. She looked up the long flight of stairs. She blew that wisp of hair out of her face. *And what the heck is it with me? Am I attracted to this guy or not? Last night I almost gave him a tonsillectomy. And if it hadn't been for the images of my father, I probably would have brought him into my apartment and jumped his bones. Gosh, Sonia. Are you hot for him? Are you hot for Brad? Or are you just so freakin' horny you're hot for anything with pants on?*

Sonia started the long walk up. When she got to the top, before she stepped inside, she looked out over her little part of town. *I really like this place. I really like my life here. Now let's hope I don't screw it up again.* Then she turned the tarnished knob and stepped into the offices of Bluegrass Confidential Investigations.

AT TEN O'CLOCK the next morning, Sonia, her blue jeans tucked into tall boots, her red cowl-neck sweater draping softly, waited for Detective Sergeant Johnny Adams to buy her coffee. She had gotten there about ten minutes early, in order to be sure to get her favorite seat in the corner. The smells in the place were, as always, unbelievably delicious.

Still, as Sonia waited for Johnny, his words from yesterday afternoon kept running through her brain. "One of your favorite pastries," he had said. ". . . meet you at Magee's for coffee and one of your favorite pastries."

That had gotten Sonia thinking. *I love the almond croissants here. In fact, everything's so good: the pecan Danish, the cherry-cheese Danish, the sticky buns. But* Sonia had grown up in an Italian family, surrounded by wonderful Italian foods. For her, her favorite pastries had to be the special treats of her youth. Sonia smiled. Good Italian *cannoli*, with that sweet, creamy, ricotta filling. Or a *sfogliatella*, with those crunchy layers. Ah, there's nowhere in this town you can get those things. How long has it been since I've had good *cannoli*?

Sonia was so lost in thoughts of the pastries that still made her mouth water, that she hadn't even noticed Johnny come in and walk right over to her table.

"Can I get you a coffee and a croissant?"

Sonia looked up. "Oh. Good morning." Dang. Tailored blue suit, white shirt, the perfect red tie. Perfect. "Just coffee, please." Somehow, the sheer thought of the pastries of her childhood had taken away her desire for anything Magee's actually offered that morning.

Eventually, Johnny came back with two coffees and a chocolate-covered donut.

How very American. That's it. He's so very American. Good looking, chiseled chin, gray eyes, light brown hair. He's tall and thin, and well-built. Yes, he's the All-American boy alright.

"Are you sure I can't get you something to eat. A bran muffin or something?"

All-American. She smiled and said, "No, thanks."

"So, how's your morning been?" Johnny asked as he took a seat across from her.

"Well, I managed to get in a good three-mile run, eat some toast, and get here on time. Not bad I would say, not bad. And yourself?"

"Honestly, I got called in to help with a domestic disturbance thing that was getting out of hand last night, so I was at work really late. I'm just now getting started on the day."

They sat in silence for a while, sipping coffee. Sonia looked him over discreetly. What is it about this guy? He's as nice as they come, bright, good-looking, and I really could jump his bones sometimes. What's holding me back here?

Johnny looked up as if he were going to say something, but then he didn't. He just finished his donut.

Sonia watched him lick what was left of the chocolate off his fingertips. *Maybe, I shouldn't be holding back. Maybe I should be pushing this thing forward, just to see what that would be like.* At that moment, however, Brad Dunham's bright blue eyes flashed across her mind.

"So, what's got you so busy lately?" Johnny asked.

"Oh, lots of little things."

"Like what? Anything a local police officer can help with? Or, perhaps, anything a local police officer shouldn't know about?" He smiled a conspiratorial smile.

She pursed her lips for just the briefest moment. *And there it is. I just don't know if it's me he's interested in or the Hensley case.*

She told Johnny about the Bob Dylan case. She told him about the Clay McCormick case, although he had heard about that down at the precinct already. She mentioned a few other cases that Jet was handling on her own. Then she turned the conversation back on him, "So what's been keeping you busy, Detective Sergeant Johnny Adams?"

She was about to ask, 'Anything new on the John Hensley case?' but she caught herself just in time. The case was officially closed, and she didn't need to raise any suspicions by implying that it wasn't. Sonia smiled at him. *I just don't know if I can trust him.*

Johnny was equally noncommittal. He told her about the domestic disturbance case he'd been called in on. He mentioned a shooting that had occurred down in Richmond, Kentucky, one that might have a Lexington connection. There was no mention of John Abbott Hensley, Dahlia Farm, or anything else Sonia would have found very interesting.

At ten forty Sonia stood up. "Well, thanks for the coffee. It's really nice to see you again, but it's Thursday and I've got a lot to do."

"Thursday?"

"Bob Dylan day, as we call it at BCI. I'll be interested to see what Jet has planned for this evening."

Johnny let a beat go by. "So, when can I see you again?"

"Soon, Johnny. I'd love to see you again soon, but I may be going out of town for a while. We'll just have to see."

"Going away? Where?" Johnny tried to look nonchalant, but the pupils in his eyes belied him. It was obvious to Sonia that he was taking a very special interest in the fact that she might be going away.

Sonia started to panic inwardly. She should never have mentioned that she might be leaving town. Scrambling, she came up with the best story she could at the moment. "Oh, a couple of girls I went to college with got in touch with me and said they wanted to get together for a long weekend." Her brain still scrambling, Sonia tried to think about which direction was the total opposite of where she and Brad might be going. After just the tiniest pause, one she hoped Johnny hadn't noticed, she said, "Atlanta. I think they're talking about going to Atlanta."

"You don't know? It's Thursday, and you don't know yet where you're going this weekend?" He sounded incredulous. This was, after all, a pretty lame story; and he was, after all, a professional detective.

Sonia ran her fingers through her hair. "Well, the girl in charge likes to surprise us. She just calls at the last minute and tells us where to go." Sonia felt the whole conversation slipping out of control.

Johnny spoke softly and slowly. "Oh, I see. Still, it must make it tough to pack, not knowing where you're going and all." His voice was just short of accusatory.

"Well, yeah, but it's always the same thing. Bring your bathing suit, one nice outfit, jeans, and tops. That almost always works."

Sonia adjusted the sleeve of her sweater. Slipping. It just keeps slipping further and further out of control. "Listen, I've got to run. Thanks for the coffee. I'll be in touch."

Sonia retreated to the door. Within a moment she was out of the bakery, headed for those blessed steps, the ones that would put some distance between her and Detective Sergeant Johnny Adams. A few moments later, she reached the sanctuary of her office. She sat down in her desk chair, swiveled around, and looked out the window. She could see Detective Sergeant Johnny Adams walking across the street toward his parked cruiser—parked in the lot right next to the white house. "Dang, dang, dang."

28

S onia had been at her desk only a few minutes when the office door opened again and Jet walked into the BCI waiting area. The look on Jet's face and the wiggle in her walk told Sonia that Jet was in one very fine mood.

Jet strode directly into Sonia's office and stood in front of Sonia's desk where she struck a pose. She stood tall, thrusting out her chest and putting her hands on her hips. Then, looking off into the distance, she said with great pride, "Today, my dear, is going to be a great day."

Sonia was usually good at placing Jet's accents, but the voice today evoked no particular character. What the? What's with the accent?

Jet continued. "Yes, today is the day that dastardly Robert "Bob" Dylan meets his demise. Oh, yes, Oh, yes. Hear ye, hear ye. Today is the day Robert "Bob" Dylan goes down in flames."

Sonia bobbed her head in recognition. Sounds like we're at the Salem Witch Trials or something.

Jet leaned down, only inches from Sonia's face, her energy suddenly erupting. "Think ye not of the wench who will lose her illicit lover, if lover be the proper term." Her voice was airy, full of venom. She slapped Sonia's desk. "No, think ye of the pure and untarnished damsel who has waited, lo these many months, for the acquittal of her suspicions. The damsel who shall, henceforth, dispense the most dreadful and demeaning punishments on this sorry excuse for a husband." Jet straightened and looked over Sonia's shoulder, out the window onto East Main, as if a crowd of imaginary commoners waited for the final words of her address from on high.

Sonia rolled her eyes and shook her head. "So, you've got a plan, I take it?"

Slowly turning back to Sonia, Jet spoke in relaxed, yet cryptic tones. "I do. I do indeed, fair damsel, and a fine plan it is."

Sonia let out a sigh. "We're sounding a little Elizabethan today, aren't we?" She took a quick breath. "And would you like to inform this poor peasant as to what that plan is?"

"Nay." Jet leaned forward aggressively and placed her hands on Sonia's desk again. She looked right into Sonia's eyes. "Your role, fair maiden, shall only be disclosed to you mere moments before you are called upon this evening."

Sonia couldn't help it. Jet was so close. She drew back.

Jet stood straight again and walked to the window. She spoke softly, her words reflecting off the glass and back at Sonia. "Only as the clock strikes eight shall ye know exactly when and where the dagger shall strike."

After a moment, Jet turned quickly and walked to Sonia's door, stopping only to say, "I'll be in my office blending some tongue of frog with eye of newt." Then she was gone.

It was only ten-fifty in the morning, and already it had been one hell of a day. Sonia shook her head and looked for the coffee she wished she had brought from Magee's. Lord knows what she's up to now, and whatever it is, I'm going to be up to my neck in it. Shaking off the thought of tonight's adventure, Sonia turned her attention to making some notes about the communications system she and Brad had been pouring over yesterday afternoon.

A little while later, Jet knocked on the glass between their offices and motioned to Sonia to come join her. By the time Sonia got into Jet's office, Jet was back in front of her computer looking at the images from Clay McCormick's restaurant, her face twisted in frustration. "I just don't get it. I've been recording out there for a week now, and the thefts keep happening. At first, they stopped, but now they've started again. Smaller amounts, but stuff is still disappearing."

Sonia moved in and looked at the footage over Jet's shoulder, although there was nothing to be learned from a quick glance. "Have you been tracking all the comings and goings? Who goes in when? Who leaves?"

Jet's eyes were still on the screen. "Of course. Each time someone enters, I write down the time they go in, and then when they leave I get that as well. Still, I haven't found any pattern of somebody going in, something disappearing, and that same person leaving. Here," Jet said, handing Sonia a yellow pad. "Here are my logs."

Sonia flipped through the pages but glanced occasionally at the screen. "Run that back just a bit. Who's that?"

"Oh, that's McCormick's son, Ralph." Both their eyes were on the screen.

"Is he here in your notes?"

"Of course. I think he went inside yesterday sometime around 9:20 AM, which is kind of early. I guess he has to set up some things for the other employees."

"And when did he come out?"

"I don't know. Check the log."

Sonia scanned the logs for Wednesday, April 6. "It doesn't say."

"What do you mean it doesn't say? I log everyone coming in, everyone coming out."

Sonia pointed to a notation at the top of the page with her

Cross pen. "No, see, here. You logged him in at 9:18 AM," she ran her finger down the page, "but you never logged him out."

"That can't be, I've been sitting here for hours watching these damn tapes. Some human walks in that door, I log it. Some human walks out that door, I log it."

Sonia grabbed the extra wooden chair in the office and pulled it next to Jet's. "Let's go back. Does Ralph work every day?"

"Yeah, sure, he has to. It's the family business."

"Okay, what does your log say for him Tuesday?"

Jet took the log back and looked over the page. "In at 9:22 AM." She ran her finger further down the page. "Out at 5:37 PM."

Sonia turned away from the computer and looked at Jet. "And was anything stolen Tuesday?"

"No."

"And the day before?"

Jet searched another page. "In at 9:21 AM and out . . . damn, I don't have him coming out."

"And was anything taken Monday?" Sonia's head was cocked.

"Yeah, stuff went missing that day. Damn it."

Sonia's head remained cocked, her eyebrows lifting. "And we can be pretty sure that whether you logged him out or not, he did eventually leave each day, correct?"

Jet dropped her chin and gave Sonia her librarian look. "Yes, wiseass. We don't think he's spending the nights inside the restaurant."

"Then how is it that you're missing him?"

Jet pushed her chair away from the desk. "Because the freakin' son-of-a-bitch is not coming out the same damn door."

Sonia smiled broadly. "I think you're on to somethin', sistah."

Jet stood and started pacing around her office. "Oh, yes, I'm on to something alright. There were only three people who knew about the video surveillance, McCormick, his cleaning guy, and little Ralphie. And now, suddenly, it appears that little Ralphie goes in the back door like everyone else, but on days that he's lifted something, he must go out the front door. Son-of-a-freakin'-bitch!"

Sonia just sat there quietly, watching her partner.

Jet's voice grew calmer. "Damn. How do I tell McCormick it's his own son that's been ripping him off?"

"Yeah, it would be a lot easier if you had the footage of him leaving with the stuff." Sonia nodded. "You could just let him watch the video. You would never have to actually say anything."

Jet sat back down and turned her chair to face Sonia. "I know. That would be great, but I just don't have that footage. Now I have to walk right up to McCormick and say, 'Clay, you know that piece of shit you call your son. He's the one that's been ripping you off. Lah de dah. Have a nice day.'"

A few minutes passed as they both thought about their predicament. Sonia doodled Roman Numerals absently on a scrap of Jet's paper. Suddenly she stopped. "Wait a minute. What if you caught him with the goods? What if you had him on video going in the back door and then stopped him out front, with the goods in his possession?" Her voice was rising. "That would do it, wouldn't it?"

"You bet your ass that would do it. But how do I pull that off?"

Sonia's smile was coy. "By doing me a teensy weensy little favor."

Jet's head rocked back an inch or two. "What you talkin' about, girlfriend?"

Sonia laughed. That voice. It was Gary Coleman on *Diff'rent Strokes*. She stood up and moved over to the more comfortable red, padded chair in front of Jet's desk. Jet's gaze followed her. "Well, I've got a problem and you've got a problem. You see, I had coffee with Johnny Adams this morning, and I can't shake the feeling that he's trying to keep tabs on me. What's worse, I let it slip that I might be out of town for a few days." She gave her shoulders a quick shrug. "His whole response kind of gave me the creeps."

Jet's attention was squarely on Sonia. "Sooo?"

"Well, your logs seem to indicate that Friday is a great day for pilfering food from the father's business, right?"

"That's right, Willis," said Jet, staying with the Gary Coleman impersonation.

"So, you'll have no trouble knowing when Ralphie's gone into the restaurant." Sonia stood and began pacing around the office. "Aaand you can be pretty sure that when he leaves he'll have a giant salmon and half a cow hidden under his coat. Aaand, since you don't know when he'll be leaving, you'll need to be watching the front of the building most of the day." By then she was gesticulating pretty emphatically. "Aaand, since you're not Gomer Pyle, when you see Ralphie leaving the restaurant with lumps under his jacket, you're not gonna run up to him yelling, 'Citizens Arreeest, Citizens Arreeest.' Therefore, you're gonna need a bona fide officer of the law standing right by your side, someone who can, with probable cause, ask Little Ralphie to show him what he has tucked away inside his jacket." Sonia stopped, squinted her eyes, and looked directly at Jet. "And which officer of the law would be perfect for such a task?" Without waiting for an answer, Sonia released her gaze and continued, "Well, it seems to me that Detective Sergeant Johnny Adams is the perfect guy. What do you think?"

"Has anyone ever told you you're brilliant?" Jet pushed off her desk and twirled her swivel chair around 360 degrees—twice. "First, you figure out that some of my log-ins don't have log-outs. Then you narrow it down to Little Ralphie. And now you've figured out how to have a police officer catch Ralphie with the goods, while at the very same time tying said officer up so he can't tail you and your merry band of ne'r-do-wells as you traipse around the country following drug dealers."

Sonia waited a moment then asked, "Okay. So, this makes sense to you?"

Jet put her hands together, as if in prayer, and bowed her head. "Absolutely, Grasshopper."

Grasshopper? Now she's David Caradine's mentor on *Kung Fu*. Yikes. Sonia jumped back into business mode. "I'll get Adams to do it." Sonia noticed the question mark in Jet's eyes. "Don't worry, I'll get him to do it."

Sonia walked to the door. "I'm outta here."

Jet lifted her hand and gave it a quick twist. "Just be back by eight, fair damsel. For tonight, tonight is the witching night."

"I'll be back," Sonia retorted, Arnold Schwarzenegger's voice ringing in her own mind.

29

A t eight o'clock that evening, Sonia walked into the BCI offices wearing her black quilted vest, dark jeans that hugged her body, and black running shoes. She was expecting . . . almost anything, including Jet dressed up as a witch. That was not, however, what she found. Jet was sitting behind her desk with a big grin on her face, clearly excited about the evening's upcoming adventures. She, too, was wearing jeans and athletic shoes, but she had on a white hooded sweatshirt, something that surprised Sonia.

Sonia chuckled. "Well, you look like the cat that swallowed the canary. Are you ready to tell me about the plan to end all plans? The plan that will rain destruction down on Bob Dylan?"

Jet stood up with a gleam in her eye. "Yes, my dear, I am."

"Wait, sit down." Sonia moved to the red chair opposite Jet's desk. "Before we get into that, I've got to tell you about my phone call to Johnny Adams this afternoon."

Jet sat, then leaned back tenting her hands in front of her face. "Do tell."

"Well, I called Adams and reminded him that at one point he had asked me if there was anything a local police officer could do to help our investigations." Sonia smiled her snarky smile. "You could almost hear him sit up in his chair at the other end of the line." She shook her head. "Of course, I believe he was sorely disappointed when it turned out that all I needed was his help with Clay McCormick's case, but by then he had fallen all over himself so much that he really couldn't back down. Eventually, I told him that we needed his assistance apprehending Ralphie McCormick with stolen goods on his person. I guess the thought of making a collar didn't sound so bad to him. When I told him that I needed him to show up by ten in the morning and wait with me for what might be the better part of the day, he really seemed to brighten right up."

Jet furrowed her brow. "I thought you were hoping to follow one of those pickup trucks tomorrow."

"I am, trust me, I am."

"Well," Jet sat forward, "how are you going to pull that off?"

It was Sonia's turn to play coy. "Simple my dear, devious, deceptive, friend. When Detective Sergeant Johnny Adams shows up in front of McCormick's restaurant tomorrow, he'll be expecting to meet me. Unfortunately, I will have been called away for a little while, so you will have volunteered to cover for me, just until I can get there. Eventually, as the time goes by, you'll feel the need to call and ask when I'll be getting there. I'll tell you that I'm just waiting to get the perfect photo and as soon as the cheating son-of-a-bitch walks out of that motel room, I'll be heading on over."

Jet bobbed her head. "Nice. Very Nice."

"Then as it gets later and later," Sonia looked coyly toward the ceiling, "you'll have to start pressing me to get there since you also have a stakeout you're working on. But I'll have to say things like, 'give me just a little more time,' or 'listen, we can wrap this up with one more photo, don't pull me out of here now.' " She looked back at Jet. "All the while, you'll just keep apologizing and apologizing to Detective Sergeant Adams. If we're lucky, little

Ralphie will walk out the door with Friday's 'catch of the day,' and at that point, Adams will have to forget about me and do his job."

"And voila," said Jet, sounding suddenly French. "Ze great magician that you are, you just made ze police detective disappear." The accent went away. "Brilliant, just brilliant!"

"Yes, yes," said Sonia, feigning modesty. "All in a day's work for a magician. What is it they say in the Bible, 'their tongues practice deceit?' But in this instance, it's all for a good cause." Sonia smiled and turned to Jet. "And now I believe you have a plan of your own you would like to share with me?"

A big smile crossed Jet's face. "Well, I'm not a fan of one-upmanship, but hang on to your hat, this one is quite a doozy in its own right."

Jet stood up and walked over to the large armoire that served as her closet. Since the entire BCI space had been fashioned out of an attic, there was no natural closet space; each of the women had brought in a large armoire to fulfill that function. Needless to say, Sonia and Jet had heard some highly colorful expletives from the men who wrangled those monsters up the stairs to the BCI offices.

With a flourish, Jet pulled open the doors, reached in, and took out two chambray shirts. Each one had embroidery over the left breast pocket.

"What are those?" Sonia stood and walked to the closet. She took the shirt Jet handed her.

"These are the key in which we will perform Bob Dylan's final song. It will be his swan song, so to speak." She gave Sonia a sly look, "In a minor key of course."

Sonia shook her head almost imperceptibly. Ah, more music allusions. Then she focused. "What are you talking about? I don't get it."

"And what does it say on these shirts?"

Sonia took the shirt from Jet, held it shoulder height on its hanger, and pulled down on its lower edge. She looked carefully at the embroidery: *Bluegrass Gas.* "That's the name of the gas company. Aren't these kind of like the shirts the guys from the gas company wear."

"Exxxxxactly." Jet's eyes were like headlights on high-beam. "These shirts are going to get us into the lair of that sicko, Bob Dylan. They will get us in, and we will end this sorry tale once and for all."

Sonia stepped back, still examining the shirt. "And exactly how will wearing these shirts get us into Bob's place?" She held the shirt's hanger under her chin, checking out her reflected image in the large window overlooking East Main.

"Well, you wouldn't want to let him and his bimbo fry, would you?" Jet tipped her chin down and a bit sideways.

"What?"

"Listen, we're getting reports that something's wrong with the gas line over at that house on Clay Avenue." Jet's pace was accelerating. "We've got to get over there and check things out. Of course, we'll knock on the door and everything, but if no one answers immediately we'll be forced to enter the premises without waiting for an invitation. Hell, the people in that room could be expiring from gas inhalation. Or worse, they could be on the verge of being consumed in a giant fireball of death."

Now it was Sonia's eyes that were wide open. "Are you crazy, Jet? We can't just barge into the place."

Jet stepped closer to Sonia, pressing. "We can't, can't we? Listen, when the gas company put these uniforms on us, we swore a solemn oath to serve and protect the members of our community. It's our sacred responsibility to crash into that apartment and save those poor souls, evil and decadent as they may be."

"I think you're mixing up your mottos there my friend." Sonia laid the shirt down on Jet's desk. She slowed the pace down. "I believe it's the police who serve and protect."

"Don't you see?" Jet picked the pace right back up. "When it comes to gas leaks and explosions, it's these brave guys and gals who put their lives on the line. And tonight," said Jet, standing tall and looking off into the distance, "tonight, you and I are going to proudly join the ranks of those who have taken the vow, the vow to save those around us from the ravages of natural gas." She was already taking off her white sweatshirt.

Sonia turned and took a seat in the red chair. Oh. My. Gosh. The girl has totally lost it. She's totally, totally lost it. She didn't say a word.

Jet followed suit and took a seat as well. "Don't you see, Sonia? We know that we're never going to get an image of Bob with the bimbo. We've tried and tried. We've got to get in there, and this is how we're going to do it. We wait until we're sure he's well into his sexual gyrations, then we walk right up to that door, bang on it, and yell 'Gas company! Gas emergency! Gas emergency!'

"If we're lucky, slippery ol' Bob won't even have locked the door. A moment after we knock, we pile into the room. I'll do the talking, telling them that there's this gas emergency and we're looking for a leak. You'll be behind me with that iPhone of yours unobtrusively recording. If we're really lucky, we'll not only catch him with his pants down, we'll catch him doing whatever disgusting thing it is that he makes that poor bimbo watch for three hours every Thursday night."

Sonia shook her head and looked directly at Jet. Her voice was strong. "No way. No way am I barging into someone else's residence pretending to be from the gas company. Jet, it's illegal; it's got to be illegal. Plus, it'll never stand up in court."

Jet leaned back in her chair and tented her fingers in front of her chin. "That's the beauty of it, honey, that's the beauty of it." She smiled. "It doesn't have to stand up in court." Then she dropped her hands and sat up straight. "Think about it. We break in. We get the shots. We show them to Mrs. Dylan. Does she have to take him to court? No. Does she have him by the balls, even though she's the only one who knows how we got the shots? Ab-so-lutely.

"Does Bob, who just got caught doing who knows what, try to take us to court for intruding on his privacy while he performs lewd acts? I don't think so. Hell, as soon as we've got the shots we're out of there. He never even knows if we're really with the gas company, no less who the hell we are. And the grateful Ms. Dylan? She's certainly not going to tell anyone."

Jet leaned back in her chair, tenting her hands again. Silence hung in the room as Jet stared into Sonia's eyes. Finally, she said, "Are you in, woman? Are you in?"

Sonia thought for a moment. She thought about their friendship. She thought about what Jet would be doing for her tomorrow. She thought about how great it was to have somebody to count on, to really count on no matter what. "I'm in, crazy lady. You bet your ass I'm in."

30

It had rained that afternoon, and it was a cold, wet evening. Having checked their watches, and assuming Bob and the bimbo were fully engaged in their regular routine, Sonia and Jet walked to the house on Clay Avenue. They climbed the slippery steps. Sonia looked around and noted the wooden porch was old and in desperate need of paint. As Jet placed her hand on the door that led into the building proper, Sonia saw it had been wedged open. "So much for security," she whispered.

"Oh, yes, security first," said Jet quietly as she opened the door and led the way into the hallway. Their bodies moved slowly, carefully—as if waiting for the floor to suddenly collapse below them.

Sonia could see tarnished metal numbers hung on the doors on either side of the main hall and could tell the building had two apartments downstairs. She assumed the same was true upstairs. From the pungent smell wafting down from the second floor, she also surmised that at least one of the tenants had a passion for Asian food.

Jet waved Sonia over to the door that led into Bimbo Babe's apartment. Ever so slowly she put her hand on the black, paint-covered doorknob. With excruciating stealth, she slowly, slowly, attempted to turn the knob. "Eureka!" she shouted in a whisper, as the door latch clicked open with just the tiniest sound.

Sonia's heart was racing. She wanted desperately to be everything Jet needed her to be at that moment. But illegally crashing into someone's apartment, to stand there and take pictures of them naked? Sonia shivered. This is crazy. She heard the sound of her own breathing and Jet's voice whispering, "One, two, three."

Sonia stood in momentary shock as Jet pounded on the door. Then all hell broke loose. "Gas company! Gas emergency! Gas company!" Jet threw open the door.

Sonia watched Jet fly into the room. She knew she had to follow.

"Gas emergency!" Jet shouted again as she pushed into the center of the room. "Looking for a leak, dangerous leak!"

Sonia had come alive. She tried to appear official as she held her iPhone surreptitiously at her side. She was glad that she had practiced shooting images from the hip that afternoon since it was going to be tough getting the shots they needed. Trusting that she was getting the right images, Sonia walked forward, bumping directly into Jet's back. Jet had stopped moving, and the room had gone silent.

Standing so close to Jet, and being quite a bit smaller, Sonia had to lean to her left and look around Jet to see what was in front of both of them. Her eyes went first to the bed at the back of the room. There she saw the bimbo, her lips red, her body robust, a stunned look on her face. She was trying desperately to find something with which to cover herself. Unfortunately for her, all she could get her hands on was a thin, bright pink, gauzy, scarf that was already covering her most private parts. Then Sonia's eyes found Robert "Bob" Dylan, the dastardly, devious, demonic, douche bag, whose perverted predilections had brought them all into this room on an evening so early in the spring.

For Sonia, it was as if the entire space were filled with water—each motion silent, each facial expression exaggerated by distress. Floating before her, she saw the bimbo's hands now clutching her breasts. She could see Jet staring at Bob, the "Oh," on his lips giving the impression of him being a large fish.

Sonia blinked her eyes, and just as quickly as the room had seemed to fill with water, the sensation of suspended animation dissipated. Bob's thin and veined hands began to shake so violently that the paint on the end of his paintbrush splattered, creating a small pattern of bright pink that illuminated the fringes of his wiry beard and spraying several spots on the gray tee-shirt he wore over his carpenter jeans. His eyes were wide behind his John Denver glasses.

Everything and everyone in the room began to move and make sounds at once. The bimbo finally let out a scream, "Ahhhh!" Bob stuttered, "Who, who are you? What, what . . ." Sonia's eyes scanned the room furiously.

Jet just stood there. "Sheeeeeet," she whispered.

Finally, Sonia's eyes found it. Right next to the easel at which Bob had been working, the wooden box that Bad Boy Bob had always carried into the sessions lay open. Sonia's eyes widened. Up close, it was obviously too small for sex toys, but it worked perfectly well for paintbrushes. Damn, he's not over here doing crazy shit, he's painting. He's painting a portrait of the bimbo. Damn it. He's painting a freakin' portrait of the bimbo.

When Sonia had first seen the bimbo, she'd thought, "Wow, she's really built." Suddenly it hit her, so was Mrs. Dylan, and they looked a lot alike as well. Sonia took a quick look around the room. Really. Is that it? Is he just painting a portrait of his own wife and using the bimbo as a model?

Sonia turned to Jet, who was still frozen, and whispered, "C'mon! We screwed up. We've got to get out of here. C'mon! We've got to go!"

Jet didn't respond. As Sonia stepped around her, trying to

move Jet out the door, the look on Jet's face told Sonia one thing: Jet was desperately disappointed that Bob was not being unfaithful. It appeared to Sonia that Jet wanted Bob to be evil, so she could help bring down fire and brimstone upon him. And the fact that Jet continued to stand there, frozen, told her Jet still had some strange hope that could all still come to pass.

Sonia looked quickly around the room one last time. "C'mon girl. Let's go!" Then over her shoulder, she shouted. "No gas here! No gas here! Wrong house, sorry. Next house. Sorry!" With that, she pushed Jet backward out of the apartment, grabbed her hand, and pulled her out of the house, onto the wet, cold porch.

Sonia kept pulling, but Jet resisted. She stood on the porch, tears running down her face. It broke Sonia's heart, but she had no words. Sonia could hear things coming to life in the apartment, the bimbo yelling, "Call the police, damn it! Call the damn police!"

Sonia spoke again, less urgent, but with authority. "We've got to go, girl. C'mon. Take my hand. Let's get out of here." Finally, with one more tug, Sonia felt Jet begin to follow. They walked quickly back to the office, Sonia feeling uncomfortable that they were still wearing their "gas company" shirts. Neither said a word.

Climbing those slick stairs was not easy, but with each step, Sonia felt like they were putting some space between them and a terrible, terrible, experience. Sonia grasped the wet, cold, door knob. Up here, no one will find the two gas company imposters. Up here no policeman will find the two PIs who stepped over the line. She looked at the hurt that was still etched on Jet's face. And up here no one else has to know how much you hurt. No one—unless you want them to know.

Together, they walked back into Jet's office. Sonia reached up and touched Jet gently on the cheek, "Can I make us some coffee, sweets?"

Jet plopped down in her chair. Her hair was damp, her face

drawn. She spoke softly. "Not unless you spell coffee b-o-u-r-b-o-n. And use the water tumbler, this is no time for a rocks glass."

"Sure, sure." Sonia found two semi-clean glasses in Jet's armoire. She thought about the bottle of Angel's Envy bourbon she kept in her own desk drawer.

Sonia wiped out the glasses as Jet spoke to the floor. "And listen, I'm sorry. I'm so sorry."

Sonia held up a glass to the light. "No, no, you're okay. It's okay." She turned to face Jet.

Jet looked at Sonia. "I lost it, I freakin' lost it, didn't I?"

Sonia didn't say a word. But her eyes spoke of understanding and acceptance.

Tears started flowing down Jet's cheeks again. "I just got so crazy. It's just that . . . I guess it's just that I never really came to grips with what that bastard did to me. It hurt."

Sonia moved close to Jet and handed her an empty glass. Then she reached over and stroked Jet's hair tenderly as Jet opened her heart. "He hurt me, really hurt me. I was so damn embarrassed. I was mortified. My husband was cheating on me in the van we bought so we could have kids, and I never knew it." She looked up. "How could I have been so stupid, Sonia? How could I have been so clueless?"

Finally, standing close to her, Sonia pulled Jet's head close to her body. "Shhhh. It just happens. It wasn't your fault."

Jet spoke into Sonia's torso. "I know. I know, but still . . ."

Sonia turned Jet's face upward toward her own. "Still, nothing. It was him. He did it. You did nothing wrong. He did it. And you dealt with it. Good for you. You dealt with it and you've moved on."

It was Jet's turn to say nothing. She just buried her head back into Sonia's torso.

The dark emptiness of the BCI waiting area created a stark contrast to the warmth and light of the friendship that Sonia felt in Jet's office. She continued. "And sure, it's going to come back

and bite you in the butt every once in a while, but you're past it.
You've started a new life and you're past it. And I'm thrilled to be
part of that new life. I'm thrilled to be your partner and your
friend."

Jet took Sonia's hand in hers and squeezed it. She looked up.
"You're the best, Sonia." Then she wiped the tears away from her
face with the back of one hand. "Now, where the hell's that bourbon. You going to hold out on me all night, or what?"

Sonia squeezed back, then turned and walked toward her
own office. "I keep the good stuff in the bottom drawer of my
desk," she said over her shoulder, "just like all those crusty old
PIs on TV. Rocks?"

"Rocks. I plan on drinking more than I can handle without a
little bit of ice melting in there. I've got a lot of crap I need to
wash away, and tonight's as good a night as any to get started."

PART V

31

S onia's Friday had started early, too early by her standards. She'd been at the office by seven-thirty in order to have a short meeting with Teresa Torres. As early in the morning as it was, Teresa had arrived with her large, well-endowed body covered in a loose-fitting, black, yellow, and red dress. Her dark, wavy hair had hung on her shoulders, sometimes obscuring the long, dangling, red-enameled earrings she wore. There had been no missing the bright red lipstick that had highlighted her broad face.

Just as Brad had coached her, Sonia had told Teresa that after two weeks of surveillance, she had no reason to believe that Marcos Torres was having any kind of extra relations with other women. "In fact," she'd said to Teresa, "it's common for stable hands to use a product called Mane and Tail on the animals, and that product can often smell like a woman's fragrance."

Sonia had thought she would be okay with the lie. She knew it was essential to keep Teresa from snooping around the farm—for her own sake if nothing else. She'd also made up some story about having been able to blend several jobs together, allowing her to charge Teresa less than their original agreement had called for.

All of Sonia's rationalizations had flown out the window when Teresa had stood up and started gyrating, doing a happy dance. "My man's okay, my man's okay, the boy's been keepin' it in his pants. *Mi viejo se porta bien!*" she'd sung, dancing herself all over Sonia's office. Then Teresa had turned back to Sonia and said, "Tonight I'm gonna make the boy the most wonderful dinner. I'll call him today, and whatever he wants, that's what I'm gonna make for him. Then after dinner, *vamos a hacerlo hasta que no padamos más!*"

Sonia's face had been one big question mark.

Teresa had smiled and translated, "We gonna do it 'til we can't do it no more! Thank you, thank you, Ms. Vitale. Thank you for your help."

Teresa had laid her money down on Sonia's desk, reached over and half-pulled Sonia across the desk. Leaning in, she'd kissed Sonia on the forehead, leaving a red lipstick impression there, along with the strong fragrance of her perfume. Then Teresa had turned and headed for the door. As she went, she'd swung her hips and her arms and sung, "My man's okay. My man's okay. The boy's been keepin' it in his pants."

As the door had banged shut, Sonia had pursed her lips, picked up the cash, and threw it in a small metal box she kept in her desk. The guilt of lying to Teresa while taking her money had made her sick—actually, physically sick. She'd slammed the desk drawer shut and spoken to the space that had just been filled with the celebratory gyrations of a happy Teresa Torres. "Yeah, and when you call him to ask about dinner, I hope he's not screwing some whore or out delivering drugs."

～

AT NINE-THIRTY, Sonia walked up the steps of the white house, through the first door, and into the offices of Semper Fi Investigations.

Brad looked up from his desk. "Hi." As she moved toward the desk, he continued, "Come on over here and sit down. I've been working on something and I need your help."

"What's that?" She moved to one of the wheat-colored chairs.

"I've been going over and over the communications we intercepted, and some of them still have me baffled. Do you have your phone with you, the one you keep your notes on?"

"Of course." She reached into her purse.

"The more I go over these communications, the more I get the sense that we're missing a key player, maybe more than one key player." He picked up a pencil and began tapping it on his desk.

"What do you mean?"

"Listen, we believe that Toro is the code name for the person at the top of this chain, right?"

She nodded. "Right."

"And we believe Forty is a code name for Hollings, the person running the operation here in Lexington."

"Uh huh."

"Well, what if Toro's not the top of the chain, but rather, only the beginning of the chain?" Brad stood up and started pacing around the room. "There are just so many different communications flying around in that system. I still don't have it all clear in my mind." Brad paused and looked directly at Sonia. "Could you write some sort of computer program that would help us sort some of these things out?"

"What kind of program?" A tiny quiver ran through her body. She knew her way around computers, but . . . .

"Something that might lock into the few actual times and dates that we know for sure certain things happened. Knowledge we've gained from your prior surveillance."

"I don't know, maybe. Maybe if I set up a few benchmark points in a database and —"

"Hold on, hold on. Something's going down. Look." Brad was pointing to the computer monitor on the far table, the one that was receiving the feed from the cameras surveilling Dahlia Farm. He walked closer to the table. "There it is, our favorite feed and hay truck." He turned to Sonia and smiled. "Looks like we're on babe. Grab your stuff. Time to roll!"

Sonia sat still for just a moment. Her heart jumped. Her brain raced. Here it was, the plan they had been talking about was suddenly exploding into reality. She and Brad were about to take off, following pickup trucks loaded with drugs—drugs that would be delivered to places unknown.

"SONIA!" Brad shouted. "Now! It's on now! We've got to roll! Go! Go! Go!"

SONIA AND BRAD both knew that they only had about thirty minutes to get out to the castle and wait for the first pickup truck to roll by. They had each gone in their own car since Brad had explained to Sonia that a long-term surveillance like this demanded at least two different chase vehicles. He had also given Sonia a walkie-talkie so they could stay in constant contact without messing with their cell phones.

As they were nearing the castle, Sonia pressed the talk button on her walkie-talkie. "Where are you? I don't see your Corvette anywhere."

"Listen, little lady. If you're going to do visual surveillance and don't want to be seen in the first two minutes, you don't do it in a brand-new Corvette. I'm driving a gray three-year-old Toyota Corolla, the most nondescript vehicle on the road. America's most popular car. Reliable, and no one ever notices them."

"Oh." She pursed her lips. Damn. I should've realized that.

By ten o'clock the two cars, Sonia's Subaru and Brad's Corolla, were waiting, parked on opposite sides of the turn onto Pisgah

Pike. That way they knew they would be covered, whichever direction the pickup took. First, the feed and hay truck rolled by. That was something they would deal with on another day. Then, as they had guessed, the first pickup, the bright green one, came to the castle and turned left. It headed toward the roads that would lead to the interstate. Sonia's car was facing that direction, so she was the first one to pick up the tail. She knew Brad would wait a few moments, then make a U-turn and begin following more than a half-mile behind.

The green pickup led them to the circle around the city, and then up to Interstate 75. It headed south, just as it had the previous week. After all three vehicles had turned onto to the highway, Brad used the walkie-talkie. *"Time for you to drop back. I've got it for a while."*

Following the pickup had been a bit nerve-racking for Sonia. The last time she had followed this truck, she had been curious as to what the heck was going on at Dahlia Farm. This time she knew she was dealing with hardened drug dealers—people who most probably had murdered John Abbott Hensley. The opportunity to drop back and let Brad take the lead for a while gave her a small sense of relief. For the first time in nearly twenty-five minutes, she took a deep breath.

The green pickup traveled south for another half hour or so. Every ten or twelve minutes Brad and Sonia would reverse positions, one dropping back, the other moving closer to the pickup. Between them, they kept the pickup in sight. Just before eleven o'clock, the pickup left the interstate and headed into Richmond, Kentucky, the home of Eastern Kentucky University. *"No surprise here,"* said Brad. *"College town. Got to be at least a few customers for that stuff."*

"How sad."

As they came off the interstate, it was Brad who was behind the pickup. Soon, however, his voice came to Sonia over the walkie-talkie. *"Your turn girl. Get up behind this guy. You can stay*

pretty close since you'll both be in traffic. If he turns, though, you go
straight and I'll follow him on the turn. But then get behind us quickly,
because if he turns again I might have to pass him and go straight
myself."

Sonia's heart was pounding as she slipped in, only two cars
behind the pickup. Fortunately, it wasn't long before it pulled into
a strip mall parking lot. The storefront at the corner housed a
low-end movie rental joint. The pickup slowed, then drove
around to the back of the building, pulling up to the rear door of
the movie store. Since there was lots of room in the parking lot,
Sonia was able to park quite a distance away and keep her eyes
on the truck. "He's pulled up behind some movie place."

"Just stay back and keep a low profile. Let's see how long he stays."

Sonia was quite certain this would be a quick drop-off since
she assumed the driver of the pickup had several other stops to
make. To her surprise, the driver stayed inside for almost forty
minutes.

Sonia pressed the "TALK" button on the walkie-talkie.
"What's taking him so long?"

"Listen, these guys are not necessarily striving for, "Employee of the
Month," awards. Our pal in the pickup might just be spending a few
moments sharing in the pleasures of the product he's delivering, or at
least in some other kind of dope these guys have on hand."

Finally, Sonia saw the driver coming out. "I think you may be
right, he's got quite a grin going. Looks more like he visited with
old friends than like he made a delivery."

"Par for the course sometimes. Now heads up. I assume he's headed
back to the interstate. I'll follow him there. You lay back a couple of
cars. But if he gets on, I'll keep going and you pick him up. You'll have
plenty of time to catch up before he has a chance to get off at his
next stop."

Sonia watched the pickup pull out of the parking lot and the
Corolla follow. It wasn't long before she saw the pickup take the
ramp down to I-75 South. Brad continued past the interstate as if

he had nothing to do whatsoever with the pickup. Sonia, on the other hand, cruised down to the highway and slowly but surely kept her speed just a little bit faster than she imagined the pickup was travelling. Within a few minutes, Sonia was about a half-mile behind the green truck and had a clear view of it on the straightaways. About ten minutes later, Brad cruised by, smiling at her as he passed. Sonia backed off for a while.

The game of leapfrog continued for another twenty minutes or so until the pickup left the interstate near the small town of Berea. Again, the town was home to a college community. This time it was Brad who followed the pickup from the interstate to his drop-off point and Sonia who picked him up as he worked his way back to the highway.

As the afternoon wore on, the pattern was becoming very clear to Sonia. The pickup kept traveling south, down the interstate. Every time the driver came to a town with a college or university, he would pull off, find a local drop-off point, spend a few minutes "visiting," then move on. There were also a few stops in very small towns, towns in which there was no college or university. Still, she knew there must have been dealers or customers looking for product.

By seven o'clock, dusk had already begun to fall and the pickup had traveled over the state line into Tennessee, up and over Jellico Mountain. Brad's voice came to Sonia. *"Well, very interesting, Nice to see we're crossing state lines. That opens up new opportunities for us to pull together federal resources."*

"Absolutely," replied Sonia, although the thought had never crossed her mind. "Do you think our boy is running out of things to deliver?"

"I wouldn't be surprised. You can be sure he won't be making any stops on the way back. These guys want to get that stuff off their truck as soon as they can so that if they ever do get stopped, they have as little product on them as possible. There's no way he passed a drop-off point, thinking he'd catch it on the way back."

Around seven-twenty, well after dusk, Sonia followed the pickup off the interstate at an exit marked Rocky Top. "Is there really a Rocky Top, Tennessee? I know the name from the song, but—"

"*Actually, the exit was called Lake City until just recently. Don't quite know why they changed it, but it might just be about that song.*" She could tell he was enjoying himself.

Sonia followed the truck for quite a while this time, further from the interstate than at any of the other stops. Eventually, the driver turned the pickup down a long street that ended in a dead end. Sonia picked up the walkie-talkie. "Brad, he's turned onto a dead-end street. It's kind of an industrial area. I can't drive past him, and I'm afraid he might notice me if I stop." The pitch of her voice was rising.

"*No choice. Just pull over as soon as you can and kill your lights.*"

Sonia did exactly that, pulling up to the curb and killing her lights and her engine.

She squeezed the walkie-talkie harder. "Now what?" Her voice rose again. "Are we going to be okay?"

"*Just sit still. Don't move around a lot in the car. Absolutely don't do anything that would make a light come on. In fact, make sure your phone is buried in your purse, just in case it rings and lights up. Don't panic, babe, I'm right here behind you.*"

Sonia looked in her mirror. She couldn't see the Corolla. Her body was frozen in her seat. She struggled to keep her breathing from shattering that stillness. She desperately wanted to slip out of the car and go back to wherever the hell Brad was, but she knew opening the car door would light her up—and that was the last thing she needed. She held the walkie-talkie close to her chest.

Sonia watched the driver get out of his truck. Maybe it was because the driver had done all the "visiting" he could handle and still keep driving, but he was less cautious than he had been. He reached into the back of the truck and pulled out two white packages, carrying them through the front door of one of the only buildings on the block that still had lights on at that hour.

"Brad," Sonia whispered, "he just went inside with two more packages. I saw it myself."

"Patience, Sonia. This is how we play the game. Just be patient."

Within a few minutes, the driver walked out and headed for the truck. As he opened the door, he stopped and looked up the street.

It seemed to Sonia that he was staring at her car, checking it out. She felt her heart pound under the walkie-talkie. Her foot tapped furiously on the floorboard. "Brad," Sonia whispered, "I think he may have made me. I'm a quarter of the way down the block. He's at the end, and he keeps staring and craning his neck—as if he's trying to make out who's in the car."

"Sonia, listen, he can't see you in the dark. He's just wondering about the car. Just don't move. Don't move a muscle. Let's see what he does."

Sonia's hand slid back and forth on her leg.

"Just hang in, girl. Just hang in."

Her hand kept rubbing. "Brad. Brad. He's getting in the truck."

"Yes, of course. He's getting ready to leave. This is going to be over in just a few moments. Hold tight, Sonia, just hold tight."

"He's started the truck. Here he comes." The words came out fast.

Brad didn't answer.

"Did you hear me . . . are you still there?" No answer.

"Brad! Brad!" she whispered in full panic. "He's driving slowly, super slowly. Brad, he's coming to get me, I know he's coming to get me!" The words came out faster and faster.

Still, no answer.

She whipped her head around. Empty street. Shit!

The truck slowly approached. As it did, Sonia slid down between the front seat and the steering wheel. Squeezing. Twisting. At five-foot-four she was not a tall girl, but neither was she tiny. Still, as panic drove her, she slid and scrunched until she was totally on the floor in front of the driver's seat—her body crammed below the steering wheel and contorted around the gas and brake pedals. The smell of the rubber mat. Dirt. Wires pressed into her neck. She desperately avoided hitting the brake pedal. Brake lights would doom her for sure.

Sonia heard the dark growl of the pickup's powerful engine as it approached her car. Then, alongside her car, the truck stopped. Her car shook in response to the vibrations coming from the muscular machine. Sonia kept her head forced downward; she couldn't look up. Still, she sensed a light beam searching through her car. She didn't move. She didn't breathe. She could do neither.

The pickup sat next to her car, rumbling ominously. An eternity passed. Finally, the light disappeared. The pickup's engine came to life with a roar. The truck pulled away.

Sonia took her first real breath. It hurt. She was still contorted in a position she wasn't sure she could ever get out of.

Suddenly, there was a rapping on the window. Sonia screamed.

32

Her scream still echoing through the car, Sonia was in full panic mode. She fought to move. She was stuck.

Sonia heard something click against the side of her car. Her heart jumped. The door opened. Her body jolted. A hand forced itself in, squeezing between her and the seat. Suddenly, the seat moved back several inches. Two powerful hands slid under her armpits and began pulling her from her contorted position—hard. She fought—wildly. Her body did not unfold gracefully. She all but fell out of the car and onto the street, her back bent, her butt on the pavement. She was pulled up to a standing position—squirming—struggling. He turned her.

Brad's bright blue eyes looked into Sonia's. She totally lost it. She threw her arms around his neck and pulled herself into him. Tears flowed. She could barely catch her breath. "He was right here. Right here." Her voice trembled.

"I know, but he's gone now. It's over. He's gone." His voice was soothing.

Sonia stood shaking in Brad's arms. She pulled back, "Where were you?" Then louder, "Where were you?" Soon, she was yelling, beating on Brad's chest, "Where the hell were you?

Where did you go? How could you do that? How could you leave me?" Her Italian rage broke through. "Where the hell were you, *figlo di puttana*?"

"Hold on, hold on!" Brad yelled back. He grabbed her wrists, stopping her from hitting him, though she tried with all her might. "Just hold on, I never left you. I was right here the whole time. I was with you."

Her foot stomped. "Where? Where were you? I never saw you! I never heard you! I—"

Brad pulled her close to him, burying her face in his chest. Though she continued to struggle, his big hand reached around the back of her head and pulled it so close to him she could feel his buttons on her face. She lost her will to fight.

"Shhhh. It's alright, it's alright. Shhhh."

As he held her, Sonia's rage slipped away. He stroked her head. The shaking of her body slowed. Finally, she rested in his arms.

Sonia turned her face away from his chest and allowed Brad to lead her to the curb. They sat down. Sonia noticed something long and thin resting against the car. "What's that?"

"What's what?"

Sonia pointed. "What's that against the car?"

Brad shook his head. "Oh. That's an M16 assault rifle, the kind I used in Iraq."

She looked at him. "Where did that come from?"

He looked straight ahead. "Do you mean where did that come from today, or where did that come from in general?"

Sonia shot him a look.

Brad looked at the weapon, then straight ahead again. "It's mine. Lots of surplus arms floating around after the war. I thought it would be nice to have the same kind I had over there."

"And today? Where did that come from today?" She sat on the curb, hugging herself.

He turned back to her. "Listen, I told you before, I'm pretty sure these boys play for keeps. You didn't expect me to go chasing one of them without bringing a sidearm and a little something extra, did you?"

She rocked back and forth slowly. "So, you brought the gun with you all day?"

His eyes went forward then down to the ground. "Of course. It was in the trunk. When you told me that you thought the driver had made you, I stopped my car before he could see me. That's why I wasn't answering you. I'd crept around the corner. The whole time he was sitting next to you, shining that light, I had him in my sights." He turned to her and his blue eyes held her. "If he had gotten out of the car, or even lifted a gun, I would have dropped him."

Sonia stopped rocking. "You would have shot him? Just like that?"

He grinned. "Well, the first shot might have been a warning, but if he went after you, I would have shot him. Just like that." He turned away again.

They sat in silence. Sonia kept running scenario after scenario through her mind, each one ending in death, either hers or the driver's. She imagined Brad was doing the same.

Finally, she leaned forward, hoping to catch his eyes. "What's that like?"

He didn't look at her. "What's what like?"

She put her hand on his leg, inviting him toward her. "Deciding you're going to shoot somebody if he does something."

Brad hesitated for a few moments. He looked down at the ground. Then, softly, he simply said, "Training."

Sonia waited for him to elaborate. Finally, she prodded. "Training?"

"Look, Sonia, you know that I was a Marine." He turned to her. "You know I was in combat. How do you think we learned to fight other men, to kill them before they killed us? Training, ma'am, training." His eyes drifted over her shoulder. "It starts the day you enter the Corps. From the moment you step off the bus, they start training you to be something you never really thought you could be. And it's not that they try to turn you into a monster, someone who likes killing. It's the total opposite. From the moment you get off the bus you're made to feel responsible for the people around you. The guys in your squad. The guys in your platoon. And then it grows and grows. You start to feel responsible for every other Marine who's there with you—and for the people you've been sent to protect." He stopped to take a breath. He looked at her. "The sense of responsibility, that's what makes you knock down a door and burst through it, hoping no one is there waiting to blow your head off."

Brad picked up a pebble and threw it. "It's that sense of responsibility that's driven into you and that drives you to do things. And it's the training that's drilled into you that allows you to know how to do it." He looked at her. "Do you want to know what crossed my mind the moment I put my hands on that M16?"

Sonia had been silenced by his passion. She shook her head.

He turned away again, searching for another pebble. "The moment I put my hand on that weapon—" He found one and threw it in the same direction as the other. "—the moment I put my hand on that weapon, these words flew through my brain:

The M16 is a lightweight, 5.56 millimeter, air-cooled, gas-operated, magazine-fed assault rifle with a rotating bolt, Sir! The M16 weighs 7.9 pounds loaded with a 30-round magazine of M193 cartridges, Sir! It can fire as a fully automatic weapon or in three-round bursts, Sir! The M16 is effective at 500 yards, 711 yards horizontal, lethal at 984 yards, and has a maximum range of 3000 yards, Sir! A skilled Marine can place a 10-shot group in a 4.3-inch grouping at 100 meters, Sir! A very skilled Marine can place a 10-shot group in a 12.6-inch grouping at 300 meters, Sir! I will be a very skilled Marine, Sir!

I said those words a thousand times and they came back to me as if I was still standing in Boot Camp on Parris Island. Training, training, and more training."

Sonia reached out and slipped her hand under and around his arm, never taking her eyes off him. "And you could have shot him from all the way down the block?"

Brad didn't push her arm away. He just kept looking forward. "Training, ma'am."

"And you would have shot him if you thought he was going to hurt me?"

"Training, ma'am. Training and responsibility." He was out of pebbles.

There was a long silence. Tears began sliding down her cheeks. Brad didn't ask her why, and Sonia was glad. Her heart stopped when he slipped his arm free, then grabbed her chin with his large hands, holding her face up to his. She closed her eyes, hoping desperately that he would lean over and kiss her. He did.

It was a brief kiss at first, but her emotions exploded and she reached up and threw her arms around him. Brad didn't resist. He pulled her so close to him she could hardly breathe.

He kissed her deeply, their tongues intertwined, dancing with each other.

Sonia wanted to melt into his body. She pulled herself closer and closer to him, losing herself in his embrace, in his mouth, in his being. Tears continued to flow down her face, mixing the taste of his mouth with the saltiness of her own tears. Every part of her body released its pent-up emotions, turning her into a wet, molten force.

Suddenly, Brad pulled his mouth away from hers and forced her face down against his chest. Though he continued to hold her tight and began to stroke her head again, Sonia could feel him turning down the heat of the moment. Clearly, he had been fully engaged with her in the incredible emotion of the moment. Clearly, he was now bringing it to an end.

They were sitting on a curb, on a deserted street in some strange town. Sonia took a deep breath. Yeah, enough. We've got to stop. Good, good. Enough. Yet, her body, her heart, and her mind yearned for more.

"Okay, then," said Brad, breaking the mood, releasing her physically. "Maybe it's time we get ourselves together and get back home."

Sonia wiped her face with the back of her hand. She felt like a wreck and a bit confused, but she had to admit to herself that she and Brad had done something dangerous and important, and that they had done it well. She gave him a tiny smile. "Maybe we should."

33

At ten-thirty on Saturday morning, Sonia walked into Magee's, pushed through the weekend crush of folks, and walked up to the counter.

"Well, don't we look like we've been rode hard and put up wet," said Hildy, smiling. Then more seriously, "Everything okay?"

"Sure. Everything's just fine. Just had a hell of a day and a hell of a night. I'm only coming in for a little while today, but I did need my coffee . . . and a little something different today."

"How 'bout one of our sticky buns. They're a real favorite. Lots of folks like 'em." Hildy gave her a tenuous smile "Tell you what. Looks like you could use a treat." She leaned forward and whispered. "The bun's on the house."

"Sounds good." There was a smile on Sonia's face, but she was bone tired. The stress of following that pickup all day yesterday—the absolute panic on that lonely street—those things had taken a lot out of her.

And then there was Brad. Oh, my gosh. What was all of that about? Sonia poured herself a cup of coffee. I was so afraid. And he was . . . . Do I really feel that much for him, or was it just the emotion of the night?

Sonia stood by the coffee station, mindlessly stirring and stirring her coffee. "Excuse me," a voice said, and Sonia almost jumped out of her skin. Somehow, with last night's harrowing experience still fresh in her mind, she had flashed instantly on a fear that this was some new threat. "Oh, I'm sorry," said Sonia, embarrassed at being so lost in her thoughts. Her heart quieted quickly when she saw a young man wearing brown chinos and a faded, black Grateful Dead tee shirt, and holding a little boy's hand. He was simply trying to get to the sugar and cream for his coffee.

She said, "Sorry," again and stepped aside. She thought about last night. And Brad? What did all that mean to him? Does he really feel something for me, or does that sort of crisis elicit powerful emotion, even in a hardened soldier? Why did he kiss me so passionately . . . and why did he stop?"

Sonia was brought back to reality again when two little children came running by, almost knocking her coffee out of her hand. Frustrated, she looked around, wondering where in the world the parents were. Finding them scrunched in the line that already went out the front door, and oblivious to their children's antics, she shuddered a tiny bit. It's a different place on the weekend, isn't it? She headed for the door.

Stepping out into the bright sun of what was turning out to be a very nice spring day, Sonia headed for her office. She turned the corner and looked up those steps—the stiffness in her body, especially her legs, made them seem more daunting than ever. Still, up she plodded, step by step until she reached the top. She turned the ancient handle and entered her domain. More than ever, it felt like home to her.

That feeling was strengthened when she heard Jet's voice sing out across the room from behind her desk. "Wellll, hello there! Didn't think you'd be coming in, it being Saturday and all. And look how bright and shiny you look, darlin'." Her southern accent kicked up a notch. "Bless your heart."

"Okay, wiseass, enough."

Jet snorted. "Oh, now *I'm* the wiseass?"

"If the shoe fits . . . ." Sonia walked into Jet's office and took her customary seat across from Jet's desk. She offered Jet half of her sticky bun, which Jet accepted gladly. "Listen, the only reason I'm here is to see how yesterday went with Detective Sergeant Johnny Adams and little Ralphie McCormick."

"Is that the only reason?" Jet looked at her over her invisible glasses. "Really?"

Sonia squirmed a bit in the chair. "Well, no. I *do* want to tell you about my day, but you first. How did things go?"

Jet's eyes lit up. "Splendid. Splendid all the way around."

"How so?"

"Well," said Jet, returning to the quasi-southern accent she often used when telling a funny story, "first, DSA—that's what I call Detective Sergeant Adams—he was disappointed that it was me waitin' for him and not you. Each time you and I talked and put off your arrival, he got just a little more agitated. By the time you told me that you wouldn't be makin' it at all, he was hoppin' mad, though he tried not to show it."

"And you were loving that, weren't you?"

"Oh, yes, I was, girl." She wore a big smile.

"And Ralphie? Did he play his part for us?" Sonia popped the last bite of her pastry into her mouth. She was surprised how much she was enjoying the sticky bun, but it wasn't just the bun that was sticky—she licked the sugar off her fingertips.

"Oh yes, he did, and in a very big way. We watched from the parking lot and saw him enter the restaurant early, before the other employees showed up for work. He was in there quite a while, doing what he does, I suppose. But then, just about lunchtime—and by then we'd moved around to the front entrance—here comes Ralphie." Jet moved forward in her chair and leaned her elbows on her desk, pushing away a stack of miscellaneous notes. She was obviously enjoying telling the story. "Now you know that yesterday was a pretty decent day, but ol' Ralphie, he's got his winter coat on and it's all zipped up like he's off to Alaska or something. That's when DSA slowly steps out of the car and walks up to Ralphie all nice and pleasant, takin' his sweet time."

Sonia cleared a spot on the corner of Jet's desk and put down her coffee. "Does Ralphie panic?"

The grin on Jet's face got even bigger. "Not at first. In fact, ol' DSA takes his time, tellin' Ralphie how much he likes the restaurant, how he likes to take his mother there for special occasions."

"And Ralphie?" Sonia used her napkin, trying to wipe her sticky fingers clean.

"Sweatin' like a pig lookin' down at a fire pit on the fourth of July."

"Nice." Sonia gave up on the wiping and threw her napkin in Jet's trash.

"And that's not all. Then ol' DSA, he starts talkin' about how his favorite things to eat there are the steaks, or is it the fish? 'No,' he says, 'I think it's the steak.' Then he goes on to say that next time he'll probably order the surf and turf and get both."

Jet picked up the pace. "By then Ralphie must know for sure that he's been caught. He starts fidgetin' and squirmin', so much so that all of sudden this huge piece of fish slides down his pant leg and lands on his shoe, just as nice as you please. You know what DSA says then?"

Sonia shook her head. "I can only imagine."

Jet got up and walked to her armoire, laughing as she spoke. "He says, 'I guess we can call that probable cause unless, of course, that's some new kind of deodorant you're usin'.'"

Jet returned to her desk with a small flask of something Sonia assumed was bourbon. She poured some into her coffee and held the flask out to Sonia. Sonia begged off.

Jet put the flask down on her desk. "Right then ol' Ralphie starts bawlin' and says that he didn't mean to steal nothin', he just needed a little bit of extra cash to take care of his sick wife." Jet sat back down, still smiling. "Of course, DSA, and everyone else in town, knows that Ralphie's wife left him two years ago. So DSA makes him open his coat and there's another big fish and several beautiful pieces of beef all stuck down in the top of Ralphie's pants." Jet smiled and smacked her hands together. "Right there, DSA reads him his rights while he's pulling Ralphie's hands behind his back and cuffin' him." Jet wagged her head, "I got to tell you, sweetheart, it was one of the highlights of my short but noteworthy career as a PI."

Sonia rethought Jet's offer and reached out for the flask. "And Clay McCormick? Did Johnny get him involved right away?" She poured a little of the amber liquid into her coffee.

"No. He said this would all seem a lot more official if Clay didn't see the boy 'til he was sittin' in an interrogation room downtown. So DSA just put Ralphie up against his car and called in a cruiser. It wasn't five minutes later that three of 'em showed up, and one of 'em took Ralphie downtown."

Jet reached out with her coffee cup, obviously wanting to toast with Sonia. "Top to bottom, girl, it was a great plan, and it was all yours. You figured it out from the videos, you made the plan. I guess on TV they would have said, 'The collar's yours, Sonia.'"

Sonia smiled, appreciating the compliment, touched her paper cup to Jet's ceramic mug and took a sip. "Well, I'm glad everything worked out. Another case wrapped up and filed away. And one that pays, as well." Then she took another long sip of her coffee and gave her fingertips one last lick for good measure.

Jet sighed contentedly. "Is that all you want to know about?"

Sonia cocked her head. "What do you mean?" She noted that Jet's accent was gone. Did that mean something?

Jet gave Sonia another sly look. "Don't you want to know what was bothering ol' DSA all day?"

Sonia shrugged her shoulders. "The fact that he couldn't be out there following me around as I was working the Hensley case?"

"I don't think so," said Jet savoring the smell of the bourbon in her coffee. "It seemed to me that he was mostly disappointed because he wasn't going to get to spend the day with you."

A tiny charge went through Sonia's body. Jet lowered her chin again, and Sonia could tell that she was trying to gauge Sonia's reaction. "Really?" Sonia tried to her best to look unimpressed.

Jet rolled her chair back and crossed her long legs on her desk. "Really. Once we settled in, and he knew you weren't going to join him, ol' DSA started talking about you. Slowly at first, a little here, a little there. But after a while, while we were still waiting for Ralphie to show, he starts telling me how special he thinks you are. That you're smart as a whip, and persistent too. Aaand, the way you look, well, how did he put it?" She tapped her fingernails on her ceramic mug. "He said he wished he could be part of our company because then he'd be able to keep an eye on you." Jet stuck her finger in her mouth. "Gack. It was almost more than I could take."

"Get outta here," said Sonia, trying to find someplace other than Jet's face to look.

"Seriously, girl. This boy's got it bad for you." Jet took a deep breath. "Are you sure you're reading him right? Didn't he make it pretty clear the other night that he wanted to, what would you call it, slide between the sheets with you?"

"Oh, that." Sonia pursed her lips and shook her head quickly. "We were both just a little drunk." She was doing her very best to keep Jet from making a mountain out of this molehill.

Another big grin crossed Jet's face. "I'm not so sure, girl. I really think you've got to give him another look. He's a nice guy. Attractive, polite, nice."

Sonia sighed, her shoulders falling. "Oh, I don't know. Maybe, but, well . . ." Sonia put her cup down. "Brad. Something happened with Brad last night."

"Girlfriend." Jet pulled her legs off her desk and sat up tall in her chair. "Come on. Spill it."

Sonia took a deep breath. "Okay, so you know that Brad and I were following one of the pickups while he was delivering drugs."

"Uh huh."

"In fact, we went all the way down I-75 to Tennessee."

Jet simply nodded.

"So, on the last stop, I kind of got caught parked behind the guy on a dead-end street. I was sure he'd figured out I was following him, especially when he just stood there for a while staring at my car."

Jet furrowed her brows. "Ouch."

"Then Brad tells me to just stay still and let the guy pass—that it'll be alright. But I know he's seen me. I know he's going to come and get me, hurt me—maybe kill me."

"And Brad didn't do anything to help you?" Jet's voice was clearly accusatory.

Sonia's hand was trembling as she picked her cup up again. "Not at first. Or at least I didn't think so."

Jet shook her head slowly back and forth. "Bastard."

Sonia's voice rose. "No, you don't understand. While the guy was in his truck right by me, and I was crouched down under the steering wheel, hiding, Brad was down the block. He had the guy in the sights of his army rifle."

"He was aiming at the guy?" Jet's eyes opened wide.

"He was." Tears began running down Sonia's checks. "He told me later he was ready to kill the guy if he hurt me. Ready to shoot him right there."

"From down the block?"

Sonia's voice reflected a combination of re-experienced fear and pride. "Oh, he could have done it. No question. He could have done it."

Jet's face softened as she spoke. "Oh Sonia, I'm so sorry." She reached her hand across her desk and touched Sonia's for a brief moment.

Sonia reached for the box of tissues lying sideways on Jet's desk and blotted her tears. Her voice was very soft. "It's okay. Really, I'm okay."

There was a long silence in the room, only the muffled sound of the cars on the street below their office filled the room.

Then Sonia spoke again. "There's more."

Jet's eyes asked the question, *more?*

Sonia took another deep breath. "Yeah. After the guy left. After Brad explained how he'd been trained to watch out for people when he was in the Marines. Then he . . . well . . . he kissed me."

"He kissed you? For real kissed you?" Jet's face came alive.

Sonia sat forward in her chair, her hands crossed in her lap. "Well actually, I kissed him, but he kissed me back, and he meant it; I could tell. He took me in his arms. He just pulled me to him. He kissed me and it lasted a long time. I felt like . . . I don't know, but it was strong. But then he stopped. He just held me close and calmed things down."

"Why? Why did he stop?"

"I don't know." Sonia slumped back and sighed, tears forming in her eyes again. "Well, it is true that we were just sitting there on a curb. But still, it felt more like he was afraid. That he felt like we couldn't, or shouldn't, really go there."

"What do you think that's all about?"

"I don't know. All I know is that he's so . . . so strong, so brave, so honorable . . . and so distant" Her voice faded. "So, so distant."

At that moment, Sonia's cell phone rang. She reached into her purse and took out her phone. She swallowed. "Bluegrass Confidential Investigations. This is Sonia Vitale . . . . Oh, hi, Johnny." Her voice was flat.

Jet leaned back in her chair shaking her head.

"I don't know, I just had a cup . . . . You're right downstairs? Oh, okay. I guess just for a little while. I'll see you in a couple of minutes." Sonia's phone chirped, indicating that its battery had just died. She realized Johnny might not have gotten those final words.

"Lover boy?"

Sonia took a deep breath, looking down at the phone in her hand. She wiped a single tear away and tried to pull herself together. "I guess." She stood up and looked out the front window at the white house across the street. She sighed. "One wants to be with me, and I'm not sure I want to be with him. The other . . . well, I just don't know."

34

Sonia was feeling less than enthusiastic as she walked down the steps and turned into Magee's. Standing just inside the door, she searched the room for Johnny Adams. She found him sitting at the most intimate table in the place, stuck back in a corner. Of course.

Johnny stood as Sonia approached the table. "Well, don't you look nice?"

Sonia thought about how tired she was, how little time she had spent getting ready that morning, how puffy her eyes must be after she'd kind of lost it with Jet. That's a crock. Still, it was nice to hear the compliment. "Thanks," she said and took a seat.

"I know you already had some coffee, but I took the liberty of getting you a fresh cup. I hope that's all right."

The sound of his voice was just a bit too upbeat for Sonia at the moment. She gave him an acquiescent smile. "Sure, that's fine. It appears to be a coffee kind of day."

"Hey, I wanted to thank you for helping me hook up Ralph McCormick." Johnny's eyes were bright and his smile genuine. "Easy day's work, and every collar looks good in the old jacket. So, thanks."

"Of course. Honestly, it was you who was helping us out." Sonia emptied the sugar packet Johnny had brought with the coffee. "We really didn't want to be the ones who tried to tell Clay McCormick that his son was the one who's been ripping him off. You took care of that for us, and we still got the credit for having solved the case. Good news all the way around." She took her first sip.

There was a lull in the conversation and then Johnny asked, "So how was your day yesterday?"

Sonia stirred her coffee absentmindedly. Her calm, everyday actions belied the doubts about his intentions that were worming their way around in her mind. "Busy. Long and busy."

"I have to tell you that I was disappointed that I wound up working with Jet instead of you." He took a quick breath. "Not that there's anything wrong with Jet. She's great. It's just that I was hoping to get to spend some time with you." A subtle smile crossed his face. "Nothing like a stakeout to give you the time to build a relationship, you know." The message was far from subtle.

Sonia took a quick sip. "Yeah, I'm sorry about that. Something came up at the last minute, and I just had to deal with it. Maybe next time." She hoped her smile wasn't lacking something in the veracity department.

"Speaking of next time," Johnny continued brightly, "I was hoping that we could get together sometime early next week. Are you still planning on being out of town?"

Sonia was caught off guard by the question. She sucked in a breath and forced a wider smile. "My plans are just a bit up in the air right now." She knew that there was every chance that she and Brad might be chasing the feed and hay truck next week, and part of her still feared that Johnny was somehow checking up on her. If she told him she was going out of town, that might alert him to be ready to follow her. On the other hand, if she told him the trip was off, she would have to come up with some other excuse for not being able to go out with him. Sonia took a closer look at

Johnny. What is it that I have against this guy? He's as nice as can be to me. He obviously does want to see me. And according to Jet, he seems to have real feelings for me. Oh, damn, I don't know. The thoughts flew through her mind in a millisecond. "Well, we'll just have to see."

"Oh yeah, sure." Johnny shrugged and swirled the coffee in his paper cup. "Maybe you can just let me know how things develop."

Sonia was about to respond when she caught sight of bright, bright blue eyes staring at her and moving quickly toward the table. Her eyes flashed to Johnny and back. By that time, Brad had crossed the room in a few long strides and was looming over the table. "Brad, what are you doing here?"

"Trying to get in touch with you." Brad's voice was terse. "I've been calling you for the last ten minutes."

"Sorry . . . my phone . . . the battery's dead."

"Well, this is important, we need to talk right now. Things could be happening." Brad's tone was anything but friendly.

Embarrassed, Sonia didn't know what to say. The tension was broken momentarily as Johnny stood up to greet Brad. Still seated, Sonia started. "Brad, this is Detective Sergeant Johnny Adams. Johnny, this is Captain—"

"Brad. Brad Dunham." Brad's eyes flicked over to Johnny.

The two men shook hands, but the feeling at the table was anything but cordial. Brad looked down at Sonia "I'm going back to my office. I hope you can join me there as soon as possible." Then he turned to Johnny. "Nice to meet you, Sergeant." He was outside Magee's in a moment. The whole episode had taken less than a minute.

Sonia could feel the warmth in her cheeks. She looked at Johnny. "I'm so sorry. You shouldn't have had to hear that." Sonia thought about the lifeless phone in her purse. It's not my fault the damn battery in my phone went dead.

Johnny sat back down. "Wow, he's pretty intense. Is he always like that?"

"Not always," Sonia responded, still looking in the direction Brad had gone. *Not always.*

There was a long, awkward silence at the table. Finally, Johnny spoke tentatively. "Listen, I should let you go. You obviously need to go meet with . . . uh, Brad? Why don't you just give me a call when you know what next week is going to look like for you? Maybe we can find time to catch a drink after work or something."

Johnny smiled and stood up. Touching his fingers to his forehead, he gently saluted Sonia and took his leave.

Sonia sat and wondered. Here's this good-looking guy falling all over himself to be nice to me, and I'm fixated on a guy who sometimes sweeps me off my feet, and sometimes treats me like crap. What the hell am I doing, anyway? A few minutes later, she stood, braced herself, and left as well, dropping her half-consumed coffee in the trash. And into the lion's den, we go. This was not the same feeling she had experienced on the long trip home last night.

35

Sonia walked across the street to Brad's office. What was *that* all about? Was that jealousy? Or was he really that pissed that he couldn't get to me in ten minutes or less? What the hell's his deal? And what the hell's my deal? Sonia reached the steps that led up to the white house and stopped. She stood still, letting out a deep breath. Am I just looking to get beat up by some guy because he's handsome and strong and . . . whatever? How about nice and kind and considerate, like Johnny? She took another quick breath and started up the steps. Crap, I don't know. I just don't know.

Sonia knocked on the door to Brad's office. It struck her that after all they'd been through in the last day, she still felt the need to knock.

"Come in!"

Sonia stepped in, but she didn't quite know what to say. "You needed to see me?" It felt very unsatisfying.

Brad was sitting at his desk. He spoke without looking up. "Yes. But also, I'm sorry for interrupting your . . . your whatever with the sergeant."

"Detective Sergeant. And his name is Johnny Adams." This

time it was her voice that was terse. She clenched her teeth. *You're not getting off that easy.*

"Okay, yeah." He finally looked up at Sonia. "Still, I was impatient and I wanted to apologize. Thanks for coming over. Can I get you some coffee?"

Sonia almost laughed. "No thanks, I think I've had my fill." ... *of a lot of things today.* She took a seat on one of the chairs in front of his desk. *Yeah, yeah, I know, you're in the power seat and I'm not. Big whoopee.*

"Can we get started? Are you ready to work?" Suddenly, he was all business.

Sonia gave in to the softness of the seat. "Honestly, I'm kind of beat. I was hoping to get some rest today,"

"Oh...."

Sonia could see the dismissive look on Brad's face. She sat up as tall as she could in the damn chair. "No, no. I'm ready. I'm ready to go. What do we need to get done today?"

Brad plowed on, seemingly oblivious to her first response. "First, we need a plan for how we're going to handle it the next time that feed and hay truck comes to town. Then we need to get back to what we were talking about before things popped on Friday."

"The computer program?" Sonia felt a little flip in her stomach. The thought of writing a sophisticated program, not being clear what it was supposed to achieve, scared her.

"Yeah, the computer program."

"Alright, we can talk about that." She felt her anxiety rising. She was more than confident in her programming abilities, but she hated the thought of working under the pressure Brad was bringing to bear. "What about the plan for the truck?" She wanted off the topic.

"Okay." Brad stood and walked over to the table with the computer and other pieces of electronic wizardry on it. He picked up a small black box with a tiny antenna and turned back to her.

"I recently did a job for a major oil company in the eastern part of the Kentucky. It involved following one of their executives as he traveled through several states." He walked back to his desk. "It was too long a trip to follow him directly and hope to go unnoticed, so they sprang for a GPS locator with a range of about fifteen miles." He held the tiny device up and turned it around in his hand so Sonia could see. "I planted it on his car. I think we're in the same situation here."

Sonia peered at the device, intrigued. "Hmm."

"My guess is that we'll be gone at least two days following that truck, and doing straight ahead visual surveillance, there's no way he doesn't pick up on us after a while." He looked down again at the device. "That's why we'll need this." He smiled and shifted his gaze directly to her. "The question is how do we get the GPS locator onto the truck."

Sonia's head and shoulders pulled back imperceptibly. "What did you do before?"

Brad slipped down into his big, executive chair. His blue eyes twinkled and he got a real "country boy" grin on his face. "Oh, that was easy. I knew when the guy was in his office and where he parked his car. I just waited for a good opportunity and walked right up to it. I looked around to see if anyone was watching, then I stuck it under his rear bumper." He leaned forward, his elbows on his desk. "I'm afraid we're not going to get that opportunity with the truck."

Sonia thought for a moment. "I agree. That's going be a tricky bit of business."

"I do have an idea though," said Brad, raising his eyebrows and smiling a sly little smile. "That's if your partner, Jet, has the cojones to pull it off."

Sonia laughed out loud, her first good laugh in the last two days. "Are you kidding? If there's anything that Joyce Ellen Thomas is not lacking, it's cojones. You should have seen the plan she came up with to catch ol' Bob Dylan? Trust me, if Jet is consistent about anything, it's that she is always 'balls to the wall.' She's up for anything."

Brad stood and walked over to the coffee pot on the counter to the left of his desk. "Sure you don't want any?"

Coffee almost always sounded good to Sonia, but her nerves were jangled enough. She waved him off.

Brad poured himself a cup and turned to face her. "Okay then. If you think she's up to it, here's my plan." He took a sip. "We'll never get an opportunity to get to the truck when the driver isn't around, not here in Lexington. So, we'll have to place the locator under its bumper while he's sitting right there in the truck. That'll demand two things. First, the truck has to be stopped. Second, there has to be a distraction."

Sonia cocked her head. "Okay . . . ?"

Brad walked back to his desk and stood between it and the chair in which Sonia was sitting. He leaned back on the desk, crossing his legs at his ankles. "Now, we know that when the truck leaves Dahlia Farm it doesn't head directly for the interstate. It turns right at the castle instead. I assume he's heading for the Blue Grass Parkway or another farm, although he might be on his way to Louisville on 60. Either way, once he's turned at the castle, we've got to get him to stop, and we can't count on a traffic light or anything else like that."

Still struggling with sinking into the chair, Sonia put her hands on the cushion and pushed herself up just a bit. "So how do you plan on getting him to stop?"

He smiled broadly. "That's where your buddy Jet comes in. You and I will be in my car. Jet will be driving her car. Instead of following the truck, we'll need to get in front of him, right in front of him. We'll be communicating with Jet on our walkie-talkies." He put his coffee down on the desk behind him and used his hands to demonstrate the different positions of the cars and the truck. "When we've got my car right in front of the truck, and Jet right in front of us, we'll give her the signal and she'll come to a full stop, right in the road way. Of course, we'll pull up right behind her and, hopefully, the truck will be so close behind my car that he won't be able to get around us. Jet will cause a regular traffic jam, with at least the three of us fully stopped on the road."

Sonia blinked. This sounds crazy. "What then?"

"Then I get out of the car and walk right up to her." He gesticulated with large motions. "I'll make a big fuss, like maybe I almost wrecked my car. It's got to be enough of a commotion to keep the truck driver's attention focused on me and Jet."

"And?" The dread in her voice was pretty obvious.

"And that's when you get out of the car, nonchalantly, as if you just need to cool your jets or something." Brad was really getting into his portrayal. He stood up, no longer leaning against the desk, his body swaying as he spoke. "You start strolling around, moving back toward the truck and all the way past it. You'll have the walkie-talkie hidden in your hand, so when you're near the back of the truck you can give me a signal. I'll hear it, even though it's still in Jet's car. When you give me the signal I'll really blow up at her and start waving my arms or whatever." He bent toward her and lowered his voice almost to a whisper. "That's when you slip behind the truck and place the locator under its back bumper."

Sonia's eyes were wide open, as was her mouth. "What if there's another car behind the truck? Won't they see me doing that?"

Brad leaned toward her. "If we're lucky, we'll be able to make this happen when it's just the three vehicles and there won't be anybody there. If we're not lucky, and someone is sitting right there behind the truck," he cocked his head and smiled, "that's when you use those chocolate-brown eyes and that beautiful smile of yours. Just do what you need to do, give them a big friendly wave, and walk back to my car."

"And they'll buy that?"

Brad stood up straighter and leaned back against his desk and grinned. "Sometimes you've just got to take some chances, you know what I mean?"

Sonia took a big breath and let it out. "Wow. That's some plan. I've got to hand it to you, that's a hell of a plan." There was a pause while Sonia thought about things. "I can tell you one thing."

He sat down. "What's that?"

She gently bobbed her head. "No one will be more into the plan than Jet. This is right up her alley. Pedal to the metal all the way 'round the track."

Brad pointed right at her. "So, you think *you* can handle that?"

Determined to prove herself up to the challenge, she winked at Brad. "I can do it."

Brad cocked his head and grinned, a little perplexed. He turned his attention to some paperwork sitting on his desk.

Finally, Sonia asked, "And what about the computer program?" It was a challenging issue for her, but she didn't want to get caught napping.

Brad looked up. "I think you're right. If you benchmark some of the times and dates from your notes, we may be able to get a clearer picture of who is actually involved in this whole mess, at least here in Lexington. How long do you think it will take you to do that?"

The question threw Sonia a bit. She wasn't quite certain how to write the program, but she was certain about one thing: she wanted Brad to know she was absolutely on top of this. "Honestly, I don't know. It really doesn't seem that difficult, but no program comes together like you see it on TV." She wiggled her fingers in the air. "The crazy technology member of the crime team, the girl who always has wild hair and wears outrageous clothing, sits down at her computer. Thirty seconds of fingers flying over a keyboard and it's done. She says, 'I've got it! The unsub last used his phone at a diner off I-70 in Terre Haute, Indiana. He was sitting next to a guy eating pea soup and drinking and ice tea—unsweetened.' "

Brad stopped and looked at her. A quiet smile crossed his face, and those bright, blue eyes twinkled with pleasure. "You can be one funny lady, Sonia Vitale. One beautiful, funny lady."

Sonia's heart stopped. She hadn't meant to be funny. She really had just been trying to say that writing a computer program wasn't like you see it on TV. Still, to have gotten that reaction from Brad was . . . nice. She could feel the warmth of his eyes flow over her body from all the way across the room.

A demure smile crossed Sonia's face. "Thanks." She let out a deep breath. "Listen, my mind was fried when I walked in here, and now I've got to go tell Jet that the three of us are going to pull off something that sounds more like a bank job than a simple surveillance. I'm sure I can write that program for you, but not before I get a little sleep. Okay?"

"Okay," said Brad, continuing to smile. And, Sonia noticed, continuing to appear to be drinking her in with his eyes. "You go get some rest. It's not likely we'll see the truck until at least Monday, maybe later. You go formulate some brilliant plan, and then see what you can do for us on that computer of yours."

Sonia stood up. She felt like she should say, "Thank you," but she wasn't sure why. Still, her time with him this morning had moved from down-right insulting to challenging, and now to pleasant. She really didn't want to break the mood before she left.

She searched for something nice to say. "Great work. I think your plan is really going to succeed. And also, again, thank you for last night. You have no idea—"

He waved her off. "No thanks necessary. Training and responsibility . . . ." His smile broadened. "And sometimes, you know, you just *want* to do it."

Those last words sang their way into Sonia's heart. Heading for the door, her back toward Brad, Sonia smiled and said, "I'll see you sometime soon." *Dunny*. When the door clicked behind her, Sonia just stood there for a moment, enjoying the first real joy she had experienced in a long time—other than last night's kiss. But that was more passion than joy, wasn't it? She walked out into the sunshine of the day. For the moment, at least, there was warmth in the air, warmth in her heart, and warmth in Dunny's smile. And there was something else as well—the growing feeling that no matter what came her way, she was going to see this thing to its end. Not a bad start to a Saturday.

36

S onia had tried to work on the computer program on Saturday afternoon, but her brain was just worn out. Instead, she had driven the few short blocks to the center of town and parked her car. She'd walked around Triangle Park, the wedge-shaped park across from Rupp Arena, the cathedral in which University of Kentucky fans worship their true religion—college basketball. She just needed a break.

Sunday had been different. After a leisurely breakfast at home, Sonia had gotten down to business. She was trying to create a database and form a query that would sort messages by the times they were sent. It would then isolate those that coincided with the benchmarks Sonia had created from her surveillance notes. By late in the afternoon, Sonia had completed the program and run it several times. Unfortunately, there was so much traffic in the system that no information of real significance had materialized. Sonia reminded herself that the reason computer programs don't give users the answers they're looking for is that the users are not asking the right questions. She hadn't yet been able to get a handle on the precise query that would give her the information she needed. Finally, she had decided to take a break and let the computer inside her head mull over better ways to approach the problem.

At that point, Sonia had been starting to get hungry for dinner. She was also starting to yearn for something else. Based on her last few moments with Brad on Saturday, Sonia had felt certain that he might well give her a call on Sunday. Maybe he'd ask to spend some time with her, even if it were only under the guise of working together. By three o'clock in the afternoon on Sunday, she had been a little antsy about things. By five o'clock, she had begun to get frustrated. By seven o'clock, she had gotten miffed. By nine o'clock, she had opened a bottle of wine and put a serious dent in it all by herself. Sonia had gone to bed that night with an empty feeling in her heart, a banging sensation in her head, and a churning in her stomach.

SONIA HEARD Jet enter the offices of Bluegrass Confidential Investigations at ten o'clock on Monday morning. She was already hard at work at her desk. Jet walked directly to the doorway of Sonia's office. "You're at it bright and early."

Sonia gave her a surly look. "Early bird . . . worm."

Jet's voice, on the other hand, sounded pretty enthusiastic to Sonia. "You think today's the day?" Sonia had told Jet about Brad's plan in a phone call the night before.

Sonia's voice was as surly as her look. "You mean, the day the truck comes and we go out and try to pull off some cock-a-maim-me plan of Brad's? I don't know."

Jet stepped into Sonia's office, hitched her leg up, and took a half-seat on the corner of Sonia's desk—something that would have been impossible on her own, given the scattered materials that always covered that surface. "Oh, you'll be alright," she smiled, "I mean, hey, it's got to have some chance of failing or it's not much of a plan."

"Easy for you to say." Sonia pushed her rolling chair back from her desk. "You're not the one who has to walk around, how did he say, 'nonchalantly,' trying to hide something on a truck driven by a guy who may have personally murdered John Abbott Hensley." She shook her head. "You wouldn't have any better ideas, would you?"

Jet held her chin in her hand. "Not right now, but let me think about it." She lifted her head higher and peeked at Sonia's computer. "Now, what are you doing there?"

"Well, I didn't have any luck with the computer program I set up over the weekend. Too much email traffic to sort out. It didn't come up with any good connections." Sonia pulled her chair back to her desk and looked at her laptop screen. "So, I'm trying out a few other ways of posing the question to the computer. We'll see how it works."

Jet stood. "Hang in there. I'm sure you'll make it work. You're the techie around here, right?" She turned and walked out of Sonia's office, speaking as she went. "I've got two clients I've got to meet with. But I'm having them come in here to talk so that if we have to jump, I'm not out somewhere where you can't get to me."

"Yeah, thanks," said Sonia, as she let the computer do its work. Eventually, she stood up and walked to the window looking out across East Main. Damn that Brad Dunham. He could have called yesterday, just to check in if nothing else. Was he so busy he couldn't even make a phone call? She sighed. Just let it go. Who knows what he was doing? Maybe he really was busy. Maybe something came up.

Forcing herself back to the computer, Sonia looked down and saw something that surprised her. Having been queried in a different fashion, the computer program had isolated only a small handful of emails, one of which could be hugely important. "Yes," she said softly. "Yes, yes, yes. Okay." She was becoming excited, really excited, and animated. She sat down at her desk and watched carefully as the computer program kept working.

"Now we've got something. Ask it the right question. That's what you've got do. Ask it the right question and it will always give you the right answer." Finally, in one loud burst, Sonia yelled, "Yes!" She turned and looked through the glass between their offices. She saw Jet smile at her.

"Is the truck here?" Jet mouthed.

"No, better!" Sonia shouted back, a big smile on her face. "Better!" A sense of pride swelled in her. She picked up her phone, dialed, and waited impatiently, as the phone on the other end rang. She paced back and forth, waiting for someone to answer his damn phone.

And that's all Sonia was able to do—wait. Brad's phone rang and rang. Finally, she got a message saying that he was unavailable at the moment and would return her call as soon as possible. Frustrated, Sonia hung up and then called right back. She knew it didn't make any sense, but she wanted so badly to get through to Brad right away. When she got the same message, Sonia grabbed her quilted vest and headed out of her office. She all but flew down those steps, and instead of walking to the corner to cross the street, she dodged traffic so that she could get to Brad's office as quickly as possible. Unfortunately, she found the door locked and no one there. "Crap," she said out loud. Stepping back out on the porch of the white house, Sonia stood there stumped and steaming. She had just located an email that could lead to some significant information, and now the one person she was dying to tell was "un-freakin'-available!"

———————

37

By four o'clock, Sonia was really pissed, tapping her Cross pen again and again on the edge of her desk. She had pulled one of the isolated emails and connected it to her notes. She knew she was really onto something and was desperate to tell Brad. But Brad was nowhere to be found, "Doesn't he ever check his messages?" she bitched to herself. She had, after all, left four of them. No truck today. No Brad. No shit!

"Well, screw him," she said out loud. She stood, picked up the phone one last time, and dialed.

"Detective Sergeant Adams," the voice at the other end of the line answered, *"How can I help you?"*

"Johnny?

"Yes?"

"Johnny, this is Sonia Vitale."

It sounded to Sonia like Johnny Adams all but leaped through the phone line. *"Well, hello. Man, it's great to hear from you."* Then the tone of his voice changed. *"Is everything alright?"*

Sonia stepped again to the window overlooking East Main. "Oh, yes, everything is fine. It's just that you had asked me to let you know how the first part of my week looked and, well, it looks like I'm free tonight. I was wondering if you would like to stop by my place for dinner? Just something light."

"Sounds great. I was supposed to be off at four, but I'm afraid I'm covering an extra three hours for a buddy. I won't be off 'til seven. Is that too late?"

Sonia's eyes didn't drift to the school district building. They went directly to the white house. "Actually, no. I'll need all the time I can get just to put something together. Seven will be fine."

"You don't need to go out of your way."

"Oh no, that's fine. I'd really like to lose myself in making a nice dinner tonight."

"Wonderful. What can I bring?"

She wasn't sure why, but Sonia felt her heart beating just a little bit harder. "Just bring yourself . . . and a bottle of Chianti, of course,"

"As you wish, m' lady. I shall arrive shortly after seven with a whole cask of the finest Chianti for you to enjoy."

"One bottle will do nicely," Sonia said quickly, remembering how she felt at the end of Sunday evening. "And don't rush. Just get here when you can."

"Don't get worried if I arrive with lights and siren on. You'd be surprised how fast a cop can get somewhere in this town if he really wants to."

"Just be careful. Don't hurt yourself or some poor civilian, just because you want a glass of wine."

"Don't worry about me. I'll be just fine. See you at seven."

"Seven. I'll see you then."

It struck Sonia that the conversation she had just had with Johnny was so . . . so normal. It was nice, his being so eager to come. It was nice just being nice.

Suddenly, Sonia's mind was racing through the cupboards in her tiny apartment. She had just invited someone to dinner and had only three hours to get ready. Now what? A simple dinner would be fine, but she didn't have time to make sauce, and her mother would die if she ever found out that Sonia had a guest over and served sauce out of a jar. For a moment, she actually considered running down to Joe Bologna's, bringing home a meal, and then serving it as if she had prepared it. And had they not just eaten at Joe's last week, she might have actually done that. Sonia quickly re-neatened the stack of the papers on her desk, then reached down and grabbed her purse. Well, one thing's for sure. I'm glad my mother always taught me to have a container of homemade, well-simmered sauce in the freezer. Now my only problem is getting it defrosted and hot in three hours. I've got to get rolling. Sonia walked out of the BCI offices and flew down the stairs to her car, leaving Jet wondering what was so urgent.

It was a scramble, but at ten after seven, when Johnny Adams walked up the stairs and knocked on her door, Sonia was ready to serve him a simple chicken parmigiana dinner. Chicken, fried in Italian breadcrumbs, covered with Sonia's homemade sauce and mozzarella cheese. On the plate, next to it were angel hair pasta and a simple green salad with olive oil and vinegar dressing.

The way Johnny's gray eyes sparkled and his lips spread into a gentle, pleasing smile, told Sonia that she had more than pulled it off. She chuckled. "*Chi mangia bene, mangia Italiano.*"

Johnny scrunched his face. "What was that?"

"Those who eat well, eat Italian." The corners of her eyes crinkled as she smiled.

Over the next hour, dinner went well for Sonia. Both the wine and the conversation flowed freely. Still, recurring visions of Brad Dunham popped up in her brain, some of which tweaked her heart—others just pissed her off. After dinner, Sonia had to apologize for not having any dessert to offer.

"Sonia," Johnny smiled across the table. "more wine and more time with you. That's all I need for dessert."

They moved to the not-so-roomy couch in Sonia's cozy little

living room. Sonia offered to put on some music, but Johnny said, "No need. Just talking with you is fine."

As they sat there chatting, Sonia became more and more aware of the fact that she was happy and comfortable just being with Johnny. She took a deep, slow breath. I wish he would touch me, just reach out and touch me. It wasn't long before Sonia found herself putting her fingertips gently on Johnny's leg, brushing it ever so lightly with her fingernails. Perhaps he's trying to be a gentleman, but I wish he would just take a hint.

Sonia thought Johnny must have had his psychic hearing engaged when, almost immediately, he took her hand in his and brought it up to his lips. Looking directly into Sonia's eyes, Johnny kissed her hand then pulled it close to his cheek.

A rush swept through Sonia's body. She wanted to reach up and kiss Johnny, really kiss him, but she resisted. She just looked at him, her eyes sharply focused, her lips gently parted—her breath quickening.

It didn't take long for Johnny to get the message. He slid his arm around her and pulled her directly to him. He pressed his lips to hers.

There was nothing tentative in the way they came together. All of Sonia's defenses and worries about Johnny's intentions seemed to fade away. At the same time, all of her frustrations over Brad seemed to push her forward. This is a really wonderful guy, and it feels great to hold him, to kiss him, to be touched by him. This is what it should feel like, easy, and natural, and good.

At the same time, Johnny's strength seemed to grow. She could feel his embrace tighten. She could feel the sexual tension in him growing as his kisses became more and more passionate. Then she felt his hand slip deftly inside her blouse and cup the breast that filled the lacy bra she had chosen to wear. She could feel his hand there and she could feel her body responding.

As Johnny caressed her breast, pulled her close, slipped his tongue gently into her mouth, Sonia's body heat rose. Her hormones were in full bloom and parts of her were dying to be touched, but her mind resisted. *No, no. It's too soon. Don't do anything you'll regret.*

Just as Sonia's body and its desires were about to win the battle, Sonia felt Johnny pull gently away. Then in the nicest, kindest way, Johnny said, "We need to stop. Really, we need to stop."

Sonia's mind and body came crashing down from the high they had been on. Fears of inadequacy jumped into her mind. Was she being rejected? Was she not appealing enough for this wonderful man? An image of John Eckel's face shot through her mind.

Fortunately, Johnny spoke quickly. "Listen, please don't get the wrong idea. I want so desperately to pick you up and just carry you to your bedroom. I want to rip your clothes off and make wild and crazy love to you. But I'm so worried about over-stepping. I know I pushed too hard the other night, and I just don't want to screw up again. Do you understand?" Johnny pulled her hand up to his lips and looked directly into her eyes. "Are you okay? Are you mad at me?"

The battle raged in Sonia. Her body wanted him to take her into her bedroom, to make love to her, to hold her, to caress her, to be one with her. But her mind knew it was good, good that he wanted to stop. *How sweet that he wants to go slowly. It's the right thing.* The words blazed through her mind—as did flashing images of Brad Dunham.

Silence hung in the room for a moment, while Johnny stared at her, waiting to see if he had gotten things just right or all wrong. Sonia sighed, looking directly into his gray eyes. "No, you're right. We can go slow. We *should* go slow." Then, though she still wished he had just dragged her into bed, she said, "Thank you. Thank you for understanding."

Sonia adjusted herself on her small couch, turning and placing her back against the armrest. Johnny shifted his body as well, unconsciously creating as much space between them as possible. After a few minutes, Johnny said, "Look, I probably should go, or I might just do something we'll both regret in the morning. Thank you so much for a great evening. Really, just thank you."

Sonia leaned forward and placed a gentle kiss on his cheek. "No, thank you. Thank you for coming, and thank you for being so patient."

Johnny got up and placed one last tiny kiss on her lips. "Good night." Then he walked out the door and down the steps.

Deciding to leave all the cleaning until the morning, Sonia walked around the tiny apartment turning off lights. She sat down on the edge of the bed. Only a few short minutes before, Sonia had been hoping that Johnny would be slipping her clothes off of her, relishing how she looked half-naked, how she felt in his arms. Now, instead, she took her clothes off herself, pulled on a nightie and crawled into bed. All the hormones that had been released as her body was pressed against Johnny's were still crashing through her body. She wondered if she would ever be able to fall asleep.

38

At ten o'clock on Tuesday morning, Sonia walked into Magee's frustrated and edgy. She was conflicted about Johnny Adams. She had started out worrying that he was somehow trying to keep her from learning more about John Hensley's death, and though she no longer had those concerns, she couldn't quite tell how she felt about him now. He was attractive, kind, and attentive. Most of all, he was obviously very smitten with her, and he was trying his best to move forward in a way that left her feeling comfortable and safe. All of those things felt good to a woman who had lost her fiancée, and her job, and who had recently been both threatened physically and snubbed emotionally.

She was also conflicted about Brad, the man who had done both. Like the wind in Kentucky, there were times when he blew warm and friendly. It felt supportive, protective, and downright appealing. There were also times when he blew cold and vacillating, creating a sense of uncertainty, sometimes even danger.

And then she was conflicted about what she had learned from her computer program. There was no doubt that she had uncovered some information that might definitely lead them forward in understanding what had happened to John Hensley and who it was that had made it happen. She was proud of what her program had uncovered. On the other hand, having discovered all of that, she was now faced with the question of how to proceed, and worse, with the danger that following that information might entail.

After getting her coffee and croissant from Hildy, Sonia marched up those long steps and walked directly to her own office. Opening her computer, she sat, drinking coffee and going over the results from her computer program one last time. It wasn't that she hoped to see anything new, it was more that she was wondering how she was going to share that information with Brad. She had been so excited about sharing the results her computer program had generated. Then he had all but disappeared from the face of the earth. For all the messages she had left, she hadn't heard from him since Saturday morning.

As Sonia sat brooding, she was startled by her cell phone emitting its silly *Star-Spangled Banner*. She huffed. I've got to change this thing. Looking at the screen, she saw it was Brad. She hesitated a moment before she answered, then took a deep breath. "Sonia Vitale."

"*Sonia, it's Brad. How are you doing?*"

"Fine, and yourself?" Her voice was cool.

"*Actually, I'm doing well. Listen, are you ready to roll? I have a feeling today is delivery day.*"

"Oh, I'm ready." Still cool.

"*And Jet? She's ready too?*"

"Trust me, she's ready to go. All we need is a call from you saying that you've seen the truck and we're on." Even cooler.

Brad seemed to pause for a moment. Then, "*Excellent. Has your program turned anything for us?*"

It was strange, but as excited as she had been about the results the program had generated, Sonia was just a bit reluctant now to share them with Brad. She didn't quite know why. After all, there was no question that she would eventually share them with him, and sooner rather than later. That was the whole point, wasn't it? Still, after he had just disappeared for two days with no explanation, there was a part of her that just wanted to . . . wanted to what? Wanted to punish him? She paused as well. "Well, it's given me some new information. Information that might lead to something." Her voice clearly lacked enthusiasm.

"Like what?"

Her voice remained flat. "Information that might lead us in a new direction, we'll just have to see."

"Oh." Sonia could hear Brad's puzzlement at her close-to-the-vest comments. Finally, he said, *"Okay, just keep your phone handy. I wouldn't be surprised if we see that truck sometime around one o'clock. You realize we may be gone a day or two, right?"*

"Of course," said Sonia. She was seething with frustration and she heard it in her own voice.

"Uh, okay . . . I'll let you go . . . Just be ready for anything."

"You as well," said Sonia cryptically. She smiled, thinking about the fact that early in the morning, before she had even left for work, Sonia had received a very interesting phone call from Jet. She loved the fact that she and Jet had concocted quite a surprise for Brad.

AT AROUND TEN AFTER ONE, Sonia's phone rang. Brad's voice was full of energy. *"Time to roll, babe. We're on."*

"Great," said Sonia, though there was still just a bit less enthusiasm in her voice than she would have expected.

"I'm on my way. I'll be in your parking lot in a moment to pick you up."

"No," she said sternly. "I'll be going out there in Jet's car. We've got the walkie-talkie, and we'll be waiting out there, somewhere around the castle."

There was no missing the consternation in Brad's voice. *"No. That's not the plan. You ride with me. Jet's alone in her car."*

"Trust me." Her voice stayed strong. "We've got this. You just get out there near the castle, and we'll all wait until the truck comes by. Then you work your way in front of the truck and we'll work our way in front of you."

"But—"

"Trust me. We've got this. We'll see you out there." She hung up and smiled. Damn, that felt good. She knocked on the window to Jet's office and mouthed, "Let's roll."

At twenty-five after one, Sonia heard the walkie-talkie squawk. *"I'm out here on Pisgah Pike, just past the farm. I'll be able to see on the laptop when the truck leaves and I'll let you know that it's go time. Where are you?"*

Sonia pressed the "TALK" button on the walkie-talkie and answered, "We're at the gas station just about a half mile from the castle. As soon as we hear from you, we'll start rolling. We should be able to lock into the truck pretty easily."

"Copy that. But are you sure I can't talk you into coming in the car with me?"

Sonia smiled and looked at Jet while she spoke. "Brad, you just need to trust me. The plan is going to work out exactly the way you designed it . . . just better."

For a few moments, there was no response from Brad. Finally, with limited enthusiasm, he said, *"You got it. I'll call just as soon as the truck is on the move."*

"Copy that," said Sonia. She almost laughed out loud. It was the first time in her life she had ever used "official cop talk." She held the walkie-talkie to her chest.

"Just another couple of minutes," she said to Jet. "Is Diogi ready?"

Jet's eyes twinkled, and she turned to look at the passenger sitting on the back seat. "He's ready to roll." Sonia put the walkie-talkie in her lap.

"Who the hell is Diogi?" Brad's voice was gruff. *"You haven't brought someone else into this, have you?"*

Sonia jumped at the sound of Brad's voice, realizing she must have held the "TALK" button too long. Then she turned to Jet and they both snickered. "No one we didn't need. Don't you worry about it, Brad. I told you, we've got this covered." Sonia made certain to release the "TALK" button.

A few moments later the walkie-talkie squawked again. *"Here we go, ladies. The truck is on the move. I sure hope you haven't screwed this thing up."* Brad was clearly pissed now.

"Copy that," said Sonia, smiling again at Jet.

Jet fired up her gold Camry. It only took about two minutes for the truck to appear at the castle and turn right onto Route 60. Sonia watched the truck, as Jet maneuvered the Camry into the outside lane and slowly passed it. Sonia, sitting in the passenger seat, made certain not to look at the truck. It was the first time in her life that *not* looking at something seemed so incredibly important. Then she watched as Jet moved over, sliding in front of the truck.

A minute later, Jet spoke. "I just picked up Brad's 'Vette in my rear-view mirror. Here he comes."

"His 'Vette?"

Jet looked at her. "Yeah, why?"

Sonia looked over her shoulder and tried to see Brad's car. "I thought he'd be driving that gray Corolla." She pushed the "TALK" button. "Why are you in the 'Vette? I thought the Corolla was better for surveillance."

"Sweetheart, that's visual surveillance." His voice was relaxed, lacking the frustration that had been so evident a few moments before. *"We're doing electronic surveillance, GPS locator stuff. And it's a hell of a lot more comfortable making a long trip in the 'Vette than in that old Corolla."*

Sonia was pretty certain his frustration had been replaced by condescension. And that pissed *her* off. She took a deep breath to calm herself. A moment later, she looked at Jet. "No one else is around, right?"

Jet checked her mirrors. "Right."

"Then let's put some space between us and the truck so Brad can slip in between us."

Jet pushed on the accelerator just a little harder. Soon, there were at least two or three car lengths between Jet's Camry and the truck. "Time for you to slip in there, Brad," Sonia said into the walkie-talkie.

Brad didn't reply, but when Sonia looked briefly over her shoulder, she could see the dark blue 'Vette pulling smoothly past the truck. Not wanting to be obvious to the truck driver, Sonia turned her head forward again. After a moment she asked Jet, "Is he in?"

Sonia knew Jet was in her glory when her language changed, and Jet was in her glory playing this kind of game. "Oh my, my, yes," she said with a southern accent so thick it seemed covered in grits and white gravy. "I believe our gentleman friend has just entered the danger zone. He's like a critter caught 'tween a hound dog and a gator. Should we commence this afternoon's festivities?"

"No, not yet. Let me check with Brad." Sonia pressed the "TALK" button and asked, "Are you ready Brad? Are we a go?"

There was a pause, then she heard back. *"This is it. We're a go. But tell Jet to move up a bit. We want to make it look good, but not so good that I wind up wrecking this brand-new car."* Sonia could hear the excitement in his voice and the smile on his face.

Jet turned her head and smiled at Sonia. "Here we go, Colonel. The fray begins."

Sonia felt herself thrown forward against her seatbelt as Jet slammed the Camry to a very sudden stop. Hearing Brad's brakes squeal, Sonia held her breath, hoping that she wasn't about to hear Brad's 'Vette smashing into Jet's car. The instant she was certain they had avoided that crash, her ears strained, waiting to hear if the truck they were trying to trap was going to plow into Brad. With a squealing of brakes and a world of squeaks and rattles, Sonia heard the truck coming to a tortured stop as well. One, two, three seconds went by . . . no crash. Sonia looked over her shoulder. What she saw half amazed her. Brad's 'Vette couldn't have been more than twelve inches behind Jet's Camry, and the feed and hay truck was no more than three or four feet away from Brad.

"Ho-ly hell," Sonia said softly, expelling a long breath.

Jet, the southern belle, followed with, "Now, that dog'll hunt."

Sonia would have laughed at Jet's use of another southern colloquialism, but she was too busy. She looked back again and put her hand on the door latch. "Here he comes. Go! Go!"

Brad had jumped out of his car and was approaching Jet at full speed. He stayed tucked in the right lane as the normally busy traffic moved past him on his left. Sonia had no idea if he was going to play the angry motorist or the concerned citizen. Apparently, it was the former, because in a moment or two she saw his arms flailing and she could hear some pretty uncomplimentary sounds coming from him, though she couldn't quite understand the words.

Jet had jumped out of her car, also hanging close to the stopped cars and playing the damsel in distress. Sonia thought she could hear a few, "So sorry,"s coming from her lips. But as Jet and Brad were playing out their vignette, Sonia noticed Brad looking inside Jet's car, as if to say, 'Time to move.'

Sonia jumped out of Jet's car on the passenger side. Then, with a little effort, she pulled the new character in the afternoon's drama out of the back seat—Jet's big, black German Shepard—Diogi. Acting as if the dog needed to be walked, Sonia led him over to the side of the road, then back toward the truck.

Sonia thought the look on Brad's face was priceless. He was obviously shocked to see the dog, but apparently pleased as well. With his back to the truck driver, Sonia could see him break into a smile, even though from behind it would have appeared that he was reaming Jet a new one.

Then it really was Sonia's turn. Trying to look relaxed, and concerned with nothing but getting Diogi to do his business, Sonia kept walking slowly back toward the truck and beyond. She knew it was important that she never look in the direction of the truck driver, but it was hard for her to resist.

The plan had been for the driver to be a bit shaken by the near accident and totally focused on the ruckus the two drivers were creating in front of him. Half-way down the length of the truck, Sonia simply couldn't resist finding out if that part of the plan had worked. Trying to look as casual as possible, she turned around and looked into the large mirror on the passenger side of the truck. Her heart rose into her throat as she locked eyes with the driver, who had anything but a pleasant look on his weathered face. What was worse was that he was on his cell phone. She could hardly breathe. She bent down slightly in order to touch Diogi's back. She did it, not because the dog required it, but in order to settle herself down—to ground herself.

As Sonia reached the rear of the truck, she was almost certain that the driver was still staring at her in his side-view mirror. She desperately wanted to look back into the mirror again to see if that were true, but she knew she couldn't get away with it a second time. She simply had to continue to play her part. With her eyes steadfastly forward, she covertly threw a small piece of raw beef onto the ground behind the truck, knowing full well that this would certainly get Diogi's attention.

Diogi all but knocked Sonia off her feet, pulling her behind the truck. Unfortunately, another vehicle had just pulled up behind the truck as well, a young couple in a faded, old, brown, Ford Taurus. Sonia didn't know what to do. She was standing right in front of their car, and both the young man and young woman were looking directly at her. She had to find some way to avoid looking suspicious while she bent down to place the GPS locator on the truck.

Failing to come up with a better idea, Sonia bent down and looked directly into Diogi's face. She scolded him for pulling her behind the truck. At the same time, she slipped her right hand into her pocket and pulled out the GPS locator. Awkwardly reaching back and to the right, she found the truck's bumper. Without looking, she stuck the locator under the bumper, hoping desperately that she was getting it attached firmly enough that it wouldn't fall off.

Sonia stood and made direct eye contact with the young couple, trying to give them a "That's-what-you-get-for-having-a-dog," smile. She thought that perhaps she had pulled off the deception until she grasped the looks of confusion on their faces. Fortunately, at that very moment, the male driver turned, looked over his shoulder, backed the Taurus up about twenty feet, then took off around the truck. Sonia gave them a sheepish wave as they passed by.

Pulling with all her might, Sonia dragged Diogi out from behind the truck as if he were simply misbehaving. Her heart pounded as she ached to see if the driver had fallen for her ruse, if he had even noticed. Sonia stood tapping her toe. Damn, this better work. Nothing to see here, just a lady and her dog. I'm not doing anything wrong. I'm just taking care of my dog.

As if on cue, Diogi circled a few times and then did his business, just as nice as could be. Sonia chuckled. She had no idea if the truck driver was watching or not, but she felt confident that if he were, Diogi's performance had been the coup de gras of the event.

Sonia marveled at their good luck. First, the Taurus had eventually pulled around. Therefore, whenever he was good and ready, the truck driver would be able to back up and go around Brad and Jet. He would be leaving them behind, or so he would think. Second, Diogi's need to take a dump couldn't have been more fortuitous if it had been scripted for her crew of "not-ready-for-primetime-players." Sonia smiled. Diogi's antics seemed right out of Jet's playbook.

Sonia gave Diogi's ear a good waggle and began walking back toward Jet's car. The truck's engine revved up and Sonia watched it slowly back up thirty feet or so. Continuing to walk forward, she looked up into the large side-view mirror on the truck one last time. A chill ran down her spine. The driver was looking directly at her. She sighed a breath of relief, however, when he gave her a big semi-toothless smile and ran his fingers through his obviously dirty, greasy hair. She smiled back at him, or at least tried to. Her lips weren't cooperating as much as she wished they would. Sonia wondered. Was he smiling because he'd figured out what she was doing? The thought sent another shiver down her spine, a deeper one than before.

Within a minute, the feed and hay truck had slowly moved around the 'Vette and taken off down the road. The only ones left standing on the side of the road were Brad, Jet, Sonia, and Diogi. A few other cars were passing them in the far lane, but the stress and fear of the experience had started to drain away from all three of them.

"Great job girls. Great job. That dog thing, outstanding. Got to hand it to you. Seriously, one hell of a job." The smile on Brad's face was radiant.

The girls hugged each other. Sonia bent down and waggled Diogi's ear again, while Jet scratched him in his favorite place, right at the base of his tail.

"Okay," Brad said to Sonia, moving to the back of the 'Vette and opening the trunk. "Get your stuff and throw it in here. We've got to get off this road before the police come and we get too far behind."

Sonia hugged Jet one last time. "You. Are. The. Best."

"Frankly, Scarlet," said Jet, "I don't give a damn." She was Rhett Butler to Sonia's Scarlett O'Hara.

Sonia shook her head and smiled. She grabbed her stuff and jumped into the 'Vette with Brad. It took off, following the truck down Route 60. Looking in the side view mirror, Sonia could see Jet making a U-turn and heading back to town. "She's the best," she said softly. A little quiver of warmth went through her heart when Brad responded, "Only one of the best. Only one of 'em."

JET REACHED out and stroked Diogi's head. He had been afforded the opportunity to sit in the front passenger seat of her gold Camry, based on his fine performance—and the fact that it was his normal seat. "Good boy, Diogi. Good, good boy. You done real well out there. We're gonna have a real nice treat for you when we get home." She had slipped back into her quasi-southern accent, this one not put on for effect, but rather, a reflection of her real upbringing.

As she watched Brad's Corvette slip around a curve, headed toward Versailles, Jet couldn't help but think of the town in which she had grown up. She wasn't picturing the quaint downtown with the big, white Methodist Church that sat perched squarely at the end of the main drag into town. It was a little community on the edge of town that filled her mind, a community in which the term *home* meant a small, two-bedroom house at the end of a not-so-pleasant street.

The sound of her own teen-aged voice rang through her memory, that and the sound of her mother's deeply southern drawl.

"Ugh, Mama. Why do we have to live in this tiny house anyway? It's so small and dark. And why doesn't Daddy paint it nice like Mr. Joseph's? I feel like we're the poorest folks on the street."

"Now you mind your tongue. Your daddy brought us up here from Savanah so he could learn to work with the horses. Someday he'll be a trainer, maybe even an owner."

She remembered a time when her mother's voice had been smooth, almost velvety. But there had come a time when it became harsh and shaky, the result of too many battles with Jet's father . . . and too much bourbon.

Those were not happy times. Nor were the days when only a quick and humorous tongue could fight off the barbs and insults a high-school girl could encounter when the clothing she wore made clear the community in which she lived. "Thank God for running," she said softly, thinking about her one saving grace in high school.

Shaking off her memories, Jet leaned over and pulled Diogi's head close, wrapping her arms around his thick neck. "Well, they're off now, buddy. They're gonna follow that truck and track them boys down. And they'll be home soon, safe and sound, God willin' and the creek don't rise."

She checked her side view mirror then pulled a quick U-ie, turning the Camry back toward Lexington. She couldn't help but chuckle at her use of that last expression, pure southern, remembering when she'd heard some preacher use those very words from the pulpit one fine Sunday morning some twenty-something years ago.

PART VI

39

There was a definite celebratory sense in the car as Brad and Sonia drove down Route 60. Sonia settled back and tried to relax, the smell of the leather seats filling her senses. But adrenaline still pumped through her system, and she started talking to Brad—fast.

"Wasn't that just epic? I mean the way you and Jet trapped the truck. I thought for sure you were going to plow into her, and worse, that the truck was going to plow into you. And then I had to walk right past that guy, and I thought he was looking at me." She was almost breathless. "And then having to stick that thing on the truck. And Diogi, wasn't he great, you know, taking a dump just when it was perfect timing. I mean, wasn't it just something?"

Brad just smiled. Sonia could tell he was definitely pumped and pleased, but he was a bit less ebullient than she. After all, she knew this wasn't his first rodeo. Still, she appreciated it when he said, "Again, babe, that was outstanding work. I almost lost it when I saw that damn dog. Whose dog is that, anyway?"

"Oh, that's Diogi. He's Jet's."

Brad gave her a quick look. "Diogi? What the hell kind of name is that?"

"Diogi!" She smiled at him. "Don't you get it? D-O-G?"

Brad paused for a moment, then he smiled. "No kidding. Very punny." He shook his head.

"Well, yes, Captain, so it is." Sonia had Jet's southern belle accent.

"Well, it worked like a charm. You guys had me going there for a while, but it worked like a charm." He turned again and looked right at her.

Sonia didn't respond, but she felt like a Disney princess, surrounded by bunny rabbits, with a bluebird sitting on her shoulder. She could almost hear a cricket whistling, "When You Wish Upon a Star."

After a pleasant moment of silence, Sonia heard Brad get down to business. "Now, open up that laptop of yours and let's get a fix on this truck before we lose him."

Sonia got her laptop open and fired up the GPS tracking program. "According to this, the truck has already left Route 60 and headed south on The Bluegrass Parkway."

Brad nodded. "I thought that was a possibility. Looks like he's headed for Elizabethtown, and probably points south. I guess it's time we settle back and just enjoy the ride for a while."

Sonia took a deep breath and relaxed into the soft, supple seat. Her eyes traveled around the cockpit of the incredible machine in which they were floating down the road. Gauges and lights. Burled wood and soft leather. Sonia ran her fingertip along the binding of the seat. I could ride in this thing forever. Especially sitting next to those blue eyes.

Sonia watched the miles slip by and finally decided she could put the laptop on the floor between her feet. She knew that even if she reclined her seat she would still have a clear view of the screen.

Brad leaned over and peeked at the laptop on the floor. He gave her a questioning look.

"Don't worry. I've got this. I can see it." When he simply turned his eyes forward again, she smiled to herself. Don't worry, Mr. Semper Fi. I *do* have this.

Sonia relaxed into her seat again, enjoying the fact that she had the situation in hand. That was until something started gnawing at her, a new feeling of distress. She remembered the heat that had coursed through her body the night before when she was kissing Johnny Adams.

Sonia drifted into silence as her mind went back and forth, excited about the man next to whom she was sitting, still aching physically for the man she had just left behind. Am I a fool for hoping that Brad will finally let his guard down and open himself to a *real* relationship with me? Or am I a fool for keeping Johnny at arm's length.

"You okay?" Brad asked.

Sonia blinked. "Oh sure, just thinking."

"Thinking about what?" He gave her a caring look.

"Oh, lots of things." She picked up her purse, which was heavier than usual, and rummaged through it looking for something to put in her mouth. "I can't believe what a beautiful day it is. It really felt like spring when I was out there with Diogi. Would you like a mint?"

They talked for a while, about the weather and other unimportant pleasantries. Sonia was fully aware that she and Brad were in a gentle place of just getting along. The rolling hills and beautiful farms passed by, and things felt comfortable. She wondered if they looked like a married couple, or at least some sort of couple, to the passengers in the cars that passed. She was enjoying that feeling until her phone cooed like a pigeon. Her heart skipped a beat when she looked at the screen: THANKS FOR LAST NIGHT. ARE YOU AVAILABLE FOR LUNCH?

Brad kept his eyes on the road. "Who's that from?"

"Oh, it's nothing. Just Jet wishing us luck." Sonia wanted to ignore the text and get her phone back into her purse as quickly as possible. She realized, however, that if she didn't respond to Johnny's text, it wouldn't be very long before he called. Damn, that would be bad.

"I better respond. You know how Jet can get if you don't deal with her right away." She was trying her best to be nonchalant.

Brad looked down at his side-view mirror. "Actually, no I don't. But go ahead."

As she typed her message on her phone, Sonia felt totally self-conscious. It was as if Brad could tell what she was typing, even though he was sitting on the other side of the car.

BUSY NOW. PROBABLY HUNG UP FOR THE REST OF THE DAY AND EVENING. MAYBE WE CAN DO DINNER TOMORROW NIGHT. I'LL GET BACK TO YOU SOON. She hit "SEND." As soon as she had, she realized that she hadn't responded to his comment about Monday night. Crap, she would need to send a second text. Sonia felt like the letters on her screen were red hot as she typed, LAST NIGHT WAS REALLY GREAT, while Brad sitting right next to her. When she was done typing, she shoved her phone into her purse as fast as she could.

40

A s they approached Elizabethtown, Sonia checked the screen of her laptop. "Looks like he's made the turn onto I-65 South."

Brad bobbed his head. "Not surprising. I'm thinking he's done with his deliveries and he's on his way back home, wherever that is. We'll just keep staying with him until he leads us there."

Sonia looked out the passenger window. "What if he doesn't stop?"

"What?"

She turned and faced Brad. "What if he doesn't stop? I mean . . . I need to stop."

"Why?" Brad's voice was rising.

"Well . . ."

"Well, what?" Brad's eyes glanced quickly to Sonia, then back to the road.

Sonia's eyes fell to the hands in her lap. Her foot started tapping. "Well, I've got to pee. And I'm hungry, too."

"You mean you didn't pee before we started this? And you didn't eat anything either?" Sonia was all too aware of his frustration.

"I was just too wound up in the morning." Now it was Sonia's voice that was rising. "All I've had to eat is a croissant . . . and several cups of coffee."

"Damn." Brad shook his head and an exasperated sigh fell to his lap. "Okay, we'll scoot off here in E'Town and get you to a McDonalds. But that better be the fastest pee in the history of the world. And while you're in there peeing, I'm buying you a burger and some fries."

"I'd rather—" Seeing Brad's scowl, Sonia just swallowed her words. She wanted to bark right back at him, but something held her back—maybe the sense that she probably should have thought things through a little better before starting this mission.

At the intersection of I-65 and The Bluegrass Parkway, Brad maneuvered the 'Vette up the off-ramp and onto a busy street. It was just two-tenths of a mile to the McDonalds, but being on a busy road and having to turn left across lots of traffic, Brad seemed really frustrated. As soon as they got into the McDonalds parking lot, Brad zipped into the first available parking space. He reached across her lap and opened her door. "Go, go."

Sonia certainly felt a sense of relief being able to use the ladies room. At the same time, she was becoming more and more pissed. What the hell? Did he think I wouldn't need to pee for the next two or three days? And does it really take any longer for me to get a chicken sandwich than a burger? Damn him. It's like he's the only one on this trip; like he's the only one who counts.

Sonia walked out of the ladies' room. She looked up to see Brad walking out of the men's room at the same time. She gave him the "So . . . ?" look. He tugged his pants up. "Since we were here . . . . I didn't want to have to stop again."

They walked to the counter. Brad turned to Sonia "What do you want?"

Sonia pursed her lips and looked at the menu on the wall. Oh, now it's 'what do you want?' you bastard. "Just the chicken sandwich, grilled, some fries and a water, please." She brushed a wisp of hair out of her face. *Why the hell am I being so compliant?*

Brad ordered a Big Mac, fries and a coke. By the time Sonia filled their drinks, Brad had the food bag in his hands. "C'mon, let's hustle. We've got to get close to that truck right away." As soon as he got the 'Vette back onto I-65, he pushed his own speed close to eighty miles an hour.

Sonia looked at her watch and realized the whole stop had taken only twelve minutes. Still, at an average of sixty miles per hour or more, that put the truck at least twelve miles further ahead of them. She could understand why that made Brad uncomfortable. The GPS range was only fifteen miles. "I'm sorry I had to stop, really I am. I'll be better about it the rest of the trip." She knew she hadn't handled things perfectly, still, it bothered her to have to apologize.

"Don't worry about it." His voice was gentler, accepting. "He'll have to stop sometime soon as well, and I'm pretty sure he's not going to be changing his route until he gets to Nashville."

Okay, Dunny, thanks. Sonia recognized the shift in his demeanor and was glad for it. *Still. Damn Jekyll and Hyde. Why is it that every time we get in a comfortable place he suddenly pushes me away—on purpose?*

AROUND FOUR THIRTY-FIVE in the afternoon, as Brad and Sonia approached Bowling Green, Kentucky, I-65 curved, and Brad pointed to an unusual building. "That's the National Corvette Museum. Every Corvette in the world is made in that large building just next to it. Of course, the museum lost three of them."

"Really? How do you lose three Corvettes?"

"Sink hole."

"Sink hole? In a museum?"

"Yup. Great big hole opened up right in the middle. Makes you wonder if the Good Lord doesn't like Corvettes or something."

The mood in the car had maintained its pleasant sense of camaraderie since the food stop, and Sonia started to consider that maybe it was time to tell Brad about the insights her computer program had led her to. She started slowly. "You know, I think I may have turned some very important information with that computer program."

Brad cocked his head and glanced very briefly at her. "I thought you said it was just pointing out a few new directions that might be worth pursuing."

"Well, actually." She took a breath. "I think it could be more than that. I think I may have discovered who's running the whole thing."

Brad looked at Sonia, then back to the road. Sonia saw his eyebrows furrow. "You know who the boss is?"

Sonia struggled to keep her voice calm and level. "Well, not exactly. I don't know his name, but I think I may know his code name, the name he uses in the emails."

"Well . . .?" It rang in her ears like a one-word command.

Sonia turned toward Brad, as far as she could with her seatbelt on. The smell of their McDonalds dinner masked the normally rich smell of the leather in the 'Vette's interior as she spoke. "Okay, let me start from the beginning." Because of her position, Sonia felt her foot wiggling rather than tapping. "You remember that with help from your secret colleague we were able to get inside the organization's network, right to all of its emails—including way back to old emails."

"Right."

"But when I spent the weekend trying to make sense of who was talking to whom, the number of messages was overwhelming, and the program I wrote just kept giving me too many possible connections. I was sure there was some important stuff there; I just couldn't ferret it out from all the other stuff."

Brad looked at her. "And?"

"And, this past weekend, it struck me that computers never fail us, we fail them." She kept her eyes on him, though he didn't return the gaze. "We don't get the answers we want because we don't ask the right questions. I had been looking for emails that were sent or received at times that matched the few benchmarks I could put together from my previous surveillance."

He checked his mirrors. "And that didn't work. I get that."

Sonia wished he would look at her, though she knew he couldn't. "So, I thought and thought about a better way to pose the question, and this is what I came up with: instead of asking who sent or received an email at a certain time, I developed a program that sorted out messages that contained some reference to time, references like, 'in one hour,' or 'at one o'clock.' Then I made the program connect those emails to any of my benchmarks, based on the time differential between when they were sent and the actual benchmark.

Brad flicked one hand. "I'm lost."

"It's like this. Someone sends an email that says 'I'll be there at one o'clock,' and if one o'clock is one of my benchmarks the program makes the connection."

Another quick glance in his mirrors. "Your program could do that?"

"Yes, it could. It was tough to get it to isolate the phrases inside the emails since there are so many ways of phrasing things and hundreds of emails. But once it did that, connecting them to my benchmarks was easy as pie . . . for a computer program."

He finally turned and looked at her. "Amen, sister. So, this really led to something?" There was a question mark on his face.

"Well, you tell me." Sonia squared herself in her seat. She was starting to feel like she was in control. "You know how we had some sense that whoever was at the beginning of the process might be using the code name Toro and that we thought there was a chance that Forty might be located at Dahlia Farm, making it most likely Steve Hollings?"

"Yeah."

"Well, among the seven emails the program isolated, most of which were absolutely irrelevant, was one sent to Forty and it said, "be there in an hour and twenty minutes.""

"So?" The side-view mirror again.

"So, it was sent at 2:45 PM. And almost exactly one hour and twenty minutes later, at 4:07, my notes indicate that a black Lincoln Continental showed up at Dahlia Farm. A thin, blond man with his hair slicked back and a goatee stepped out of the car and went directly into the barn. At 4:18, just eleven minutes later, the guy got back into the car, and he and his driver took off. Nothing else happened on the farm until six minutes after nine, when the police arrived with lights and sirens and the whole place erupted into mass bedlam."

Brad looked quickly at her. "So, you think that the guy who showed up had sent that message, telling them he would be there around four, and that's when he showed up? To do what?"

"First, yes I do think the blond sent the message. And more importantly, so does my program. Second, 'To do what?' I don't know. But it could be that he was sent to check in, or came to give an order or something. Trust me, I saw the guy. He was no messenger. It was more like he was the guy in charge. And I believe he may have come down, checked things out, and then given the order to kill Hensley."

"Whoa." Brad bobbed his head.

"After that, he gives himself plenty of time to get back to wherever he came from, and no one knows that Hensley's been done in until this guy is safe and nowhere near the scene of the murder."

He glanced at her. "And you figured all this out from your

computer program?" Sonia could see the twinkle growing in Brad's blue eyes.

Sonia lifted her chin. "No. I figured it out using deductive reasoning . . . based on the information my computer program generated." She turned to him. Her confidence shifted momentarily to real questioning. "Do you think I'm way off base?"

"Actually, no, I don't." His eyes were on the road, but his voice was clear and strong—and supportive. "It sounds plausible, very plausible, *if* your program got it right. So, who is this guy?"

She was reveling in his reaction, but the next answer was difficult. "That's the thing. His code name is Sofia."

"Sofia?" He cocked his head. "A woman's name?"

"I know. It's confusing." Her head wagged. "Maybe a woman named Sofia sent this guy. But then again, they're all using code names, so it's not likely that the woman in charge, or who might be in charge, used her real name." She sighed. "I just don't know."

Brad was silent. Sonia knew that he was pondering the whole scenario.

"But I've got more." She waited for his reaction.

"You do? Well . . ." He was clearly into this.

"Okay. So, I tried to find a town or city that was about an hour and twenty minutes from the farm. Actually, it wasn't very hard for me, because I grew up in Cincinnati, which is, roughly, an hour and twenty minutes away from Lexington. So, using that as a reference, I sat down with my Rand McNally road atlas and plotted a circle that would take you about an hour and twenty minutes away from Lexington. I wanted to catch every possibility, and it was easier on that then on Google Maps. Then I started looking at all the towns and cities that were close to the perimeter of the circle."

"And you found?" His eyebrows were raised.

"Mostly I found a whole lot of nothing. Very rural southern Ohio, very rural south-central Kentucky, and one other big—."

"Of course, Louisville." He turned to her and smiled.

"That's right." She smiled back. "Both Louisville and Cincinnati are about an hour and twenty minutes away from Lexington."

"Yeah, but that doesn't quite give us what we need, does it?" He furrowed his brow. "I mean, we know, or think we know, that Sofia came to Dahlia Farm, or sent someone, from either Louisville or Cincinnati. We think he, or the guy Sofia sent, came there to give final approval to the disposal of John Abbott Hensley, maybe because he had stumbled on the drug operation."

"Yes. That's what I think too," excitement rose in her voice, "that Hensley stumbled onto the drug operation. I went back to my notes, and when Hensley arrived at the farm he seemed happy and carefree. Then he started over toward the barn, where, as you recall, the feed and hay truck was sitting. And now that I think about it, perhaps it wasn't that Hollings was trying to show Hensley something out in another field like my notes had indicated. Maybe it was that he was simply trying to keep Hensley from going into the barn."

Brad's head bobbed. "Makes sense. It really does. But which city did he come from, and how do we figure out who the hell he is?"

Sonia turned toward Brad again. She was enjoying taking charge of the conversation. "And here's something else. Do you remember I spent several days out at the farm trying to catch Marcos Torres in the act?"

"Yeah."

"Well, I finally went back to my notes from the first day I spent out there, a day in which I felt nothing important had happened."

"And..."

"And a black Lincoln, very much like the one I saw on the day Hensley was killed, showed up on the farm that first day. Nothing much happened with it then. The blond guy wasn't in the car, and the driver was only there for a few minutes." She paused. "But I just can't help but think those two cars are connected."

"Maybe, but ... ?"

"Well, if they are connected then I've got something else to tell you that could be crucial."

Brad looked at her. "Don't hold back now. Tell me."

"Look, because things weren't so busy, so complicated, and because unlike Kentucky, the 'Great State of Ohio' has decided that people should have license plates on both the back and front of their car, I got the license plate number of that Lincoln. That might lead us to the one that showed up the day they killed Hensley."

"You got a plate number?" His voice was full of excitement.

A big smile crossed Sonia's face. "I got a plate number. It's, let me see here," She pulled her phone out of one of the cup-holders. "It's MDB-619."

"Awesome, babe. Incredible." He smiled. But then he said, "You've been sitting on that information the whole time and haven't said anything?"

Brad seemed excited, but there was something in his question. To Sonia, his tone implied that she'd screwed up.

Sonia turned her head forward, her voice tightened. "Well, it just didn't seem important until the program got me started making some other connections." She wasn't going to let him take this away from her. This was *her* information she was bringing to the table. Information *her* hard work had developed.

"Plate numbers from a car that showed up at the murder scene didn't seem important?"

Now he sounded incredulous, but Sonia wasn't going to take it. "It wasn't a damn murder that day, was it? And it wasn't the same car that came the day Hensley died. It all just didn't come together in my mind until the program led me through the whole process. No way I screwed this up."

"Hey, don't worry about it." Brad's voice was upbeat, but Sonia was convinced that he was pissed. Then again so was she. She was the one who had generated this information.

After several moments of tense silence, Brad said. "Listen, that's how it goes in this business. We've all watched hundreds of TV shows in which something unimportant finally pops into the mind of the hero and he says, 'Wait a minute. I just remembered. The dog didn't bark.' "

"What?" She cocked her head.

"The dog didn't bark. It's a famous line from a Sherlock Holmes mystery. The reason he figured out who done it was that the dog should have barked and it didn't."

"So?" Sonia wasn't sure where this was all going.

"Well, that's really how it goes. We pour over information and pour over information and then sometimes something new comes in that brings it all together. Or sometimes, it's just that somebody looks at something differently and sees it in a new light. Yeah, you could have told me right away about the Lincoln, but you got there. That's the important thing, you got there." He turned and smiled at her, a big smile. "Now we can plug into one of my old colleagues and find that car. That just might lead us to this Sofia guy . . . person." His head was bobbing up and down. "Great job Sonia, great, great job. I just might have to hire you to work for me at Semper Fi, you and your crackerjack computer skills." Another quick glance. Another big smile.

Sonia enjoyed the smile. She even enjoyed the notion that they might work together again after all of this was over. But what made him think that he would be hiring *her* to work for *him*?

41

B y a little after five-thirty, Sonia and Brad were approaching
Nashville when the GPS locator program indicated that the
feed and hay truck had left the interstate and stopped.

"Probably stopped to get some dinner," said Brad.

"Does that mean we can get some dinner too? I hate to say it,
but I'm a little hungry."

Brad looked at her and raised his eyebrows, but Sonia could
tell he was just teasing. "Fair enough." He gave her a quick smile.
"Let's pull off at the next exit and see what we can find. But it's
going to be another fast food meal. We can't afford to get caught
doing anything else if he's only stopped for a quick bite."

Sonia rolled her eyes, making certain that Brad could see her
reaction.

"Isn't this what you signed up for? The glamorous life of a
private investigator?" He gave her a little smile. Dinner turned out
to be an Arby's sandwich.

"Now what?" Sonia asked as she climbed back into the car.

"Now we wait." He sighed. "We wait until our friendly truck
driver has had enough to eat and takes off again." It made Sonia

think about the hours she had spent surveilling Dahlia Farm, hoping to catch Marcos Torres cheating on his girlfriend.

An hour and ten minutes later, the alarm on the GPS program went off. Brad gave Sonia a quick look. "There's our boy. He's rollin'. Here we go." Brad took off, following the GPS signal, watching the truck move from I-65 South to I-40 West. "Looks like our boy is heading in the direction of Memphis. If he's going all the way there, it's going to be a while. It's about three hours to Memphis from here."

"And so it shall be," said Sonia softly.

SONIA WAS WHIPPED and needed to close her eyes. She was aware, however, that Brad wasn't the least bit weary or worn out. She could tell that this kind of operation was exactly what brought him to life.

Moments later, or so it seemed, Sonia opened her eyes and looked at the car's clock. The bright green digital display read 9:14. "I guess I fell asleep there for a while."

"Well, you were quiet for a while, and then, about an hour ago, I heard your breathing change. When I looked over, I saw that you were conked out, head back, mouth open, a little drool trickling out of your mouth." His tone was totally snarky.

"No, it wasn't," said Sonia, quickly checking both her cheeks.

"Yeah, yeah, it was. Flowing like a river down onto your clothes. It almost filled that whole side of the car." Then Brad let go a hearty laugh.

"You bastard." But she couldn't resist the urge to pull down the passenger side visor and look at herself in the mirror. She smiled at the camouflage smudge her fingers had left the night Brad had sent her on a wild goose chase through the fields of Dahlia Farm.

"Don't worry about it, babe."

She gave Brad a quick look. Is he talking about the smudge or my drool?

"You look great . . . for a woman who just passed out and snored herself through a few hundred miles of Tennessee."

Sonia reached out and smacked Brad, playing pissed. This was fun. It was like . . . Suddenly, she remembered long car trips with John Eckel . . . when they were in love. It sent a chill through her. She took a quick breath. "So, where are we?"

"We're coming into Memphis." He pointed through the windshield. "You can see the lights ahead. And I'm damn curious about this guy. Is he going to blow through Memphis? Is he going to stop for the night? There's really not much past Memphis until you get to Little Rock, and that's another two hours or so." He gave her a quick glance. "Or maybe, just maybe, this has been his destination all along. We'll just have to stay with the boy and see what happens."

Sonia was hoping it would be the last option. She was ready for this part of the trip to end. "Wait," she said, looking down at the laptop. "Something's happening." She lifted the computer to her lap and studied the screen. "It looks like the truck is leaving the interstate. He's taking the exit for South Parkway. I think we need to move up closer to him. It'll be harder to follow the GPS once we get on local streets."

"Yeah, it will." Brad checked his mirrors then moved into the faster lane. "My guess is that he's not just looking for a quiet place to stay. This might be it, his home base."

A few minutes later Sonia was watching the sights and sounds of downtown Memphis go by. "There's a sign for the South Main Historic District. Do you know where that puts us?"

"I really don't." He shrugged his shoulders. "I don't know Memphis all that well."

A few more moments went by, and Brad had pretty much closed the distance between the 'Vette and the truck.

"According to the GPS," Sonia squirmed in her seat, "he's

right up ahead. Are we getting too close?" She was afraid to look at him. It had been less than a week since she had been scrunched down below the steering wheel of her car, wondering if she would survive the next few minutes. She didn't want her eyes to betray the fear she couldn't shake.

Brad seemed confident. "Well, we can't see him, not for real, so he can't see us. And I don't want to lose him if he turns into some building or something."

Sonia's voice rose involuntarily. "This is it. He got off here. Take this ramp right here."

Brad looked at her. "Yes, Captain. Whatever you say." He gave her a little grin.

Sonia didn't mind the tease. She was telling him what to do because *she* was the one who knew what to do . . . and that felt good. She was also glad that Brad hadn't picked up on the fear that she was keeping in check.

Brad pushed the 'Vette down the ramp and onto the surface street. "What street are we on? Can you tell?"

"Florida Street. We're on Florida Street."

Brad drove on past a number of warehouses and commercial buildings. "This must be what we're looking for. His base has to be right around here somewhere."

"Hang on." Her voice was terse. "This might be it. He's stopping, and it's not at a cross street."

Brad pulled the car to the curb and stopped. He stole a look at the laptop. "Now comes the tricky part."

"What do you mean?"

He looked down the street. "Well, you can follow someone with a GPS locator, but you can't catch them that way. In order to really know where he's stopped, and what he's doing, we're going to have to drive right down this street, right past him." His gaze never shifted. "Let's hope the truck is still outside, and that the driver is too busy getting out or getting into the building to notice us as we drive by."

Another shiver ran through Sonia's body. "I'm with you on that." But then she had an idea. "Look, let's just blow on by like you're some stupid teenager driving his daddy's 'Vette. You drive. I'll keep my eye out for the truck. It'll work. I'm sure of it."

Brad turned to her. He smiled, and the look on his face told her he agreed. He shifted in his seat. "Ready?"

Sonia took a very deep breath and let it out. "Ready."

Brad started down Florida Street, while Sonia kept her eyes on the GPS monitor. They approached the blip that represented the truck.

Sonia spoke softly. "One more block."

Brad hit the gas and started cruising down the street—fast.

Sonia shifted her gaze from the laptop to the street. She hoped that if anyone noticed the car, they would think the people inside had no interest whatsoever in the buildings they were passing.

"There it is," Sonia whispered, "on the left."

As they passed the truck, however, Sonia's heart flipped. At that very moment, one of the men near the truck turned and looked directly at them. She almost screamed.

A block later Brad slowed down. "Did you catch the address."

"1800. 1800 Florida Street." Her voice quivered. "But one of those guys looked right at us."

Brad's head whipped around to look at her. "Really? Right at us? Did he look . . . concerned, suspicious?"

"I don't know. I just know he looked right at us."

Brad pulled the car to the curb and waited a moment to speak. "Don't worry about it. Could have been anything. Maybe he just likes 'Vettes. Nothing we can do about it anyway. Just don't worry about it." His voice sounded reassuring but did nothing to calm Sonia.

Sonia took a deep breath. "Now what Kimosabe?"

Brad looked in the rear-view mirror. "Now we wait . . . again."

"Wait for what?" Sonia's foot started tapping. She just wanted to get the hell out of there.

"We keep watching the laptop, waiting to see if this is just a pick-up or something, or if he's really in for the night."

She hated asking the question. "That could take a long time, couldn't it?" She knew what the answer would be.

"It always does, babe."

∼

AN HOUR AND A HALF LATER, it was Sonia who spoke first. "Are we done? Have we waited long enough? It sure looks to me like he's shut it down for the night."

"Yup. Now we find a place to spend the night ourselves. I'm bushed, aren't you?"

Sonia was grateful to hear his words. "Yeah. Long day." She closed her eyes. She couldn't get the picture of the man standing next to the truck, looking directly at them, out of her mind. It was going to take quite a while for the knot in her stomach to go away.

Sonia felt those blue eyes smiling at her. She opened her eyes and turned to him. Somehow, the knot in her stomach began to unravel.

"Nice job." Brad's voice was warm.

"No, really, *you* did a great job . . . babe." Sonia all but choked on the last word. She had so wanted to end with a term of endearment, but it certainly didn't come naturally to her yet. She turned and looked out the passenger window. Babe? That's what I came up with. Geez, how lame. Couldn't I have done better than that?

42

B rad pulled the 'Vette into an empty parking lot. "Why don't you get your phone out and see if you can find us a place to stay?"

"Do you want something cheap?"

"No way we're going to find something cheap in downtown Memphis. And no way I'm driving too far away from that truck. You never know what could happen. Hell, they could load up and move out in the middle of the night. This could just be a stopping point on the way to Mexico. Just find something decent, a Holiday Inn or something."

Sonia used her phone and finally found a Holiday Inn not too far from Florida Street, on Union Avenue.

"What is it?"

"Holiday Inn Downtown."

"That'll do, especially if it keeps us close to our prey."

"You got it, boss."

Brad had to drive several blocks, down to Kansas Street, before he could get them turned around and heading back downtown. He certainly didn't want to drive past the truck on Florida Street again. After a few more minutes, and with a few turns, he got them to the Holiday Inn on Union Avenue, close to the famous Beale Street music clubs.

As they walked into the colorful lobby, Brad said, "Wow, really nice." When he went up to the front desk to check them in, Sonia overheard the associate behind the desk ask, "One room or two?" Her heart moved up into her throat, unsure of which answer she preferred.

Brad turned to her and smiled warmly, then he turned back to the desk clerk and said, "Two please." Sonia sighed. She was both relieved and disappointed.

Brad carried Sonia's light green duffel and his own black overnight bag to the elevators and down the hall. It took only a few minutes for them to be standing outside Sonia's room. "Listen, you'd better give me the laptop. I need to be listening for that alarm on the GPS program just in case they decide to move out sometime during the night." A warm smile crossed his face. "Who knows? You may be seeing me well before for morning." He slipped the electronic key into the card reader on the door to her room. "Maybe in just a little while." He turned to her, leaned forward, and placed a gentle kiss on her forehead, just the way he had on that deserted street in Rocky Top. His bright blue eyes twinkled. "Later." He walked down the hall to the next room and stepped inside.

Sonia pushed her door open. She stepped into the plush room, with its huge king-sized bed. All warm reds, yellows, and browns, the empty room still had a chill in it. She threw her duffle on the duvet. What the hell did he mean by that? Might see me before morning? Later? Damn him, can't he just be straight with me?

Sonia took out her phone, turned it on, and left Jet a voice message. She told her about the trip to Memphis and following the truck to what seemed to be its final destination. She shared a little of her frustration with Brad. "God only knows what's going on in his mind? Listen, I've got to get some sleep. I'll check in with you again tomorrow."

Sonia opened her bag. She pulled out the extra white sweater she had brought along, her makeup bag, her hair dryer, her toiletries, and three pairs of shoes. She sighed, thinking about what having long wavy hair entailed. She pulled out her spritz bottle, her hair product, her pick comb, her paddle brush.

Then she came to *them*—two sets of sleepwear. One, from Target, the dark blue, two-piece cotton pajamas with pink fringe around the neck and the bottom of the legs. The other, from Victoria's Secret, a white, silky pajama top that she could wear with its matching silky pants or just the silky white panties she'd also brought along. She laid both sets out on the duvet. Now, what the hell do I put on?

Sonia picked up the silky pajama top and held it up to her body. The top would look really sexy on her—especially if she also put on the small, black, lacy bra she'd stuffed in her bag at the last minute. She crossed to the mirror beside the door. But as her eyes slid upward from the bottom of the pajama top to her face and her hair, she was dismayed. She'd run out of the office over twelve hours ago, pulled a dog around in a crazy theatrical display, eaten two fabulous fast-food meals, and fallen asleep in the seat of a car. Her hand unconsciously touched her face to check for any drool. And her hair—it was terrible. Not actually dirty, but certainly flat and stringy.

Screw it. He's not coming. She folded the top and slipped it back into her duffle. He never said he was coming. He was probably just thinking about that damn truck and following it to Kingdom Come if need be. Screw it. She slipped on her cotton pajamas.

Sonia went into the bathroom, washed her face and began to brush her teeth. As she stood there brushing, more energetically than usual, she saw herself in the mirror. Hair mussed up, toothpaste foaming out of her mouth. Not a stitch of makeup. "No . . . .

No . . . . Not like this. If that bastard comes, he's not going to find me looking like this." She spit out her toothpaste and rinsed. "And you know what, he *is* coming." She marched back into the bedroom. " 'Might see you in a little while. . . before morning . . . later.' Oh, he's coming, damn it. He's coming, and I'm going to be ready."

Slipping out of her cotton pajamas, Sonia spent the next fifteen minutes doing the best she could with her hair. She put on just enough makeup so that her complexion had a nice subtle blush and her chocolate-brown eyes were magnified.

Satisfied that it looked like she didn't have a bit of makeup on, she slipped into the silky pajama top and bottoms. She liked their feel on her skin.

Then she slipped off the bottoms, slipped on the silky panties, and slipped the bottoms back on.

A moment later, she took off the silky top. She put on the lacy bra. Yes.

Finally.

She looked at herself in the full-length mirror, wearing just the bottoms and the bra. How do you like them apples, Captain Dunham? Sexual desire ran through her body.

Too much?

She put the silky top back on over the bra. Looking back into the mirror, she opened the top one more button.

She pulled down the covers, crawled into bed and turned off the light.

A few moments later, she turned the light back on, slipped out of bed, took off the bottoms and put them back into her duffel bag.

Crawling back into bed, wearing only the bra, the top, and the panties, she turned off the light and lay back in bed, hoping the pillow wasn't flattening her hair.

Sonia lay perfectly still. The bed seemed to absorb her body. Her breathing deepened.

Suddenly, she shot up in bed. "Just a minute." She'd heard a noise at her door. Stumbling to the bathroom, she turned on the light and pulled the door mostly closed. In front of the full-length mirror, in which she could barely see herself, Sonia fluffed her hair, used her index finger to check her mascara, breathed into her hand to check her breath, and fluffed again. She turned to the door. "Who is it?" she asked. There was no immediate response, so she asked a little more loudly, "Who is it?"

Getting no response a second time, Sonia stood on her toes in order to look through the peephole in the door. She saw nothing. She moved around, trying to use different angles to see more of the hall. Finally, keeping the safety chain hooked to the door, she opened it and looked into the silent, empty hallway.

Sonia turned back into the room. She saw the green numbers on the digital clock. 3:07 AM. "That son of a bitch," she whispered. "*Figlio di puttana.* Son of a bitch. Ugh." She pushed open the bathroom door. The light spilled over her, dissolving the seductive shadows in the room. She stepped into the bathroom and turned on the water as hard as she could. She scrubbed and scrubbed her face. She walked back to the bedroom, yanked off the silky top, wrestled off the uncomfortable bra, and tugged off the panties, which had found a way of creeping up into places they should never have gone. She tossed them all across the room, the top resting sprawled on the TV. She put on her much warmer dark blue pajamas with the pink lace around the neck and the bottom of the legs, said, "Son of a bitch," one more time, and crawled into bed.

43

S onia was rudely awakened by a knock on the door at precisely five thirty in the morning. After such a terrible night, her nerves were jangling. She popped out of bed and walked to the door. This time, when she looked through the peephole she saw Brad Dunham standing outside her door. The bastard had a smile on his face.

"What is it?" she asked. She knew her voice sounded less than entirely pleasant—just the way she wanted.

"Open the door." It sounded like he was having fun.

"Why?"

"Because it's five thirty in the morning and I'm trying to talk to you without waking up every other person in the hotel." He was half whispering.

"Just a second." Sonia stepped back from the door and ran her fingers through her hair. She put her hand in front of her mouth and breathed out, checking her breath once again, then opened the door a few inches. She stood there in her dark blue cotton pajamas, with the pink lace at the neck and the bottom of the legs. *No way I was hoping you'd come knocking in the middle of the night, asshole,* was the message she hoped her attire was sending.

"Well, good morning, Sunshine." His smile broadened, and Sonia could tell he wanted to step into her room. "Listen, we've got to be ready to move out early if necessary. We have no idea what these guys will be up to today, and it may not even be today. We—"

"Wait. You mean we might have to stay here a whole day just waiting?"

"Could be." He shrugged. "I guess it could be a couple of days."

"Ugh." She turned and walked back to her bed, finally letting him into the room, but scooting quickly past the TV to remove the silky top from its unseemly perch. Plopping down on the bed she asked, "So what do you want from me?"

His eyes roamed around the room as he spoke. "I need you to get dressed and ready to leave. We'll go down to the restaurant and order some food to go. If we have time, we'll stay and eat. If we hear that GPS alarm go off, we'll just grab the food and run."

"Sounds delightful," Sonia said, using the same tone of voice people use when telling their dentists they understand why they need a root canal. She stood, waiting for Brad to take the hint. She felt him linger. "Okay, get out of here and let me get going."

Brad looked at her, confusion darkening his expression. Then he seemed to let it go; he turned to leave. "Be ready to go in half an hour." Just as he reached the door, however, he looked back at her. "By the way, you're beautiful in the morning." Then he slipped out the door.

"Son of a bitch!" Sonia shouted silently, as she threw a pillow at the door. Then she marched right into the bathroom, took off those freakin' dark blue pajamas with the pink fringe at the neck and at the bottom of the legs, and jumped into the shower. When she got out, she simply ran her fingers through her hair, put on a marginal amount of mascara and lip gloss—just enough for her own self-respect—slipped into the same clothes she'd worn the day before, and walked out of the room.

Sonia knocked on Brad's door, her light green duffel dragging on the floor. "Forty-five minutes," he said as he opened it. "Not bad." He nodded his head in the direction of the elevator. "Come on. Let's go downstairs and get you some food."

The restaurant was nearly empty at six-fifteen in the morning and chilly. The temperature had been turned down during the night and the space had not yet been warmed by any human-body heat. It was made even chillier by Sonia's disposition.

She sat staring at the silverware that was waiting for its first use of the day. He looked across the table at her. "Not much of a morning person?"

"Depends," she said. *On who the hell I'm with*.

Sonia watched him order an egg, ham, and cheese biscuit. She wound up ordering oatmeal in a Styrofoam cup. "Don't order anything you can't pick up and run with," he'd said. They'd each ordered a large coffee to go as well.

They ate in silence. Brad was finished, and Sonia almost so, when the GPS alarm went off. "Before seven and our boy is moving out," said Brad smiling. "I guess they're still trying to make up for the deliveries they missed right after the Hensley thing." He threw a twenty-dollar bill on the table and started for the door. "C'mon babe. Time to roll."

Without a single word, Sonia stood up, grabbed the duffel bag and her purse, picked up her coffee, and followed.

Within a few minutes, they were able to use the GPS locator to find the truck, and Brad established a position a reasonable distance behind it. "I'm guessing this guy is going to drag us through some pretty heavy traffic this time of day."

"Uh, huh." Sonia's reply articulately communicated a whole world of information. She was pretty certain that Brad's silence indicated that he was getting the message. She twisted her lips. Or are you so wrapped up in yourself you didn't even notice? She watched in silence as they drove on through the heavy morning traffic. Eventually, they were out of the city and on I-40, heading back toward Nashville.

"Bet that boy's pretty tired after yesterday's haul."

Sonia watched the computer in silence.

A few minutes later Brad tried again. "At least we're not following him in the rain or anything."

Sonia let that comment go as well.

Finally, Sonia relented just a bit. "Looks like we're on our way back to Lexington."

Brad didn't let the opening slip by. "Pretty sure you're right. But I'd be surprised if it's a direct shot. Who knows what this guy's route really looks like."

Sonia's eyes never left the computer. One tiny break was all she was willing to give him.

They had ridden in silence for well over an hour when Sonia's phone rang. She looked down at the screen. Her eyes flashed to Brad for an instant.

"Hello . . . ." Her voice was syrupy. "Oh, good morning, Johnny, how are you? . . . Well, I'm already out on the road for the day, but I hope to be back in town by mid-afternoon. Would you like to get together for dinner? . . . That sounds great, I'll give you a call when I get into town and you can tell me where we're going . . . . You have a great day as well, Johnny. I really look forward to seeing you tonight, you know, for dinner, and, well, whatever."

Sonia ended the call. She looked straight ahead—silent.

A full minute went by before Brad asked, "Sergeant Adams?"

"Detective Sergeant Adams." Her tone was terse. "He's taking me to dinner tonight. I'm sure we'll have a pleasant time. He's a very nice guy . . . a real gentleman."

Brad made no response. And although Sonia was dying to see

what the expression on his face was like, she avoided looking at him in the same way she had avoided looking in the side-view mirror of the truck the day before. Silence filled the car for the next hour and more.

Around ten o'clock, just southwest of Nashville, Sonia looked down at her feet and noticed a change on the computer screen. "Wait a minute. Looks like the truck is leaving the interstate. He's turning left. He's heading north on 48." She put the computer on her lap. "He'll pass a travel stop almost immediately."

"Okay, then." She could hear relief in his voice. "We may well be on our way to the first drop-off."

"I guess so," said Sonia, mustering zero enthusiasm. "It looks like the road has a couple of big turns on it before it kind of straightens out." Her foot started tapping.

The 'Vette reached the interstate exit for Route 48. "This is us," she said. "Get off here and start heading north."

Brad maneuvered the 'Vette off the interstate, turned left, and started following the truck's GPS signal through some beautiful Tennessee forested areas and then past some small farms.

As much as she tried, Sonia was unable to keep herself from getting excited—and fearful. After several minutes, her tapping quickened. "It looks like he's just turned left onto a real local road. I'll bet it's small and secluded, just like Pisgah Pike. And he must be going pretty slowly on the smaller road because we're getting pretty close. Be careful not to run up on him."

"Yes, ma'am" Brad responded.

Sonia noted the sarcasm in his voice. "Look!" she exploded, banging her fist on the 'Vette's console. "I'm pretty sure that guy saw us last night, and I damn well don't want to run into some trap. So just be careful that he doesn't see us now. Is that okay with you?"

Brad was silent for several long moments as he turned onto the road the truck had taken. Finally, he said softly, "Farms again.

Use a feed and hay truck to deliver the drugs, you've got to deliver them to farms. But I don't think these are horse farms."

Sonia didn't respond. They rode on in silence for several minutes, then Sonia said, "He's stopped. I can't really tell if he's on the right side of the road or the left, but he's definitely stopped. What do we do now?"

Brad slowed the 'Vette to a stop. "Well, I'm guessing that as soon as he's made his delivery, he's going to head back to the interstate. That means he'll be coming right back at us. There's no big parking lot or anything for us to hide in, so he'll eyeball us for sure. I think our best bet is to try to get close to the farm he's on and then make a decision about whether or not we can drive past it without getting seen."

"Right past the farm?" Her anger at Brad was starting to be overcome by her fear of what was about to happen next. Her foot was tapping again. She brushed a wisp of hair out of her face.

"Right past the farm . . . if we think we can pull it off. That way, we get beyond the farm, turn the car around, and wait for him to leave. We give him enough space as he drives toward the interstate and he never sees us. All we have to do is make a note about which farm he stopped at."

"Sounds crazy to me," Sonia said, almost inaudibly. Tapping, tapping, tapping. She was slouching down in the seat, her arms crossed.

Brad gave her a quick look, his eyes appealing for trust. "Look, I know it sounds risky, but we don't have a lot of options out here. How far away from the farm are we?"

"Looks like it's just around that curve." It was not the answer she wanted to give him.

Brad inched the 'Vette slowly forward. "Okay then, nice and slow, hoping no one comes up behind us, and we just creep our way around the curve until we get a sense of what things look like." Eventually, they could see the farm.

Brad's voice brightened. "Excellent. Look how long that driveway is. And it curves. I can just barely see the end of the truck. That's the best we'll get." Without another word, and certainly without asking Sonia's opinion, Brad hit the gas. The 'Vette flew quietly past the farm at a speed that wouldn't attract attention but that left only a few moments for them to be noticed.

As Brad pulled off the maneuver, Sonia kept her eyes down. She swallowed hard. I hate this.

When they were past the farm, Brad asked, "What was the name of that farm? Did you get any kind of address?"

"No." She looked straight ahead.

Brad glanced at her quickly. "No?"

"No, I wasn't looking."

His voice rose and he glanced at her again. "Why weren't you looking?"

Sonia's head turned away from him. "You didn't ask me to look, did you?"

Silence filled the 'Vette for a moment. Brad's eyes stayed on the road. "Are you okay?"

"Oh yeah, I'm fine. Just fine." Her arms were still crossed. She stared out the window. Nothing she saw registered.

"What's wrong babe? What's going on?"

Sonia hated that word—"babe." She kept staring out the window. "Nothing. It's just a lot of pressure, and I didn't get any sleep last night. It's just a lot to handle. I'll be okay."

Brad's voice softened. "Yeah, you'll be okay. I tell you what. As soon as this guy has gotten us back on the interstate we'll try to find a place to get you another cup of coffee. And we'll get the name of the farm as we drive out of here."

"Sure." Clueless. He's so damn clueless!

Sonia watched as Brad tried to find a place to turn the car around. The country road was narrow and full of curves. Sonia realized that every place Brad might have tried a three-point turn, he would have been at risk of having some truck or farm vehicle come around a curve and T-bone them.

After passing on a few options, Brad did find a spot along a little bit of straightaway, and with a small patch of grass on either side of the road. "This will just have to do." He cranked the steering wheel hard to the left. With a few other quick moves, he had the car turned around and pulled as far off to the side of the road as he could get it.

The 'Vette purred quietly as they sat in silence, waiting for the truck to make its delivery and get rolling again. Finally, Brad asked, "Is it something I've done? Have I said something to hurt your feelings?"

Sonia let out a long breath. Oh, Dunny, don't you know? Can't you tell how you hurt me last night? Why did you make me think you might come to my room and then not show up? Why can't you just be honest with me, one way or the other? She said nothing.

Brad was left with nothing to say as well. The silence in the car was palpable. It went on for minutes. Suddenly, the silence was broken by the sounding of the GPS alarm. "Okay," Brad said with noticeable relief, "Here we go."

Sonia watched the blip on the GPS screen move closer to them as it came down the long driveway. Then it turned right. "It turned right." Then with real alarm in her voice, "It turned right. He's heading right for us."

"No shit. Are you sure?" Brad leaned over to look at the screen.

Sonia pointed at the blip on the screen. The intensity in her voice rose. "I'm sure. He's heading right for us."

"Holy crap, what the hell is he doing?" Brad checked his mirrors. "Damn, we've got to get out of here." He threw the 'Vette into reverse, laid on the gas pedal, and took off backward down the road.

"Turn around! Turn around!" She couldn't believe they were going backward.

"Can't! No room! No time! Got to keep going 'til we can turn!"

Sonia swallowed. She looked down at the screen. "He's coming right at us. He's coming fast. Faster than before." The roar of the engine filled her ears.

Brad's not-so-*former*-Marine voice rifled the words. "GPS shows a place we can turn?"

"No, nothing changes on this road for forever."

Brad kept the 'Vette flying down the road backward, veering at times as he struggled to keep the car stable around all the curves.

"Still coming at us," said Sonia, her voice now flat.

"Just keep watching, keep watching. Ho-ly shit!"

Sonia instinctively knew to turn around and look out the 'Vette's back window. Her heart stopped. Behind them was a large green tractor, pulling a flatbed that filled almost the entire expanse of the road. She screamed.

Careening toward the tractor, Brad had just an instant to react. "Hold on!" he yelled. He stomped the 'Vette's gas pedal as hard as he could. The four hundred and twenty-five horsepower engine made the 'Vette respond as few cars in the world could. Brad cranked the steering wheel hard to the right. That forced the car off the road, to the right of the tractor, and up one of the few grassy embankments the road offered. Flying more than three feet up the embankment, the 'Vette was literally suspended sideways as it flew past the tractor and flatbed, held up only by the centrifugal force created by the powerful engine and the speed at which they were tearing up the soft surface of the embankment.

At the top of the arc created by his maneuver, Brad cranked the steering wheel hard to the left. Not only did that bring the car back down to the road, it threw it into a wild, one hundred and eighty-degree spin.

Sonia had closed her eyes just as the 'Vette left the road. When she opened them, she found that they were facing almost completely in the opposite direction of the farm they had just passed. Whipping her head around, she looked out the car's back window, only to see the tractor and flatbed still bouncing down the road, away from them. All she heard from Brad was, "Let's get the hell outta here."

44

B rad jumped on the gas pedal. The 'Vette took off down the road, flying around hairpin curves. Sonia was thrown from side to side in her seat while Brad braced himself with the steering wheel. Both he and Sonia were silent for long seconds. Then Brad asked, "What are we headed toward?"

Sonia had lost control of the laptop. Reaching down between her legs, she pulled it back into her lap. She was relieved to see the blinking GPS marker. Manipulating the image as best she could as the car leaned hard left then hard right, she yelled, "Nothing but country roads out here!" Her foot, which had been trying to push its way through the floorboard a minute ago, started tapping again.

"Got to keep moving. Find something we can turn onto. Could be forever out here in farm land." Brad was breathing normally again, but still sharply focused.

Sonia's mind started to clear. "How'd he know we were out here? How'd he know to come after us?" The words were fast and clipped.

Brad's speech slowed. "Actually, we don't know for sure that they were coming after us. Any chance they were just taking another route?"

Sonia looked back at the GPS map and manipulated it, trying to see what other roads were near them, her hands still shaky. Brad had the 'Vette flying down the winding country roads at speeds the local sheriff would have frowned upon. Finally, she said, over the roar of the engine, "I've got it. Not the next right, but the one after that. That'll take us back to the interstate, but at a different exit."

"Got it." It seemed to Sonia that Brad was almost enjoying this.

Sonia started to speak in measured tones as well. "First right coming up almost immediately. Looks like about one or two miles to the turn. It's possible that's where they were headed. Possible."

The first right blew by. And at eighty miles an hour, it took the 'Vette just over one minute to cover the approximate mile and a half to the next turn. Applying the brakes hard, the motor screamed as Brad downshifted to make the ninety-degree turn onto the crossroad that would lead them back to their original path. Accelerating immediately, but only to sixty miles an hour, Brad asked, "How far to the interstate?"

"Looks like five or six miles."

Brad kept the car moving steadily but slowly lessened the pressure on the accelerator. Sonia squirmed and adjusted her seatbelt, glad that this road was straight and even, running smoothly along neatly parceled pieces of farmland.

It seemed only the blink of an eye to Sonia and they were approaching the interstate. "Here it is," she said calmly, her voice now back where it belonged in her throat. "Take a right onto this next road and go over the interstate. The ramp is on the left."

Brad took the turn, but as he let the 'Vette blow right past the entrance to the interstate, Sonia exclaimed, "There it is! You're missing it!" Then she saw a smile on his face and a twinkle in his bright blue eyes. She turned her head forward, as if speaking to no one in particular. "Okay, you want to tell me what you're doing?"

"Well, sweetheart, we're going find out if those bad boys are actually after us or not." He turned back to her and smiled. "If they keep coming past the interstate, they're definitely planning to track us down and do bodily harm to that beautiful, sexy body of yours . . . and of course, my own studly body as well."

Those words sent a ripple through Sonia.

His eyes returned to the road. "If, on the other hand, they turn onto the interstate, then one of two things is true. One, they were trying to catch us but they've lost us and have no idea where we are. Or two, they never even knew we were out there, and they just chose a different route back to the interstate." He looked back at her. "Maybe this just all made sense to them in purely geographic terms."

Having gotten past the entrance to the interstate, and far enough around a curve to not be seen by anyone turning onto the highway, Brad slowed the car. Looking over his shoulder, he pulled a smooth Uie, the 'Vette's tight suspension and steering making easy work of the maneuver. He pulled to the side of the road and stopped. "Now we wait." Brad took a deep breath and relaxed. A few minutes later he said, "Check out your GPS reading. How far are they from the interstate? In fact, are they even following the same route?"

Sonia picked up the computer. "Looks like it. Looks like they're headed right to that interchange. Maybe only another mile or two and they'll be there."

"Won't be long now and we'll know if they're still after us." Brad locked his fingers, twisted his wrist, and stretched his arms. "Of course, if they're not, we won't know if they ever were."

Sonia had no response. The car sat on the side of the road, its engine purring quietly. Finally, Sonia spoke. "Okay. I've got a question for you."

Brad kept his eyes peeled on the curve in front of them. "Shoot."

"If there's still a chance that they may be following us, why have you turned the car around? Don't we want to get away from them if they're still coming after us?"

Brad turned toward her, a wry smile on his face. "Well, Grasshopper," he said, trying to do his best Kung Fu accent, and reminding Sonia immediately of Jet, "let us think this through. You have noticed that we are just around a bend in the road, have you not?"

"Yes." She felt something coming.

He raised his eyebrows. "And what does that tell you?"

"That they can't see us from the interstate?" She shrugged. "I don't know."

"Well," said Brad, continuing with his accent. "Let us suppose they were following us and were somehow wise enough to cross the interstate to try to catch us? Would it be best for us to run from them by continuing out into the farmlands of Tennessee?"

She shrugged again. "I guess so. I mean, they're in a truck. They couldn't catch up with this car, right?"

"Ah, how true, grasshopper. But then where would we be? Where would we be going? How long before we might have an unfortunate accident on a winding road? Now, is there a better strategy?"

Sonia was silent for a moment. Then her eyes brightened, and a smile crossed her face. "I've got it. You've got us tucked up against the curve in the road. If, by chance, they really are coming to get us, when they come around the curve we'll be ready for them because of the GPS." She was getting excited. "They may see us, but by the time they do, they won't have time to react. You'll hop on that gas pedal and Mr. Corvette will go rocketing right past them before they can even come to a stop. Then we've got a clean shot to the interstate and we're miles down the road before they even get the truck turned around." Her smile broadened. "Brilliant, Holmes, Brilliant!"

Brad's bright blue eyes popped open at that last statement. Sonia said, demurely, "After that comment about the dog that didn't bark, I didn't want you to think that I hadn't read my share of Sherlock Holmes." They both chuckled softly at that. There was a softness in their eyes as they looked at each other and smiled.

Sonia looked down at the computer. "And I guess we'll never know if your plan would work or not."

His brow furrowed. "And why's that?"

She looked up at him and smiled again. "Because the truck just turned onto the interstate and is heading for Nashville, and I assume, points north."

45

Sonia watched the GPS locator program. "There it is. They're well on their way toward Nashville."

"And here we go." Brad put the 'Vette in gear and took off. Sonia watched as, within moments, they slipped smoothly onto the highway. Then she asked, "Why so close?"

"Because, my dear, I'm guessing we could both use a tiny breather and something to put in our stomachs. We'll stay pretty close. Not close enough for them to see us, but close enough that we can hop off the interstate, get ourselves something to eat, and get back behind them well within our fifteen-mile limit. I'm not guessing that they'll be stopping again soon so we'll have to make it quick."

They rode on in silence for a few minutes, then Sonia said, "Have you noticed that every car we pass seems to be staring at us."

"Nerves, honey. Just nerves. After being chased like that you can't help but be a little paranoid."

"Yeah, I guess you're right." Two minutes later she said, "Exit coming up. Mickey D's. That's us."

"You got it." Brad slipped the car smoothly off the highway, took a right, and pulled directly into the parking lot of a McDonald's. "Here you go, babe. I'm guessing you need to use the ladies room, so tell me what you want and I'll get our food."

"Egg McMuffin, no cheese, black coffee with sugar. The breakfast of champions."

Sonia and Brad got out of the car and were headed for the restaurant when Sonia noticed a man and his wife, both in their sixties, staring at the 'Vette. Sonia smiled a sad smile. Ah, another older man fantasizing over the car of his teen-aged dreams. Then she turned around and stopped. "Brad. Brad."

"What?"

"The car. Look at the car."

Sonia watched Brad's face as he turned around to look at his dark blue Corvette. A smile crossed her face as she watched the shock grow on his. Then she looked back at the car herself and broke out in quiet laughter. The sides of the car were covered in grass and mud. "Looks like we've been out runnin' with the boys from *The Dukes of Hazzard*," she said.

Things got even funnier to Sonia as she watched Brad walk slowly back toward the car, shaking his head. "Good thing we were able to get away from Sheriff Rosco P. Coltrane and Boss Hogg," she continued. "Maybe Uncle Jesse can come and help clean this thing up for us by drivin' it through the fishin' pond." By then she was laughing so hard she could hardly get the words out.

Sonia paused, suddenly afraid that Brad was going to burst into a tirade about the car. Then she watched his face soften. He turned to her and said, "Listen, Daisy Duke. Get your fine country ass into that there McDonald's and use their privy. I'm a'gonna get us some food and we'll be drivin' the 'General Lee' outta here right fast as we can. And by the way, how do you know so much about that show? You're too young to have watched it."

"They made a movie about it a while ago. Didn't you know that?"

A big smile still on her face, Sonia went inside and used the ladies' room. When she came out, she saw that instead of waiting with the food, Brad was standing near the car, talking on his cell phone. As she walked up to him, he stopped talking and covered the phone with his hand. "Same thing you're having, but with the cheese," he whispered. Then he reached into his back pocket and handed her his wallet. As she walked away, Sonia could hear that he had restarted his conversation, but she was focused on the fact that their minutes were flying by.

When Sonia got back to the car with the food, Brad had the 'Vette running and ready to roll. Back on the interstate, Sonia reached into the bag and pulled out the first Egg McMuffin. "This one's yours," she said as she unwrapped it, handing it to him carefully. Once again, she was struck by how much they seemed like a couple.

"Thanks," said Brad, taking a bite. "How far ahead are they?"

"Fourteen miles, just within our range."

"Good. Now let's see where these boys make their next stop."

Within a few minutes, the Egg McMuffins having been scarfed down quickly, and the coffee still too hot to drink, Brad was moving the car from I-40 East to I-65 North, back toward Kentucky. As they made an arc around downtown Nashville, Sonia looked out toward the same skyline she'd seen the night before. It had been a skyline of music and romance and dreams of stardom when lit up at night. But in the daylight, the city appeared to be a stalwart center of commerce, a true American city.

"Well, they're heading north," said Brad. "My guess is that we'll follow them past Bowling Green and on up to Elizabethtown."

"Do you think they'll have a drop off in Bowling Green?"

"Probably not, too close to the last one. Could be one in E'town."

Time passed. They crossed into Tennessee. Just after one o'clock, Brad spoke. "Okay, let's see what's going to happen now."

"What do you mean?" She looked at him.

"Well, we'll be at the junction of 65 and The Bluegrass Parkway in a moment. If they get on the parkway, they're headed directly back to Lexington. If they stay on 65 it's almost a sure thing that they're headed toward Louisville."

Sonia and Brad sat silently as they followed a few more minutes, their eyes focused on the road ahead. Sonia looked down at the computer screen. "And there it is. They're headed for Louisville."

"Ah, makes sense. If you're bringing stuff up from Memphis, you want to hit as many cities as you can. You wouldn't want to skip Louisville."

Sonia settled in for another tiring segment of the trip when her eyes caught something on the computer. She lifted it into her lap. "Hang on. Something's happening . . . Yeah, they're leaving the interstate . . . Looks like it may be the very next exit . . . Yeah, they're getting off on 313, headed west."

Brad glanced briefly in her direction. "Okay, then, we're following."

"The same way we did last time? That really didn't work out so swell." She hoped the angle of her head made it abundantly clear that she was not simply stating a fact.

Brad kept his eyes on the road. "No, it's too dangerous. We'll just follow until we see them stop. We'll make a note of the distance from where we are to where they are. That'll give us a pretty good idea which farm they've stopped at. Then we'll go back to the interstate and use the same strategy we used before. We'll wait for them to get onto 65 and then we'll get on behind them and follow." Turning to Sonia and smiling, he said, "It's not as complete a strategy, but certainly seems to have less downside."

"Sounds good." Sonia turned and looked out her side window then smiled. *I knew you'd come to see things my way.*

Sonia watched the beautiful farms go by as they drove along the two-lane road. Dark brown creosote fences. Circular hay rolls, eight to ten feet tall. Wooden barns—with the occasional bible verse painted on the roof. The purr of the powerful engine, barely working hard, had a soothing effect on her. "Wow, they're going a long way out into the country."

Brad checked the rearview mirror. "Yeah, seems strange, doesn't it? I guess you can't just pick the farm closest to the interstate, walk up to the front door and say, 'We'd like to use your farm as a drop-off point for drugs. Will that be okay with you?' " His voice was relaxed.

"Yeah," said Sonia softly. She was trying to reflect Brad's confident mood, but the possibility of another harrowing confrontation had gotten a knot started in her stomach again. It was working its way up into her chest.

Brad must have sensed her apprehension. He looked at her. "You okay?"

"I'm fine, I just want to get this trip over with and get back to Lexington."

"So you can have dinner with the Sergeant?" His eyes went to the side mirror.

Sonia turned away from him. She had forgotten about her phone conversation with Johnny Adams earlier that morning. She couldn't tell from the tone of Brad's voice what he was feeling. She knew she had certainly meant to hurt him when she spoke openly on the phone with Johnny that morning. Sonia looked down at her fingernails. *Wow, was that really just this morning? But that was before everything that had happened back in Tennessee.* Sonia's foot started tapping. She sucked in her lower lip. *Oh, crap. Have I messed this up again? Is he mad? Is he hurt?* She simply didn't know how to respond. She said nothing.

As they drove on, the tension and the silence were again

palpable in the car. Brad looked up to the mirror. "Uh, oh. Looks like we've got company."

Sonia spun as far around in the seat as she could and tried to look out the tiny back window. The knot moved from her chest to her throat.

Sonia saw Brad's shoulders hunch forward as he braced himself. "You can't see them right now, they're hanging back, but they're out there."

Sonia twisted a little harder—straining. "How do you know?"

"They got a little too close. I saw them on a bit of a straightaway."

Sonia turned to the front, her hand steadying the computer on her lap. She saw his eyes flick up to the rearview mirror, then the side mirror, then back to the rearview.

Sonia checked her own side mirror. "Who do you think it is?

"No question, it's not a welcoming committee."

"How do you know?" The panic in Sonia's voice was rising.

"Big black Suburban, shiny clean, no farm dust on it. Trust me, I know." Brad's voice tensed. "And shit, here they come."

He laid on the gas pedal and the 'Vette jumped like a toad that had just landed on a hot stretch of blacktop. The car could do zero to sixty in 3.7 seconds. Already going fifty, it hit eighty in a lot less than that. "Open the console," said Brad calmly, but with authority.

She looked at him, panic in her eyes. "What?"

His voice stayed calm. "The console, open the console."

Sonia zeroed in. She opened it.

Still calm. "Push the button, the red button."

"This one?" She pointed.

Brad didn't look down. "The only one down there."

Sonia pushed the button. "Now what?" She was almost without breath. She felt her body pulling into itself.

Brad bore down. "Now, this is where you look at the screen

and tell me we've got plenty of options. These boys ain't gonna give up 'til they've tracked us down or we've lost them."

Sonia desperately scanned the GPS map. "Nothing! There's nothing! Just one road coming up real fast on the left. If we keep going straight, we'll run right up on the truck. We're almost on them now."

"On the left?"

"Yes. Here it comes." She almost screamed it.

Brad stood on the brakes and downshifted hard, pulling the 'Vette to a screeching, sliding stop just before the turn. Then, laying a patch of rubber, he took off again down the new road. Not ten seconds had gone by when Sonia's head snapped to the right. A "Road Closed Ahead" sign whipped by.

"Road closed! Road closed!" she yelled.

"Not for us! We've got to go somewhere!"

At that very moment, the macadam road turned into gravel. Sonia could hear rocks and pebbles being thrown up inside the wheel wells of the car as it plowed on, kicking up a plume of gray-white dust.

"Hang on, babe," Brad said as the 'Vette flew past a hand-painted "Bridge Out" sign. Downshifting and palming the steering wheel all the way to the right, Brad turned the car perpendicular to the dismantled bridge and brought it to rest right at the very end of the gravel road. Piles of wood planks, torn from the bridge, were heaped next to metal railings which once served to keep cars from falling off the bridge into the shallow river below.

"Get out! Get behind the car and get down!" Brad's voice was calm but commanding.

Pushed by Brad's words, Sonia jumped out of the car, the knot in her throat dissolving as she was finally able to take action. She could see the black Suburban charging toward them, still on the macadam. She ran. She reached the front of the car and stopped. She ran back. She opened the door.

"What are you doing? Come on! Come on!"

"Getting my purse!" She reached into the front seat and grabbed her purse. She ran around the front of the car. She slid down behind it. Brad wasn't there. "Where are you?" Panic in her voice. The knot returned. She heard the trunk lid close. She looked up. Brad stood at the back of the car, his M16 in his hand. He moved slowly, deliberately. He took a kneeling position behind the wheels of the 'Vette. The Suburban came to a skidding stop, a cloud of dust settling slowly behind it.

"Fifty yards," he said softly.

Sonia looked at Brad along the the length of the car. "What were you doing?"

Brad kept his eyes on the Suburban. "I had to let them see that I was armed, really armed. It'll give them something to think about."

"What are they waiting for?" The Suburban hissed.

"They're trying to figure out what to do. They've treed the critter, all right, but they didn't expect it to have teeth like this." Brad checked the sites on the M16, then continued to stare out at his adversaries. "And what was the deal with your purse? Are you crazy or something?"

"I don't think so." Sonia pulled out her loaded Glock and an extra magazine filled with seventeen rounds of nine-millimeter ammunition. Brad turned. Sonia could see his astonishment. She smiled. "You didn't expect me to go chasing bad guys all over the place without at least bringing a sidearm and a little extra, did you?"

"You are one piece of work, Sonia Vitale." A huge smile crossed his face. "One very, very, fine piece of work."

Sonia let those words soak into her—through her skin, through her body, into the very heart of her being. She *was* one very fine piece of work, and whatever the next few moments brought she knew she was ready for the challenge.

Not fifty yards away from them was a large, ominous Suburban, in which, she guessed, were at least two men, maybe more—men who were certainly there to do them harm. She and Brad, on the other hand, were trapped by a dismantled bridge, on a road that was no longer passable, kneeling behind a car that was made of fiberglass, hoping, somehow, to avoid being killed. This was not at all what she had signed up for when Joyce Ellen Thomas had offered her a job doing technology work for a small private investigation firm called Bluegrass Confidential Investigations.

The doors of the Suburban opened. Two men got out of each side of the vehicle and shielded themselves with its front doors. Sonia's stomach clenched as she caught a glimpse of the large handguns they were holding.

Brad lifted his weapon. "Hang on. Here we go."

Sonia kept her eyes on the Suburban. "What do you think is going to happen?" She felt somehow calmed by the realization that whatever was about to happen, she was by the side of a man she knew she could count on, a man who would do everything he could to save them both— if possible. That *if possible* part blazed quickly through her brain several times.

Brad sneaked a quick look at Sonia, then brought his gaze back to the Suburban. "Well, I don't think even they know what to do next. There's probably one guy left in the Suburban, telling them to get out there and do something. We'll know soon."

Sonia let out a scream as her ears were filled with the sounds of exploding gunfire. "Get down! Get down!" yelled Brad, and they both slid backward until they were lying on their stomachs behind the car.

Thirty, forty, fifty bullets exploded through the body of the 'Vette, flying past Sonia and Brad. Even through the roar of the guns firing and bullets tearing through the car, Sonia recognized the pop of one of its tires as a bullet burst through it. The front end of the car sagged.

Sliding even farther back and down a slight embankment,

Brad yelled, "Stay down! Stay down! They'll stop to reload soon! Then I'll take them!"

"Not without me, damn it. Not without me!" Sonia pulled the slide back on her Glock, chambering her first round. She yelled, "Locked and loaded!"

"Locked and loaded!" Brad replied.

Sonia looked at Brad. She saw his tight smile and those bright blue eyes.

The firing from the Suburban ceased.

"On my command!" said Brad. "Just move up and lay down suppressing fire. Just keep on shooting. This weapon will tear right through those doors. They're gone in the first ten seconds. Ready? In three, two..."

From behind the 'Vette, Sonia heard the soft, muffled sound of sirens. "Sirens!" she yelled. "Sirens! Someone's coming!"

"It's about time," said Brad, letting out a long breath.

46

The men who had been firing at Sonia and Brad jumped back into their vehicle. They spun it around, attempting to get back to the main road. Within moments, the sound of the sirens manifested itself as three large, black Suburbans. Her heart racing, Sonia saw the three new vehicles quickly create an effective roadblock, stranding the attackers on the gravel road.

Several men and women wearing DEA bulletproof vests jumped out of each of the three vehicles. They were aiming automatic weapons at the men who had, just moments before, been attempting to kill Sonia and Brad. Stepping out of their Suburban, the shooters quickly dropped their weapons and put their hands on their heads. Within moments, the driver had exited the vehicle as well. He and each of the shooters were soon on their knees, their hands cuffed behind their backs.

Suddenly, Sonia felt Brad next to her, pulling her upward and into his arms. Without a word, he kissed her. He kissed her long and passionately. She could hardly breathe, though she wasn't sure if that was because of the hormones and desire that were flooding through her body, or because he was holding her so tightly that no air could get into her lungs. He stopped for a moment and pulled back. "I can't believe you. You're so . . . so . . . wonderful. I just have to . . . You're just so . . ." Then he pulled her close again and kissed her for a long, long time.

"My man!" A big, deep voice startled both Sonia and Brad. "How are you this fine day?" Sonia looked up to see a tall, handsome man, not as tall as Brad, but still six feet or so, with black eyes, black wavy hair, and a lean muscular body. He was an imposing figure in his dark blue slacks and light blue button-down shirt, no tie. The dark blue Kevlar vest with the bright yellow DEA letters across it did nothing to soften the image. Sonia checked out his face and was taken aback when he smiled a bright, white, movie-star smile. Hmmm. His skin. It's almost the color of cinnamon.

Brad looked at him. "Well, my friend. I am damn well, thanks to you and the rest of the cavalry." He hadn't yet let go of Sonia.

The bright black eyes turned toward Sonia. "And you, ma'am. You're okay?" His looks were Hispanic, but he spoke with only the tiniest lilt of an accent.

"Yes," said Sonia haltingly, still unsure of what was going on. "Yes, I'm okay." Sonia brushed a wisp of hair out of her face and realized she was covered in dirt. Brushing herself off, she realized, as well, that her hand was still shaking, and in it was a Glock 17. It was still locked and loaded, and dangerous as hell.

The man saw her look down at the handgun. "You might want to make that thing a little safer at this point. You wouldn't want it to go off and take ol' Dunny out, now would you?"

The man's use of the name, Dunny, startled her.

Brad let Sonia slip out of his arms. She dropped the magazine out of the handgrip of her weapon, pulled the slide back, and allowed the gun to eject the live shell that had been waiting in the chamber, waiting to lay down suppressing fire while Dunny took aim and killed those four men in less than ten seconds—able to kill them because they had been foolish enough to think a car door would protect them from an M16 round fired at fifty yards.

Sonia turned to Brad. "And now, would you like to explain?"

"Well—"

The handsome man stepped in between Sonia and Brad. "My name is Roberto Alvarez, miss." He gave Brad a snarky look. "My friends call me Robbie. I'm with the DEA. Dunny and I are, well, good friends I guess you could say. You see, I've done a lot of favors for him, but he's done nothing but get my ass in a sling. So, in an effort to make things right, Captain Dunham, here, decided he would figure out this whole drug delivery scheme, you know, where the drugs come from, where they go, who does the delivering, all of that stuff."

Sonia looked at Brad. *He* was trying to figure things out. *He* was going to discover all that stuff.

"Then he would call me in to wrap things up, and I would get all the credit. Of course, as part of his whole deal, he drags a civilian into harm's way. They go driving all the way down to Rocky Top, where he almost has to pop some guy."

"Now wait a minute." Brad put his hand on Robbie's arm.

Robbie looked quickly at Brad, his smile wry. "Oh no. Let me finish." Then he turned back to Sonia. "So, last weekend ol' Dunny here makes a quick trip down to DC to let me know what he's planning."

Sonia's mind snapped like a trap. *That's* why I couldn't get in touch with him all weekend.

Pointing at Brad's bullet ridden, front-end sagging, mud and grass-covered car, Robbie continued. "You see, after he almost got you killed down in Rocky Top, he figured it was time to give me a heads-up so that we could get a GPS locator on this fine-looking vehicle. That way we could track the two of you all the way from Lexington to wherever-the-hell you all were going."

Sonia gave Brad a look of disbelief. "The whole time? They were following us the whole time?"

"Oh yes, little lady." A big grin crossed Robbie's face. "Oh, and thanks for picking that Holiday Inn Downtown. It's my favorite place to stay in when I'm in Memphis."

Sonia got the implication immediately, and shot Brad a look that would freeze the balls off a polar bear.

Brad turned his palms upward. "Now, in all fairness."

"In all fairness, nothing," Robbie wagged his head. "So, this morning, while my team and I are just cruising our way from Memphis to Nashville, I get a call. He's telling me some cock and bull story about this Corvette flying through the air while you guys were possibly, *possibly*, avoiding detection by circumnavigating some poor farmer down southwest of Nashville. Hard to believe, but he tells me it might just happen again, so I should close ranks a little tighter and be ready to come to your rescue."

"And that you did, my friend." Brad gave him a subtle thumbs-up. "That you did."

Robbie bobbed his head. "That's right. We came running, scooped up these bad boys, who, by the way, are pretty likely to spill their guts about the whole operation, and absolutely nothing bad happened." As he finished his sentence, Robbie smiled and looked directly at what remained of Brad's dark blue Corvette.

Sonia was dumbfounded. All the time that she had been looking at her computer and tracking the feed and hay truck, Robbie Alvarez and his team had been tracking her and Brad. Then it hit her. "Wait a minute. How did you know we were in trouble right now? What made you come to our rescue just at the perfect time?"

"You want to tell her?" Robbie looked at Brad.

Brad, in turn, looked at Sonia. "You called him."

"What?" Her voice began rising.

"You're the one who told him we needed help and that he should come right away."

"No way. I did nothing of the sort." She was emphatic. "I

didn't even know he existed, no less how to tell him we needed help."

"The red button."

"Huh?"

"The red button," he said nonchalantly. "I told you to open the console in the 'Vette and push the red button."

Sonia looked at him blankly. "What the?"

"That was our panic button." Brad broke into a big smile. "You pushed the red panic button and it sent out an SOS to Robbie and his team. They knew it was time to come runnin', guns ablazin'." He turned to Robbie. "And come they did, just in the nick of time."

Sonia was dumbfounded again. "You son-of-a-bitch," she said softly. Then she turned the volume up a serious notch. "We'd called for help and you didn't tell me?" Her face was turning red.

Brad just shrugged his shoulders.

Sonia hit Brad's arm as hard as she could with her open palm then turned and faced the broken-down 'Vette.

"Sonia." Brad's voice fell away. "C'mon Sonia. We didn't have—"

Behind her back, Sonia heard Robbie clap his hands and interrupt. "Well, listen, boys and girls. I've got a team to check on, and we've got some serious agency work to do. You know, questions to ask, stories to take." She turned around just in time to see Robbie give Brad a crooked grin. "Can you take it from here good buddy? Or do you need a ride back to Lexington?"

Sonia took a step back toward both men as Brad was about to speak. "You know, I believe I've had enough of his driving. I think we'll take that ride if you don't mind." She gave Brad a sardonic smile and Robbie a nod of thanks.

PART VII

47

A t ten-forty on Thursday morning, Sonia stood at the bottom of those dreaded stairs and looked up. She was holding her coffee and her croissant and was hoping she could just sit and enjoy them in her own space. She felt tired, fragile, spent. A little over twenty-four hours ago, she had eaten breakfast in a Holiday Inn in Memphis. Since then, she'd almost been killed in a Corvette that had literally crawled up an embankment. Then she'd almost been killed when bullets tore apart that very same car. The thought of it all still rattled her.

When Sonia walked into the BCI offices, Jet waved at her from her desk, then pantomimed that she would talk to Sonia as soon as she finished the call she was on. Sonia smiled and headed for her own office. It had gotten chilly again, and she slipped off the light jacket she'd worn that morning. Five minutes later, when Jet finally walked into Sonia's office, Sonia was sitting there, mindlessly writing out her Roman numerals, her coffee and croissant untouched. XXI, XXII, XXIII . . .

"Well, girl, how'd the trip go? You catch any bad guys?"

Sonia squinted. "Actually, yes." Jet took a seat opposite Sonia's desk, and Sonia went on to describe all of the travails of the second day. There were times her voice cracked, but there was a clear sense of accomplishment in it as well. She had held her own in one of the most dangerous situations she could imagine and she knew it. Still . . . .

Jet shook her head. "Well, honey, you've really been through it, haven't you?"

"I know, damn it. I feel like Alice."

Jet looked at her strangely. "Who?"

"Alice. Alice in Wonderland."

"You mean because you've been out there running around with The Mad Hatter?"

Sonia sat up. "No. Because I feel like I've fallen down the rabbit hole. I mean this whole thing started with just trying to catch Marcos Torres messing around. Then there was Hensley's suicide, which is really a murder. Next thing I know, I'm down in Rocky Top and I'm sure I'm going to be murdered. Then it's off to Memphis, tractors, getting shot at behind a Corvette . . ." Sonia stopped for just a second. "And then there's Brad."

Jet's eyes flashed. "Did he do something bad to you?"

"Not really." A little energy came out of her voice. "Actually, he kissed me and told me that I was wonderful."

Jet gave her a cock-eyed grin. "That son-of-a-bitch."

Sonia wagged her head and started again. "When the shooting was over, he swept me up in his arms and kissed me more passionately than I've ever been kissed. He held me so tight I could barely breathe. Then he looked at me and told me how wonderful I was." A tiny smile started on her face. "We were literally ready to go into combat together . . . as partners. I was his partner." Saying those last few words felt especially rewarding.

Jet held her tongue.

"Of course, he never told me that he'd been in touch with Robbie, that we had backup the whole time. He just left me hanging out there, thinking we were going to die."

Sonia hadn't touched her coffee. Without a word, Jet leaned over and pushed the coffee closer to her.

Sonia waved it off. "Then on the way home, it was like he'd never kissed me, never said those things to me." There was a real edge in her voice now. "He's an honest to goodness Jekyll and Hyde. When we'd left E'town, I was sure we would come home to my place—or his—spend the evening with each other, just enjoy being together. But when we did get home, he just had Robbie drop me off at my place. "He said, 'I hope you enjoy your date.' Idiot! Then he went on with Robbie."

Jet looked her. "Date?"

Sonia wet her lips before speaking. "Well, that morning, after he didn't come to my room in Memphis—"

"Come to your room?"

"Yeah, but he didn't. Then Johnny called me on the road and asked me out. And I said, 'Yes.' But I didn't really want to go. I was just mad at Brad . . . . It's complicated."

Sonia stopped talking and took a slow sip of her coffee. Her croissant sat there untouched.

Jet cleared her throat. "What do you think gives with him? Why do you think he does things like that?"

"I don't know." Sonia turned her head away as if looking for something important.

Jet leaned forward, putting her elbows on Sonia's desk. "No. Seriously, what do you think might be going on? He's clearly not some total bastard. He's treated you nicely at times, sometimes wonderfully. Then he pulls away. Right?"

"I guess."

"But he really doesn't do anything bad to you, does he? He doesn't really mistreat you, or physically hurt you. He doesn't even say anything mean to you, right?"

"No. No, he doesn't ever do anything like that. It's just that he pulls me into his arms, into his world, then he pushes me away. It hurts like hell and it sucks."

Jet's voice softened. "You're right, but that's not my point. It just seems to me that there's something else going on, something that makes him do this to you."

Sonia sat silently for a moment. "Well, if there is, I sure as hell don't know what it might be."

"Tell me," said Jet, sounding more like a detective than a friend. "What do you know about this guy, beyond the obvious? He's a former Marine and NCIS, he's got a good practice as a PI, he's got a cool—I mean, *had*—a cool car. But what do you really know about him?"

Sonia reminded Jet that she had already told her how both Brad's father and mother had been killed, "doing the right thing." Her body language softened as she gave Jet a thumbnail refresher on how he had served in the Marines but left because he no longer felt like he was doing the right thing. How he had served with NCIS. Finally, having run out of steam, she said, "I guess Dunny's just always been a good person."

Jet's head twisted. "Who?"

"Dunny. That's what his friend Robbie called him." Her voice perked up. "That's what all his close friends call him I guess."

"How do you know that?"

Sonia shook her head. "That computer lady he set me up with mentioned it. She seemed to know him really well. In fact, now that I think about it, she said something very strange to me. She said, 'Good luck with your investigation.' " Sonia cocked her head. "Then she said in a weird way, 'Good luck with everything.' It was like there was a secret message there, one I didn't get."

"And that's all she told you. Just that everyone called him 'Dunny?' " Jet's energy was rising.

"Yes, but there seemed to be some sort of subtext there for her. It was like she was trying to communicate something to me, but I never grasped it." Sonia reached for her coffee again.

Jet stood up. "Well, don't you think it's time you found out what that secret message was?" She walked behind Sonia, put her hands on Sonia's shoulders, and massaged them gently. "Honey, it's time you got in touch with that lady and found out what you're missing. You've earned it. You've earned the right to know what she knows. And if she was willing to hint at it when she didn't even know you, I'll bet she'll flat out tell you if you just ask her the right way."

Sonia dropped her head and shoulders, trying to let her muscles relax in Jet's hands. "But I don't even know who she is. I don't even know her name."

"Then how the hell did you get to talk to her?" Sonia could hear the confusion in Jet's voice.

"Brad. Brad set it up." Sonia stretched her back and rolled her head from side to side. "He just told me to be in his office at a certain time and that there would be a clandestine phone call from some computer geek he used to work with. He said the person would help me hack into the drug ring's communications, and he—I mean she—did."

"So, the only way you can get to this woman is through Brad? Is that true?"

"I'm afraid it is. And I can't do that. I can't ask Brad who that woman is."

Jet stood behind Sonia for another moment, though she had stopped massaging Sonia's shoulders. "No, but you could ask for more help, couldn't you?"

"Oh, I don't know." Sonia kept rolling her head, trying to lose the headache that wanted so desperately to afflict her, the same one she always got after she got angry. "We've already gotten into the system. I really don't think I need any more help."

Jet swiveled Sonia's chair around and looked directly at her. "Trust me, girl." She was completely energized. "You need help. You need help, and the only person in the world who can help you is that woman. You're going to go right over to that Captain Dunham and tell him you've got another great idea, but you need more computer help to do it. And you don't just need computer help. You need computer help from that same lady."

Sonia's eyebrows, shoulders, and voice went up. "Come on. How do I do that? I can't make him call someone without giving him a good reason. What if he asks about my great new idea?"

Jet leaned forward and put her hands on the arms of Sonia's chair. Her face was only a foot or so from Sonia's. "Don't you worry about that. You'll think of something. You just need to have him set up another phone call between you and her, and you need to tell him he can't be there when you're talking to her."

Sonia leaned back in the chair. "But why? Why would I need that?"

Then, in her favorite southern accent, Jet said, "Oh you got reasons, my dear. Lord-a-mercy do you have reasons. They're right there below your eyebrows and on either side of your nose."

Sonia's hand went unconsciously to her face. "What?"

"Honey chil', do you think the good Lord gave you those beautiful chocolate-brown eyes just so you could see better? No, no, no, my little honey lamb. Those eyes are powerful tools, tools you're gonna use to help Captain Dunham realize how important it is that you speak to this woman—and that you do it alone. Oh, my, my, my. It could be a matter of national security."

Sonia smiled for the first time in hours. "I can always count on you, can't I?"

"Well, sugar plum, that's what we women do. We stand together through thick and thin, no matter what those damn Yankees do to us."

"Enough already." Sonia shook her head. "I get it. I know the plan. Now quit talking like you just made a dress out of one of the curtains at Tara and get back to work." She turned her chair around and faced her desk. "Just pray for me that I'll be able to come up with something to say to Brad and that I'll be able to pull it off."

Jet put her hand on Sonia's shoulder, squeezed, then walked around Sonia's desk and left the room.

Sonia looked for something to straighten on her desk but found nothing. She turned her chair around again, looked out the window, and started planning how she was going to get Brad to help her speak to her secret technology guru. She heard a soft tap on the doorjamb of her office. She looked up.

Jet leaned back in and asked, "By the way, what's the deal with Johnny Adams?"

Sonia sighed. "Oh, that. I told him that we should get together for dinner when I got back to town, but when he called, I just had to tell him that I was too beat to do anything last night."

"And tomorrow night?" Jet's voice and eyebrows went up.

"No, I'm done." Sonia shook her head gently back and forth. "Right now, I'm not sure I have the stomach for being with any man."

Jet nodded. "Good enough, girlfriend. He wins some. He loses some. And this was a monumental loss." She pursed her lips. "For Johnny, that is," she crossed her hands over her breast, "bless his little heart."

48

J ust past a quarter 'til twelve, Sonia walked across the street and knocked on the door of Brad's office.

"Come in!"

Sonia walked through the door and found him sitting at his desk. "Good morning." She took a seat in front of him, sitting forward on the chair. "How are you?" Sonia sounded a whole lot more chipper than she felt.

"I'm good. A little worn out from the past few days, but good. How about you?"

"Oh, I'm fine, doing great. So, is Robbie still in town?" She smiled. It wasn't easy.

Brad's hands were still, his facial expression neutral. "I know that he spent the night here. I haven't seen him this morning, but we did talk on the phone."

Sonia struggled to stay upbeat. "And how's he feeling about what happened yesterday?"

Brad leaned back in his chair. "Well, bad news and good news. As you would expect, once we were made by those guys and they came after us at E'town, the whole surveillance plan was pretty much blown." He shrugged his shoulders. "Our bad, but that's just the way it goes. You seldom get to roll up the entire operation at once.

"On the other hand, we were able to give Robbie a pretty good idea about this side of the delivery chain, including southern Kentucky and some of Tennessee." Brad's pace quickened. "Also, and this is great, Robbie had left some guys watching the Memphis hub, and two more feed and hay trucks took off from there early that morning. Of course, his guys followed them and eventually picked them up as well."

Brad leaned his elbows on his desk. "Given that all the men they've rounded up are only drivers and delivery guys, it won't take much of a deal offer to get them to spill their guts. All in all, you and I have given Robbie quite a nice picture of the operation to show to his superiors. I hope he gets a lot of credit."

His words lifted Sonia's heart. She knew it hadn't been a perfect operation. They had, after all, been "made" by the drug dealers. Still, to hear that everything they had done and been through in the last few days had led to the DEA arresting not just one group of criminals, but several, made her happy—made her proud. And the fact that Robbie Alvarez believed those arrests would most likely lead to the unraveling of the whole operation . . . well, that was something. She took in a deep breath. We did it . . . *together*. She felt a sense of pride and accomplishment. "Well, I'm glad it all worked out."

"Are you kidding?" Brad became more energetic, his face full of satisfaction. "We did great. You get what you can get when you can get it. That's how it goes in this business." He let out a big breath and relaxed back into his chair.

Sonia paused, then decided to move forward. It was great to hear all of this, but she had another agenda for this meeting. "So, listen. I know we still haven't quite figured out what happened with Hensley, and I've got another idea about how a computer program could help."

Brad's eyes opened wide. "Really?"

Sonia sat up taller, her body language keeping him at bay. "Now, don't get too excited, it's just an idea. In fact, I'm not quite sure how to do it. Do you think you could set me up with that same technology geek who helped me the last time so she can get me started?"

He shook his head slightly. "Well, maybe not her, but I'm sure I can get someone."

"No," said Sonia, trying to keep her voice calm. "I really want it to be her. We had such a nice working relationship and, you know, I'm a little embarrassed talking to these real pros. Can't you make it happen with her, please."

"If it's that important to you." The expression on his face made it clear that he didn't quite understand why it was so important that she worked with the same expert, but he seemed willing to go along. "You did, after all, get us a real lead on the whole set-up. Let me see what I can do and I'll get back—"

Sonia took a quick breath. "Also, I'd really like her to call me at my office. That way I can be at my own computer . . . in my own space."

Brad sat silent for a moment then leaned in. "Can't you bring your laptop over here?"

Sonia leaned in as well and looked directly at Brad with just a slight pout on her lips, "Well, I'm really a little embarrassed about this whole thing. It just seems like I'll be able to think more clearly and work better with her if I don't feel any pressure from anyone."

Brad squinted. "From me?"

"Well, you know, you're the pro." She sighed. "You've got all that experience." Sonia's head rocked a little to her left. Her eyes opened wider. Her face softened.

Brad leaned back in his chair again, this time tenting his fingers—searching for an answer. He unconsciously let out a sigh. "Okay, but are you sure you can't share anything about this with me now?"

Knowing that she and her chocolate-brown eyes had already won the day, Sonia didn't back down. "No, I'm sure. I wouldn't want to embarrass myself. Just help me talk to what's-her-name and I'll let you know if something comes of it."

Sonia had cast a line, trying to find out the woman's name, but Brad didn't bite. He had brought the woman in on the down low; years of experience made it easy for him not to stumble and let her name slip.

Brad sat forward again and planted his hands on his desk with a distinct thud. "All right. I'll give you a call as soon as I have it set up. Now, do you want to talk about how we're going to wrap this Hensley thing up?"

"Not right now." Sonia popped out of her seat and headed for the door. She had gotten what she'd come for and she didn't want to take any chances. "Let me run down this other thing, and then we can talk." She just tossed a, "Thanks," over her shoulder, stepped into the hallway, and closed the door. She felt the distinct urge to whistle "Zippity Do Dah" as she left the building.

AT FOUR O'CLOCK in the afternoon, Sonia was sitting at her desk when her phone rang. It was Brad, saying he could set up a conversation with the NCIS technology expert if she could do it immediately.

Sonia's stomach flipped, but she tried to speak nonchalantly. "I'm available right now." She stood up and walked to her office door, closing it gently. Then, with a quick, "I'll be waiting," she hung up and sat back down at her desk, absentmindedly still holding her cell phone. What if she won't help me? What if she can't? What if she tells me things I don't want to hear?

Suddenly, the phone in Sonia's hand rang, startling her. She took a deep breath. "Hello. This is Sonia Vitale."

"Sonia, this is your friend. I understand I might be able to help you with some technology questions." The voice was bright and friendly.

Sonia wouldn't have said she was prepared for this, but she did know there was no point in beating around the bush. She jumped right in. "Thank you so much for calling, but I'm afraid you've been lied to. You see, I don't have a technology question. I've got a much more important question."

There was a pause on the other end of the line, but before Sonia could go any further, the woman at the other end said, *"It's about Dunny, isn't it?"* The tone of her voice had changed.

There was another moment of a silence. Then Sonia answered tentatively, "Yes, it is."

"Somehow I just knew."

Sonia's voice rose. "How—how did you know?" Slowly, Sonia spun her chair around until she was looking out her window onto East Main.

"I knew the first time Dunny asked me to help you that he was all about you. I knew the first time I spoke with you that you were starting to fall for him as well. Just starting, but definitely there."

"How could it have been that obvious? I didn't even have feelings for him then."

"Oh, yes you did, sweetheart. You just didn't know it yet. And now?"

Sonia waited for there to be something else before she realized she'd been asked a question. It was hard for her to give an honest answer, but she knew that if she weren't honest with this mystery woman the whole phone call would be a waste. She plowed ahead. "And now, I guess I just need to know where I stand."

She had trouble going on, but the voice on the end of the phone went on for her. *"And you think, even hope, that he cares for you, right?"*

For some reason, tears were welling up in Sonia's eyes. "Right."

"*But you can't tell, because he keeps pulling away from you, holding back, like he's protecting someone, right?*"

Sonia reached back and grabbed a tissue from her desk. She blotted her eyes, trying not to smear her mascara. This woman she'd never met was telling her more about her relationship with Dunny than she knew herself. She'd never thought about him protecting himself, but now that she heard the woman say it, she knew that's exactly how it felt.

"You're right, you're so right about that. But I don't know why. I don't know what to do. What do I do? What do I say to him?"

"*Let me ask you a question. Do you know why he's like that? Do you know his story?*"

Sonia stopped for a minute and thought. "Well, I guess I do. He told me that he lost his father, and that he lost his mom. Is that it? Is that what's made him like this?

The voice on the phone rose. "*Wait a minute. You know about his dad being killed and about his mom dying. Is that all you know?*"

"Well, then he went to the university here, he joined the Marines, he worked for NCIS."

"*And that's all you know? You don't know anything else?*"

Sonia began to panic. What is it? What else is there? Has he done something terrible? She said nothing.

"*Let me fill you in.*"

The phone call lasted another twenty minutes. When it was over, Sonia sat quietly at her desk, tears running down her face. She couldn't get her mind around what she had just heard.

49

S onia was still at her desk when a quiet knock interrupted her thoughts. She looked up and saw Jet. Sonia didn't say anything. She didn't motion Jet in. She just sat there.

"Are you okay?" asked Jet quietly. She took a tentative step. "Is it okay if I come in?"

Sonia nodded her head.

Jet slipped into the room and sat on the edge of Sonia's desk. "Can you tell me about it?"

Sonia blotted her eyes, protecting her mascara from the tears that were welling up and the ones that had already fallen. She sat up a little taller and took a deep breath. "It's Brad. It's what he's been through. Oh, Jet, I feel so sorry for him. And I feel so bad, like I've just walked all over his feelings like . . . like a careless teenager."

"That's not true," said Jet, firmly. "I know that's just not true. That's not who you are. Tell me. What happened to him?"

Sonia looked around for her coffee. She and the cup had both been sitting there quite a while and she had to settle for a tiny sip of cold liquid. She spoke in a flat, neutral tone—numb. "I told you that his dad and mom had been killed and that after Iraq, the

Marines assigned him to NCIS." She swallowed hard. "Well, while he was stationed in Maryland, he was assigned to the same unit as a certain female agent. She was beautiful and he was, well, he was Dunny; and they seemed to be in love. And everybody loved seeing them be in love. He was happy, maybe for the first time since his folks died."

She took another breath. "Then one day this whacko sailor who was totally pissed at the government starts shooting up some post office in the city. It's not the job of NCIS to jump in, they do investigative work; but his girlfriend is nearby and she's armed, so she goes right in there to try to save anybody she can."

"Oh my God," said Jet quietly.

"Well the whacko sailor sees her and tells her that he's got three hostages, three postal workers, and he's going to kill them all. And she . . . she tells him that if he lets the others go that he can take her as a hostage. She says she makes a better hostage because she works for the Navy, just like him."

Sonia tried to take another breath but couldn't. She coughed several times instead. "So, he tells her to put down her weapon and he'll let the others go. And she does it." Sonia's body leaned forward and her brown eyes reached out to the empathy that was written on Jet's face, on her lips, in her blue eyes. "And she *does* it," she whispered softly.

Sonia stopped for a moment and looked blankly out into the BCI offices. Then she continued. "So, the guy lets the three hostages go and then he makes the girlfriend call her office, you know, the NCIS office. Brad is there and he hears all about it with the rest of his guys. They all go flying down there. The police and MPs, the Military Police, they have the place surrounded by then but Brad sneaks past them and walks right into the place."

Sonia's pace quickened. "The guy and the girlfriend are behind one of the counters by then, and he's got some sort of box cutter right at the girlfriend's throat. Without drawing his gun, so the guy doesn't freak out, Brad walks right up to him.

"The guy knows Brad must have a gun so he tells him to put it on the counter. And Brad does it. Then Brad says, 'Time for another trade. If you're any kind of man, you'll take me as a hostage, not some little lady. Hell, she's half your size.' The guy doesn't answer, so Brad says, 'You got the balls to take a real man hostage instead of some woman?' "

An image of the anger and fear Brad must have felt at that moment flashed through Sonia's mind. "But then the guy loses it. He says, 'Cool, I'll take you as a hostage, hotshot. But that means I don't need this bitch anymore,' and he just pulls the blade across her throat, killing her instantly."

Sonia stopped again. Jet didn't say a word, she just reached out and took hold of Sonia's arm, squeezing it firmly, tears running down her own face.

After a moment, Sonia took a breath and continued. "So, Brad goes nuts and charges the guy. But the guy gets to his gun first. The guy gets off a few of rounds and Brad's hit several times, but he goes flying over the counter anyway and takes the guy to the ground." Sonia sat up taller and gave Jet a weak smile. "Well, of course, as soon as the shots were fired, all kinds of police and MPs come rushing into the place yelling and stuff and they don't see anyone in there. But as they come around the end of the counter, they see Brad holding the girlfriend in his arms. They're both covered in blood, her blood, his blood." Sonia stopped there and was still.

"And the guy?" The words were shaky in Jet's throat.

Sonia swallowed hard. "They found him dead. Brad had grabbed his head and twisted it so hard he broke the guy's neck and spinal cord. Brad said later that all he was doing was using the skills the Marines had given him before they sent him off to Iraq."

It took a few moments for Jet to digest the story. Sonia sank back in her chair, her shoulders slumped, her chin dropped to her chest. As she did, a thought clarified in her mind. She knew she wanted to work with Brad, to be his partner, maybe more than his partner. She knew as well, however, that if he came to see her in the same light he saw this other woman, as a victim, they would never be equals—in their work—in a relationship. No, she would have to come through this whole thing as the strong, competent person she knew she was—that she knew she had always been.

Jet broke into her thoughts again. "And Brad. Was he okay?"

"Yeah. Well, kind of. He was in the hospital for a week or so while the bullet wounds started to heal, but his friend said he was never the same."

Sonia stopped speaking. Jet let the silence hang in the room as she moved to the red chair across from Sonia's desk, the same kind that sat across from her own.

Eventually, Sonia took yet another deep breath and forced herself to sit up. She looked at her coffee cup but decided to pass. "You know, one night they were out drinking, Brad and the friend. I think she had it bad for him. And I think he liked her too. So, they're out drinking and he tells her that it was all his fault that the girlfriend died."

"Because he rushed in to save her?"

Sonia's voice became stronger. "No. That's the thing. Not because he rushed in, but simply because he loved her. It's like he feels that once he loves somebody it puts them in danger. When she started to talk to me, she said something about it feeling like he was protecting someone. Well, I thought she meant he was protecting himself. That wasn't it. He was protecting the other person." Sonia touched her chest, covering her heart. "Jet, he's been protecting me."

50

Sonia had gone home with Jet that evening and slept on Jet's couch, simply because she didn't want to be alone. Without waking Jet, she'd gotten up early Friday morning, gone back to her own place, packed a few things, and left town. Driving up to Cincinnati, to the predominantly Italian neighborhood in which she had grown up, she'd spent the weekend with her folks. They, of course, had been able to tell that she was deeply shaken, but they'd had the good sense to mostly leave her alone and, in true Italian fashion, feed her well. Several times over the course of the weekend her mother had said, "*Mangia. Mangia figlia mia.* Eat, my child."

The only difficult moment in the weekend had come when Johnny Adams had called Sonia on her cell. Sonia had slipped off into the bathroom for a little privacy, sitting on the closed toilet, holding her phone to her ear—not on speaker. Though she had spoken softly, her voice had echoed in the old, black and white tiled bathroom. "Okay, Johnny. Thanks for waiting. How are you? . . . Oh, I'm fine. Just thought I'd get away and spend some time with my folks." Her tone of voice had been much more subdued than her words. ". . . Monday? Oh, I don't think so. Actually, Johnny," she'd brushed that wisp of hair out of her face, "we really should talk . . . . No, no, it's not that. It's just that I think we need to take a break. There's so much going on right now . . . . Yes, but . . . . Really, Johnny, my life, well . . . ." She'd run her fingers through her hair. "I guess I've just come to the conclusion that I need a little space right now. I'm just not ready to be in a relationship, and I don't want to be unfair to you . . . . No, it's nothing you've done. You've been so sweet and kind. It just wouldn't be right . . . . Honestly, I just think it's best we don't see each other at all for a while. But I hope we can still be . . . Listen, Johnny. I've got to run. My mom's putting dinner on the table. Thanks for calling. I'll talk to you . . . Thanks for calling."

Sonia had hung up. She'd shaken her head. My gosh, Sonia, could you have been any more lame than that? There must be a better way to do that.

SONIA DROVE the hour and twenty-five-minute trip back to Lexington on Sunday afternoon, the light green leaves of spring giving the rolling hills through which she drove a sense of freshness, of new beginnings. By Monday morning at ten o'clock sharp, she knocked on Brad's door and entered his office. Robbie Alvarez was already there, and he and Brad were standing by the coffee pot, well into discussing how the DEA was trying to roll up as much of the drug operation as they could.

"Good morning," Brad and Robbie said almost simultaneously. Then Brad added, "Have a good weekend?"

Sonia put on her best casual smile. "Nice. Just went home to see the folks and get in a little family time. Are we finally ready to talk about John Hensley?"

Brad gave her a long look, a look that made it obvious that he wasn't buying her smile. "That we are." He held a coffee cup out to Sonia as an offering. She shook her head.

He continued. "Generally, a local murder is not a DEA issue, but since solving it might well help us bring in the real kingpin of the drug operation, Robbie believes he can help us with DEA resources. I've just been bringing him up to speed on your computer program and some of the characters we believe we've identified."

Brad sat down at his desk, while Sonia and Robbie sat in the two chairs across from him. Robbie turned his attention to Sonia. "So, you think this Sofia is up in Ohio, probably Cincinnati, and that he or she is the head of the whole thing."

Sonia nodded.

"Then you've got this Forty, who you think is running the Lexington operation. Is that right?"

Sonia sat up a little taller, remembering that the chair she was sitting in was meant to make her feel less important than 'the man.' "Yes, as far as we can tell from the emails. There's an awful lot of traffic, so it's hard to be sure. Also, there seem to be one or two other names that pop up a lot when you look at Forty's communications."

Robbie looked to Brad, then back to Sonia. "So where do we go from here?"

Sonia and Brad looked at each other, but neither jumped in with any answers. Robbie cleared his throat. "Well, clearly our first task is to find out who these folks are, but our real goal is to prove their involvement, not only in the drug operation but in the murder as well. That's where the real leverage lies. If we can get them on the murder charge they'll sing like canaries about the drugs in order to get a lighter sentence on the bigger deal."

Brad gave Robbie a wry smile. "Sounds easy. All we have to do is find out who runs this gigantic drug operation and then get them to very politely tell us that they just happened to have ordered the murder of Hensley. Nice." Brad chuckled and smiled at Sonia. "What do we do *after* lunch?"

"Okay, wiseass," said Robbie, his bright, white smile reflecting his respect for his former colleague.

"Of course, we've got that license plate as a starting point." Brad's blue eyes drifted to Sonia. "Thanks to Ms. Sonia, here."

"That's right." Robbie reached into his pocket and took out his smartphone. He scrolled around, checking some notes. "In fact, it leads us to a company in Cincinnati, Allegro Imports. They fly in inexpensive leather goods and wicker items from all over the world." He gave them both a sly look. "There's every chance something funny could be going on there as well." Then he got more serious again. "The paperwork lists an Alexi Dimitrov as the head guy."

Sonia slid back in her chair. Brad and Robbie looked off absently, silently—pondering. Finally, Sonia sat up taller. "Actually, I might just have a plan that could help us find these folks. And after that, who knows."

Sonia didn't go on, so Robbie looked to Brad, "Does she always hold back like this?"

Brad's blue eyes honed in on Sonia again. "Hold back? Those are not words I usually think of when I think of Sonia Vitale." He smiled.

"Okay," she started. "What if we get back into the operation's emails and generate a few of our own? We send one to Sofia, making it look like it comes from Forty. It could say, 'Need to see you as soon as possible. Meet at my place at eight tonight. DO NOT RESPOND!' Then we send one to Forty, making it look like it comes from Sofia. That one could say, 'Need to see you at your place. Be there at eight tonight. DO NOT RESPOND!' "

Sonia could feel Robbie's eyes on her. "Go on."

She turned directly to him. "Do we know where Allegro Imports is located? Do we know how to find the car Sofia uses?"

"Honey," Robbie chuckled, "in today's computer world, we can find anything." He smiled. "That is if we know what we're looking for."

Sonia sat farther forward in her chair, right at its edge. "So, we can do two things. First, we can just go out to Dahlia Farm and wait to see who shows up. Second, since we're pretty sure it's going to be Dimitrov, we put someone on that car to follow it. Most likely they follow Sofia and his car right down to Dahlia Farm, and then by implication, we have a pretty good chance of proving who those two folks are." She could tell the guys were with her. "We prove Dimitrov is Sofia and Hollings, the farm manager, is Forty."

Robbie shook his head. "Well, that might leave us a bit short of proving who they are, but it sure gets us a reason to bring them in for questioning, and probably enough to get a search warrant as well." He shrugged his shoulders. "We just see where it goes after that."

Brad sat back in his chair and turned to Robbie. "Sounds like a plan." Then he smiled at Sonia. "A good plan."

"One other thing." Sonia looked back and forth from Brad to Robbie. She spoke with a new-found authority. "I'll find a way to send copies to those two or three other email accounts that seem connected to Forty. I'll just make it look like they've been accidentally copied or something. Maybe, just maybe, one or two of them will show up as well."

Robbie stood. "The more the merrier." He smiled down at Sonia. "Okay, let me call the Cincinnati office and get a team ready to tail Dimitrov's car tonight." He looked down at Brad. "We are doing this tonight, right?"

Sonia jumped in. "Absolutely. Tonight."

"Okay," said Robbie. "Sonia, you send those emails today. I'll get the teams in place to follow Dimitrov and back us up." He turned his attention to Brad. "Alright then, it's a go. Seven o'clock tonight." Robbie took a step toward the door, then turned back to Brad. "Why don't *you* spend the day trying to talk the Chevy dealer into giving you a new Corvette, seeing as the other one didn't hold up very well."

Brad smiled politely, then sat forward and rested his left elbow on his desk. He made a cranking motion with his other hand, slowly raising the middle finger on his left hand to indicate that he thought Robbie was number one in his book.

A broad smile crossed Robbie's face. "Back at ya, buddy." He left the office.

Sonia stood up to leave as well.

"Wait a minute," Brad said. But when Sonia stopped and looked at him expectantly, he seemed to be at a loss for words. She watched him struggle. Finally, the words came out. "Uh, nice job."

"Thanks," Sonia replied. She walked out the door.

51

A t seven o'clock that evening, Sonia and Jet walked up the steps to the white house. They were both wearing, black shoes, black tops, and dark jeans. Sonia was wearing her quilted vest, Jet her dark blue jacket. Sonia had copies of the emails she had sent that afternoon. Without knocking, they walked right into Brad's office and found Brad sitting at his desk, Robbie sitting in one of the soft chairs. Sonia smiled and put her purse down by the umbrella stand near the door. "Good Evening." She noted the surprise on their faces.

Brad cocked his head. "What are you doing here?"

Sonia looked quickly at Jet, then back to Brad. "What do you mean? We're doing this tonight, right?"

Brad answered quickly, nodding his head toward Robbie. "Yes. *We're* doing this tonight. Robbie and I."

Sonia's voice rose. "And Jet and I." There was no question mark at the end of that statement.

Robbie stood and turned to them. "No, no, ladies. I'm afraid there's been a bit of a misunderstanding here. This is now an official DEA operation, and I'm afraid there's no place for civilians here."

Sonia's head bobbed back. Her foot started tapping. "Oh, no you don't. You're not keeping me out of this. If it weren't for me, everyone in the world would believe that John Hensley committed suicide. Everyone, that is, except the people who killed him." She wagged her finger at Robbie. "And if it weren't for Brad and me, you would have no idea about the drug operation, or the distribution line down into Tennessee. Hell, the hub in Memphis for that matter." She shook her head. "Oh, no. Brad's going and I'm going too." Sonia glanced at Jet and then back to Robbie. "And so is Jet, my partner."

Robbie shot her a look. When he answered, he was almost condescending. "Well, of course Brad is going. We can make an exception for an 'essential civilian,' and he'll come as one of those. But you and Jet, that's not going to happen."

Sonia turned to Brad seeking support. Suddenly, his history of losing people he loved shot through her mind. She did understand, but still . . . . She looked directly into those bright blue eyes. "Brad?"

Brad stood, walked around his desk, and approached Sonia. "Listen, babe." His voice was soothing. "This could get dangerous. These could well be the people who killed John Hensley. I couldn't stand it if somehow you got hurt," his eyes turned to Jet, "or Jet either."

"No." Sonia turned away from him, walking toward the window that overlooked East Main. At the window, she turned back to Brad, her expression firm. "Now you look here. I get it. I get that you don't want me or Jet to get hurt. Well, you know what? I don't want *you* to get hurt either. You or your buddy Robbie." Her voice was strong, very strong. "But I'm not telling you to not go, am I? No. This is my case, our case, as much as Robbie's. And if anyone is an 'essential civilian,' " her fingers wiggled quotation marks in the air, "it's me; me and Jet."

Neither Brad nor Robbie responded at first, but then Robbie spoke. "And exactly how do you come to that conclusion?"

Sonia's mind spun. "Well . . ." The words formed in her mouth as quickly as they formed in her brain. They flew out of her. "The car. The car you tracked down. With the license plate. That's not the same car I saw on the day Hensley died. What if those two cars aren't connected at all? Don't you need someone to verify it's the same car Sofia came in? And . . . ." Her mind was spinning. She knew how lame that first reason was, but she had to make her case. "And . . . . And as a matter of fact. How do we know that Dimitrov has anything to do with any of this? That he's the guy who got out of the car and walked into the barn that day. Don't you need an eye-witness to identify him as the same guy? Don't you?"

Robbie took in a breath and turned to Brad. "She may have a point there."

Brad's head was slowly shaking back and forth. Sonia knew he was scrambling to find the one thing that could shoot down all of Sonia's reasons.

Sonia beat him to the punch. "And come to think of it." She stuck her chin out. "Why didn't you call Robbie in sooner?"

Brad didn't answer.

"No, come on." She walked toward Brad, almost belligerent. "Answer my question. Why did you wait to call Robbie in on this whole thing?"

Brad's voice was quiet, small. "Well, I'd gotten him involved in something else earlier." He stopped.

Sonia wouldn't let it go. "And?"

Brad stood up taller, spoke stronger. "And it turned out that I was wrong. And that brought down a bunch of shit on him. Screwed him up good."

Sonia was winning this argument and she knew it. She glanced at Jet, who had been silent but following the verbal battle closely. She turned back to Brad. "And how would it look, now that Robbie has brought in DEA resources, if it turns out that Dimitrov owns Allegro Imports and that's it? He just owns

Allegro Imports. And the blond guy I saw that day on the farm isn't Dimitrov at all. Do you want to arrest this guy, only to find out that we're wrong about all of this? That you've dragged Robbie down the dumper again?" She brushed that wisp of hair out of her face—with energy.

Brad walked back toward his desk. He turned and leaned against it. He spoke softly. "No. No. That can't happen." He turned to Robbie. "What do you think?"

Robbie shrugged. "I think she's got us, partner. I sure as hell don't want another bust to go south on me. And she's right. Hell, we're looking at a blond guy, while we're chasing someone with a woman's name. And, we've made a bit of a leap from one black Lincoln to another as well. I think we go in there together and make sure we're taking down the right guy."

"Okay." Brad's voice tightened. "But she's not coming any closer to these guys than absolutely necessary. She gets to come along, but only as far as it takes for her to ID Dimitrov as the guy who was there on the farm that day." He looked at Sonia. "And no guns, okay?"

Sonia was about to argue when she felt Jet lean subtly against her. She glanced quickly at Jet and then turned back to Robbie. "And Jet comes too."

Robbie took a deep breath and sighed. "And why is that?"

Sonia stuck her chin out again. "Because you need *me,* and I'm not going anywhere without *her.*"

Brad and Robbie exchanged glances, then Robbie spoke, looking directly at Jet. "You do understand that you're doing this of your own free will and that if, God forbid, anything bad happens, the agency is taking no responsibility what-so-ever."

Jet gave all three of them her biggest, warmest smile. "Oh, Colonel. You needn't worry about little ol' me."

Sonia rolled her eyes and watched Brad and Robbie exchange a glance. Damn it, girl. Drop it. Sonia's chocolate-brown eyes flashed Jet a warning. Let that go.

A car horn sounded outside the offices of Semper Fi Investigations.

Robbie looked around the room. "Okay, then. Let's roll."

Sonia grabbed Jet's hand and gave it a quick squeeze. She reached for her purse.

Brad stopped and gave Sonia the look. "No. Guns. Robbie and I go in. Both of you stay in the car. Something goes south, the two of you just get the hell out of there."

Sonia hesitated, but it was too late to argue. She reached into her purse. She pulled out the emails and stuffed them into her jeans, leaving the purse, heavy with her Glock, on the floor. Jet followed suit. Then all four of them filed out of Brad's office and into a big, black suburban. It struck Sonia that for all the movies and TV shows she'd watched, she'd never actually seen the inside of one of these vehicles, especially one that could carry them to a possible confrontation with some very bad people.

52

B y seven-forty, the black DEA Suburban was sitting across the street from the castle. They were hoping to see a black Lincoln approach from the east and turn onto Pisgah Pike, headed for Dahlia Farm. Brad and Robbie sat in the front seats, Sonia and Jet in the back.

Just a few minutes after they had settled in, Sonia looked forward between the two men. "Wait a minute. Who's that?"

Robbie spoke first. "What?"

"That pickup truck, the one that's just coming down Pisgah Pike. I'm sure that's Steve Hollings' truck."

Jet leaned over and looked between the men as well. "Are you sure? How can you tell? It's so dark."

"Trust me." Sonia watched the truck turn left toward town. "I watched that farm for days, and there's enough light here for me to know one thing. That's Steve Hollings' truck. It's the one with the roll bars behind the cab."

Brad turned his head to follow the truck as well. "I thought your messages told them to meet at Dahlia Farm. Why would he be leaving now?"

"No." Sonia's voice was stern. "My message said, 'Meet me at my place.' We're the ones who assumed it would be at the farm."

"Could be Hollings' home," said Jet. "Couldn't it?"

"Well, we can't just let him drive away." Robbie started the Suburban. "We're just going to have to trust that Sonia is right about everything and follow this guy." He touched the transmitter in his ear. "DEA unit six. You guys still on Dimitrov?"

Sonia couldn't hear the response, but she could sense that the plan was still in place.

Robbie spoke again. "Looks like this whole thing may be going down somewhere other than Dahlia Farm. Just keep me informed on your end."

The Suburban took off and followed Steve Hollings as he drove down Route 60, into town. After a few zig-zag turns, he stopped his car on Second Street, near the intersection with Spruce. Hollings got out of his car, looked around, then crossed the street. He turned around the corner of a long, one-story building and disappeared.

Sonia looked to her left and saw that Jet was already on her phone, using her Google Maps application. Jet whispered to herself. "247 East Second Street. Got it. Whoa!"

Sonia was trying, with no luck, to read the phone upside down. "Whoa, what?"

Jet looked at Sonia, then at the two faces that were looking back at her over their shoulders. "That, ladies and gentlemen, is the County Coroner's Office."

Robbie turned forward while Brad put his hand on the Suburban's hefty door handle. "Here we go. You ladies stay in the car."

Sonia's hand shot out and grabbed Brad's shoulder. "And how do I make a positive ID from inside the car? I'm going in. I've got to go in." She felt Jet's elbow poke her in the ribs. "*We've* got to go in."

Brad hesitated, then let out a quick breath. "Okay, but just long enough to make the ID. Just as soon as we know it's the right guy, you're out of there. Got it? You go back to the car."

Sonia responded softly. "Okay."

Brad spoke pointedly. "Right now, stay behind us. You stay behind us. Got it?"

Sonia exchanged a look with Jet. She was determined to be a part of this, but that didn't mean she wasn't apprehensive. She was glad to do what Brad was asking.

The four of them crossed the street and turned the same corner Hollings had. Robbie silently pointed to another Suburban sitting across the road on Spruce Street. Sonia got the message. Those were Robbie's agents. Then Sonia grabbed Brad's elbow, stopping him in his tracks. She, too, pointed, this time at a black Lincoln parked further down Spruce Street.

"Is that the car?" Brad whispered.

Sonia shook her head. "Same kind, but I don't think it's the same one. That one looks a little different. Maybe he has a bunch of them."

They moved on and came to an area lighted by a small outdoor lamp. Below the lamp was a metal door which had been propped open. Robbie turned to the group and nodded his head toward the door. *Here we go.*

The foursome slipped through the metal door and moved as slowly and quietly as possible down several halls, finally, passing through double doors marked, "Medical Examiner." They heard the muffled sounds of a conversation. Following those sounds, they found themselves standing outside another door, this one marked, "Autopsy." It was wood and glass, with a small curtain over the window portion.

Brad whispered to Robbie. "Sounds like two males and a female."

"Agreed." Robbie leaned closer to the door, straining to hear more.

Suddenly, the conversation ratcheted up to a full-blown argument. Robbie pulled his weapon and held it down along his side. Brad followed suit. Robbie gave Brad the "Are-you-ready," look.

Brad turned toward the girls but looked directly at Sonia. "Stay here. Stay put. When we get in there, I'm going to push that curtain aside. If Dimitrov is in there, don't do anything. Just let us take care of it. If he's not, if everything seems normal in there, you come in and keep us from doing something we'll all regret."

"Oh, don't you worry, Colonel, we—"

"Shut up!" Brad whispered. The level of his intensity made it clear that he'd had enough of Jet's southern drawl.

Sonia had had enough as well. This wasn't play acting. This was real. This was the third life or death situation in which Sonia had found herself in the last week. Jet, it appeared, didn't seem to grasp the gravity of the moment.

Robbie tapped Brad on the arm. "Time to roll, buddy." Without waiting for Brad's response, Robbie stepped into the room, his weapon drawn but held behind his thigh.

Brad's eyes bored into Sonia's and gave her a look that clearly said, "You stay here." He quickly followed Robbie into the room. Even though he was no longer a federal agent of any kind, he had his handgun drawn and hidden as well.

Things were starting to spin out of control for Sonia. On the one hand, she had been glad to acquiesce to Brad's instructions and stay behind him—safe. On the other hand, as things were developing right in front of her eyes, she knew that she wanted to be with him, right beside him, his partner, bringing down the people who had killed—*murdered*—John Abbot Hensley.

Sonia wished she had her Glock, but she remembered clearly all the instruction she had received when getting her Concealed Deadly Weapons License. She knew she could only use her weapon to protect herself or someone who was in imminent danger. She was quite certain that helping Federal agents arrest criminal suspects didn't qualify. She was also very clear on what her task was that evening—identifying Alexi Dimitrov as the man who had shown up on Dahlia Farm just before John Hensley was murdered.

Sonia all but held her breath as she heard Robbie's voice ring out. "Federal agent. DEA. Everyone stay where you are!" She *had* to know what was going on in that room. Fortunately for her, it was only a moment before Brad subtly pushed the curtain away from the door's window, exposing the entire scene. She could see that the three people inside the room stood stunned by the intrusion.

The autopsy room was just as Sonia expected it would be—cold, sterile. The trio inside stared at Robbie and Brad. Sonia recognized each of them: Steve Hollings, the farm manager, Dr. Xin Li, the Medical Examiner, and the man with the blond, slicked-back hair and the goatee, whom she now was quite certain was Alexi Dimitrov.

Dr. Li stepped forward. "I am Dr. Xin Li, the Medical Examiner. What is the meaning of this?"

"DEA investigation," said Robbie, with his official voice turned onto 'INTIMIDATION.' His eyes scanned the room. "We're just wondering what has brought you three together this evening. It's a little late for office hours, don't you think?"

Both Dimitrov and Hollings seemed to be content to let Xin Li do all the talking, and she responded. "We're just discussing the possibility of re-opening the file of some unfortunate person who recently died in an automobile accident."

"Well," said Robbie, "I'm not going to ask you to go through the trouble of trying to flesh out that lie on the spot. Let me just ask this question. Which one of you is Sofia?"

Sonia could see the looks of fear that shot back and forth between the eyes of the trio. She whispered to Jet. "Clearly, these are our guys, but what is Dr. Li doing here?" She watched as Dimitrov, Hollings and Dr. Li drifted slowly apart. Dimitrov and Hollings moved outward, while Dr. Li remained in the center, standing in front of one of the ominous-looking metal autopsy tables.

"I have no idea what you're talking about." The Medical Examiner stood tall, indignant.

"Fine then." Robbie looked directly at Dimitrov. "Perhaps you could identify yourself, sir."

The blond spoke with a heavily accented, smoky voice. "My name is Alexi Dimitrov. I'm a friend of Mr. Hollings and I am just here to help him with this matter."

Robbie turned to Hollings. "And you, sir, are Steve Hollings, the farm manager at Dahlia Farm?"

Hollings just nodded, running his fingers through his hair. Sonia noted it was the same the movement she had observed on that fateful day.

Robbie's eyes bore down on Hollings. "Isn't that where John Abbott Hensley recently took his own life?"

"Yes," said Hollings. Even from the hallway, Sonia could tell his mouth was so dry the word hardly came out.

Xin Li took a step forward and spoke dismissively. "Gentlemen, I did the autopsy on Mr. Hensley myself, and if you are implying that something else happened to Mr. Hensley I would direct you to the report I filed with the Coroner's Office. That report indicated there were absolutely no signs of any foul play as regards Mr. Hensley's death."

"Well, I hate to disappoint you all," Robbie almost chuckled. Sonia could tell he was enjoying himself. "But it seems that we have reason to disagree. You see, we're quite certain that Mr. Dimitrov, here, is a central figure in a huge drug operation, an operation that has a sophisticated email network that we've infiltrated. In that system, we believe Mr. Dimitrov uses the code name, Sofia." He turned his attention to Hollings, who was sweating profusely. "We think that Mr. Hollings is in charge of the Lexington branch of this fine business endeavor. We're quite certain that he uses the code name, Forty." Sonia saw Hollings' head whip around and look at Dr. Li.

Turning to Xin Li, Robbie said, "And you, Dr. Li. You're a bit of a surprise to us. But now that I think about it, what better way to have a murder declared a suicide than to get the Medical Examiner in on the whole thing. I'll bet they paid you a pretty penny to come on board at the last minute and help them out with this."

Dr. Li took another step forward, her hands balled into fists at her side, her severe bangs and wireless glasses matching perfectly the intense pitch of her voice. "This is absolutely absurd."

Fully aware that at any moment the tension inside might explode, Sonia swept the autopsy room with her eyes. Suddenly, she whispered to herself. "Oh, my God."

Jet leaned closer. "What? What is it?"

"Look at her desk." Sonia pointed through the window. "The nameplate on her desk. Dr. Xin Li. It's her. She's Forty."

Jet craned her neck. "What?"

"Xin Li. *She's* Forty. Someone's got to tell Brad. She's Forty."

The conflicting forces crashing in Sonia's heart and mind came together in one great crescendo. Torn between not wanting to hurt Brad by putting herself in danger, and not wanting to fail Brad by withholding the information he needed—torn between being the good little Italian girl the nuns had trained to obey instructions at all costs and exercising the new-found strength she had acquired from all she had experienced in the last few days and weeks—torn between real fear of the dangerous situation in the room and her desire to do the right thing—she opened the door and stepped in.

53

Every head in the room spun around. Their eyes landed on Sonia simultaneously. There were only two eyes that concerned Sonia, however, and they were bright blue. They were also more than not pleased.

"Brad. Brad. Wait." Her voice was full of energy. "You've got to know this." Sonia pointed at the nameplate on Dr. Li's desk. "Look. She's Forty. It's right there. She's Forty."

Brad and Robbie spoke almost simultaneously. "What?"

"Look. Xin Li. Her initials. They're XL."

Brad looked at her, his brow furrowed. "What the hell are you talking about?" His voice cut with a sharp edge.

"Don't you see, XL?"

"Forty." The sound came from behind Sonia. "Forty, in Roman numerals."

Sonia turned and realized that Jet had entered the room as well. She turned back and looked imploringly at Brad. "Xin Li. She's Forty. *She's* the one in charge here in town." Then Sonia turned to Dr. Li. "*You're* the one who used that code name, the one who received the emails."

The Medical Examiner shook her head vehemently. "I have

no idea about your email system. Or your so-called code names." She held out her hands toward her colleagues. "Neither, I'm sure, do these men" She waved both hands in a dismissive gesture." Leave my office immediately. I'm calling the police."

"Go ahead." Sonia stepped out in front of Robbie. "I just happen to have copies of those very emails right here." Pulling the folded copies of the emails out of the back pocket of her jeans, she walked over to Dr. Li, wagging them in the Medical Examiner's face.

"You bitch" Xin Li hissed. She reached out to grab the emails away from Sonia. Sonia spun and turned her back to the Medical Examiner, hunching over, avoiding the attack and protecting the emails. The next words she heard came from an unexpected voice.

"Everybody freeze!" It was Steve Hollings.

Looking over her shoulder, Sonia saw that in the commotion of Dr. Li's yelling and grabbing at her, Steve Hollings had pulled out a semi-automatic handgun that looked a lot like the Glock she owned, just smaller. It was only a moment later that Alexi Dimitrov yelled, "Hands up!" as he drew a small, silver-plated revolver.

There was an incredible moment of silence as each of the seven people in the room came to grips with what had just happened. Sonia quickly realized that not only were Hollings and Dimitrov pointing *their* guns, Brad and Robbie had *theirs* raised as well.

Sonia watched a certain calmness come over Robbie's face. "Okay, gentleman. Kudos to you both. Nice move. Unfortunately, with several DEA units surrounding the building," he nodded at the blond man, "the very ones who followed you down from Cincinnati this evening Mr. Dimitrov, I don't think that this little display is going to get you very far. Are you really going to kill several DEA agents and then try to walk out of this room alive? I don't think so."

"Maybe not," Hollings said. The black weapon in his hand shook while beads of sweat appeared on his brow. "But I just might be able to use this situation to my advantage. Just let me say that—"

An idea flashed through Sonia's mind. She looked at Brad. "Brad, Brad. It was her." She glanced over her shoulder at Dr. Li. "She didn't just cover up the murder. She was in on it. She's probably the one who ordered it, and Sofia, he just came down to give his final approval."

Hollings words followed Sonia's quickly. "That's right." He waved the gun toward Brad and took a step forward as if to make a point. "And let me tell you something else. I can tell you that—"

Suddenly, a voice exploded from behind Jet, through the barely opened door. "Police! Drop your weapons!" One second later, BLAM! A gunshot exploded in the room. Another second, BLAM! Another gunshot.

Sonia stood frozen. But she sensed from the movements around her that both Hollings and Dimitrov had fallen to the ground behind her. Time slowed to a crawl for Sonia. For the first time in her life, she had been in a small, tiled room while her unprotected ears were being exposed to the sound of a large-caliber handgun being discharged. She couldn't believe the ringing in her ears, the fact that, for a moment, she could hear nothing else. The smell of cordite and smoke filled the room. She turned, as did everyone else in the room, toward the door from which the gunshot had come. She was stunned when she saw who stepped into the room. His name crossed her lips silently.

Sonia was shocked out of her stillness when Dr. Xin Li grabbed her and pulled her backward. Sonia's eyes bugged open, but all she could see were the shocked looks on the faces of Brad and Robbie . . . and Detective Sergeant Johnny Adams. Their weapons were all pointed right at her.

Sonia felt an incredibly sharp blade being pressed against her throat. She knew immediately that Dr. Li had somehow gotten her hands on a medical instrument, probably a scalpel, from a tray of surgical instruments that had been on the metal table.

Dr. Li's voice was cold with precision, hot with intensity. "Do not think that I don't know exactly where to use this blade, gentleman. My training has been very complete. And if you do not let me take this beautiful young thing and walk away, you will see how well a trained surgeon can inflict damage on a lovely young face." She snorted. "After that, if need be, you will see how I can slice the carotid artery, causing a flow of blood that will leave her dead in less than thirty seconds."

As she felt the razor-sharp edge of the scalpel against her throat, Sonia's mind scrambled, clawed, for some thought of how to escape, how to free herself from almost certain death. Mindlessly, her left hand clutched the paper copies of the emails she had thought would be such a powerful weapon. But her right hand, frozen, hung empty at her side. Empty, until her mind filled it with the object that so often resided in the right pocket of her vest. The symbol of her parent's love, old-school as it was.

Dr. Li turned her attention to Brad, momentarily removing the scalpel from Sonia's throat and gesturing at him while she spoke. "By the way, you, the one with the panicked look on your face, her lover. You should know that when that has happened no life-saving efforts would ever be able to save her."

As Dr. Li's voice cut through the air, Sonia slipped her right hand into her pocket, tightly grasping her Cross pen. Still, she remained stuck, her mind unable to push the idea of attacking the woman from thought into action.

The Medical Examiner's voice dripped venom as she almost smiled into Brad's eyes. "She would be dead before you could hold her in your arms one last time."

It was those words that launched Sonia into action. Spinning, raising her left arm as hard and high as she could, Sonia knocked Dr. Li backward and off-balance. Snatching her pen out of her pocket, she swung it in a great arc, driving the pen deep into the woman's throat.

Sonia had no thoughts as to whether or not the pen had found the carotid artery, but she did know two things. First, blood was spouting out of the woman's neck, soaking her clothing, spilling over the floor, specks flying in Sonia's face. Second, Dr. Xin Li's eyes were stretched wide, blazing with hatred, and directing the scalpel in her hand to the precise point in Sonia's chest that would lead it to her heart.

Sonia gasped. Suddenly, her ears were racked with pain as once again a large-caliber handgun roared in the pristinely-tiled room.

54

Sonia watched as Dr. Li's head rocked back and her body crumpled instantly to the ground. The roar of the firearm in her ear, she was unable to hear the clank of the scalpel as it hit the tile floor. She turned. Sonia's eyes focused on the black weapon that had launched its deadly projectile into the brain, the mind, of the woman who was about to kill her. In a flash, they shifted to the brightness behind that weapon, the eyes of Brad Dunham.

Before Sonia could say or do anything, she heard Johnny Adams speak, the roar in her ear dissipating. "Everybody freeze. Let's get those hands in the air." Everyone obeyed.

Sonia stood motionless, her mind still reeling, trying to grasp what she had done. Her hands shook. Her body trembled. But it had been necessary. She was sure of it.

Robbie spoke up, still looking forward, his hands in the air. "I'm DEA. Give me a chance and I'll show you my credentials."

"First," Johnny was moving around to the front of the group, "every weapon on the floor. Slow and easy, I want every weapon on the floor, and everyone's hands in the air."

Brad and Robbie both bent and laid their weapons down.

Sonia watched as they stood up and put their hands in the air. Jet as well.

Still standing in front of the autopsy table from which the implement that nearly caused her death had been taken, Sonia watched Johnny as he surveyed the cold, sterile room, a room still filled with the smoke and smell of firearm discharge. "Okay, let's see those credentials."

Sonia looked across the room. "Johnny?" Her voice was small, pitched upward. Her hands were still in the air.

Johnny nodded to Sonia as he stepped forward and took Robbie's credentials out of his hands. He gave them a cursory glance then handed them back.

By then, Robbie's backup had piled into the room, three men and a woman—all wearing Kevlar vests and yelling. They quickly took positions pointing their weapons at Johnny and indicating that he put his gun on the ground. He complied.

Sonia stood at one end of the room. Across the room, next to each other, were the two men she had kissed in the last few days, the two men who had each saved her life. For just the slightest moment she was caught between her feelings for both men. Suddenly, she was completely overcome by the depth of her feelings for Brad. As she rushed toward him, Brad reached out and scooped her up.

He held her in his arms, the side of her head pressed against his. "Why, Sonia? Why did you come in here?"

She pulled back and looked into those bright blue eyes. "Because I had to, Brad. Because, just like you, I had to."

He did nothing to break the connection between them. "I guess I'm going to have to get used to that, aren't I?" Touching her face gently, he wiped away specks of blood.

She smiled. "Well, I guess that depends, Captain Dunham. If you want me around . . . ."

"Oh." His fingertips ran lightly down her face. "I very much want you around."

Sonia quivered at the sheer intimacy of the moment. "And why is that, Captain Dunham?"

Brad didn't say another word, but Sonia was pretty sure his eyes were saying, *Because I love you, Sonia Vitale.* Then he pulled her close and kissed her.

Tears welled up in Sonia's eyes, tears of joy, her own unspoken response.

Finally, as his people watched, Robbie turned to Johnny Adams and said, "And I guess you won't mind showing me your badge?"

"Sure," said Johnny, reaching for his shield.

Jet walked up behind Sonia, smiling at Brad as she did. She put her hands on Sonia's shoulder and nestled her forehead in Sonia's hair.

Sonia half-turned, put her arm around Jet, and pulled her close, relishing the feeling of being held simultaneously by her best friend and the man she loved. A long moment later, she turned. "Johnny, what are you doing here? How did you know?" She let go of Brad and Jet and turned fully to face Johnny.

Johnny answered slowly, haltingly. "Well, it's kind of hard for me to say it now, Sonia, but I was hoping you and I, maybe . . . ." He looked around the room. Every eye was on him. "I've been so worried about you that I've been following you as much as I could ever since you got back to town. So tonight, after I'd followed you out to the castle and then back into town, I somehow sensed you were on your way into trouble. I'm just glad I managed to get here in time. In time to, well, you know . . . ."

By then, Robbie's DEA agents were dealing with the bodies of Alexi Dimitrov, Steve Hollings, and Dr. Xin Li. Several Lexington police officers had entered the room as well and the room had become a noisy, confusing scene. The officers and the DEA agents exchanged credentials and tried to make sense of what had happened.

Sonia walked over to Johnny. She gently put her hands on the chest of the tall, handsome man. "I'm so sorry. It's just that . . . ."

He shook his head. "You don't have to say anything. I can see that you and Brad, well . . . ."

Sonia stepped back as some LPD officers came to collect Johnny's weapon. He looked at her and shrugged his shoulders. "All part of the normal procedure after an officer fires his or her weapon." As he walked away with his colleagues, Johnny looked over at Brad and mouthed, *Take good care of her.*

Brad nodded, then looked across the room at Sonia. Their eyes met and they walked slowly toward each other. Sonia stood tall and whispered. "Do you think we could get out of here?"

"If it's okay with Robbie." He looked at his friend. "Can we tie this up in the morning, Robbie? I'm beat, and I'd like to get a little rest."

Robbie grinned. "I'm not sure that's what you're going to get tonight old friend." He shrugged. "But I'm sure we can tie up the details tomorrow."

"Problem is," said Brad, "I don't have a car." Then realizing the truth of his own statement, "No seriously, I really don't have a car."

"That's alright," laughed Sonia. "I'm sure one of these nice policemen will give us a ride somewhere." She reached up and touched his face then slipped out of his arms. "Oh, but we'll have to give Jet a lift home."

"No need for that," Robbie interjected as he tugged briefly on his slacks. "I can give her a lift. Plus, there are still some questions I need answered for my report. You guys go on."

Jet pulled her ever-present ponytail through her hands. "Yeah, you guys go on. I'll be okay." A silent message passed between Jet and Sonia.

Brad took Sonia by the hand. "Come on, babe, time for you and me to get a lift back to my place." Then he bent down and whispered in her ear. "Or your place. It doesn't really matter much to me."

55

A t ten the next morning, Sonia walked into Magee's as she always did. This time, however, she was leading Brad by the hand. They greeted Jet, who was already there, and who was holding one of the larger tables for them. Instead of her perpetual ponytail, Jet's hair hung softly down around her shoulders.

Walking up to the counter, Sonia smiled at Hildy, who responded with a special smile of her own and asked, "Your regular?"

"Yes please." Sonia glanced back over her shoulder at Brad. "But make it a double, would you?" Hildy smiled even more broadly.

Croissants and coffees in hand, Sonia and Brad joined Jet. Three or four minutes later, Roberto "Robbie" Alvarez walked in, got himself a pastry and some coffee, and sat down at the table. "Everyone get some good rest last night?"

Brad gave Sonia a quick smile. "Slept like a baby." Then he turned to Robbie. "And yourself?"

Robbie lifted his cup in a tiny toast then took a quick sip. "Couldn't have been better." His eyes darted to Jet and back.

For a moment or two, there was a pleasant silence at the table as everyone enjoyed their treats. Then Brad asked Robbie, "What do you think about Adams? He going to be okay? That was a pretty fast shoot, wasn't it?"

Robbie rocked his head back and forth once or twice and pursed his lips forward. "Oh, I think he'll be alright. You know. Bad guys. Guns drawn on innocents. No way you take the chance they fire first. And Hollings. Looked to me like he was about to lose it, maybe go ballistic on us. I think this goes down as a justifiable shoot." Robbie took another sip of his coffee. "And you're pretty lucky yourself, Brad. With Adams and me vouching for you, you weren't even taken into custody. That's pretty sweet."

Jet took a sip of coffee then turned to Brad. "Brad, I know things worked out, but with Sonia and Dr. Li standing almost on top of each other, I can't believe you took that shot. How did you know you wouldn't miss and hit Sonia by mistake.

Sonia looked at Brad and quickly turned back to Jet. "Training, ma'am, training." She gave Brad a big smile. He responded with a tiny grin of his own.

After a quick laugh, Sonia asked Robbie, "But what about the case? Did we ruin the case?"

"Not really." Robbie flicked his coffee cup with his fingernail. "Look, you never get it all. But with Dimitrov and Hollings showing up in response to your brilliant email scheme we had no trouble getting some search warrants this morning. I've got teams executing those warrants at Allegro Imports, Dimitrov's home, Hollings' home, and Dahlia Farm as we speak." He looked at Brad. "We've already been inside the hub down in Memphis. We got the location of the distribution point in Louisville from the driver we picked up." Robbie turned his attention back to Sonia. "Thanks to you and Brad we know some of the drop off points in Southern Kentucky as well. We're putting an awful lot of stuff together. And we'll get more as we squeeze all the different players we pick up."

"But what about Toro? What about the point of origination?" asked Brad.

"Well, unfortunately," Robbie responded, "right now we don't know if Sofia worked for Toro or if Toro worked for Sofia. Again, we've got three different drivers who worked out of Memphis, and the guys from the Memphis hub itself. I'm pretty sure somebody's going to make a deal with us and tell us how it was all set up."

"That brings up something else," said Jet. She raised her coffee cup. "How about a toast to Sonia, for having figured out that Dr. Li, not Steve Hollings, was Forty?"

There was a round of "Here! Here!" at the table. Sonia blushed. And as the congratulatory sounds rang in her ear, she couldn't help but think of how all that she had experienced in the last few weeks had changed her. She knew she was still the same person. Yet, she was now more convinced than ever that whatever her new job, her new life, demanded of her she would be up to the challenge. She raised her coffee cup. "And let's hear it for having to practice writing Roman numerals over and over again in elementary school."

When the laughter died down, Brad looked at Robbie. "But that does leave one other question. Why was Alexi Dimitrov using a woman's name as his code name?"

"I think I know the answer to that one." Robbie looked around the table and paused before continuing. "He wasn't. Ever since Ms. Sonia gave us that license plate and we tracked down Allegro Imports, we've been doing some research on Mr. Dimitrov. It turns out he's Bulgarian. Would anyone here like to guess where he grew up?"

Everyone at the table was silent, looking around at each other.

"Well then, let me tell you. Alexi Dimitrov grew up in the capital of Bulgaria, Sofia," He pronounced it "*Sew*-fee-ah."

Sonia noticed that although Robbie was answering everyone's

questions, his eyes kept making contact with Jet. Finally, she broke in. "So, that's it. I guess you'll be leaving today to go back to DC and wrap up all the loose ends on this case, right Robbie?"

"I don't know." Robbie's eyes flashed to Jet for the briefest moment. "I haven't found a place in DC that makes an almond croissant that compares to this one. I may just have to stay around a day or two to see what other delicious treats a man can find in this backwater town."

Sonia sent a silent message in Jet's direction and received one back. "You may just have to do that." Then she added, "And me, I've got a phone call to make."

Jet furrowed her brows. "To whom?"

"To Teresa Torres, who I'm sure is not related to, and probably never will be related to, Marcos Torres."

56

On Friday morning, Detective Sergeant Johnny Adams walked around the room shared by all the detectives in his unit. Shaking hands, he wished them well and thanked them for all their support. After his actions on the previous Monday evening had been declared justified, he had been cleared to return to duty. He had declined, however, saying that the stress of having killed two people, even in the line of duty, had led him to reconsider his choice of career. Privately, he had shared with some of his closest colleagues the fact that losing Sonia Vitale to Brad Dunham was turning out to be very difficult for him. Therefore, he had decided that moving to a new city just might be the best thing for him.

After collecting his few personal belongings, Johnny Adams walked out of the police station for the last time. Entering his small apartment, he was surprised at how few boxes it took to hold all the things he would bring with him to his new home. He was convinced that it was time to start over, to start a new life, and maybe find someone else to love. He was certain of something else: the eight hundred and twelve thousand, six hundred and forty dollars he had stashed in two old Samsonite suitcases would certainly help him get the start he wanted in that new life. He was sure of one other thing, as well. Thanks to his quick thinking and bold efforts, the three people with whom he had worked to accumulate that money, Alexi Dimitrov, Steve Hollings, and Dr. Xin LI, would never be able to open their mouths again.

AUTHOR'S NOTE:

For those of you old enough to remember the original television series, *Dragnet*, I'm sure you can still hear in your mind's ear the rich voice of the announcer saying, "The story you are about to see is true. Only the names have been changed to protect the innocent." In the case of this book, however, THE STORY YOU HAVE JUST READ IS *NOT* TRUE. NONE OF THE EVENTS OR CHARACTERS PORTRAYED HAS ANY RELATION TO ACTUAL EVENTS, OR TO ANY PERSONS LIVING OR DECEASED.

On the other hand, should you ever visit the wonderful city of Lexington, Kentucky, bring this book with you. It may lead you to wonderful things: some interesting places and things to see; some great Italian food, served with incredible breadsticks; some excellent coffee; and some delicious pastries—especially the almond croissants.

PS: As an independent author and publisher, my most valuable assets are the comments and recommendations of the folks who take the time to read and share my novels. If you would like to help, please take a few moments to write a review on Amazon, or wherever you purchased the book. Or just tell your friends about the adventures of Sonia, Brad, and Jet. I'm certain they would appreciate it.

CURIOUS ABOUT WHAT SONIA DOES NEXT?

Wondering about her relationships
with Brad and Jet?

Like to know a little about the future of
Bluegrass Confidential Investigations?

Then Take a peek at:
The Bluegrass Files: Twisted Dreams

1
———

"They should call me Lucky," she whispered out loud as she drove her car through the early morning darkness and onto the property. Her eyes followed the headlights as her car moved along the winding driveway.

She smiled and nodded as she thought about her life. Lucky. I'm lucky to be doing what I love, working with these majestic beings. Lucky to be working on a farm that's so lovely I can see its beauty all around me, even before the sun really comes up. Lucky to be helping these animals, and those I'll never even have the chance to see. Life is good; I'm blessed. And soon, soon things will be even better. Soon this will have all been worth it.

The first to arrive, as usual, she pulled her car into the same spot she used every day, just next to the old east barn. She stepped out into the somewhat chilly morning, a quick shiver running through her body. Dang, they say it'll be a great day, but it's brisk enough this morning.

The sound of her car had moved the giants inside the barn to life. Her heart lifted as she heard the rumble of their voices and the sound of their thousand-pound bodies moving on the old wooden floor. She didn't want to pull open the large sliding door the horses would use later in the day, so she stepped through the human-sized door and turned on one bare-bulb light, creating a dim, almost surreal atmosphere in the barn. Heads bobbed and hooves clumped, stretching long, powerful muscles. The sweet smell of hay and straw and grains filled her senses. Her already-muddied boots moved quietly over the well-worn floors of the barn. Big brown eyes stared at her, while snorts and the occasional whinny welcomed her into this special domain. This was where she felt most comfortable and a warm rush of satisfaction rose in her as she looked at each of the beautiful creatures—creatures who counted on her for their well-being.

As she headed for the large bin in which breakfast was held, a blend of oats and other grains, a strange sensation crept up her spine. She turned her head to peer into the dim recesses of the building. Pausing, she saw nothing. She went back to her task. But as she scooped out the first bucket-full of grain, the sensation returned, this time verified by the shifting and nervous responses of the animals. She spun completely around. She was stunned. He was right there.

"Oh, you scared me. What are you doing here?" It was almost a whisper. A deeper, much darker chill ran through her body.

His voice was smooth, almost soothing. "Oh, my dear. Now, you didn't think our last conversation was really going to be the end of it all, did you?"

She took a small step backward. "Wait, wait. We can talk about it. We can—"

He stepped into the space she had vacated. "No, child. I'm afraid the time for talking is over."

She just barely saw it coming out of the corner of her eye. Her head was wracked by the sudden blow from his large hand. It would have sent her reeling to the ground if he had not caught her himself. He pushed her backward into one of the stalls; he struck her again. This time the back of his hand sent her down into the straw that covered the wooden floor.

He was on top of her almost immediately, the weight of his body sitting squarely on her tiny hips, pinning her to the ground. His powerful hands wrapped around her sleek, thin neck.

"Believe me, child. This is never what I wanted. I never planned it this way. But now, now this is where we are, and this is what we must do."

She struggled, kicking her mud-covered boots, trying to get even a tiny bit of that cold morning air to descend down into her lungs. But his now-monstrous hands, hands she once admired, were crushing her windpipe. His eyes bore into hers. She could just barely hear what he was saying as her mind and body screamed out for oxygen and struggled against the pain. A few phrases came to her, "long trip . . . your own car . . . before they find you." Darkness began to creep into her mind. She struggled even harder. Her eyes perceived less and less, until all she could see, in the center of her vision, was his face. Then, as her body relaxed and the struggle ended, one last thought crossed her mind. Love in his eyes.

AT TEN O'CLOCK on Monday morning, the mood in the offices of Bluegrass Confidential Investigations was somewhat festive. The recently-installed television in the waiting area was rarely on; this morning, however, things were different. This morning the two young women who ran the firm had a special interest in a local morning show. Jet leaned against the molding in the doorway to her office, her arms crossed. "Well, look at that. We're TV stars."

Sonia took a seat on the brown leather couch in front of the TV. She smiled and wiggled two fingers on each hand in the air. "I'm not sure the word stars actually fits, but it is kind of exciting to watch, isn't it?"

"Sho 'nuff is," Jet replied, slipping ever-so-briefly into one of her many accents.

A quiet sense of pride filled Sonia's heart as she watched the images of Jet, Brad Dunham, and her being interviewed on the local morning news program. Sitting on the interview set at the local TV station, in three wooden chairs with dark red cushions, they were all facing Mark Sullivan, the young, attractive male host with the blonde hair and the quasi-beard. It being March, both women were wearing heavy sweaters, Sonia red, Jet white. Both had on dress pants. Brad was wearing a navy V-neck sweater over a white shirt and snug-fitting jeans.

"I'm here with Sonia Vitale, Joyce Ellen Thomas, and Brad Dunham," Mark had started as he sat on his matching chair, a small jungle of artificial plants behind him and to his side.

"Jet," Joyce Ellen had corrected. "Everyone just calls me Jet." She smiled. "And Sonia's name is pronounced Vi-*tah*-lay, with an accent on the "tah" and a long "a" sound at the end."

"Yes, thank you." Mark turned, speaking directly to the camera. "Over the last few weeks, these three local private investigators combined the resources of their two firms. Together, they discovered illegal activities that were taking place right here in Lexington and beyond." He'd turned to Sonia. "Now, Sonia, is this the kind of work you usually do at Bluegrass Confidential Investigations?"

Not used to being on TV, even local TV, Sonia's voice had sounded a bit tenuous. "Well, we generally have more of a local focus at BCI. You know, helping people find missing loved ones, checking up on missing things. Personal matters."

"I understand." He'd turned to Jet. "So, Joyce," he shook his head quickly, "excuse me, Jet. This must have been exciting work for you all."

Sonia had been a bit surprised when Jet, who was also not used to being interviewed on TV, had come off cool and collected. "Really, I have to say that it was mostly Sonia and Brad that did all the heavy lifting. They followed some of those folks right down I-75 into Tennessee; then they followed others all the way to Memphis." She tipped her head. "And things got pretty intense after that."

"That's true, isn't it Brad?" Mark turned slightly in his chair.

Given Brad's experience as an investigator with the Naval Criminal Investigative Service, NCIS, it had been no surprise to Sonia that Brad had seemed even more at home on set than Jet, although much less enamored of the attention. "Well, I can't deny that things got a little dangerous for a while. And I do have to thank my good friend from the DEA, Special Agent Roberto Alvarez, for saving our bacon on the way back from Memphis."

Mark Sullivan had looked down and checked his notes. "Now Sonia, am I correct in saying that it was your interest in the John Abbott Hensley suicide that got you involved in all of this?"

A quick image of Dahlia Farm and a man dressed in a madras shirt had flashed through Sonia's mind. "That's true, Mark. And at this point, I think we all have a better idea of what was going on there."

Sitting on the couch in the BCI offices, Sonia's eyes drifted from the screen. She remembered well how she had felt at the beginning of the Hensley affair—committed to doing the right thing, but fearful that the whole situation might be beyond her. She didn't feel that way anymore. She'd seen the case to its completion. She'd actually been the one who had figured out who the key players were. She'd stared death in the face—three times. She was no longer the same person.

Her attention returning to the TV, Sonia watched as Mark continued. "Now ladies, your offices are right here in town, correct? Right on East Main, over Magee's bakery?"

"Well, yes they are," Jet had answered, her perpetual blonde ponytail swinging as she turned her head toward the camera and licked imaginary sugar off her fingertips. Everyone had chuckled.

"And Brad, your office is right across the street?"

"That's correct." Brad had answered evenly, with no emphasis.

"In the white house, right next door to the school district's Central Office."

"And I assume the name, Semper Fi Investigations, implies that you're a former Marine?"

The mention of his time in the Marine Corps had brought Brad's bright blue eyes to life. "Yes, sir. That it does."

"So, Brad, how is it that you all started to work together?"

Brad had looked quickly at Sonia, then back to the host. "Really Mark, it's a long story."

ABOUT THE AUTHOR

After a long career as a professional musician and educator, having written several instructional texts along the way, Frank Messina turned his attention to writing fiction in 2016. He holds a Doctor of Education degree from the University of Massachusetts at Amherst.

A native of Long Island, New York, Frank moved to Lexington, Kentucky in 1978. Having lived there for almost forty years, he now considers Lexington his home and is excited about sharing the beauty and culture of that wonderful little city as he leads readers through the exciting, albeit fictional, world of Sonia Vitale and the ladies of Bluegrass Confidential Investigations. *The Bluegrass Files: Down the Rabbit Hole*, is his debut novel and the first in a multi-volume series.

Please feel free to contact Frank or learn more about him at: fjmessina-mysteries.com or fjmessina.author@gmail.com

LOOK FOR:

The Bluegrass Files: Twisted Dreams – Coming July 2018

As Private Investigator Sonia Vitale tries to find a missing young woman, she is unaware of the dangers facing her heart—and her life!

The Bluegrass Files: The Bourbon Brotherhood – Coming September 2018

Bourbon and horses, the life-blood of Kentucky culture. Sonia Vitale and her team race to solve a crime, save an industry . . . and save a life!

Made in the USA
Lexington, KY
26 June 2018